Courting Laura Providencia

A NOVEL BY
Jack Pulaski

ZEPHYR PRESS
BROOKLINE, MASSACHUSETTS

Various chapters have appeared previously in slightly different form in
the following publications: *Ploughshares, New England Review, Agni Review,
The Ohio Review, Tikkun*, and *The Longwood Introduction to Fiction*, edited
by Sven Birkerts.

Cover illustration and design by Anna Herrick
Book design and typography by *typeslowly*
Printed in Michigan by McNaughton & Gunn

"In My Craft or Sullen Art" by Dylan Thomas, from THE POEMS OF
DYLAN THOMAS, copyright © 1946 by New Directions Publishing Corp.
Reprinted by permission of New Directions Publishing Corp., and by
David Higham Associates & JM Dent.
Italian text from Dante's INFERNO reprinted from the Meridiani edition,
copyright © 1991 by Arnoldo Mondadori Editore S.p.A., Milano.

Zephyr Press acknowledges with gratitude the financial support of the
Tiny Tiger Foundation, Charles Merrill, and the Massachusetts Cultural
Council.

MASSACHUSETTS CULTURAL COUNCIL

Library of Congress Cataloging-in-Publication Data

Pulaski, Jack.
  Courting Laura Providencia : a novel/ by Jack Pulaski.
    p. cm.
  ISBN 0-939010-67-4 (pbk. : alk. paper) — ISBN 0-939010-68-2
(hardcover : alk. paper)
  1. Immigrants—Fiction. 2. Courtship—Fiction. I. Title.
  PS3566.U36 C68 2001
  813'.54—dc21

                                            2001004024

98765432 FIRST EDITION

ZEPHYR PRESS
50 KENWOOD STREET, BROOKLINE, MA 02446
www.zephyrpress.org

Contents

Acknowledgments

I wish to express my gratitude to Christopher Mattison for his sound judgment in the editing of this book. His susceptibility to the written word has significantly mitigated my pessimism, and helped to spur me on to new work. The encouragement of Leora Zeitlin and Jim Kates has made this novel possible. Jody Beenk, Nina Moeller, Sarah Pulaski, Anna Herrick, Douglas Herrick, Martin Bock, Roberta Shafer, Barry Goldensohn, Lorrie Goldensohn, Howard Norman and Jane Shore all deserve my thanks for the years of discussion, support, and the telling of stories. This book is also dedicated to the memory of Ed Hogan who started it all.

And as it continues to be my good fortune to inhabit the earth while the poet Paul Nelson and the painter Judith Nelson are here, my profound thanks, as I continue to learn from them.

Por Margarita, mi esposa, mi amiga, mi amor

LAURA PROVIDENCIA
IN THE NEW WORLD

Ｈigh up in the towers of the public housing project, Laura Providencia and her mother, her brother Angel, and her little sister Rosita lived under siege. In the elevator that smelled like a urinal, the junkies bobbed devotionally. The walls of the long hallways teemed with the exploding alphabet, the declamations, white, screaming, *Paco of St. Ann's Ave, Hector El Corazón, The Bishops* ... the worm-like letters spawning words, the words clamoring over one another kept pace with Laura Providencia as she walked down the long hallway toward the vestibule where the mailboxes were plundered.

During the first months in the new country she had longed for letters from her cousins on the island to corroborate what she thought she remembered. She learned the new language quickly and felt like a guest in her own life. Laura's mother, Señora Milagros, was astonished, and suspected that the rapidity with which her daughter learned the new language was symptomatic of some unnameable contagion of the barbarous new world. Although, in the new world, shoes were plentiful. Stunned, Señora Milagros looked at the dark girl budding into a woman, the pretty girl mouthing with such facility the noise of the new incomprehensible words, and she forgot the occasion of Laura Providencia's fourteenth birthday. But Angel, who was one year older than his sister, celebrated his birthday on the same day, and as Señora Milagros remembered her son's birthday, it seemed to her that Laura had loitered in her womb as a reproach for the passion that had made her.

Señora Milagros regaled her neighbor Señora Ramirez with the story: she told it tenderly, and Laura knew she was meant to overhear, as God was meant to overhear. "Dios mio, a day and a night in labor, the pain like knives, she came out of my body, tore me to pieces. I was nursing her brother and she was not supposed to happen; but she was in me, growing, and dried up the milk in my breasts. I had to hire my cousin Teresa to nurse Angel. I paid Teresa with my shoes. After a year, to the day her brother was born, she came. And then this one," Señora Milagros said, caught her breath and braced her back against the couch pillow. She spread the fingers of her large right hand, held and encompassed the top of Rosita's velvety head. Señora Ramirez said, "Pero, pero," her hands twitched in her lap, her face disfigured with a disappointment as profound as a child's, she struggled against the desire to weep, shocked by the audacity that had compelled her to interrupt Señora Milagros. Laura Providencia noticed that although the women's gestures mirrored one another, they sighed in harmony and breathed in unison, the black sheathed swelling cushions of their breasts, a rising tide of dark moons obscuring their chins, but they weren't identical, though Laura had seen them that way; except now, the crack, the sudden momentary fissure in Laura Providencia's vision precipitated by Señora Ramirez' interrupting "but, but" allowed Laura to see again that her mother's face was round and brown, and Señora Ramirez' was teak-colored and narrow, but these distinctions did not alter what the two women found in the greater affinity, their one fate. And it was up to Señora Milagros to tell it; this Señora Ramirez could not do, she was not the talker, it was up to Lucia Milagros to tell the truth of her heart which was their one life, uniting them deeper than blood. Lucia Milagros telling it, and Dolores Ramirez nervously attentive, until finally she was still, and only listening, and at home in her silence. And now in telling it, Señora Milagros had elected to leave out a part, didn't say it — without explanation, discarding perhaps, foreshortening maybe, was this, all that was left out of the recitation to be tacitly understood — could such a telling be trusted? Out of the wreckage of Señora Ramirez' trance fell language that was all distress, even as her body paid homage duplicating every movement and gesture of Señora Milagros.

Señora Ramirez' mouth labored, her tongue slowly hefting one word at a time, attempting to place each word in a coherent order, and failing, she held up two fingers. Señora Ramirez nodded. Señora Milagros sighed and nodded and told once more of the two children who had died: one in the womb, that she had known was a boy because her belly had come to a point, and she, who had been pretty became ugly within a month, which was as long as that son had survived within her; and Luz

Divina, the infant girl deserted by life after only a week on the earth, taken while napping in her little hammock, without cause or reason that God would reveal to the midwife or priest, all fathered by Noel who appeared almost as regularly as Christmas. Señora Milagros shrugged and was silent. Señora Ramirez searched Señora Milagros' face for the cause of the altered narrative. Had her friend discovered that she needed to keep some part of the story for herself? Señora Ramirez, who could never presume to tell it, offered the names of her living children, "Dolores, Rafael, and Venus (named for the popular song)," long before anyone knew that the girl would have the face of a Pekingese dog. Señora Ramirez' face closed as though she were submerging her head beneath water and for a perfect minute her face became the mask of an enduring Pietà; saying more would achieve nothing, and her friend, her sister in misfortune knew and didn't need to be told again. Venus, the adolescent girl with the dog's face, hated her mother and hated her name: the name that clung to her long after the song ceased to be heard from the windows of the housing project, and there was no point in telling Venus that her mother hadn't intended the irony that adhered to her name like a chronic illness. Venus looked at her mother and couldn't imagine anyone's innocence.

Señora Ramirez' silence puffed out her lips and turned the lobes of her ears red; the silence she kept as long as she could hold her breath wheezed. She gulped air and didn't name the two children she had lost, but genuflected once for each, and the howl that burst open her mouth called "Julio, Julio," not because she expected the man who had fathered her children to ever appear again, but calling out the provisional name she had given to her loss might prime the recitation Señora Milagros had stunted. "Julio, Julio, mi vida," she called. Señora Milagros said, "Entonces, well, Noel was merely useless as other men, he could never understand why any more should be required of him except to be handsome and in love, although he aspired to be dangerous, but was only brutal in manly commonplace ways. Luz Divina who lived only a week was the most beautiful of my children, her face a sublime version of her father's. I mourned for that child six years. During the six years of mourning, Noel's long absences and brief visitations began; during the ever more rare visitations he claimed his husbandly rights. More memorable than Noel's appearances were the soups that my sister Titi prepared and fed me, deepening my sleep. One scalding afternoon, after the hot bath my sister prescribed, and a bowl of her steaming soup, which had the head of a whiskered fish in it, but smelled of jasmine and had the taste of the best Spanish brandy, my sister Titi helped me into the hammock, strung up in the cement whitewashed bedroom between two open windows where one could watch the blue air boil. I breathed out the fumes of the soup, which tickled my temples, swung in the hammock in pursuit of a breeze, slipped out of my sweat-soaked body, and sank into the most refreshing siesta of my life. At first I didn't recognize the voice as my mother's; it was the voice of a young woman for whom death did not yet exist. The voice brought with it from beyond the grave a cooling breeze, and when she said 'Pay attention' I knew it was mother, the easy and confident way she took authority was unmistakably Mama. The cooling breeze from somewhere else bathed me, and I was aware of never before having been so effortlessly attentive, and then Luz Divina said to me, in the calmest and sweetest voice, 'Mami, don't mourn anymore, six years is sufficient; if I had lived longer your suffering would have been inconsolable, because at the age of six, in New York of America, I would have been struck by an automobile and killed, and then your pain would have been unsupportable. Mami, do not mourn for me any longer.' And at that time, I'd never had any idea of coming to the United States."

Laura Providencia watched the last tremors ripple at the top of Señora Ramirez' bosom, her hands opened in her lap, and her face resolved itself into an inconsolable autumnal softness. Laura noted that her mother hadn't significantly altered the catechism of narrative, she had only paused and reordered the sequence in which she spoke of her children. She concluded as always, patted Rosita's head, and said, "And then this one, who now has," and she raised both hands raising five fingers of her right hand, one finger of her left, one digit at a time, took a breath, and said, "six years." Rosita fidgeted, waiting. Laura stroked her little sister's thin arm, kissed her cheek and whispered, "Don't worry." Laura thought of how it was easiest for her mother to express affection for Luz Divina. Laura recalled a past when she had envied this sister she had never seen, but now she merely thought of Luz Divina as one of the family; and Rosita's unhappiness had grown more insistent. Laura Providencia's caresses and explanations calmed the child for brief intervals. Laura could see Rosita's face working, consuming the poor fictions and caresses she had reached for, and would reach for again, before feeding these comforts to her agitation. Laura knew what Rosita was waiting for, and she knew it wasn't going to happen.

Rosita, thin and brown as a fistful of twigs, at the center of the trembling pink ball of the dress, pushed, and Señora Milagros' hand flew from the top of Rosita's head to her own mouth, to catch and cup the small frightened laugh. The stem of Rosita's neck, and her scrawny shoulders shuddered; she pushed her head between her mother's huge knees, which looked to Laura like shrouded boulders about to part, as if Rosita were trying to return to the place of her making; but Laura knew that wasn't it, it was only the long waiting, the endless waiting that had commenced on the day they had left the island, after her mother had told Rosita they were going to visit somebody special. Rosita thought they might be going to visit her grandmother; it was, she knew, a long walk and a car ride to Abuela's house. A car would have to be hired, this usually happened after the long walk to Uncle Nestor's village. Laura wondered why her mother never told the children their destination when they went on trips. Always Señora Milagros just took the children out and they walked and walked and arrived eventually, someplace. Laura had once thought that her mother might have believed that walking about without knowing the destination would give them a feeling of freedom; or on that day when they left the island not telling where they were going would obscure the pain of leaving, or maybe her mother thought the children really didn't have to know. Although Laura knew, after a while she figured it out, and Angel knew too; but Rosita was so little, she became tired of walking and began to cry.

It was a hot, brilliant day. The dust, sparks in the sheen of blue air, the ocean beyond the road boomed and gurgled enormously, Rosita's weeping as distinct and sinuous as the drone of insects hovering about their heads. Señora Milagros stopped in the road, put down and laid open the suitcase at her feet. Rosita plodded to the right of her mother's hip, veered off the road, and stood there, kneading the hem of her dress. Laura Providencia, Angel, and Aunt Titi were strung out in the road not far behind, each weighted with a portion of boxes, bundles, and shopping bags. Aunt Titi bobbed along the road, pressed and scoured into her sacramental essence, a little taller than a dwarf. The huge crucifix swinging from her neck, driving her forward; she halted, and her smiling face, which might have been carved out of a plum pit, peeked out from the pyramid of bundles she carried unerringly. Señora Milagros bent over, her eyes on the extravagant horizon of the sea, as her hand probed in the suitcase under the folded bed sheet, felt the smooth warm glass of the sealed jar of holy water, and grasped and brandished a hand mirror in the air as a magician might pluck a dove from a bystander's dumb ear. She thrust the mirror in front of Rosita's face. "Look child! Fea! See how ugly you are when you cry." The face Rosita saw flashing in the mirror was the gaping face of a fish, just before the sun burst an explosion of silver light from the mirror, and then Rosita could see nothing, and she wanted to scream, "I'm blind," but the scream cracked in her throat, and even after Angel had swept her up, and the world came back into her eyes after the successive blinding blows of silver and blackness, she knew it all could be taken away, immediately, anytime; and many years later as a middle-aged woman, as she told it all to Laura Providencia, Laura still providing the words so that she could tell it, Rosita remembered living in an infinite and inexhaustible longing; this recollected as the centuries of someone's childhood she had been told about. "But anyway, it was true," she said, that despite the wanted and unwanted attention of men throughout her life, and much testimony to the contrary, she knew herself to be ugly. Although Laura Providencia had helped her to say it, she shook her head, no, no; Rosita smiled.

They paused in the road parallel to the sea. The surf boomed and hissed, the skittering blotches of green neon spit out from the sea, and moving on the white sand toward the road defined themselves as crabs as they crawled out of the glaring light. Aunt Titi gestured for Angel to load his bundles into her arms. Angel obeyed, and divided his bundles and boxes between Aunt Titi and Laura. He could not deny Aunt Titi what she asked for, anymore than he doubted her capacity to carry the load. She had planted this belief in him, and in Laura, long before the children could resist belief, long before belief required effort. She, Aunt Titi, Titi diminutive for Tía, Tía Titi, which became Aunt Titi in the United States, but always she had been known as Auntie, even in some past when she must have been a child, although neither Laura nor Angel could imagine that; but Aunt Titi in the long ago had not so much told them, as allowed Laura and Angel to be in the presence of her soliloquies, which said, nuns were married to God, and she Titi, was betrothed to God, forever. Giddy as a Pentecostal with the thought of the end of the world, she'd mentioned the care of this niece, that nephew, her younger sister, Lucia Milagros, so-and-so who's dying, and the still nameless she assisted in being born, all of this merely an aspect of her devotion; and Angel and Laura marveled at her abiding contentment.

Angel hung a shopping bag from the crook of Aunt Titi's elbow, and stacked parcels in her arms up to her eyes. Aunt Titi, in her devotions, and under the weight of her burdens, grew smaller and smaller, happy finally to disappear altogether in the service of God.

They continued. Angel carried Rosita. Rosita's skinny legs swung, her sandaled feet bouncing off Angel's thighs. Laura Providencia walked alongside, carrying her pile of boxes, purring at Rosita's ear. Rosita, in Angel's arms, her head on his shoulder, kept her eyes opened and whined. Up ahead, Señora Milagros marched under her load of belongings, and in the rear, a motley of parcels jiggled and moved inexorably down the road, behind and under which, Angel and Laura knew, was Aunt Titi.

They arrived in Uncle Nestor's village. Uncle Nestor, the youngest and most obliging of Aunt Titi's and Señora Milagros' brothers, made the arrangements for the hired car and drove them to the airport.

Handsome Uncle Nestor examined his mustache in the rear view mirror, stroking with his forefinger the black lushness of hair on his lip, and navigated the automobile with the barest touch of the steering wheel with his left hand. The car screeched down the mountain road. Inside, amid their tumbling belongings, Uncle Nestor's dog, El Capitán, who traveled everywhere with Nestor, howled. Aunt Titi, Señora Milagros, Angel, Rosita and Laura Providencia bounced and bobbled. Rosita screamed. Angel was fascinated by El Capitán. The animal appeared to have been bred from a Russian wolfhound and a goat. Angel, swaying and bouncing, applauded the acrobatic dexterity of El Capitán. The dog managed to remain upright on the floor of the car, his four shivering legs scrabbling in perpetual motion, seemingly sustained by the legato of his wolf howl. The rainbow-hued mountains and God's gaudy sky fell with them in the side windows of the car hurtling toward cataclysm. Angel looked out of the window at the flamboyant mountains in the distance, heard the screeching tires at the edge of nowhere; the sun's light gleamed in the windows and Angel imagined the long fall, deep enough to confound all physics, far enough to have one's life pass before one's eyes, suffer remorse for the life lived, and enjoy the disorientation of one's first evening in eternity before ever hitting bottom. The car spiraled down and down. Uncle Nestor, happy and calm, almost succeeded in taking his attention away from the vision of his face in the mirror.

When the car had come down from the mountain, and they were hurtling along the long flat road, El Capitán stopped howling. Rosita was screaming. Señora Milagros turned in the front seat and made a motion with her hands, as if she were going to take the mirror from the suitcase and thrust it in front of Rosita's face again. Aunt Titi fished in the shopping bag between her legs, pulled out a melon, an orange, a pink bow of shiny fabric, and a hairbrush. Aunt Titi gave Angel the melon, Laura the orange, and put the glistening pink bow in Rosita's lap. Titi began to brush Rosita's black hair, the slow powerful strokes yanked Rosita's head back. Rosita cried. Titi fixed the pink bow in Rosita's hair and said, "One must suffer to be beautiful." Laura Providencia knew that the point was not beauty, but the virtue in pain. Rosita threw up.

They stopped the car, fetched buckets of seawater and cleaned up the mess. They stripped Rosita, standing in the road; Aunt Titi, Señora Milagros, and Laura Providencia shielding the near naked child from the sight of Angel and Uncle Nestor. El Capitán ran in circles and barked. Uncle Nestor held his nose and strolled beyond the range of the bad smell. El Capitán ran after him. Aunt Titi opened one parcel, removed various herbs and ingredients she had named, but whose names she would not share, and brewed the special tea for Rosita. The heat of the day was such that Titi did not need a fire to cook the ingredients; she poured the tea from a jar into a baby bottle, snapped on the rubber nipple, and vigorously shook the contents.

Rosita stood, washed and in a clean frock, near a palm tree whose shade was obliterated by the noon-day heat, and sucked the bottle dry.

Back in the car Angel cradled her. When they reached the airport Rosita was still sleeping. Laura Providencia said, "Look

Rosita, an airplane! We are going to fly." Rosita snored. Angel carried Rosita on the plane. Once during the flight Rosita's eyes flickered. Rosita awoke in Nueva York, America.

"I want to go home." Rosita was waiting, still waiting. Señora Ramirez reached over and stroked Rosita's head. It seemed to Rosita that her mother, through her meanderings, had misplaced home as she must have misplaced the man who was her father.

This, at least, was what Laura thought Rosita was trying to say, as Laura retrieved her little sister's words, one at a time, from the wet, hiccupping sobs. "And this one," Señora Milagros said, tugging down the heavy folds of her dress, and lifting Rosita's chin from her lap, "this one is never still."

Later, in the sketch Laura would make of Señora Ramirez and her mother, and hide in her closet, Laura depicted the two women as nearly identical, the women's ballooned and shapeless childbearing bodies shrouded in the black, sack-like dresses. Laura's mother wore the heavy woolen dress with the thick, abrasive rope around where her waist used to be. From the rope's two ends hung two large weighted knots, each shaped like the clapper in a church bell.

After the third month in the United States, Laura's mother had asked Laura if she would wear the heavy black dress, and the rope, for a while. Señora Milagros explained that now that Laura was a señorita, having menstruated, she could help pay some of the debt that her mother owed to Our Lady of Perpetual Succor. "Many years ago," said Señora Milagros, she had promised the saint, that if she granted her cousin Teresa, who had once nursed Angel, but had, several years later contracted tuberculosis — if the saint granted Cousin Teresa one more good long year to live, she, Lucia Milagros, would wear the heavy penitential dress for two years in return for the one year granted Cousin Teresa. "But," said Señora Milagros, she was still a young person when she made the vow, and not capable of the necessary seriousness; she had only worn the dress five months. She was not sure that the misfortune in her life was due to the unpaid debt to Our Lady of Perpetual Succor, but she felt that the debt had undoubtedly made her susceptible to envious people, and the evil eye. Now she had been wearing the dress for almost a year, and the ponderous rope pulled at her back as she sat at the sewing machine in the factory. The pain in her lower back slowed her hands, and she was being paid, she reminded Laura, on the basis of piece work. "So," she said, if Laura, who was now a señorita, took on a small portion of the debt for only a couple of months, there would be relief to her mother's back, and she would bring more money into the house.

Laura knew that when her mother referred to herself in the third person, and invoked the title "Mother," her mother had marshaled the moral force of all creation; and as Laura steeled herself to say no, she felt herself complicit in her mother's martyrdom. Laura's voice shook. She explained again why she couldn't wear the dress to school. Señora Milagros frowned. Laura said, that although such a costume was not expressly forbidden, it was inappropriate. Laura offered to wear the penitential dress during the summer, when she was not attending school. Her mother said, "In the summer I will not need you, by then my debt will have been paid."

Rosita fidgeted in Laura's arms. Laura pressed her cheek to Rosita's temple, and tightened her embrace. Looking out from the periphery of Rosita's hot brow, Laura's vision lingered for an instant on the smear of pink icing on her mother's mouth. Señora Milagros looked into Laura's face and saw what Laura was seeing; Señora Milagros' eyes went black and accusatory, as if Laura's seeing was itself a mockery. Laura felt suddenly like a child caught in a shameful act; she managed not to blurt out that it was Angel's fault. He had handed the plates of birthday cake to his mother and Señora Ramirez and run off. It was, after all, his birthday cake, and of course he was gone, out in the street. Laura felt again the presence of his absence, the weight of it in her chest, and then she wanted to apologize to him too, for the readiness of her heart to heap blame on him. What did it matter that it was the icing on his cake that had smeared mama's mouth with the gaudiness. Laura spoke, "But mama," she said, "but," and was startled by the sound of her own voice, which she recognized as her own although it sounded false to her. She reminded herself that she had not denounced her brother and she made cooing noises in Rosita's ear.

Señora Milagros, with her thumb and pinkie, deftly pinched the corners of her mouth and the blotches of pink icing disappeared. She looked down at her well-shod feet, and, when Señora Milagros looked up again, Laura saw on her mother's face something like confirmation, a look, benign and tantamount to forgiveness; she had almost smiled.

In that first year Rosita had begun the first grade, and the black girls beat her up. Laura talked to her mother about the hazards of the public school. Children not much older than Rosita were seen making deliveries of drugs in the school yard. Señora Milagros had heard of the thirteen-year-old expectant mothers who would not complete the seventh grade. Señora Milagros and Aunt Titi decided on St. Ann's school for Rosita.

Laura delivered Rosita into the custody of nuns. Nothing in the street frightened Rosita as much as the Sisters at St. Ann's School. Laura had turned away from the sight of the nun in the arched doorway, and all she could remember of the nun's face was that it was an inspiration to abstinence and chastity of every kind, and Laura did not wish to see the face again. The school and the church attached to it were the only buildings left standing on the street. Beyond the church and the gray mortuary stone of the school and its fenced in box of graveled yard was rubble, and the smoke of blackened walls of burnt out buildings.

Rosita hung on to the wrought iron fence in front of the school. She sat down, bunched and anchored herself on the sidewalk, her small fists clutched around the iron bars were difficult to get at through the barrier she had made of her hunched upper body. Laura struggled, she reached in through the crevice between Rosita's upper arm and forearm and tried to work Rosita's fingers loose. Laura begged, she pulled at Rosita's shoulder, wedging Rosita a little way from the fence. Rosita clung, her fists knotted around the iron bars. Laura heard herself wail, and she ran from the sight of Rosita clutching the fence, and the nun whose face neither she nor Rosita wanted to see moving out from under the arched doorway.

Laura ran and remembered Rosita rising obediently from the sidewalk, and following the nun into the school; although Laura could not have seen this, running as she was, not wanting to see, but when she remembered it she remembered always, Rosita letting go, rising with a look of sudden forbearance on her face, and following the nun into the school. Laura Providencia described it this way in memory, as over the years Rosita forgave her sister again and again.

The white lady with blue hair had come to their house. She was a very tall, thin old lady with a stern, dignified, but kindly face. Laura answered the door. She thought that Miss Quire resembled a great white bird, a bird bringing her the fulfillment of her dearest wish; she would attend a school where she would be required to do what made her happiest, draw pictures for hours on end. Señora Milagros and Aunt Titi thought of Laura's drawing as an aspect of her tendency for inattentiveness, an eccentricity that could become a vice, if left unattended, but here was this woman of great dignity who had come to their home, the white woman with blue hair, whose tremulous and patrician voice was itself blue. Aunt Titi did not understand a word the blue-haired blue-voiced old white woman said, but she felt and knew an immediate and deep affinity for the magisterial chaste presence who had honored them by coming to their door. Before Laura was allowed to translate for Miss Quire, the dean of student affairs at the High School of Music and Art, Laura's mother and aunt sent Laura hurrying off with a glance at Laura's bare feet.

In the dark closet Laura studied the long seam of light in the crack of the slightly opened door, waiting and knowing that the light would tell her nothing beyond the possibilities of its design and radiance. She stood in the dark and fondled the everyday shoes cradled in her arms; she had put her special Sunday patent leather shoes on her feet. She knew she had injured her mother and Aunt Titi by answering the door and admitting Miss Quire into the house while she was still barefoot. A letter had come from the school announcing the time and date of Miss Quire's visit and asking if the designated time for the visit was convenient. But Laura Providencia — who had translated the letter — and her mother and aunt had trouble in believing in what the letter said, believing that it could happen, and so they forgot about it; or on Laura's part, not so much forgetting the portentous visit, as placing the time of the visit in some messianic future that could never be imminent.

Through the crack in the slightly opened closet door and its seam of light, Laura breathed in the powerful hospital smell of the disinfectant her mother had insisted Laura use when she washed the floors. Suddenly, Laura was certain that Miss Quire had seen the drawing she had made of the immaculate grotto that was her home. The drawing was one of twelve Laura had submitted in a portfolio to the entrance committee. In the drawing Laura had rendered with colored inks, the living room and the peach-colored wall where the flock of pink, tin, cherubim ascended toward the thorn-crowned, bleeding Jesus pointing to his heart in flame. Down, diagonally from the cherubim, on a transparent plastic console, in which a three dimensional waterfall cascaded beneath a flickering rainbow, a flock of doves, whose wings beat to the mysterious tides of light in the transparent console, supported a large tank of tropical fish. The gloriously colored fish darted about in the water, a miniature glass castle, wrecked schooner, and a thumb-sized mermaid with silver breasts imbedded in an ocean floor of candy-colored marbles. Adjacent to the underwater life, which was stacked above the waterfall, and past the television set and the clock on the wall, a smiling sun with golden spokes supporting neon stars, was the altar loaded with votive candles, the profusion of small, erect flames spuming thin scrolls of smoke, surrounding the foot-high statue of the Virgin Mary.

The composition of the drawing suggested an inventory of the too fecund miracle of creation, threatening to overwhelm the hallowed space where one might pray. It was funny. Laura had not known the drawing would be funny when she began rendering the sun clock with the radiating spokes and stars her mother had purchased at the five-and-ten, but when she completed the drawing, she smiled. She was, after she thought about it, tempted to destroy the drawing, but she could not. She included it in her entrance portfolio. Now in the dark closet she heard her mother and her aunt offering Miss Quire coffee, and Miss Quire, not understanding a word, making flattering statements about their home, which neither her mother nor aunt understood; and her mother and aunt were calling, "Laura, Laura Providencia por favor." Laura decided not to bring her everyday shoes into the living room to display what her aunt and mother provided; the patent leather shoes on her feet were sufficient. But she came out of the closet knowing she had exposed a nakedness, revealed something of the inner life of her family in a way that the living room itself, and her mother and aunt standing there, could not. In the walk from the bedroom to the living room, Laura had time to change her mind several times. First she concluded that she was not really guilty of betraying her family. What her drawing revealed was something she had not known or intended, and she was, she told herself, as surprised as any stranger to discover what the completed drawing revealed; but there was something else she could not exonerate herself from, and it festered and thrilled her. The white, blue-haired lady carried some idea of who Laura Providencia might be. Laura didn't know exactly what the idea was, but she suspected that it must be something grand and fine, and Laura knew she had given the picture she had made, the blatantly funny picture of where her family lived, in partial payment for the wonderful idea the white lady with blue hair had of her, and she had answered the door barefoot.

Señora Milagros, Titi, Laura Providencia, and Miss Quire sat down to coffee. Rosita was napping in her bedroom. Angel was somewhere in the street. Miss Quire sipped the inky coffee, and her transparent eyes became avid, while her kindly and dignified smile remained fixed. She said that Laura Providencia was one of three Puerto Rican students accepted at the school. She said that that very day she was going to visit the other two new students, and welcome them to the school; would it be possible, Miss Quire wanted to know, for Laura to accompany her to welcome the new students to the school? Laura translated the request. Señora Milagros hesitated. She looked at her sister. Aunt Titi nodded yes. Señora Milagros said, "Si."

Down in the street the white lady with blue hair moved through the neighborhood like an apparition. Laura felt it was her presence that lent Miss Quire visibility.

Laura was surprised by what her innocent and purposeful hand continued to render. She stacked her drawings on the shelf of the closet, under the shoe boxes and above the rail where her Communion dress hung. She knew herself to be alternately innocent and guilty, but mostly innocent, except for the irreducible something in her that saw, and all that her hand made visible without a trace of charity for the world it made manifest, or the maker, ostensibly, herself. Aunt Titi was certain that the old white-white woman's visit was a sign, evidence, and vindication for the journey to the United States. Señora Milagros and Aunt Titi did not say so, would not utter it, who knows what malevolent spirit might be present to overhear, but they nodded, furtively in affirmation, and insisted on the present of the new special outfit Laura Providencia would wear to her first day of school.

Angel and Rosita slept. Señora Milagros, Aunt Titi, and Laura Providencia were up most of the night. Laura stood, in her slip, on a kitchen chair. She dressed and undressed many times. Aunt Titi and her mother sewed and altered the various parts of the garment she would wear. Laura Providencia endured their gift. Wearing it, she would be wearing what her eyes saw, what her hand would render, so that if her hand mocked anything, it mocked her also; willing, compliant, accepting the gift, she was not completely apart from what she saw and rendered, and there was, Laura Providencia hoped, some form of dispensation in this. She owed it, as her mother owed time in her penitential dress.

Aunt Titi had traveled downtown to Orchard Street to purchase, from two pushcart vendors and Molly's Millinery, a pink pillbox hat with a white-netted veil; the white elbow-length gloves, and a salmon-colored, cake-shaped purse with shoulder straps, large enough to carry lunch, books, pencil and a handkerchief. Señora Milagros worked very hard to get the bodice of the dress to fit Laura properly; it was shaped and layered like an artichoke, vibrant green, and would have obscured Laura's waist if not for the tufted, creamy white sash culminating in a large bow on Laura's thin hip. Aunt Titi stitched on the bow. The skirt flowed down in night blue velvet pleats, pocked with silver stars, the lace hem of the skirt was circled by a flock of doves chasing each other around, just above Laura Providencia's feet, sheathed in white socks and the Sunday black patent leather shoes.

That morning Señora Milagros and Aunt Titi dressed Laura with great care. Laura stood on the kitchen chair, one white-socked foot gracefully extended, her mother bent beneath her, and slipped the gleaming black shoe on Laura's foot. Aunt Titi, just a little taller than the chair Laura stood on, and in a posture that looked like a frozen curtsy, reached up to hold Laura's hand and steady her balance. The early morning light washed over the dark of the kitchen window and turned one shimmering pane into a mirror. Laura perched on the chair, her mother tenderly held one foot, Aunt Titi held her hand. Laura Providencia saw herself mirrored in the kitchen's window, gowned as some tropical plant, floating above the clothesline she could see through the window mirror that let in some of the morning, and the vista of clotheslines and rooftops as the window also reflected the inside of the kitchen. Laura recollected having dozed off, and waking surprised many times through the long night. She opened her eyes and her mother asked her to get undressed, or to raise her arms and turn around, or to step down from the chair. Laura stepped down from the chair, her elegant descent mimicking a choreography she could vaguely remember having seen somewhere, perhaps in a movie, or maybe she had read it; and it occurred to her then, that she might only be momentarily trapped in her mother's story; but the dress was so heavy.

Señora Milagros slipped the white elbow-length gloves on Laura's outstretched arms. Aunt Titi stood on her tiptoes holding the pink pillbox hat with the white-netted veil just above Laura Providencia's head. Señora Milagros whispered, "Esperate." Laura closed her eyes. Her mother's hands touched her face softly, rubbed her cheeks, caressed her temples and neck. Laura felt the coolness of the cosmetic smeared with the most meticulous care over every inch of her face and neck. She felt her mother's breath on her cheeks, and knew her mother's belief in this concluding act to be the most she could bestow.

Laura Providencia opened her eyes. Her mother stood an

arm length in front of her, aiming the large hand mirror in which Rosita had seen her face as that of a gaping fish. Laura saw in the mirror that she was white, her caramel brown face had been turned into a mask of ghostly white. The pink pillbox hat with the white-netted veil came down in Titi's hands, crowning her head. Señora Milagros and Aunt Titi applauded softly, and went to awaken Rosita.

Laura Providencia moved down the street under the weight of the garment, in her white-gloved hand she clasped Rosita's small hand and tugged her along the sidewalk. She kept up a steady patter of talk as her little sister seemed to recognize her voice, even as Rosita looked at the strange person with the ghostly white face with suspicion. Laura saw the street, people hurrying towards the subway station, and Rosita, through the gauzy film of the netted veil. The whitish haze softened everything she saw, as if the whiteness of her skin were giving off the largess and privilege of its color, everything seen at a remove and modulated by a mist as subtle as dust.

People rushed by them hurrying to the subway entrance. Laura kept on talking to Rosita, trying to reassure her that she was herself. Rosita glanced at the person holding her hand, tugging her along the sidewalk. Laura could not lift the veil, it hadn't been necessary for her to put words to her tacit understanding; she was under the obligation of a covenant; she would not lift up the veil. When they reached the street of St. Ann's School, Laura was dragging Rosita. Rosita howled. Laura realized that she had lost or left behind the large cake-shaped purse containing her books, pencils, lunch, and handkerchief. She could still feel the phantom weight of the heavy purse's shoulder strap. Rosita was hunkered down, clinging to the wrought-iron fence. Rosita peeked at the ghost face that claimed to be her sister, and at the nun in her black habit with the most forbidding face in the world moving out toward her from under the arched doorway. Laura's scream billowed out the veil curtaining her mouth as she swung, she glimpsed the blood gush from Rosita's nose, and several streets later she saw the blood on her white gloves.

Laura Providencia walked slowly down the long hallway. On either side of her, venerable oaken doors emitted a silence she willed herself to inhabit. The crowd following her was noisy and laughing. A series of bells went off, louder than a junkyard of alarm clocks, shrill and persistent in the space of half a minute. Many of the students who had been following her ran off, but many stayed, surrounding her, blocking her path so that Laura couldn't go forward, although she had no clear idea of where she was going. Many of the students were shouting questions at her, some seemed concerned, some were laughing. The old white lady with the blue hair and blue voice broke through the crowd. Her face asked a question. Laura Providencia thought she had said, "Yes Miss," or "Yes Missis, may I help you," but she wasn't sure. Somehow, through the long walk down the interminable hallways of the school, Laura Providencia had lost her English. The old white lady with the blue hair didn't recognize her. She looked about the crowd to locate the student who might identify this apparently lost elfin parent. Laura clenched the silence in her throat. Miss Quire lifted from the flat terrain of the breast pocket of her tweed gray tunic the lorgnette, pinned and hanging from a ribbon. She squinted through the lorgnette she held between thumb and forefinger; bending down, and peering into the face behind the gauzy veil, she exclaimed, "Oh my, my." The face behind the veil was weeping brown streaks into its whiteness. Laura Providencia threw her white-gloved hands up in front of her face. Miss Quire saw the bloodstained palms. She touched Laura's arms looking for injury. She fluttered her hands and spoke kindly and authoritatively in her blue voice, and the students dispersed.

Miss Quire led Laura by the hand through one of the oaken doors with a pebbled opaque window. In the women's faculty bathroom Miss Quire removed the pink-veiled hat from Laura's head and put it on a stool. She stripped the white, bloodied, elbow-length gloves from Laura Providencia's arms, dropped the gloves in the sink, and turned on the water faucet. She did all this slowly, softly asking questions until finally Laura answered in Spanish, and Miss Quire seemed to grasp the gist of Laura's responses. Miss Quire produced a handkerchief from the sleeve of her gray tunic. She soaked the handkerchief under the running faucet.

Laura stared into the mirror above the sink and watched the old white lady with blue hair wash her face with the wet handkerchief; in slow circular motions the old white lady restored Laura Providencia's face to brown. Laura glanced at the adjacent sink brimming with water turning red, the bloated fingers of the floating glove waved at her.

THE TRUANT

On the street of the Lovenest Candy Bar Factory the air is thick and sweet. The clouds above the smokestacks keep pace with my slow trot.

The factory whistle shrieks. I move past a series of barred factory windows, and know, as though the void were a great weight suspended in me, I have never seen or touched through anyone but me, have no memory of ever being anyone or anything else. Seasick as Jonah in the whale, I'd climb out of my eyes if I could. A number of kids on their way to the schoolyard pass by me, their faces contorted, mimicking, I realize, the idiot trance of my face. Peggy lingers behind the others. She is in my fourth-grade class. Miss Hamilton, the teacher, assigned me to sit with Peggy and help her with her reading. Peggy's face is clenched around a secret. Sitting at the desk next to Peggy, she looked put-upon, and I felt I ought to apologize for something. There on the street, after the others have gone some distance, her pretty face puffs up with hatred. "You," she says, "Kilt God!" "What?" I've heard, but the words pass through me. She spits on the sidewalk, turns, her long black braids swinging, and she runs off, joining the others. Peggy's accusation and the amazing transformation of her face lack the power to dispel the other fear; I run. I run for a long time through many streets.

It's too late to go to school now; and I have lost my books. The air stinks of malt. I've run all the way to the beer breweries.

Strolling on my block, I wonder what to tell Mother. How to explain what happened? I'm not in school, and I have left my school books somewhere. She will have to tell Father when he gets home. She will not tell him before he has been fed. Still, it will be bad. I decide to go off, walk around, explore, think what to do. The street is empty except for the janitor of the building next to the one where I live; old man Kropotkin is sitting on the stoop, bantering with the widow, Mrs. Fleischbaum. Thick-bodied Kropotkin sits on the bottom step of the stone stoop, elbows on his knees, his large white, moulting head in his hands, rocking from side to side. On the top step of the stoop Mrs. Fleischbaum waddles on parade; her bony chin held high, one white-gloved hand at the throat clasps the fur coat which is bald in spots, the spring breeze riffling the wretched fur. "Well Lillian," says Kropotkin from the bottom step, "I ask you only once more today, will you marry me?" Mrs. Fleischbaum puckers and says, "Mebbe." "Mebbe?" booms Kropotkin, "mebbe is not no." He claps his hands, "And so Lillian, what about the dowry?" "The dowry?" says Mrs. Fleischbaum, "the dowry!" The fur wings of her arms unfurl, wide and trembling. The blue-veined, beribboned wreckage of her throat is rigid with dignity. The white-gloved hands shake, grasp the collar, and slowly the coat opens. "Mr. Kropotkin," she says, from the top step of the stoop, "Mr. Kropotkin, mine body is mine dowry."

Kropotkin shudders, his laughter comes out in a thin whistle, "Aha! That! That belongs to the undertaker," and he winks; in the batting of his eye I see myself appear in his vision. Will he tell Mama he saw me? Mrs. Fleischbaum hardly regards me at all; I might be some aspect of Kropotkin's shadow. She turns, slowly, the fur mantle swirling, and I'm off. At the corner I slow down, turn, cross the street.

I pass several people who take no special notice of me. A police car goes by. I wonder whether Dead-Finger Ryan the truant officer can be lurking anywhere near. I begin to gallop. With my mouth I make the sound of galloping hooves, I bounce in the saddle past a Chinese laundry, around another corner, and I'm under the El, and the noise of the train consumes every sound in the world all the way to the Williamsburg Bridge. During the High Holy Days Grandma took me onto the bridge so that I could throw my sins away in the river.

I walk over the bridge. The seagulls in the sky pivot and wheel, the river below blinking back the lights on the bridge. I watch the water and the tugboats. Under the sky spotted with birds, I pass the hunched figures of bums. Water music plays in my stomach.

As I reach the Lower Manhattan side of the bridge I come on a large company of mothers sitting on benches rocking baby carriages. I march by; they look at me and rock the carriages silently. One of the mothers stares at me. Will she call a cop? Report me as a hooky-player? I avert my eyes and walk briskly, as someone with an important destination. Very soon I'm off the bridge and on Delancey Street. Even though it is a weekday the street is busy, people coming and going, vendors and push-carts. I pass under the grand marquee of the Loews Delancey movie house.

On Orchard Streeet I stop and watch from a distance; the skinny shill for a clothing store is hanging onto the lapel of a reluctant customer; the shill is thin and wears a black, tight suit; he is dragging a fat man, slowly, over the pavement toward the store's doorway and singing, "A zoot, a coat, a gabardine." I re-member an ant in the park moving a leaf thousands of times it size.

I wander through many streets, losing and finding my way. Now I'm waiting for three o'clock. I want to go home. The wait-ing is infested with endless time — it's passing slow, clogged with my meandering. I trace my way back through many side streets. The weather has turned hot.

Walking over the wet black gutter littered with pieces of sparkling ice, I bend down, pick up a chunk, and suck on it. I stand there sucking the ice, the cold of it wonderful in my mouth.

"'Ey, who died and left you king?"

"What?"

"Who gave ya permission?"

I turn around. There are three. They're older, fifth or sixth graders. The littlest one, my size, is smoking a cigarette. He walks up to me and repeats the question. Nose to nose he blows smoke in my face. I ask "What?" "Who tol'ya y'could have the ice?" I shrug. "You a wise guy?" "I thought it was free." "It's my uncle's ice." "Oh." "You a wise guy?" I shake my head no. "See," he says, "since Geronimo moved to the Bronx these little punks come to our block and think they can get away with anything." The other two come forward. The three stand in front of me passing the cigarette from mouth to mouth. They take turns blowing smoke in my face. The tallest one says, "You afraid?" I am afraid, but I don't know how to answer. Is it a test? The one who asks has an old face stuck on his boy's body. He sounds solicitous. I look at his face and see benevolence. I smile. "He's a wise guy," he says, "mark him, Petey." Petey is holding a pen-knife cupped in the hand at his side, and he says, "Eh, he's just a kid." The third one blows his nose through his fingers and wipes his fingers on my shirt. "Y'know that ice is from offa Uncle Impereteli's truck and this ain't your block!" "Pay attention! Oh, he gotta learn." "And look!" the one who is my size says, astonished, pointing at my belt buckle, "He's grabbing at the family name." I look, the belt which mother bought me has the initial "I" on the buckle, for me, my name, Isaac. The big one says, "Gimme the belt!" I take a step backward. He grabs at my waist front and yanks me forward, the other two swarm over me, twisting my arms. My right arm is pushed up behind me. I scream. I hear the other screaming. A woman's voice from far away, in the other language. They let me go.

I reach for my pants which have slipped down past my hips. With my left hand I hold my pants up and swing my right arm at my side; the pain ebbs. From high above, the woman's voice goes on haranguing the boys. There is a smudge of light from a window five stories up. From the window the shrill voice scolds, filling the street. The boys shout, answer placatingly, one says in English, "hide and seek, it ain't nothin," their backs are to me. The tall one is holding my belt. It dangles down, the buckle with the letter "I" shining in the gutter among the puddles of melted ice and the smoking stub of the cigarette. I reach and grab hold of the belt hanging from the tall one's hand with my two hands and jerk it hard. His arms fly up from his sides, letting go of the belt as he tries to keep his balance, and he falls.

I'm halfway down the street, one hand holding up my pants, the other grasping the snaking belt, the buckle ringing off the pavement. They're after me, their sneakered feet exploding from the concrete echoes as the lady's voice fades. My knees pumping high, I careen around the corner.

The street I have pitched myself into is filled with women hauling shopping carts and pushing baby carriages. Old people sit in front of tenements, on milk boxes, sunning themselves. One, two, three young men, stripped to the waist push hand trucks loaded with bolts of cloth. I run, holding up my pants with one hand, the belt hanging from my other hand. I zig-zag past a young man with a red bandanna around his head; he is pushing a hand truck. He looks at me, lets go of the handles of the L-shaped hand truck which veers forward with the weight of the piece goods. He doubles up with laughter, points at me and yells, "Hi-ho Silver!" I whiz by between two women pushing baby carriages. One woman screams, I glance over my shoulder. Petey, the one with the knife, is a quarter of a block behind me, weaving and darting between the hand trucks. The one with the wrinkled, old man's face is pacing a little behind Petey. I turn the corner and zip by another flock of old people sitting on boxes in front of a doorway, and dive for the hallway that has no one sitting out in front.

In the vestibule that goes on and on it is nighttime; the vestibule has its own dank weather. Ahead of me there is a dim snaking light. I run in the murky light until I reach a stairwell. Something is moving in the dark behind me.

I charge up numberless flights of stairs, every breath stabbing in my side. Several flights below me, I hear feet pounding up stairs — Petey with the knife, and his friend with the old man's face? Slow now, I make my way up, up. I run out of steps. There is a wall with a door in it. I yank the door open, stumble through to a smoky savannah of floating rooftops and endless sky. I lay flat, hide, close my eyes. Sprawled on the rooftop, aching, the pigeons throb and coo around me.

After a time, time and the world return. The giant stone finger of the Empire State Building gooses a forbearing heaven. It is humid. The tar on the roof is sticky. Looking down between my legs I see that someone has excavated out of the malleable black a valentine heart and two names. In large beautifully crafted letters, with doves fore and aft, and haloed with stars, *Lena Pishota, love forever, Apache Ramos.* Beyond the exquisitely carved arrow-pierced heart that says, *Forever,* Lena's name again, in chalk, *Lena I would let you piss in my eye just to see what it looks like — Stanley.* Surrounded by the strutting, clucking, soft cooing pigeons, and the declarations of love carved and scrawled between my sprawling legs, I lie down.

It is quiet. Everyone waits. In his undershirt, nose open to the smell of pot roast, Father's jaw works. The glossy white oilcloth on the table mirrors him into twins. His reflection is stretched across the table, the kitchen light ripples the terrain of his headless muscular double, the bowl of pot roast steaming from the region of his groin up to the actual him, dead to the world, eating. He scoops the last of the meat up to his mouth, and mother ladles out a pile of gravy-soaked potatoes. He finishes off the second helping. Mother quickly loads the plate. He looks up, sees me. He says, "Ess, Ess, mein kind." He chews and his eyes go out. There is a ding, ding, ding in the radiator pipes, one neighbor signaling another. Mother whispers, "Where were you?" I shrug. She will not make an issue of it, not now. I finger the length of clothesline holding up my pants. My kid brother is seated next to me. He leans against my shoulder. Father wipes the gravy from his plate with a heel of rye bread and pops it into his mouth; his puffed cheek jiggles up and down. His eyes roll around dreamily. He swallows; his eyes light up. He looks startled. He looks from me, to Mother, to my brother. "So hello," he says. He pours himself a water tumbler full of schnapps. I stop holding my breath. My brother swings his feet under the table. Mother begins to pick at her food. Father stares at me; his mouth gapes. I wonder what my face is doing. He bellows, "Eat!" Mother says, "Please eat." I look at the food on my plate, the immaculate kitchen; the kitchen smells of stewed meat and dis-infectant — like a hospital corridor. On her hands and knees she has purged the place. Father turns away; he can't stand to look at whatever it is he sees in my face. He has another drink. "I ran into your cousin Eddie today," he says to Mother, "Eddie and the shiksa hit the jackpot again, she's pregnant." — "Three boys they got already." Mother says, "So more soldiers for the Czar." "What?" says Father, "We're in America, no?" Mother says, "Women shouldn't make soldiers for them." Father says, "Who's them?" Mother sighs and says in Yiddish, "Armies is armies. Eat, horse." Father answers in Yiddish; he says something about Mother's side of the family. Mother answers him in Russian, which I do not understand. Father's eyes flash. He lights up the stub of a cigar and has another drink. He looks at me in disbelief. "What," he says, "are you starin'? Eat!" My brother laughs and wets his pants. I feel the wet against my leg, it smells. "Oy," Father moans, "Sarah, look at him, the world is gonna eat him alive!" Father's shivering hawk's head comes close. I can't move. His hands beg, he screams, "Wake up!" and the blow lifts me out of the chair.

Lying on the floor I can taste the blood in my mouth; there is a whistling inside my head and I can see through one eye. Furniture and dishes are being smashed. Mother is shrieking. My brother is doing the Indian dance he learned in kindergarten; he is circling around and chanting, "Hiya-hiya-hiya-ha!" Looking straight up and squinting through one eye, I have a telescopic view of the water-stained ceiling. Suddenly, Father is on his knees hovering over me. "Listen," he says, "you have to understand, I'm a very emotional person. You know you're the apple of my eye," and he bursts into tears. Mother is yelling, "Lunatic, murderer! You should burn in hell!" Her voice takes on an odd calm as she speculates in Yiddish to someone invisible. "Ah no, they won't be able to make it hot enough for him in hell, never." I envision Father down there, foreman of the conflagration, sweating, laughing, and exhorting the ranks of the damned. "For cryin' out loud, it's freezin' down here." Harry who works at the factory with Father stumbles, gasping, out of the cloud of steam to ask, "Allo Abe, how's by you?" Father answers, "I make a living." The two dance around, huffing, puffing, trumpeting a ballet of hernias, the distended broken muscles shimmy from their hairy groins; they point, compare, and bless the heat.

Lifting me up by my shirt front, Father says, "I'm sorry, okay? I'm sorry." He's crying wet tears on me. Mother comes up behind him with the bread knife. "Lunatic," she says, "close your eyes in this house tonight and you won't wake up." Father gets up and explains, "Y'know Sarah, I'm an emotional person," and he punches a crater into the wall. My brother has taken off the Indian headdress of red feathers. Now he is a reporter. He thrusts a soupspoon under my nose and says, "Talk into the microphone sir, pul-ease, a few words for our listeners on the West Coast." Then he wails like a police siren and speaks into the spoon, "Call-ing all cars! Call-ing all cars!" Father lifts brother up and tosses him back. I hear my brother bounce and roll on the floor laughing his weird wet-pants laugh. Father bends down beside me, lifts me up by the shirt collar, rattles my head on my shoulders; he's weeping salt water on me. "I'm sorry, alright?" Mother waits with the bread knife, "Animal," she says in Yiddish, "close your eyes in this house tonight and I'll fix your sleep." Father says, "Izzy, son, come, get up, we'll go to the Turkish baths, have a sweat, and good sleep, come." I lie there, and it's not just that I can't talk. I would say I'm all right, all right — only how to explain the other fear languishing into oddness — seeing through my one open eye that maybe I am the entire realm of the kingdom, only me, me.

Angel and Geronimo

When Angel thought of the Machine and Metal Trades Vocational High School, he envisioned enormous and gleaming complex machines purring and miraculous, awaiting his participation in scientific marvels. He hadn't thought of this as his calling, it hadn't been his dream, but the higher faculty of the school committee knew something, and decreed this as part of his destiny in the United States. He was courteous, happy, he would accept the designation of this school as part of the adventure of his new life in the new country.

It was a week before school was to start. He wasn't lost, really; and it was not difficult for him to find his way back to his home block, once it occurred to him that he was somewhere else. He had begun to retrace his wandering. The street he found

himself on was nearly identical to the street where he lived. He'd
been imagining towering machines and corridors, brilliant as
crystal where he moved in good faith and found a vocation,
given as arbitrarily as life is given. He squinted, the light he
dreamed in collusion with the bright day, and he didn't begin
to run as the group of boys ran at him, but then knew suddenly
that he must run. He heard a cry as if his passing had torn loose
a wail of devotion. He'd meant no intrusion, perhaps running
was a mistake, his flight itself a provocation and he stopped,
willing to explain, although he couldn't think of what it was he
was supposed to explain.

They were all over him, and had him on the ground twice.
The kicks were bad. He went out of himself and came back. He
wondered if he was dead.

The next day, awaking to a life he could not believe was his
and on his own street, Jose and Paco, offering friendship, taught
him that he had wandered into the territory of the Sicilian
Comanches.

He had scrambled up on his feet twice, fending off punches
with his arms, and a blow to the back of the head took him
down again. He hit the pavement hard, the breath knocked out
of him. Someone's foot rolled him over. There was the briefest
pause as they seemed to study him. He hadn't wet his pants
until he saw their faces, outraged, and on the face of the leader,
Geronimo Balducci, indignation. Angel felt something shameful within himself, perhaps they had seen it and knew what it
was. He wanted to know what it was. On his scraped knees and
scraped palms he crawled over the sidewalk. They watched and
said things, and then he was running again, and they were chasing him. He ran pressing a wad of newspaper to his bleeding
head; and the Sicilian Comanches chased him through the

streets, all the way home.

Every morning Señora Milagros and Aunt Titi went to church, and then to work. Laura delivered Rosita to the Sisters at St. Ann's. When Laura and Angel weren't attending school, Laura tried to prevent Angel from going into the street. She didn't say it, but Angel knew Laura was remembering their trip to the hospital emergency room, where the doctor had sewed up his head. It had been necessary to shave his head; on Angel's monkish pate slightly above his right ear, the doctor stitched what looked like a livid crucifix, two inches in diameter, and on the top of his head, above his temple, the doctor's needlework left a furrowed "X" nearly as large as the cross above Angel's right ear. Laura tried not to stare at the markings on her brother's shaven head as she placed herself in front of the door and refused to move. Angel said that he was obligated to go out again, and asked Laura to please move from the door. She said she could not. Angel cried out and went after Laura with a hammer. She moved from the door.

During her lunch hour, Aunt Titi, who worked in the same factory with Laura's mother, would hurry to the apartment, sprinkle holy water around the door, and leave money.

Occasionally, perhaps once a year, there was a visitation from the man Noel, dapper and reeking of cologne. Laura saw Noel as an aspect of their mother's religious life, the manifestation of some principle she sustained. Angel was astounded by the man who claimed to exist, and sometimes even bragged that he was his father. When Angel laughed, Noel smacked his face. Angel promised Noel that someday he would take his life. Noel laughed and said he did not doubt Angel's sincerity. Noel continued to send, once a year, a Mother's Day card to Señora Milagros, by way of announcing the forthcoming visit to cel-

ebrate his paternity. Señora Milagros kept all the Mother's Day
cards in a bundle, tied in a ribbon, and placed them in a drawer
in her dresser, beneath her marriage certificate. In that first year
in the United States, some time around Easter, Noel invited
Angel to visit the half-brothers and half-sisters he had never
met, and Noel's woman, Patria. Noel didn't offer an address,
and Angel had no desire to ask. Angel barely shook his head,
no, to acknowledge the invitation, and reposed in the sense of
his certain privilege to annul Noel's existence, and his annual
claims of fatherhood and husbandly privilege.

   Laura tried to speak to Angel. He answered, but his voice,
soft and remote, came from far away. Laura was accustomed to
what her relatives interpreted as her mother's state of distraction. Señora Milagros never distinguished between her waking
and sleeping life. If Señora Milagros dreamed of her mother,
who had not been in the world for twenty years, she simply
said, "Mama said it rained all of Easter Day. I got off the burning trolley and bought some aspirin. See, the swelling of my
feet has gone down." Laura had noted with great and recurring
relief that despite her mother's disinclination to explain, she
was not handicapped by her inclusive reckoning of causality.
She could tell time. She was adept at piecework. So many blouses
an hour, so many button-holes a minute meant the rent. But
Laura saw something more estranged in Angel's eyes.

   She thought of when they were very little and slept in the
same bed, and Mama bathed them in the yard, together, in the
metal tub. They shared what had never been confessed to anyone. Laura shrugged, Angel nodded, they felt themselves beyond complicity, and even if they weren't, the discoveries of look,
see, and touch, had happened before the world existed. They
lived on the Island then. Everything was green. The air which

was shot through with wet light was green. On the green, steaming, perfumed hill above the shack, where Mama was still laughing, and Noel an indolent presence who hummed, Laura and Angel sat, wearing only their soaked underpants, and on huge banana leaves rode a fog-shrouded stream down the hill into a bed of sweet mud.

Eventually big people appeared. Mama said this is Uncle So and So, and Aunt So and So. Whenever the grownups asked a question of Angel and Laura, Laura answered. Angel, the older brother, noticed that when Laura answered their uncles and aunts smiled, and they got candy. Angel was amazed by the enormous store of his sister's words. She interpreted him to the world, and to himself. Mama would ask Laura, as Angel stood holding his sister's hand, "What does he want?" Laura answered. Mama would give him a coconut, which he shook at his ear; later he cracked the coconut open with a rock and sank his teeth into the sweet white meat of it.

Many people mistook Laura and Angel for twins. She looked into his face as into a mirror, saw in her reflection the future, and she wanted to run away. Then she felt like a traitor. She begged Angel to be careful. She followed him in the street, but he ran, disappearing around a corner into an alley, a hallway. When Angel's ghostly loitering was discovered on a hostile street, he had to fight and run.

After a time Laura recognized that Angel had his life in the city of the new country apart from her. She gave up following him. She missed him. However, she also had the responsibility of Rosita, and she had to wash all the floors of the apartment every day, with the disinfectant that made her eyes burn and her nose run. Her mother's life was made of work at the factory and sleep, with the exception of the one sumptuous thing: prayer.

Sometimes Señora Milagros complained that so much prayer had bloated her stomach. At home, spider-limbed Rosita was well-behaved except for her acrobatics and walking in her sleep. Rosita used the living room couch for a trampoline, catapulted herself from chairs, and hung head down in closets. Laura kept the front door of the apartment locked. She made up Rosita's bed with a rubber sheet under the bedclothes. Late at night, when Rosita's bed was awash, she began her somnambulist wandering. Immediately Laura awoke, her sleep attuned to the sound of water. Rosita moved about the apartment, eyes opened and asleep. Laura took Rosita's hand, spoke softly to her, and led her back to bed. She made Rosita's bed with fresh sheets and dry blankets. Laura spoke to Rosita as she fixed the bed and Rosita seemed to understand. Laura tapped a hollow in the pillow for Rosita's head. Rosita spoke in some Pentecostal language of her sleep, the only comprehensible word was the distressed call of "sister," and Laura never knew whether Rosita was calling her or beseeching the nuns at St. Ann's. Once Laura had slept too deeply to hear, and Rosita wandered to the door and unlocked it. Barefoot and in her nightgown, she drifted through the halls of the housing project, startling a junkie nodding out on his feet, somewhere between sleep and coma. Rosita glided by declaiming her sleep language and the junkie screamed.

Laura changed the lock on the front door. The new lock was more difficult to open; and with Angel's help she attached a bell at the top right corner of the door.

At home, Angel appeared to be in a state of protracted meditation. But Laura was confident that Angel's life would open to her again, when he understood whatever it was he needed to understand. Now when Laura sketched her brother, she studied him closely, and discovered after she completed his portrait that, despite her concentrated observation, she had drawn him from memory. She could still see herself in his face, but there were asterisks in the folds of flesh around his eyes, and the exquisite definition of his features was being hammered into something blunt.

It was in the street, late in August of their second year in the United States, that Laura first heard rumors of Angel's preeminence. Jose Ponce de León, who was nervously in search of his own valor, told Laura that the Bishops were courting Angel. Jose and Angel were enrolled at Machine and Metal Trades Vocational High School. During the winter months Jose and Angel would sometimes attend school; but most often, and especially in spring, they would check in for attendance, and then leave, each going his own way to explore the city.

Jose Ponce de León was courtly and polite when speaking to Laura. He brought her gifts of brushes and paints. Laura knew these were stolen, but she did not want to shame Jose by refusing his gifts. Jose told Laura how proud Angel was of her artistic accomplishments, and the special recognition she received at school. Jose explained his aspiration to be accepted by the Bishops. The Bishops were considering some test so that he might prove himself worthy. However, Jose said, it was clear that Angel would not be required to submit to any such test. The Bishops would not risk offending Angel. With an enthusiasm that Laura found embarrassing, Jose went on to say that the Bishops had limited the territorial expansion of the Sicilian Comanches, exiled the Sultan Morenos, the principal black gang, from the housing project playground; and the Bishops had even succeeded in imposing some governance over the anarchy of the project's junkies. Moreover, the unaffiliated heroin vendors, who sold smack and reefer out of the ice cream carts during the summer months, paid tax to the Bishops. The Bishops used the tax to assist those who needed help with low interest loans.

Jose was so overwhelmed by the beneficence of the Bishops that Laura did not answer him. She merely thanked Jose for the brushes and paints and rushed home.

It was Señora Ramirez who showed Laura, Angel's picture in the *Daily Mirror*. The next day the same photograph appeared in *El Diario*. The newspaper photo seemed composed of fading gray dots and Laura had to study it closely to delineate what she was seeing. It was Angel. At first he appeared naked. A man who was clothed and had his back to the camera was lifting Angel in the air. Angel's arms were raised above his head and his hands looked like large mushrooms. The caption under the photo said, "Angel Milagros, Catholic Youth Organization Contender for the Golden Glove Lightweight Crown Stops Noah Sims in Two."

When Laura questioned Angel about this, he was sitting at the kitchen table. He moved his head like someone who was hearing impaired and could not be sure who was questioning him, or what the question was. Angel smiled. He was accommodating. He had faith. If he answered the questions he had been asking himself, eventually, he would answer whatever it was Laura was asking. Laura remembered that in her sleepy flight to the United States, Aunt Titi had said that they were going to a country where there was a remedy for nearly everything. Then when they got here Laura was shocked by the ugliness of the place, and the people who were without courtesy; but she thought, as Ponce thought of the test of the Bishops to see if he were worthy, perhaps the apparent ugliness and people without courtesy were an aspect of truth, the beginning of a remedy.

Laura called into the living room where Rosita was balancing herself on her head in the easy chair, watching television. Rosita did not answer. Laura went into the living room and lowered the volume of sound on the television set. On the screen, ranks of mice in tutus and ballet slippers danced to the polyrhythmic clanging of pots and pans. Laura said, "Rosita, the blood will rush to your head. You'll get dizzy." In the kitchen Angel said, "Ruby told me I got the aptitude." Rosita somersaulted, landing ass first in the large soft cushioned chair; she folded her hands on her knee. Laura returned to the kitchen and got the bottle with the leprous looking nipple on it, filled the bottle with warm milk and a splash of coffee, and brought the bottle to Rosita. Rosita burrowed into the soft bulk of the chair and sucked on her bottle. Her eyelids flickered as she watched the mice dance on the gray television screen pulsing with static snow.

Laura seated herself at the kitchen table facing Angel. She took hold of both of his hands. She said, "Please," and kept her face in front of his face; his eyes turned to stare peripherally beyond the horizon of her shoulder, but she wouldn't let him look away. "Angel, disme que pasa? Who is Ruby? What is this business of the Bishops?" Angel smiled his sweetest smile, and all at once he was there, present; he knew the word he needed but had difficulty saying it. Laura knew that now she must not supply the initial words necessary to furnish his silence with meaning. His mouth opened, and closed. Laura realized that the near weeping that hadn't happened, and had been a weight in her throat for months, was the knowledge of their separation. In the living room Rosita was snoring.

Laura kissed her brother's cheek and said, "Esperate," got up and went to the living room. Laura adjusted the bottle in

Rosita's mouth. She propped the bottle on a heart-shaped pillow, which she placed under Rosita's chin. Rosita would not choke. Laura rearranged the sharp angles of Rosita's limbs into a symmetry that would avoid cramping, and Rosita's awakening to numb extremities. When this happened, Rosita awoke screaming. Laura lowered the sound of the television to a murmur, but she did not shut it off; if the sound were turned off, Rosita would wake up.

She returned to the kitchen table and took her brother's hands in hers. Angel was able to declare easily enough his willingness to tell her everything he had learned up to that moment. But when he opened his mouth, nothing but air came out. They heard the sprinkling of water against the door. A single dollar bill slid under the door onto the kitchen floor; then another and another, gliding under the door jamb and unfurling in the motion of a caterpillar. Three dollars. Laura and Angel called out, "Gracias, Titi." As usual, Titi did not answer. They could hear huffing and puffing as she rose from her knees on the other side of the door. They listened to the muffled clapping of her slippers as she went down the hallway to the elevator to join her sister at work.

Laura did not get up to retrieve the money. There was time for that later when she would shop for supper. She tugged at Angel's arms across the kitchen table. He said, "Fear." The word just fell out. Later, though not much later, he said, "Degradation." Laura whispered; she made suggestions, and avoided the appearance of collaborating enthusiastically. Finally Angel said, "Si, si," yes, certainly that was it, the experience of fear was a degradation. He continued without help, fluent, digressing only to linger over details which Laura understood as hesitation. In the boxing ring, he explained, there are rules. Laura could see that Angel was reassured by the rules, and she was supposed to be reassured too. You contest against one individual. There are limits and one may know them. Ruby, the trainer, had told him that he had the aptitude, a significant talent, and if he could sustain the necessary devotion, he might be a champion. Although Angel said, this was not of particular interest to him. Sometimes Ruby became angry with Angel. There were many things that Angel learned too easily. He did not lead with his head, he kept his elbows tucked in at his sides, he moved well; unlike most novices he learned quickly to throw combinations, and in his weight class he was a heavy hitter. What infuriated Ruby and left him wonderstruck was Angel's capacity for dreaming. Often, after a minute of study, Angel could anticipate the moves of a sparring partner; and Angel was gone, leaving his body behind to drift around the ring while Ruby screamed at the sparring partner, "Get him, bang him!" Inevitably there was some lapse in his body's knowing, and he was hit hard, bloodied, and restored to attentiveness. Ruby screamed, "Thank you, thank you. Now we got your attention. Circle to the right and counter with the jab when he hooks."

Laura asked Angel to continue speaking while she got up and put the beans in a pot of water to soak for supper. Angel did not pause. The thing was, he explained, and blushed addressing the top of his hands, the thing was that he had learned that he did not fear confrontation. He did not fear fighting. He could master his body's fear of pain. One day after a particularly rough sparring session, he had been hurt and then hurt his opponent, and he began to suspect that his anger was only the bright side of his fear. But there was the other fear and it was humiliating.

He saw it on the face of Geronimo Balducci, profound, ferociously alive, righteous. They hated him. He was it, the hated thing. He had succeeded in reducing the various fearful things that may have been responsible for the feeling of shame to the one irreducible thing. The fear had been diminished; and he could look on the baffling thing of hatred with some humor and irony. In the ring all such emotions were beside the point, rage and hate, a compost to nurture the art of becoming dangerous. Ruby hissed, "Concentrate pretty bastard, concentrate." But something lingered. Angel had seen their faces transfigured, passionate. He felt himself stupid, "un pendejo," incapable of the mysterious passion that moved Geronimo Balducci, and it occurred to Angel that he might be suffering from some form of impotence.

Two weeks before Christmas, Angel shot Geronimo. It was an odd balmy December. By this time Ponce de León had insinuated himself into the company of the Bishops. Because of what Jose had left unsaid, Laura surmised that Jose had failed his test, and his status among the Bishops was that of unofficial bard, chronicler, and sometime ambassador. Jose told Laura that again there was a territorial dispute with the Sicilian Comanches, and that Angel, who was no longer boxing, had been chief negotiator at a meeting that had broken down. Many in the housing project speculated on when the inevitable would happen. Several social workers, their rhetoric as diffident and careful as anything heard at the United Nations, intervened; a priest intervened, promising eternal damnation, and a detective from the local precinct made use of some outstanding warrants to thin the ranks of the belligerents. These efforts succeeded in forestalling and diminishing the war, although there were several spontaneous skirmishes. In the last of these Angel put three bullets into Geronimo Balducci, who survived to spend the rest of his life in a wheelchair pissing into a plastic bag attached to his leg.

Laura had begged Angel not to hang out with the Bishops. She told her mother and Aunt Titi. They went to the church and lit candles. The resignation of the two women made Laura feel hopeless. Years later, during one of Laura's visits to the prison to see Angel, after Angel had become an omnivorous reader, he described the prison as a place of hopelessness that was very much like hell. Laura was struck by how much Angel's neutral tone resembled his mother's; and Laura remembered when she had first spoken to her mother of Angel's association with the Bishops and the trouble it would bring. Señora Milagros' griefs were deepened. This was, she said, one more thing to be endured; and she explained to her daughter that yes, she loved her son, she had carried and nurtured his body in her womb, but the souls of males were fostered on some other planet and there was nothing a woman could do to alter the folly a man commits himself to.

Laura tried. One night some time before the shooting, Laura sat at the edge of Angel's bed. He was stretched out with one arm thrown across his eyes. Señora Milagros and Rosita were asleep. Titi was downtown caring for her niece Lydia, who was pregnant and suffering from a morning sickness that lasted all day and all night. All the lights were out except for one votive candle on the dresser illuminating the statue of the Virgin Mary. The movement of the small flame made it seem that beneath the white of the Virgin's gown her belly was breathing. From the bedroom where Rosita was sleeping a small red light threw a shadow across the cave-like floor. Laura whispered, depicting several wonderful futures that might belong to Angel and the alternative futures that were certain if Angel continued his association with the Bishops. He answered that he was with them but mostly with himself. The Bishops had accepted his singularity; they even found it attractive. In the quiet of the dim bedroom Laura felt as though she had been running and singing at the same time. She had gone on and on endlessly, afraid to stop. Her throat felt strained and she gasped for breath. Angel's mouth opened in sleep. Later she could not be sure whether she realized that he had been sleeping for some time, or that the sudden flaring up of the candlelight revealed the track marks on his arm. She beat him in his sleep; bringing her fists down on him, pounding, pounding; he moaned, rolled over onto his stomach, his arms scooping at the mattress to dig deeper into his sleep. His back arched and his head pressed against the mattress. Laura choked and beat on him. The brass bell went off, the ringing clear, soft, a call to prayer from a distant mountain village. Laura paused in the long monastic instant of the ringing bell, suddenly happy, as if she had trespassed into a life that had never been hers; and it was gone. Her longing for it began immediately; she felt herself in exile as she turned to chase after Rosita, who was tugging at the chains on the front door and chanting in another language. Angel was up on one knee on the mattress, shaking his head.

Señora Milagros had gotten up out of bed. Laura reassured her mother that everything was all right and Señora Milagros returned to bed. Laura changed the sheets, blankets, and pillowcases on Rosita's bed. She put Rosita into a fresh nightgown. Laura imitated the sounds of Rosita's sleep language, muttering softly, stroking her hair; she put Rosita back to bed. Angel paced in the kitchen, hugging his ribs.

In reform school Angel was allowed to write and receive mail without restriction. Laura visited him regularly. Toward the end of the first year, just before Angel was transferred to a medium security prison and had his sentence extended for reasons he would talk about when that circumstance was history, he did finally respond to what Laura had been trying to ask in letters and visits all of that year.

This was the last time she believed him. It was not that Angel lied. He continued to be forthright concerning facts. But now when he spoke there was an excess of interpretation, a mania to understand. She had begun by saying she did not believe him to be a criminal, and that the reasons the Bishops had shot the three boys could not have been her brother's reasons. Angel smiled and said that he had had plenty of time to think about it, and that the correctional institution's psychologist, whom he was required to see, insisted that Angel think about it. Although, Angel said, that what he confided to Laura he would never divulge to the psychologist. True, Geronimo Balducci called him terrible things, and a coward; he insulted all of the Bishops. The Bishops were offended and it was sufficient. But Geronimo had sought out Angel in particular. Angel said that there were people watching it all from the windows of the housing project. Someone must have called the police; they got there very fast, but too late. The kids who had been shooting baskets ran off; one remembered that he had left the basketball and returned. The kid hung at the edge of the court. Geronimo nodded, giving the kid permission to get his ball and leave. Paco gave Angel a significant look, noting the Italian's presumption; the playground was Bishop territory. Angel knew he was supposed to care about this. The skin on his neck itched, he did not crave a fix, but he wanted one. Paco was far gone on bennies. Angel looked above Geronimo's head through the basketball hoop at the bucket full of beer-colored cloud. Paco, peering over

Angel's shoulder at Geronimo Balducci, said to Angel in Spanish, "He thinks he's the priest of your town, your priest." The
bodies moved slowly around the court as if they were rehearsing a strategy for a basketball game; all but Angel and Geronimo,
who stood still, facing each other. "I'm talking to you,
motherfucker," said Geronimo. Astonished, Angel almost answered, asking, "Yes?" and watched the spectacle of Geronimo.
The sounds came at him as though traveling a great distance,
the full meaning delayed by the sight; Geronimo, fantastic, livid,
bellowing, heaping the vilest curses on, yes, his, Angel's sister
and mother; but what Angel heard first, in the interval after
Geronimo's intake of breath, and then the crooner's glissando
down a complete octave, the tone almost conversational, nearly
whimsical, was Geronimo's outrage at Angel's prideful walking
of the streets. Angel's fighting in the ring didn't mean shit. "Understand this first motherfucker, the Golden Gloves was nothing, proved nothing." Geronimo's nose was open, his nostrils
dilated, his black opaque eyes gleaming in their slits. If Angel
tangled assholes with him, Geronimo said, Angel would have
to take his life, would have to know that he was willing to do
that, at least that, for openers, but Angel had shit for blood and
better get off the street, go home and stay home.

Angel said later to Laura that he really didn't know. He had
never considered this principle. He thought about it. He hesitated. The other Bishops saw him thinking. He turned toward
Paco. The Comanches laughed. Geronimo didn't laugh. He
waited, full of authority. The itch on Angel's neck had spread to
his back; he scratched it. Angel knew the Bishops were waiting
for him, but that wasn't it, nor even the curses on his family, or
being called a coward. Even after the rage took him, and it
seemed to him that he had been standing on that spot for years;

it was not just because Geronimo had attempted to put a coward's face on him, but any face; he didn't want it, nor the burden of a personality. He didn't want it, any of it. He wanted to be nothing and no one in the world, just there, seeing everything, whatever there was. And Geronimo had tried to violate him, putting a face on him and the weight of all the things that go with having a face.

Angel had turned to Paco and taken the pistol out of his hands. As he fired he felt himself shrugging his shoulder. He heard shots from the near distance. The gun shots made the sound of corks popping from wine bottles. The pistol in his hand jumped like a living thing, and after the first shot, the second two came as his fingers squeezed to quell the writhing thing. He struggled to hold on to it with both hands, wrestled it to his side. He couldn't drop it, wouldn't repudiate the act he had just committed, but his body rebelled, his arms jerked, his stomach rolled, and he managed to hold his legs steady. Geronimo bent forward in a kind of mock Japanese bow. Angel would have sworn that Geronimo almost looked pleased; it was a look of vindication, only a little weary and revolted by his inordinate effort. Geronimo held his hands to his gut and toppled. Angel's arms sprang up to catch him, his right hand still clutching the wriggling pistol, and they appeared to be embracing. Geronimo peered into Angel's face, as if in contemplation of the species. From the windows of the housing project, screams as of birds very far away. On the ground near Angel's feet, moaning. Others around him running. Angel could hear a fire engine's siren. Whistles blowing. It occurred to Angel that the kids who had been chased off the basketball court had probably pulled the fire alarm boxes as they ran away. And then Geronimo's words from before reached him, reached him again, no longer mitigated by the obvious, provocative intent, "My dick in your mother's mouth, your sister takes it up the ass." Angel's arms thrashed, flung upward, as if he were trying to swim up into the sky and the pistol flew through the air. Geronimo fell from Angel's upthrust arms. Angel's face twisted in disgust; and it was not true, as the prosecuting attorney would later say, that Angel had then kicked Geronimo as he lay on the ground. Angel had shoved the body of Geronimo with his foot, wanting to get as far from it as possible, wanting to get away; and as he started to walk off, shedding his blood-smeared windbreaker and tee shirt, kicking off his blood-splattered shoes, naked to the waist he flung his jacket, shirt, and shoes in the air. Paco impeded his going for a moment; crawling on his hands and knees, he brushed Angel's legs. Paco wasn't bleeding anywhere that Angel could see. On all fours, Paco swung his head about, looked, and appeared to fall dead from what he had seen. Angel, naked to the waist, and in his stocking feet, walked in the peculiar balmy December air. Behind him, those of the Bishops who hadn't run, and some of the wounded followed. Several mothers ran from the surrounding buildings, screaming. Angel walked, he didn't want to look over his shoulder, didn't want to see what followed, and felt as though he were being pursued by an enormous multitude. He walked, overcame the temptation to run, and wrapped himself in his own silence. He would not, did not speak again until after he was incarcerated. He was certain, beyond anything he had seen, that Laura Providencia was somewhere at the howling ragged end of what followed him; and as soon as he spoke again, he would speak to her first. He walked, turned a corner out of the housing project on the avenue, strolling in determined silence; behind him, screaming humanity. Just beyond the curb, the fire engine, and a bunch of little kids skipping in the wake of the gasoline fumes; the parade of vehicles and children moving at the creeping pace of a cortege, governed by the slow tread of his footfalls. And why shouldn't he turn his face and let them all see him seeing, it wouldn't breach his silence, looking at it all: the world, the fire engine at the forefront of the parade, idling slowly and parallel to his slow marching. Among the row of firemen in their big hats and enormous boots, bulky coats, all clinging to the long horizontal ladder running the length of the great red truck, rolling slowly, the black suited priest hung from the ladder, calling. Angel could see the priest calling to him. From the window of the patrol car, behind the fire engine, a policeman yelling, trying to get his attention. Angel could see their faces, urgent, the firemen, priest, and policemen in the slow moving cortege, their words dying in the pandemonium of sirens, bells, screams, horns and shrieking children, and anyway, he couldn't think of a reason to talk to any of them.

Days of Awe

A ir conditioning hadn't been invented yet, childhood had, my existence privileged beyond my father's. I could go to The Rainbow for sixteen cents, sit in the dark, and watch the smoking cone of light shape shadows into shipwrecks, and cowboys, galloping, mounted on horses too noble to sweat. Like something with gills, I knew how to breath through those summers. I brooded at the window. The street boiled beneath me. I wanted my father to take me to the park, or the ball game, like other kids. But my old man took me on tours of where the Hoovervilles used to be. "Here, yeah, was the soup kitchen," he would say, and stamp his feet on the pavement, and see a line of bundled, shivering men. My old man's teeth chattered. I wiped the sweat from my smarting eyes, licked the salt from under my nose. "A chicken in every pot — you son of a bitch, you should live so long," he hollered.

I told the guy who had stopped and stared, "He ain't talking to you." The man was wearing a sweat-drenched, lightweight summer suit. He hugged a briefcase to his chest. He had stumbled and regained his footing. For a moment I was sure that the man saw what Father was seeing: the gray men in their ragged steaming coats, bunched together in the long bread line strung out all along the ice-white street, the line of men stretching past the thoroughfare, beyond sight in the falling snow. "Here's a laugh," my old man gasped. "Pros-per-ity"…he doubled over, gagged on the word. The men on the bread line stamped their feet, shrugged snow from their shoulders. Father laughed. The haggard men laughed, snorting little wreath clouds; my old man coughed, straightened up, flailed one arm in the direction of the horizon. "We been told," he sputtered, "prosperity is just around the corner."

The man with the briefcase ran in that direction. For an instant I wanted to follow. My head hurt — a whole life in outrage — how to get away?

Father shifted his stance, backed up and moved in a circle, circumlocuting toward summer. "Gus' joint we should go," he said. So as usual, after the tour, it was Gus' Cafeteria.

I retraced Father's words all the way back to Union Square, and there the pavement replayed how the cop on horseback had opened up his head. "The first time," he said, "my skull was still practically a virgin, boy did the blood run." He said he was embarrassed. The policeman on horseback was singing. The cop had a beautiful voice, the lilt of it gave Father pause. He hesitated. He had grabbed at the cop, would have dragged him down. But the beauty of the man's voice seemed a joke, and Father's momentary enthrallment, the butt of the joke.

Despite the ambrosial steam of the cafeteria, the chimes of spoons, the great gong of the machine that dispensed the tickets to entering patrons, tickets with numbers on them, each number redeemable for brisket of beef, barley soup, melon or fish, my nose in the mist rising from my meat loaf, I noted that the tour of the Hoovervilles was not just Father's way of stoking his appetite. He had to return again and again to the place of his greatest fear. I knew. I had something to compare it to. In autumn, after the Days of Awe, I had gone with father to the cemetery in Jersey, where Grandmother was buried.

I was following my Father's words, thinking we were lost. We had walked for a long time. I was tired. Hiking a labyrinth of endless headstones, smaller stones piled on the headstones to commemorate the visits of the living, we passed one of the cemetery's presences — maybe a man — nearly visible, but I was not yet thirteen and I could still see him. Kissed by Yahweh, doused by several drops of stinking eternity, this was a face gentiles could love. His flesh had suffered the proof of the relation between mind and spirit. Father walked right through him, and made a deal with one of the more enterprising ghosts. This one smelled human and my old man hired the specter to facilitate his catharsis. The scrawny, bent-over ancient might have been taken for a crone if it were not for his unruly beard, which appeared to breathe on its own. He wore a black gabardine frock coat that had been threadbare when Lithuania was a prairie. The yarmulke hovered an inch over the old man's bald head, and was clamped with a butterfly barrette to the one remaining tuft of wiry gray hair, sticking up out of a dent on his skull.

Before prayer they bargained. I only blushed. When I was seven, I had been mortified. They exchanged accusations, "You take the bread out of the mouths of my children," for openers; and denunciations, pleadings, self-condemnation that calibrated the value of pity in the fallen world. They mimicked renunciation, throwing up their hands, wept for the fact of the price of the word. "From your mouth to God's ear," the old guy hissed. Bent over, in the most eloquent staggering I had ever seen, the old man, flogged by the clouds in heaven, shuffled a circle of dust around Father. High-octane spleen fueled the blue rage in Father's eyes. To be hustled in God's name, at the foot of his mother's grave, this last most combustible offense lit something in Father's face. I turned away. The old ghost glimpsed it, and considered retirement. The birds in the trees shut up. Father found his human voice; he quoted Odets, the only author he had ever trusted, to the extent that any scribe was to be trusted: "Life shouldn't be printed on dollar bills." And, "This is a way to make a living?" he asked the ghost in high Yiddish. "This is an honorable vocation?" Looking toward the beyond to beseech somebody who probably wasn't home anyway. Father identified himself as one of the cadre who was going to bring heaven to earth by annihilating all such rackets after they kicked the asses of landlords and bosses. Fat, human tolerance oiled the old ghost's eyes. "Yeah, yeah," he whispered with an inexhaustible exhaustion, "Waiting for the Messiah doesn't pay very much, but it's steady work, and," he asked, "your mother's name?"

Father's chest heaved, torrents of water Father didn't know were in him, quantities of briny snot, all this stuff ran out of his nose, mouth, eyes, the great barrel of his chest shuddered, thumped by something beyond, truly beyond. Father uttered his mother's name and experienced again, once a year, every year, the genesis of what is everlasting — Momma, the giver of hereafter and hereafter. The old man asked my name and my father's. He reached inside his gabardine and withdrew two yarmulkes shaped like cakes. Father and I covered our heads. The old man began to rock; his Adam's apple shimmied in his gaunt throat. He coughed, greasing his larynx. His rocking gathered momentum and he gave out a shriek entreating heaven with our names. Shivering, Father managed to show his teeth. "For a fee he'll mention me to God," he said, loud enough so that the other half dozen ghosts who inhabited the cemetery, and who were similarly employed, heard him. Pop's intermediary rocked, faster and faster; he put in my father's mouth the language that had been old when the Romans were nailing rabbis upside down. Pop and the old man rocked furiously. They wailed. Oh, how they wailed. I felt naked. They exchanged riffs, the most heart-rending wails, sobs, piercing screams — a harmony with a life of its own. Throbbing and rocking they seemed engaged in a contest to see who would make the stones weep first.

At Gus' Cafeteria I watched my old man, hunched over his meat loaf, arms on the table, surrounding his plate. His eyes rose for a quick, desperate reconnoiter of the room. He eats, I thought, as though he were about to be arrested any minute, and no amount of work will not make his eating a crime. Having the work that pays for the meat loaf is the whimsy of the people who own the numbers; nothing can be earned. Over the revolving door, which is the entrance and exit, is a sign that reads, "In case of fire, yell fire!"

But at the cemetery, after prayer, he was surfeited, purged, far gone in beatitude. He belched and purred, his eyes finally blank. The fragment of heavenly coma was not of the duration of a session at the Turkish baths. There at the shvits we cooked and steamed ourselves into a night's sleep as deep as a Bodhisattva's waking dream of life before creation. But this, at the cemetery, was as much as prayer could do.

Father had slipped some coins into the hands of the specter who had conducted the prayers. The old ghost studied what was in the palm of his hand and screamed rape. Father claimed that that had been the agreed-upon price. They reprised all that had gone before, the accusations, denunciations, screams for justice, and pity. Father slipped the old man another fifty cents. This too, I finally realized, was part of the ceremony, to facilitate our reentry into the known world. Father and the old guy hugged one another, cursed one another, and hugged one another. We went home.

THE RUMBA LESSON

Isaac sensed that rituals he initiated were not entirely of his making. His life was interesting, good as literature, and his trouble real.

Laura said she was sure he was the father. She said Isaac was the sweetest boy she had ever known, and "a rare thing, muy singular, a Jewish drunk." Isaac wanted to say that was not exactly right, but he was drunk at the time and so he sang to her. Laura settled herself in a chair, smiled, and let him sing. For a moment Isaac was stunned. It happened often, looking straight into the face of Laura Providencia could cause amnesia, sleepwalking, and archaic longings which might require several lifetimes to understand. He had seen it happen to others.

There was the man on Seventh Avenue who had moaned when Laura passed, and she had stopped traffic on Sixth Avenue. The truck driver had slammed on the brakes, jumped out of the cab of his enormous sixteen-wheeler, and presented a card with his name, address, and phone number on it. Traffic was tied up for blocks. The huge, red-faced trucker began to recite his history, presented his bank book, said he lived with his old mother, was practically still a virgin, and a Catholic. Isaac felt then as though he had suddenly become invisible. Laura endured it with patience, good humor, and skill, as someone who was born with a handicap — say one leg shorter than the other — and had learned forbearance and how to cope cheerfully; like a nurse, or midwife, she seemed to guide the truck driver through his frenzy, as he sweated, blushed, and declaimed his life, virtues, and especially his capacity for loyalty. Laura listened quietly and said she appreciated and valued loyalty and honesty, and she waited until the man was calm enough to get back behind the wheel of his truck. Up and down the avenue car horns blared, drivers and pedestrians howled, and a policeman blew on his whistle. Isaac had seen it happen to his father. It was just before he finally moved out and they had the terrible fight. Isaac was shaving, getting ready for his date with Laura. His mother was in the kitchen grieving. His father hovered around the open bathroom door. "What is it with you, you got a prejudice against Jewish girls?" Isaac moved the razor slowly over his throat, flicked with one finger the soapy foam from under his chin into the sink. He scraped at his face and thought that perhaps it was true. Whenever he had dated a Jewish girl he could read the girl's angst so quickly, knew the intricacies of her family struggles so thoroughly, that it felt incestuous, like he was romancing a sister.

Isaac looked into the steamy mirror, and beyond his own divided face, half clean shaven, half bearded with white soap, he saw his father's worried face. The old man stood behind him, still in his work clothes. "Of course," he said, "what do I know? I'm just a working man and you read all them books." Isaac squinted into the dripping, foggy mirror, disconcerted again by the sight of his father's aged, tired head sitting on the squat, powerful body. "Pa, I'm sorry, I'll be out of here in a minute and you can get cleaned up." "Izzy, you know I'm not a great believer in religion; that's not the point, I can live without hocus pocus, but for them it's something else." "Them?" "Them! them! the Christians, you read so many books and still you don't understand. One Jew they took and made a God, and so now they got to kill the rest of us; but even they get tired of it sometimes, so once in a while we have a little peace. Izzy, this is the world we live in." Isaac's mother called from the kitchen, "To him you can talk till you're blue in the face." Isaac's fathered hollered, "Sha quiet, Sarah, be calm." Isaac's mother lowered her voice and addressed the tribunal residing in the air somewhere above the gas cooking range. Beginning with the havoc Isaac caused in her womb, Sarah reiterated Isaac's delinquencies. "And with the first tooth he grows in his head he bites, he don't suck, he chews. I give him milk, and my nipples run blood. I sit and I nurse, my breast burning. Chicken pox, whooping cough, strep, and measles, this one he don't miss a thing. Five years old he is and you turn your back for a minute and he's gone, disappearing acts he does." "Izzy," his father said, "you got a kind of curiosity that scares me, it ain't healthy. Everything you can't find out in college, this I understand. But you can take my word, let me fill for you the blanks. According to them we invented all their troubles. Capitalism we invented, communism we invented, whichever way you look, we did it. Only they need us to prove they're innocent. You want to marry that? You want to take that history in bed with you every night? Believe me, one fine morning you'll get it in the neck."

Isaac looked through the steam rising up from the sink of hot water, and saw in the wet mirror his father, waiting. "Please, Pa, enough." "Please," his mother said in the kitchen, addressing the invisible tribunal, "explain to me how it is some people study and become human beings. My son, he reads and becomes a wild thing. A beatnik, a hippie, a bum," his father pleaded, "this is a future?" With his pinky Isaac removed soap from his ear. Slowly he guided the razor over the last soapy inch of his chin. "Nu? So answer." Isaac said nothing. His father grasped fistfuls of the gray hair at his temples and shook his head, to empty from his skull the dreadful premonition of his son's future. Isaac stared into the mirror. His father said, "So you're going out with the Spanish broad again." Blood jumped from Isaac's chin, spattering his neck and undershirt. He dropped the razor into the sink, spun around, grabbed his father's shirt front, and shoved; it was like trying to move a wall. His mother, who could see through walls, screamed, "A son raises his hand to his father!" The old man held him tight, one iron arm clamped around Isaac's waist. Nose to nose the two wrestled. With his free hand Isaac's father pressed a towel to his son's bleeding chin. In the kitchen Isaac's mother keened and asked, "So what can be next?" Isaac squirmed in his father's embrace, feeling his side grow numb. His father dropped the towel he had held to Isaac's chin and snatched a scrap of toilet paper. The roll of toilet tissue whirring, he spit into the scrap of tissue, and with his thumb, as though he were affixing a stamp to an envelope, pressed it to Isaac's bleeding chin. The breeze blowing through the open crack of the bathroom window smelled of autumn, and Isaac was a little boy again, standing still with his eyes clenched as his mother spit into a handkerchief, and with the damp hanky, polished his cheeks. Isaac opened his eyes. Close enough to kiss, he whispered in his father's face. "Don't ever, ever, call her the Spanish broad again." His father stared into Isaac's burning eyes and said, "Oh yeah? From where do you know her?" Isaac said, "From City College. Last spring she was in my philosophy class." His father blushed. "Izzy, I'm sorry." Isaac could see that the old man was contrite. "I swear," his father said, "I didn't know she was a college broad."

Isaac yelled that his father was a bigot, and squirmed out of the old man's grasp. His mother rushed from the kitchen. She reminded Isaac that his father was a life-long progressive, and she followed Isaac as he walked from the bathroom down the vestibule through the living room that led to his small bedroom. In the living room she reached for Isaac's hand and the two paused for a moment under the framed portraits of Franklin and Eleanor Roosevelt. "Remember?" his mother demanded. Isaac didn't trust this voice. She clung to his hand. Isaac thought how Catholics made pilgrimages to Lourdes. His parents had taken him once a year, as regularly as the Yom Kippur visit to the cemetery, to the shrine of the Roosevelt home in upstate New York. He remembered when he was very young getting carsick on the long journey. From the living room wall Franklin Delano Roosevelt smiled triumphantly, the cigarette holder clamped in his teeth at a jaunty angle. Eleanor in the frame next to her husband looked out at the world beatifically. Isaac thought, as he had when he was a boy, that Mrs. Roosevelt, despite her patrician air, bore a resemblance to Mickey Mouse's dog, Goofy.

Isaac smiled. His mother's eyes pleaded.

In the bedroom he put on a clean, freshly laundered shirt. His mother recounted the trips to the Roosevelt home in Hyde Park, New York. Isaac ran for the front door. As he made his way down the steps, his parents called from the landing above, "Don't forget." Isaac jumped down the steps three at a time. His father called, "Izzy!" Isaac didn't answer.

On the subway ride to Greenwich Village, where Isaac was to meet Laura, he picked at the tissue congealed on his chin. The bit of paper came loose under his fingernail and blood dripped on his shirt.

Isaac's aunt Sophie telephoned after she had received a telephone call from Uncle Sol. Aunt Sophie told Isaac that his father's blood pressure was dangerously high. His mother's days alternated between depression and migraine headaches. Sophie's voice was flat, objective, and damning. She explained that in the month since Isaac had moved out his parents had not been able to make peace with Isaac's transferring to night school to take only those courses which interested him, or his clerking in the bookstore, his life in Greenwich Village, and his relationship with the Spanish girl. However, they acknowledged facts as facts. It was not necessary for Isaac to cut himself off completely. His parents would be happy to have him come visit and bring the girl. Unless, of course, Isaac was not willing to settle for anything less than killing his parents. Aunt Sophie did not allow Isaac to interrupt or comment. She had not said hello and she did not say goodbye.

Laura said okay, she would go. She understood, she was sympathetic to family obligations. She wore a tailored suit and had her black hair done up in a bun behind her head. She wore the glasses she needed only for reading.

They did not have to knock. His parents had been listening for their footsteps. The door that opened from the hallway into the kitchen was open. Isaac was again startled by the appalling cleanliness of the place. His mother hugged him. His father stood by the kitchen table which was loaded with pastry, cookies, a bowl of fruit, walnuts and figs, cold cuts, bagels, cheese, smoked whitefish, soda, wine, and the old man's bottle of slivovitz. His mother clung to Isaac in the doorway. Laura stood behind Isaac. His father said, "Sarah, let go already; let him out of the doorway." They entered. Isaac introduced Laura. Everybody shook hands and then they stood for a full minute in silence. Finally Sarah said, "Have a little something, we'll have a meal later." His father gulped down a glass of Slivovitz. Isaac helped himself to the slivovitz. His mother frowned. Isaac's father poured Laura a glass of wine, handed it to her and began to execute a bow. He turned away, groaned, "My God it's Dolores Del Rio," yanked open the door, and ran out of the apartment. Sarah called after him, "What? Where are you running? Abe, we got!" her hand gesturing toward the table. She turned, inventoried the table, opened the refrigerator, and scanned the shelves; she lifted the lid off the pot bubbling on the gas range and seated herself again at the table. Isaac marveled once more at the efficacy of slivovitz. There was heat behind his eyes. A fragrance of plums smoked in his nostrils, a scorched fog in his head leaked the taste of fruit. Somewhere doors were opening. He wanted to say yes. Isaac held his mother's hand and Laura's hand. He could feel himself smiling and he didn't mind.

His mother said to Laura, "You're beautiful." She said this as though she had been looking out the window and had observed that it was raining. "Your father is not wearing a hat," she said. The sky in the window remained bright. The rain poured down. Isaac felt that the autumn sun shower was happening for him. Laura, making conversation, spoke of her younger sister Rosita, who was a great worry and concern to her. Isaac's mother said, "Wait." She got up, went to the living room and returned with a book. "A present," she said, and handed the book, which was titled, *What To Do Until the Doctor Comes*, to Laura. Laura said, "Thank you," her pronunciation crisp, and without the slightest trace of a Spanish accent. Sarah shrugged, "I know it by heart anyway," she said. "I knew it before I read it. Again they sat in silence, Isaac holding the hands of both women. He glanced at the ring of blue flames under the boiling pot. The lid on the pot tapped, playing on a froth of bubbles. The clock ticked. The kitchen window, washed by his mother into invisibility, appeared to be a thin sheen of sunlight, off which the rain splashed. Isaac waited for the table, cargoed with fruit, meat, fish, nuts, and wine, to rise in the air. Sarah said, "I got a younger sister named Rose too, born on the other side. His father is American born. My husband, the Yankee." Laura said, "Really." Sarah said, "Yeah," and smiled. "I was fourteen when I came to this country," Laura volunteered. She appeared serene. Isaac looked at her and marveled. He reached for the slivovitz to steady his joy. He remembered that one hour before they went down into the subway to come here they had made love. Laura was getting dressed and had asked Isaac to hand her her shoe. He did, they touched, and then they were on the floor. When her moans began to sound like hurt, his eyes opened. Laura struggled under him as though to save herself from drowning. She thrashed and wrestled herself free. Wearing only the half slip that had bunched up around her waist, she crawled away into a corner and sat there. Naked, Isaac searched for his pants in the dim disorderly apartment, bewildered. Laura had fled from the wonderful dark ahead of him, and once more he had followed her out. He ached, he raged, he felt he could take the whole building down with his bare hands. He looked at her. She sat on the floor in the corner, her lovely face resting on her knees. She told him a wonderful story. His Scheherazade. Often, after she had wept and struggled free of their world-annihilating love, she told him a story, always a wonderful story.

He stared at her. She said, "I have my grandmother's face. My brother also has it, and a cousin in New Jersey. On my brother, the face of my grandmother has been badly punished. I was named for her. Did I tell you? She was nearly buried alive. Grandmother was afflicted with the sleeping sickness. Medical care in those days on the Island was only for the rich, as you can imagine. She lay in a kind of coma for a month; she was finally assumed dead. Narcissio, her novio, was ten years older than Laura. They were to have been married. Narcissio was inconsolable. He remained at her bedside. He wept, kissed her hands and her lips. She did not awaken. No one seemed to know that it was necessary to move her about in the bed; that is why Grandmother Laura's beauty was marred with bed sores, one hole in each of her heels, and one small crater at the base of her spine." Laura told it as it had been told to her. Only she had her hand on the inside of Isaac's thigh as she described her grandmother, laid to rest in the coffin on satin pillows. "The coffin was carried in parade on the shoulders of Narcissio and his brothers. The music drowned out Laura's pounding on the lid of the coffin. The village band played "Besame Mucho" all the way to the cemetery. Where, Laura said, the pallbearers heard a rhythmic pounding, out of tempo with the band, and pried open the lid of the coffin. Grandmother Laura sat up, wiped her eyes, and there was a week-long fiesta. Narcissio and Laura were married. Narcissio was a farmer, and he trained his fourteen-year-old wife as he would a dog. If the meal she served him was not just so he beat her with a stick. Grandmother Laura came to long for and fear the sleep she had escaped from. Narcissio looked into the face of his wife and began to fear her as one who had returned from the dead."

Isaac thought, before Laura the world had never been worth the trouble; and her knees, her knees were worth a decade of devotion. His mother was saying, "So I understand your mother is a widow? She works?" Laura said, "Yes." "In a factory?" "Yes, she takes home piecework; she makes dresses. She made the suit I'm wearing." "It's very fine," his mother said, taking up the hem of Laura's skirt in her hand and examining it closely; and, "It's not easy for a woman alone." Laura nodded. "You met Isaac at City College?" "Yes." "That's nice, your mother — a widow alone — to work and maintain like that. She must be a wonderful person." "Yes, she is," Laura agreed. Isaac thought, this too is a story, and it's almost true. Mrs. Milagros worked in a dress factory, she had made Laura's suit, and she was certainly alone. It could be said that her life resembled the life of a widow.

Sarah heard and identified her husband's footsteps first. They turned and listened as he struggled with the door. Sarah sat, incredulous. She heard him fumble with the keys, scratch at the door like an animal, and rattle the door knob; he shoved and pounded. Sarah rose slowly from her chair, dumbfounded. Abraham, who was always so deft with tools, a skilled master at making things work, could not negotiate the door he had been coming through for thirty years, and he was hammering the door off its hinges. Sarah unlocked the door and pulled it open. Abraham stood there, one fist still raised in the air, grinning, drenched from head to foot; in one hand he held a paper bag from Stern's Pharmacy. His white, dripping hair was plastered to his head. He stepped into the kitchen, smiled, grasped the lapels of his light topcoat, and in the manner of a subway exhibitionist yanked open his coat and an ocean fell out. Sarah ran for a mop.

Isaac had another slivovitz. Laura said, "Please, Izzy, no more." Isaac kissed the palm of her hand. His mother returned to the kitchen and mopped the floor.

For the next hour Isaac, his mother, and Laura discussed the benefits of education. Abraham had disappeared into the bathroom. Whenever Sarah called her husband, he cried from the bathroom, "Soon! Soon!" Sarah filled up a plate for Laura to nosh. The scent of the brisket filled the kitchen. The light in the window matured toward early evening.

Sarah was the first to recognize the man who had entered the kitchen as her husband. His hair was gleaming black, slicked down to the contour of his skull and reeking of Brilliantine. He was wearing his navy blue pinstriped suit with the wide lapels and the padded, enormous shoulders. In the breast pocket a white handkerchief was folded into a peak. Isaac thought of this as his father's George Raft outfit, gangster chic, circa 1935. "Please Izzy," his father said, "do me a favor. Go to the phonograph and put on Xavier Cugat." Isaac went to the living room, searched through a stack of old records, found the "Miami Beach Rumba," and put it on the machine. Isaac returned to the kitchen. His father said to Laura, "Please Miss, you'll teach me to dance?" Laura looked from Abraham to Sarah. Sarah studied her husband's gleaming, perfumed head and said, "It'll wash out —" and to Laura, "Little boys is little boys. Nu, go dance." Abraham took Laura's hand and they went into the living room. Sarah leaned toward Isaac and whispered, "Y'know this girl, she says different, but she seems to me an orphan."

Sarah remained in the kitchen, added something special to the brisket of beef, and contemplated the ways in which Laura might have learned to be her own mother and father. Isaac went to the living room and watched his father and Laura rumba.

On the couch, under the portraits of Franklin and Eleanor, Isaac watched his father labor to a conga beat, trying to mimic the steps Laura demonstrated. Diligent, sweating and enchanted, with his arm arched high over his head, he held the tips of Laura's fingers and lumbered into a pirouette; the leg that he had held aloft for an instant landing so hard on the waxed floor that Franklin and Eleanor trembled on the wall. Laura instructed patiently. "Bend your knees, yes, good." She put her hands on Abraham's flanks and gently rotated his hips. His eyes glazed over. Isaac saw that the pinstriped jacket tight across his father's broad back was dark with sweat. It was difficult to detect the movement of Laura's feet. Yet her body seemed to move, hips, belly, and shoulders, suggesting undulations. She held her head high, smiling benignly, as though acknowledging obeisance.

The record came to an end. Isaac's father wailed. "Minks and diamonds! Izzy, minks and diamonds!" Then he began to sing "Dark Eyes" in a butchered Russian, and the song devolved into "Ochicherni got no money, ochicherni, minks and diamonds! Izzy! Minks and diamonds." Isaac thought for a moment of the Cuban with the grocery store who had been courting Laura for the past year. Laura had joked about it. Abraham dropped to the floor, propped on one extended arm, the other arm raised in the air, he held his body parallel to the floor and kicked his legs out and back, demonstrating for Laura the Kazatski. Sarah appeared under the living room's arched doorway. "Abe," she said, "You looking for a stroke? A heart attack maybe? Come, supper is here."

They sat at the kitchen table. The black stuff Isaac's father had rubbed into his hair began to run. Sarah wiped the dripping from his temples with a damp cloth and wrapped his head in a white towel; the towel folded on Abraham's head looked like a turban. The scimitar tie clasp, pinned to his tie of exploding red carnations, spelled in glowing zircon letters, "ABE." He clapped his hands and commanded, "Eat."

Laura looked to Isaac in alarm. As they had filed into the kitchen Laura whispered that she did not wish to offend anyone, but after the cold cuts, figs, halvah, and banana, she could not eat anymore. Laura stared at her plate, heaped with brisket of beef, smoldering onions and the side plate of noodles and carrots. "What?" said Sarah, "No bread?" Sarah cradled the loaf of rye between her breasts and sawed away with a huge kitchen knife. Laura closed her eyes. When she opened her eyes she saw a wedge of bread lying on top of the noodles heaped on the side dish. Isaac watched his father, who, for the first time that Isaac could remember, paused over his food, in a trance, staring at Laura. Sarah studied her husband, looked to Isaac and Laura, and said that it had happened once before; on the day Roosevelt died. Overcome with grief, Sarah explained her husband had been thrown off his appetite. Sarah watched Abe. He sat, transfixed. "So," she said, "he's not a professional man, but he's a provider — in the worst of times he found the rent, grocery money. A doctor, a lawyer, would be nice of course, still at least a serious working man tries to do, he's in the world. On dreamers and bums a woman can't depend." "Ma," Isaac protested. "I got to talk to her like she was my own," Sarah said. "The truth is the truth, you're a very confused boy." Isaac turned to his father who had not taken his eyes off Laura; he seemed to have heard a little of what Sarah had said and announced from the depth of his reverie, "My father used to say if the rich could hire the poor to die for them, the poor could make a good living." "You're talking conditions mostly from the other side," said Sarah. "Over here is better. A man with common sense, a realistic outlook, can make do in bad times, and in good, build a future." "The other side," Abraham said dreamily. "Terrible," said Sarah, "terrible, and Eat! No one is eating." Laura said hurriedly that she had come to this country by plane, and with her fork moved the noodles around on her plate. Sarah said, "My family came by boat." Abraham began to eat and told Laura the story of his brother-in-law Max who had made a fortune in scrap iron. "They tell me when Max was ten years old in Russia there was a pogrom in his village. He bit off part of the ear of a Cossack. The Cossack threw him against a wall. Max still walks with a limp, but now into a limousine." Abraham laughed until his eyes were wet. "My brother-in-law's daughter, God bless her, goes by the title Doctor, is a big time scientist, studies bugs." "Entomologist," said Isaac. "Feh, bugs," said Sarah, and her fingers went to the clean, penciled lines of her eyebrows. In her battle against dust, dirt, and the subversive possibilities of hair, she shaved her eyebrows. Sarah took a large swallow of seltzer water and waved her cloth napkin in the air. "Tuberculosis," she said, "took my sister on the other side." Laura said, "Malaria." Abraham was about to remind Laura that she was not eating, and looked to Sarah; she gasped. "Malaria. When I was a little girl in Puerto Rico many died of it. "My mother," said Laura, breathlessly, "made dresses for the dying women. She took me along to their homes. They would say I want ruffles here, pleats, a bow at the waist, and lace at the neck."

Isaac took a sip of wine. He saw that Abraham and Sarah were listening. They forgot to remind Laura to eat. They ate. He felt Laura watching him as she went on with her narrative. He thought, it's only wine. And Isaac felt, as he had on the occasion when he first heard the story, the hurtful throb of his sex. He thought of the *Thousand and One Nights*. The sultan was haunted. Scheherazade needed to escape bed. But she was there in her story, and he was taken by it.

"The dying women would request that their favorite song, it was often a popular romantic song, be played by the village musicians at their funerals. I, along with the other children of the village, would dance behind the coffin, which was carried on the shoulders of the male relatives." Sarah said, absentmindedly, "Our practice is to get the dead underground quick." "Excuse me?" Laura asked. "You danced," said Sarah. "Oh, yes," said Laura, and she hummed a bolero, her body moved slightly, vividly dancing in the chair. Abraham groaned, "Oy isz zie scheyn!" Sarah sat up straight, listening. Isaac could see that Laura had been taken by the story she was telling. "I danced," Laura said, "with the other children in the road, and the musicians played, and the coffin traveled on the shoulders of the men. The sun was so hot. It was something like happiness. Only I knew always what the dead woman in the coffin looked like. Mother took me to the last fitting. If the dying woman was too weak to get out of bed, sick with fever, I would help Mama get the woman into the beautiful new dress. Mama and me, we'd move the body around in the bed. Often, I would help fix the hair. Mama sprinkled perfume and put on their makeup. The skin looked so terrible, yellow and greasy. Mama used a lot of powder. Then we had an oval mirror, from the bedroom at home. When we finished putting on the dress, and the makeup, perfume, and flowers in the hair, Mama and me, each holding an end of the mirror, standing at the two sides of the bed, we would pass the mirror over the bed. And the dying one lying in bed could see she was beautiful."

"And," Sarah asked, without an edge to her question, as if there was something she might have overlooked, "beautiful is so important?" "Yes, maybe. I think so," said Laura. "Perhaps it is only the effort of dignity." "This," said Sarah, "I can agree." "But the fever," said Laura, "the fever made it difficult. And heat, unbelievable heat." Sarah leaned forward in her chair. "My sister Lillian, who went from TB, in the last year of her life had fever almost all the time." Then the two women were holding hands, discussing fever.

Laura reprised her coming to America. She leaned sideways and whispered in Sarah's ear. Sarah laughed. Abraham adjusted the turban on his head, and said, "Okay ladies, you can laugh, but please, secrets ain't nice." Sarah said, "I could tell you stories," and lapsed into silence. Isaac's arms felt heavy, as if he were swimming under water, but the slivovitz had also blunted some inhibitions and he enjoyed a sense of clairvoyance. Isaac knew his father wanted to tell the story of his honeymoon. But the old man had noticed that Laura's plate was still piled with food and he appeared brokenhearted. Isaac read his mother's face. She was born knowing nearly everything, and the only thing left to learn was how to bear it. Sarah rocked in her chair and began to mutter in Yiddish. Isaac identified several nouns. Isaac's father spoke in the soft voice of a convalescent. He offered a plum. Laura pleaded that she could not eat another thing. Abraham nodded bravely and continued to explain that his mother-in-law had never been able to understand that in this country a dowry was not essential. Also, battling for so long the infestation of the tenements, Sarah's mother had, on the day of Sarah's wedding, washed her daughter's red hair in kerosene. Alone with his bride in the hotel room, the groom sniffed and said, "Kerosene," and he thought of burning buildings. His bride laughed and said, "It's all in your mind." Abraham laughed. Laura seemed not to have returned from all she had related. She smiled politely. Sarah stopped rocking and said to Isaac, "You could do worse," and to Laura, "You could do better." Laura said, "It's late, we really should be going." Abraham said, "Don't go please." He got to his feet. The turban slipped and tilted rakishly on his head. He hollered, "You'll take her home in a cab, y'hear? No subway, a cab." Before Isaac could speak his father had stuffed money into his shirt pocket. Isaac tried to return it. His mother said plaintively, "Isaac," and tangled Isaac's arm in a hug. Isaac managed to put the money back on the table, weighing the ten-dollar bill down with a pear. His father snatched the money from the table and shoved it deep into Isaac's pants pocket. Isaac pulled the tenner out and stuck it into the breast pocket of his father's jacket. Abraham took the bill out of his pocket and clenched it into Isaac's hand. Laura watched. Sarah, Isaac, and Abraham went round and round the kitchen, embracing, wrestling, the ten-dollar bill passed from body to body, ring-around-the-rosey. The bill fell to the floor. Laura picked it up and said, "Please, all right, yes, a taxi ride home would be nice."

Abraham stumbled and caught his breath. "Thank you," he panted, "thank you." Sarah wheezed, "Darling, good luck," and embraced Laura. "Izzy," she said, lifting his hand to her heart, "don't be a stranger."

Ten minutes after their departure, Sarah realized she had forgotten to give Isaac and Laura the shopping bag she had filled with food. "Go," she said, "go take it to them," pointing to the bag set on the floor next to the gas range. Abraham glanced at it. It was filled to the brim with canned goods and jars, a stalk of celery stood up out of the bag wedged between the tightly packed cans, and the neck of a headless pullet draped over the side. "Take your raincoat for in case," Sarah said, as she rose and tucked the pullet's neck into the shopping bag, and re-wrapped the chicken and the stalk of celery in wax paper and rubber bands. Abraham got his coat on and looked at the kitchen window, which lit up with a flash of heat lightning. He smiled, "My mother wouldn't send me out into such a night." Sarah said, "Hurry." He scratched his head, said, "Yeah, yeah," and thought how his wife had given birth to their first child and became a virgin. He wondered if his son's life with the gentile girl could be different. Sarah snatched the towel turban from his head, and covered his head with his slouch hat, pulling it down firmly above his brow. She went to the food closet, but could not fit anything else into the shopping bag; and so she loaded his coat pockets with cans of sardines. She opened the door. "Hurry," she said, "maybe you can still catch them." He walked through the door, down three steps, paused and sang, "Ochicherni, got no money." Sarah called, "Abe, hurry please, the children."

A Little Learning

I stood at the kitchen window, one story above the street. Autumn was not far away and some species of tropical weather, made more potent and other worldly by the various stuff drooling from factory chimneys, turned the air into soup. The heat had stopped time. People stumbled about as though a carnival had spewed up out of the smoking manhole covers, dumb mercy, and giddy homicide in the chewable air. The cops were cavalier and slow about making the rounds of the streets to turn off the fire hydrants. The johnny-pump gushed a great fan of water, arching over the gutter, raining down on the screaming children and some of the grown-ups surrendering the last of their dignity after another sleepless night. In the great fan of water canopied over the gutter from sidewalk to sidewalk was an honest-to-God rainbow, shimmering jeweled lights flashing in the wet haze.

The water cut a swath, one tunnel of breeze in the simmering expanse of the street. At night people were crapped out on their fire escapes, the roofs were loaded with tossing, muttering bodies, and the stoop fronts inhabited till dawn with the indefatigable talkers, and on our street where the secret was that there are no secrets, the mystery of the weather that might have migrated from hell, pried loose the last of our secrets.

Momma, arbiter of the real, stood behind me, testifying to the back of my head. She repeated how blood was thicker than water, and that brotherhood, real brotherhood, began at home; for example, my kid brother Jacob, who was nearly ten years old, and at that very moment up on the roof talking to pigeons, or maybe up in 5G, the vacant apartment adjacent to the roof, feeding and talking to the stray dogs he had rescued from the streets. "So," she said, "my Jacob is a little what some people might call socially backwards, but he shouldn't be made a pariah, and he has a brother, if he made the effort could help his brother make a friend. So the child wouldn't run errands for the pigeon fancier, Mickey One-Eye Callandrillo, that boy who is on parole from reform school, and will end up, like his father, in the electric chair — that such a one should be your brother's benefactor and companion? You're satisfied with this? Think what's doing on the roof this very moment!"

If I kept my back to Mother, this disrespect would provoke a recitation of her history, her inventory of betrayals, the universe, God, Mr. Him, had inflicted unspeakable things on her and all mothers, and I, the older brother, my father's son, was bound in the very nature of things to betray her. She sighed the sigh of the damned and I, flesh of her flesh, was actually part of

the cosmos, stacked up against her — part of what was damning her. "So," she asked the ceiling, "I should be so foolish to
expect help from him?" The him was me, and when Mother
asked, I answered trying to mitigate God, and the universe. I
turned from the window just in time, saw a pair of flaming trousers churning in the air, headed for the street. A burning jacket,
a puff of socks, and a shirt of smoke waved its arms as it thrashed
on the other side of the sweating window. Mother saw too. She
wasn't impressed. It was only Mrs. Cheechko up on the fourth
floor setting her husband's clothing on fire, and launching each
burning item out the window with the cry, "bum, son of a bitch."
Everything was unraveling in the heat anyway, and Mrs.
Cheechko's tragedy was chronic in all weather. Mr. Cheechko
would return in a day, a week, beat his wife, buy a new ward-
robe, and Mr. and Mrs. Cheechko would love each other to pieces
again. And besides, to Mother's way of thinking, romantics were
not worthy of a minute of serious thought.

"He talks to you," Mother pleaded. "When he talks," I reminded her, and once more attempted to reassure her with as-
sessments and hopes I almost believed. I explained that my
brother was just going through a phase, another phase. It was
true that my little brother, all through spring and summer, had
given up almost all talk with human beings, and relied on gestures, sign language, and rolling his eyes. The fact that Jacob
resembled Harpo Marx was not reassuring to Mother. I had a
hunch that my brother had concluded that everything uttered
by human beings that was not false was hurtful, and so he tried
to learn the language of animals, cooing with pigeons and barking with dogs. When I mentioned this notion to him he made a
monkey noise that sounded like Tarzan's Cheetah in the movies;
then he meowed, and that was real enough to precipitate my

first allergic sneeze. Mother paused to wish — in Yiddish — cholera on the principal of my brother's elementary school. The principal had suggested psychiatry, and the possible necessity of institutionalizing Jacob; but Mother was sure that if only I were a little more forthcoming and made use of my social skills, I would lead my brother back to human fellowship.

Mother was coaxing me up on the roof. "To make a look," again. I had climbed the five flights of stairs to the roof twice in the past hour. I repeated that as far as Jacob was concerned, Mickey Callandrillo was not a danger. Mother made a face. I made a face back. It turned out we were both right. Mickey Callandrillo was destined for the electric chair. But despite his cyclopic brow with the one eye alternately blind with hate, or avid with it, his perception would occasionally short circuit into idiotic rage; Mickey One-Eye, who was seventeen, did make it to twenty-one. Jacob helped Mickey One-Eye with the pigeon coops. I reminded Mother how happy Jacob was up there; Mickey up on the roof with his long pole stirring his flock of pigeons round and round the sky was blissful. Mickey never got in trouble when he was up on the roof, it was only when he came down to the street that bad things happened.

But this was different, Mother reminded me. The unnatural heat. Every day an accident. Things were out of control. What next? The roof of our building was like the crowded deck of a ship of fools all about to drown, everybody confessing everything to everybody. I said that people were up there just trying to catch a breath of air; and everybody knew enough to keep their distance from Mickey One-Eye and his pigeon coops, so they wouldn't be tossed into the wide, slow moving blue. Mother thought of the principal of P.S.141 again. This time she paused to wish him a black year and hemorrhoids. I paused to dream

of the library on Bushwick Avenue. I could walk through one
door and then another and be in Sherwood Forest. I longed to
swashbuckle through the woods with Robin and his Merry Men.
"And Leo's mother?" Mother asked. "Mrs. Chernow?" "Yeah,
right," Momma said, "that nut job." She's not gonna jump," I
said, "Nobody takes her serious anymore — call the fire department, call the cops, they won't come. She won't jump."
Mother gave me another of her looks which said I was being
willfully stupid and missing the point. She knew, I knew, everybody knew that Leo's old mother would stand at the edge of
the roof, trying to get the nerve to jump, until maybe she grew
old enough to die from natural causes and fall off the roof. Mrs.
Chernow had first gone up on the roof in nineteen thirty-something, when Leo's brother George said he was going off to fight
in the Spanish Civil War. She screamed that if George went she
would jump. George went. Mrs. Chernow didn't jump, and
George was buried in Spain. Now George's brother Leo was
down in the street, sitting on the stoop with my father. I could
see them from the window. Father had his arm around Leo's
shoulder. Leo was crying. Leo's wife had left him; he had lost
his job as a gym teacher and had been run out of town, that
town with trees, upstate, pretty as a picture on a magazine cover.

Leo's wife, described by Mother as an American girl, also
pretty as a picture, couldn't bear the disgrace. And Leo, Mother
said, never a clever man, one to anticipate complications, poor
Leo seemed to grow dumber with the hardships he endured.
Leo's wife, a nurse in a veteran's hospital when she met him,
hadn't realized that Leo, a war hero, survivor of Anzio, with
lots of medals and a steel plate beneath his reddish pate, was a
traitor. She had never been inclined to think about politics. Leo
had refused to sign the loyalty oath and disavow the Communist

party. The school board declared him unfit to work with children. Leo's father-in-law, the town postman, had resented and felt tainted by his handling of the *Daily Worker*, which he was obliged to place in the mailbox in front of his daughter's and son-in-law's house.

Mother moved so I could not avoid her eyes. "You lay down with dogs, you wake up with fleas," she said, and I knew she was thinking of the malevolent ways of infection which are not accessible to soap and hot water. Mother's point, of course, was not whether Leo's mother would jump or not; what she feared was the contagion of Leo's mother's madness. My brother was up there in the vicinity, also hanging out with Mickey Callandrillo, and there was Mickey's craziness to be considered; and if the whole neighborhood was up on the roof, bearing witness to my brother's companionship to crazy people, public opinion would confirm that my brother was crazy and perhaps persuade Jacob that he was nuts and he might as well spend his life barking and cooing. "Hear me?" Mother hollered, "You lay down with dogs, you wake up with fleas. You're almost a man, thirteen years soon. Go! Do something. He's your brother. Remember?"

Looking into her eyes, the pupils dilating, the lids swelling and growing red as the decibels of "Hear me? Hear me!" climbed, I knew I'd better go before she reached the octave where she harangued the unseen powers until her voice, after a day and a night, became a squawk, her eyes went blind, and she collapsed into something we called sleep for a day or so. Always she awoke and launched into a marathon cleaning of the apartment that lasted nearly as long as her sleep, but never as long as the juggernaut oration to the unseen powers that preceded oblivion.

When the signs promised that mother's soliloquy would become an epic, falling into coma, and concluding in rebirth and catharsis, Father and I would call Doctor Schacter. The doctor came to the house, gave Mother a shot and the scope of the tale and recrimination, oblivion, and soap and suds purging of the reborn world was foreshortened into the practical constraints of an eight-hour work day. But it was not always easy to read the signs correctly. Sometimes Mother simply confided a story to the unseen powers. The something in her that became convinced of the futility of speaking to her husband, or me, or Aunt Tessie, the sister she was closest to, prompted her speaking to some larger disposition in the cosmos, whose silence suggested an as yet uncommitted understanding. When my father left for the street to comfort his comrade Leo, after Mother had reported that my brother had already departed for the roof, she laughed and turned open the faucet in the kitchen bathtub. I heard water tumbling. The water ran, splashed and gurgled. I thought that perhaps Mother thought that she had already sent me off to the roof to check on my brother. I heard Mother yawn noisily, and laugh again. She said to no one present, "Sleep fast, we need the beds." She laughed, and from the bedroom I laughed into my cupped hands. I'd heard the joke and the story many times before. When Mother's family had come from Russia there weren't enough mattresses for all her sisters and brothers, an uncle, an aunt, and her mother and father, so everyone slept in shifts, and Mother's mother said, "Sleep fast, we need the beds." The water ran. Mother forgot to put the stopper in the drain. She repeated the old joke, and a new story, told with a vehemence that edged her closer to waking.

She was a little girl. She had a friend, Natalie Ginsberg. The Ginsbergs were well-off, they lived in a fancy apartment house, an apartment with a bathroom that had a bathtub in it. My grandmother encouraged Mother to play with Natalie. Sometimes Mrs. Ginsberg, whom the neighbors had dubbed, "The Duchess," would give Natalie's old clothes to grandmother. Mother said Natalie was a nice kid, a little dull, but a nice kid. Mother entertained her friend by inventing games and stories. One day as Mother was telling her friend a story about a lost prince, Mrs. Ginsberg came into the room carrying a tray of cookies, and said that Mother's father was as handsome as a prince. Many women in the neighborhood talked about how handsome Mother's father was.

Mother stopped talking. I thought maybe she was thinking about how handsome her father was. When she said that her father was handsome she seemed to be reporting the result of a census, nothing she had seen herself; and in the same breath that reported her father's princely handsomeness, she recalled that in their tenement her family shared a water closet with four other families who lived on the same landing, and their railroad flat didn't have a bathtub.

Mother said that Duchess Ginsberg invited her father to bathe at her house. The privilege was not extended to anyone else in the family. One day after Mother had told her friend Natalie a story, which Mother illustrated on the brown paper of a flattened grocery bag with a crayon, the Duchess summoned Mother to the bathroom. Mother said she was almost eight years old at the time. Duchess Ginsberg began to yell at her, curse her. The Duchess' eyes brimmed. She screamed, "What! I'm supposed to clean up after him too?" She pointed to a dark rim that ran around the inside of the tub. "Filth," she screamed at Mother, "Clean it up!" Mother scrubbed and scrubbed. The Duchess screamed, "Filth!" Mother cried and scrubbed. She couldn't get the tub clean enough for the Duchess.

I peeked from the door of the bedroom. Mother said to the white concavity of the tub that she never told her mother, never told anyone. Her head and shoulders disappeared into the bathtub and she scrubbed.

"So what's going to be? Your brother he's going to have the life of an orphan? With nobody to look out for him? What are you just standing there, nu? Go!"

I repeated, "Not to worry," while I saw that for Mother, worry was prayer. I walked to the door mumbling reassurances, my tongue dumping me into the resonance of my words, meaning dwindled to comforting sounds.

I made my way down the long dark hallway and caught the leaking voices of the inhabitants echoing in the dark, a humming babble out of which I discerned Mother's voice, riding the Slavonic gutturals of someone else's scream. She might have begun a more monumental telling. An itch radiated up my spine. The dark smelled of cooked cabbage, cut through by the sharp ammonia of disinfectant. I climbed the stairs. Whistling in my head. Voices seeped into the air, and growls and someone laughing.

On the second flight of stairs I heard water splashing, someone filling a tub in a kitchen, sitting and dreaming in cool water.

I continued on, up the steps, at the next landing there was a dirty painted-over window, and a small lightbulb cast a dim shimmer on the ceiling. I climbed the long droning cavity of dark, my body slick, dripping. Flies buzzed around my head. "Duchess Ginsberg," I'd never heared that one before. I wanted to surface, reach the light. I climbed, my feet infallibly finding the steps beneath them. No one passed, up or down. I heard evidence of life beyond the barely visible doors, groped my way up toward what might be nowhere, and reassured myself I would arrive by inventing a memory of the world.

My father writhing in the dark becoming light. The theatre dark. The band rising into the orchestra pit on an elevator. As the band rose, dazzling light, a dawn, governed by music, light exploded from the brass instruments. I sat in my plush seat, my feet swinging. The most ferocious, lyrical song pounded around me, in me, my father shuddering beside me in the dark yielding light. Gene Krupa wailed away on the drums, reprised "Sing, sing, sing" and the "Angels Sing" a trumpet insinuating a wedding frailech. Years before the rabbi would prepare me for bar mitzvah, attempt to make a Jewish man of me, and tell me that Zion referred not only to a hill in Jerusalem on which Solomon's Temple was built, but to heaven as the final gathering place of true believers, I rocketed through the dawn of creation, orbited heaven. My father lurched, grabbed my face in his hands and kissed my eyes. Together, womanless, heaven a place of exile.

I grasped the rusty handle and yanked, the hinges squealed, a stream of mortar sprayed down on my head, and the sky fell through the door. I was high above the earth. Clouds drifted in the yellow sky. The barely perceptible movement of the clouds tugged shadows across the black tar of the roof. Each shadow, a wobbly egg about to blossom into some preposterous shape, held within it an inhabitant. Mrs. Goldie Applebaum, the new mother, barefoot and in a housedress, crawled within her shadow after her infant daughter, wriggling out of her diaper in her own yolk of shadow. Round Mr. Sugarman vendor of vegetables had his eyes closed. He was in his undershirt, suspenders at his haunches, belly down on a towel and tilted slightly upward on his paunch, his short legs rotated slowly, as though he were still pushing his pushcart.

Above Mr. Sugarman, my brother in a funnel of gleaming light sat on a milk box. He wore a boat-shaped admiral's hat made of newspaper, and on his face, the ecstasy of Saint Francis. Bird wings fanned out from the sides of his face. On his shoulders, on his lap, on one outstretched arm, palm up, pigeons stood and cooed. People wandered on the roof, gasping for air. My brother saw me and laughed. His laughter sounded like a seal barking. I yelled, "Hello," hoping my good cheer might induce him to say something. Jacob just went on smiling and laughed his seal bark laugh. He turned his eyes toward Mickey Callandrillo. Mickey stood on a rotting brick parapet that divided the roof in halves; his back to me, Mickey held the pole up in the sky, turning it round and round, he conducted a flock of pigeons around and into the feathery white island of a cloud. The birds sailed and disappeared into the whiteness, and then burst through the boiling white, trailing radiant scripts of light, a vaporous indecipherable alphabet, dissolving in heaven as my brother barked delight.

On my side of the parapet Goldie Applebaum had caught up with her crawling infant daughter and scooped the giggling baby into her puddle of shadow. I turned, thinking I could report to my mother that Jacob was fine. Old Mrs. Chernow melting in the sun sat very near the edge of the roof, legs splayed out, in her carpet slippers, her teeth in her lap. Rivulets of sweat dripped from her waxy pallor onto the black tar of the roof. She moved her head in my direction, and made a motion with her hand, as though she were going to put her teeth in and say something. The wrinkled pouches of her cheeks fluttered. She knew that my father was down in the street talking to Leo. She sat there, at the edge of the roof, chewed at the inside of her cheeks, and stared at me.

I could hear Mrs. Chernow's eyes ranting. My vision, locked, captured by hers; I couldn't turn away, neither could I move out of the glare of my mother's vision as she had shrieked the tale with which she immolated herself, only oblivion provided punctuation, rest. I knew everything Mrs. Chernow's face said. Yes, George the elder brother and son is dead and buried in Spain. Morris the father, unable to feed his family, vanished in nineteen thirty-something. Now, Leo the veteran, one leg loaded with shrapnel, and a steel plate in his head, insisted on being true to a belief that would make him an American pariah, an untouchable. And my father down in the street, comforting Leo, would do nothing to stop Leo from letting go of the sweet American life that had nearly been his. It was up to women and their children, fate's true hostages, to do something practical, allow happiness to find its own means. My face almost agreed with what Mrs. Chernow's face said. I tried to change the subject. I suggested that she get out of the sun, move over to the shade. She looked at me as if I were crazy. Her gaze echoing my mother's imperative, should I forget, I am my brother's keeper. I glanced over my shoulder at Jacob; there he was, wearing the great boat of an admiral's hat made of newspaper, his head steeped in the sky of birds, barking like a seal. Mrs. Chernow's face couldn't silence itself.

I'm not sure why I did it, and I hope it wasn't meanness. Perhaps it was only the desire to provide an end to Mrs. Chernow's story. I jumped off the roof. Mrs. Chernow screamed.

The last time I made the leap I had a cape. Charlie Lanza had made our capes out of a bed sheet. Charlie was fourteen and he could sew and he could fly. I was eleven then, and I was Robin. Charlie was Batman and he jumped first. The distance between the roofs seemed vast. Charlie coaxed and hollered from the other side. The wind fluffed the cape up on his shoulders. He was lying belly down, waving for me to take off. His eyes were slits in the black mask he'd swiped from the five-and-ten. The black rubber bathing cap fit tight over his skull, the two crayoned black cardboard bat's ears stuck up on his head, and were held in place by a rubber band threaded through the base of the ears and stretched tight under his chin. I wore the same mask, mine was green. Charlie had swiped the mask for me. I was too chicken to steal for myself. Charlie's mouth, bordered by the black mask, sprayed spit as he yelled, "Jump, you gotta jump, Robin, they're after you, jump!" I backed a good distance from the edge, took a running start, and jumped.

The sound of my heart booming in my ears prolonged the flight, my legs bicycled round and round, my arms windmilling the air, the stench of the alley below rushed up dousing my head, blinding the glimpse of the cloud that had chased me, and this time I landed on my feet.

I had seen for a brief moment before I leaped that the distance had narrowed since the last time.

I caught the shock of landing in my legs, tottered, giddy to be staggering in a circle on the solid other roof. I had been scared again, and wondered if I would be scared every time I did it. My eyes felt washed; my gut emptied out, except for the feeling of overrichness I hoped wouldn't last too long.

There was scattered applause from the other roof. Mrs. Chernow screamed. I hadn't meant to frighten her, I think. Mrs. Chernow was backing away from the edge of the roof, traveling on her tochis, pulling with her arms and pushing with her legs. She stopped near the parapet where Mickey was still conducting the pigeons around the sky. My brother had his back to me, Mrs. Chernow was screaming. People laughed. It wasn't my fault.

Mrs. Chernow's scream followed me down the dark, heating my ears, forever on the point of dying, echoing and illuminating her teeth, which I saw again, like cubes of ice melting on the black tar of the roof.

The tenement shared a connecting basement with the one I lived in. I could walk down, climb up and be home again. There was a door down in the basement just past the coal bins that opened up into the hallway of my building.

Mrs. Chernow's last damning look, as people on the roof laughed at her, said that my leap had orchestrated the laughter, that I was complicit in the humiliation of her life. What my nose knew of the dark, what my feet and hands had learned by rote, carried me down the steps, and I argued with Mrs. Chernow's last accusatory look, which might have been born in my mother's eyes. I defended myself. I would remind my mother that Jacob would get hungry, he would come down from the roof for supper. She would be serene again, at the close of day. She would blow on my brother's soup, cut his meat, ladle words into his mouth. My brother would make musical sounds, a recitative of sweet animal creatures, his sounds close to speech, a promise, Mother's respite.

I sank ankle-deep into the mountain of coal. Walked on my knuckles and knees, crawled, slid on my belly, and peered through the haze of coal dust at the mountains of coal I would climb before reaching the stone corridor of basement that led to the seven steps and up to the door that opened into the hallway of my building.

Climbing the last mountain of coal, sinking and sliding backwards, I argued with myself and Mrs. Chernow. I said into the dank, dark air, which I hoped would carry the message, that I was Leo's friend too, practically family — Mrs. Chernow's scalding look confirmed kinship. I would never intentionally do harm. I hadn't meant for my leap to be a retort, really.

But when Mrs. Chernow screamed I thought I'd heard the word "goy" hurled at me, or was it "murderer"? In her vocabulary the words were synonymous. Getting blacker by the moment as I clambered the landsliding hill of coal, I considered what I thought might really be true, and at least a mitigating circumstance — one which Mrs. Chernow would never understand, nor would my mother.

The first time I jumped the roof, I did it at Charlie Lanza's instigation. Charlie had explained that the jump was the real price of admission to the Saturday matinee. The privilege of bearing witness, chapter by chapter, to the adventures of Batman and Robin had to be paid for in some act that duplicated the bravery of the dynamic duo. This, Charlie insisted, would set us apart from the other kids who were just going to the movies.

Struggling in troubled sleep I thrashed on the mountain of coal, and the basement, a place I knew, became strange to me. The steps up to the door that would lead to the hallway of my building, and the stairwell, those steps that led to the first crucial door, receded. I crawled near the summit and the mountain under my belly shifted and slid, carrying me down where I came to rest in the indentation that had taken the shape of my body, a lumpy and jagged cradle. One notion calmed me. I would question what my leap said. See, Mrs. Chernow, it's like this: I wasn't saying jump and be done with it — I was only demonstrating some heavenward lurch — I swore to Leo's momma, and myself.

I stood up on the mountain of coal and unearthed my ankles. I crouched. It occurred to me that my father would hate the question I had been compelled to ask myself. This was a confusion he wasn't able to tolerate. It would only make him mad. But I could talk to Uncle Sol. He would listen. My uncle's thoughtfulness suggested everybody's extenuating circumstances, another thing that made Father angry. Father's friends accused Uncle Sol of being a Trotskyite. He worked in the same factory as my father. In the apostasy of Uncle Sol's complex heart I found a place where I could confide even what was shameful; and I never stopped to think that my parent's childhood friend, who had always been present and known to me as uncle, wasn't actually my mother or father's brother, this kinship formed by something as primal as blood.

Two autumns, a thousand years, and a moment ago when I had been humiliated by long division, and my teacher, Miss Adam, looked upon me as something hopeless, I went to Uncle Sol. It was a Sunday morning. He was still in bed and barely awake. I stood at the bedside ready to confess that I was an idiot, and apologize for being a sham, having no right to mouth the glory of bright words. I sensed that Uncle Sol had been grooming me for a conversation that could last a lifetime. I stood there trying to say some kind of farewell. I blurted how I had been degraded by long division, seeing again Miss Adam's disdain, as powerful as disgust. Uncle Sol rubbed his eyes and asked what day it was and what grade I was in. I said, "The fifth and it's Sunday." He asked how old I was. I said, "You know." He began to talk about time and numbers. The pyramids were involved and the stars — something called "geometry." He said, "The origin of so-called Arabic numerals is obscure. The zero was unknown till the twelfth century, when it was invented by Muhammad Ibn-Mousa, who was also the first to use decimal notation, good morning Isaac." He yawned and smiled. I said, "Good morning." He said, "Go to the kitchen and tell Aunt Leah to give you a pencil, two glasses of milk, and two seeded rolls with butter."

In the kitchen Aunt Leah was serving breakfast to Emily and Daphne. Emily was a year younger than I, Daphne two years younger. I was sure they were having no difficulty with long division. Daphne was eating an orange and squinting through her thick glasses at a book propped against a bottle of milk. I could hear Emily eating her breakfast, behind her book. There were books everywhere, on chairs, shelves, stacked on the floor. Aunt Leah was the smallest-breasted Jewish woman I had ever seen. She read a lot too, I thought, so she could keep talking to Uncle Sol. I asked for the milk, the rolls with butter, and a pencil. Aunt Leah dropped the thin volume she had been reading into the pouch of the apron tied around her narrow waist. Aunt Leah had the competency of the adept blind. She was able to do all kinds of tasks as she was reading, her feet finding their way and the hand not holding a book, attending to business. However she did use two eyes and two hands to set up a tray with the two glasses of milk and the buttered rolls. Her gaze, as always, assessing, scouring my face, any face, about to be in the presence of Uncle Sol; her scrutiny modulated all soul's claims to honest weight. Everybody's rhetoric, all sophistries boiled down in the glare of Aunt Leah's look, a bath one was required to take before one was allowed to visit her husband. Leah, the lioness protecting the bed chamber throne, where Uncle Sol was a thought thinking itself awake. When she bent over to rummage in a drawer to search for a pencil, she began to read again from another book, left open on the countertop just above the opened drawer. Aunt Leah read, her hand felt around in the drawer where I glimpsed buttons, bobby pins, scissors, a thicket of sewing needles stuck to a small horse-shoe-shaped magnet, ribbon, torn and ragged pieces of newspaper, and a bread knife. Bent over the counter reading, Aunt Leah took the bread knife and the pencil out of the drawer. Reading, she sharpened the pencil at both ends. I watched and waited for her to slaughter her hands. Daphne and Emily continued reading and eating breakfast. Aunt Leah sharpened the pencil at both ends. One point of the pencil was green, at the other end the point was red. The morning light flowing through the kitchen window that needed washing, spilled into the opened drawer stuffed with newsprint, brimming with the alphabet. I stood holding the tray in front of me, the buttered rolls danced on the plate and the two glasses of milk on the tray trembled, as the people in the apartment above galloped across the floor that was the ceiling of Aunt Leah's kitchen. Aunt Leah thrust the pencil behind my right ear. I flinched and spilled a little of the milk on the tray. There were paper napkins on the tray. I hadn't seen Aunt Leah put them there.

Uncle Sol took the pencil from behind my ear and put it behind his ear. He was sitting up in his bed, his long legs stretched out and crossed one over the other. He wore royal blue puffy pajama bottoms, and at the far end of the bed his two enormous feet towered up at the tapering juncture of the trunks of his legs. He was a big man. He ate the roll and brushed crumbs from the gray washed-out sweatshirt that made up the other half of his sleeping garment. I ate my roll. We drank our milk. Daphne wandered into the room. She read a book as she walked. In one outstretched hand she held an orange. From behind the book she said, "Here, Daddy, we forgot," and, "You want one too, Isaac?" I said, "No thanks." Uncle Sol took the orange and said, "Is that all?" The book came down from Daphne's face. Her eyes filled with the sight of her father. Her face brightened. "Oh Daddy," she said, "Daddy," and kissed Uncle Sol on the cheek and hugged him. He kissed Daphne on the forehead. The book went up in front of her face. She went the way she had come, reading. She didn't bump into anything. Uncle Sol said, "You want a piece of the orange?" I said, "No thanks." He said, "Take it."

I ate a piece of the orange and wiped the juice from my chin. I looked at Uncle Sol. It was true, I thought, he did look like Abe Lincoln — a young beardless Lincoln, the kind you would see in a movie, very handsome. Uncle Sol reached out from the bed to the nightstand, and put the orange peels on top of a gigantic tome, the title on the broad spine said *Gray's Anatomy*.

Uncle Sol, who worked in the factory with my father, hauling and lifting, swinging a baling hook, was, and remains, the most amazing autodidact I have ever known. He seemed to have the capacity to learn anything that had been written in a book; and he helped people. He confided in me. I confessed to him. After a time we really talked. Our talk talked, so that when I was away I was storing and rehearsing much of what was best and most baffling in my experience for him. I'm still doing it. Eventually he told me that he considered the capitalists and communists primitive materialists, although, he said, the socialist idea was not without some nobility. He pitied the utopians and yet knew himself susceptible to the belief that the hope of humankind was to fall in love with reason; just as soon as everyone got a library card a far better world was on the way.

The scope of Uncle Sol's self-taught learning was dizzying. Beyond his study of history, philosophy, religion, the sciences, and psychology, Uncle Sol functioned as a paramedic; he was the doctor of our street. Doctor Schacter had at first been skeptical, then impressed, and finally humbled by Uncle Sol's knowledge of medical science. Doctor Schacter often consulted with Uncle Sol when he came to make his hurried house calls. Doc Plotkin, the pharmacist who provided front-line emergency care for the neighborhood, found Uncle Sol to be his indispensable resource; more than once Uncle Sol had been crucial in saving a life, and he had delivered two babies and taught himself four languages, so he translated for and dealt with the various bureaucracies on behalf of the neighborhood's immigrants.

My mother, indeed, nearly every woman on our street was, in one way or another, in love with Uncle Sol. When one of the women would exclaim, "Doctor oh Doctor," Uncle Sol begged, "Please don't say that, please." Any woman had the power to bring the blood to his face and make him turn away, but everybody's dream life was enhanced. The family romance of all enriched, Uncle Sol, the eroticized Abe Lincoln figure, figured as every mother's most beloved son, every sister wedded in spirit to her brother was willing to forgo consummation in exchange for the tantalizing and invincibly innocent dreams of this most beautiful brother, to say nothing of all the good and faithful wives who dreamed of an illicit romance with him, and in those dreams their lives became, at long last, their art.

I knew before I knew I knew, and learned more, as I would bring Uncle Sol the befuddlements of my own first love. Uncle Sol did, on occasion, indulge in infidelities. My mother was incapable of judging Sol harshly. This galled my father, whose appetites seemed a threat to himself and the world at large, as he was often condemned for what he dreamed of doing, as well as what he had done. Aunt Leah claimed not to be bothered by her husband's extramarital activity; she saw it, she said on those occasions when she felt called upon to explain, as an eccentric but not unheard of need of intellectual genius to keep itself, willy nilly, grounded in this world. Moreover, for Aunt Leah, who had endured the process of becoming a mother, the contemplation of her husband's extramarital episodes provided a sensual flush — sex on the brain — which was the place she preferred to have it. Besides, Aunt Leah was busy preparing her daughters for something momentous, a relationship to the world unlike anything women had known, and Uncle Sol was useful to this process in ways he couldn't imagine.

My mother noted Aunt Leah's haphazard housekeeping, but acknowledged her kindness, and admitted a grudging admiration for Aunt Leah's peculiar industry. Aunt Leah, through her connection with Rabbi Shankstein, was employed bathing corpses in preparation for burial. She was also a capable seamstress and was often commissioned to make wedding dresses. But all this work, dreadful and celebratory, was in Mother's view, futile, if not crazy. Aunt Leah, at the sewing machine, like some doomed creature in a fairy tale, endlessly spinning flax into gold, worked to pay for the constant purchase of books — the making of which there is no end.

Aunt Leah and Uncle Sol were satisfied with the arrangement. Uncle Sol's salary took care of household expenses, Aunt Leah's earnings paid for the books, and they and their daughters wended their way through the pathways between the stacks of books quite comfortably. Uncle Sol could look down on the ziggurats of volumes, no higher than his hips and flanking him on both sides as he moved to the bedroom, and wonder about the mystery of motherhood. Leah was a vigilant and industrious mother, without any special fondness for children. She had endured sex, and it was Leah, Sol remembered, who'd declared that she wanted children, because of what recondite Marxist principle, Uncle Sol could never quite surmise.

There were also Uncle Sol's peculiar shortcomings, things left unfulfilled, which Aunt Leah brought to fruition, as though tidying up. For example: Uncle Sol had assimilated the literature of psychoanalysis, and studied the various methods of hypnosis. Doctor Schacter told Uncle Sol about Mrs. Gertie Dresnicky. Mrs. Dresnicky was diabetic and addicted to chocolate and port wine. This passion for chocolate and port wine, Doctor Schacter said, was sure to kill her. Uncle Sol attempted to hypnotize Gertie Dresnicky in her kitchen. His idea was to persuade Gertie Dresnicky, once she was deep enough in susceptible sleep, that water had the taste of port wine, and saltless crackers the flavor of chocolate, while port wine tasted like vinegar and chocolate like cod-liver oil. Sitting in Gertie Dresnicky's clean kitchen, Uncle Sol swung the gleaming house key suspended from a cord before Gertie's eyes. Gertie, overflowing the straight-backed kitchen chair she sat on, drifted in a trance, her eyes fluttered, but Uncle Sol induced the wrong kind of enchantment. Gertie Dresnicky, eager to please, began to confess the secret recipe for pirogi and sausage bequeathed to her from her mother. She enumerated, her eyes blinking, the culinary delights she could offer the man who shared her life; her husband Sergei, she added, was so thin he didn't cast a shadow, and he was indifferent to food. Sergei seemed to subsist on cigarette smoke and tea; his only earthly passion, said Mrs. Dresnicky, was chess. Where Uncle Sol failed, Aunt Leah succeeded. He had taught her the technique and designed Aunt Leah's reading program; and when Aunt Leah launched the swaying key before Gertie Dresnicky's eyes, the no-nonsense aura emitted from Aunt Leah's breath wouldn't allow digression, and she was able to install in Gertie Dresnicky's proliferating dream life the eating regimen prescribed by Doctor Schacter.

Doctor Schacter said that Aunt Leah had undoubtedly saved Gertie Dresnicky's life. Also there was the case of Mr. Peter Napoli the iceman. Peter, a fine figure of a man, a burlap cloth draped over his right shoulder as he toted huge cakes of ice to those households still aspiring to the convenience of a refrigerator, conveyed the sense that with equal ease and dignity, he could transport Mt. Everest, nested on his burlap-napkined shoulder. Peter Napoli also believed that hospitals were places where people went to die. He would never go to a doctor, and he lived in terror of dentists, whom he believed to be gratuitous torturers, the pain they inflicted degrading the soul, rather than offering the kind of hurt that humbled the body and released an ennobled soul. He had endured a toothache for a week. Finally he persuaded Mrs. Napoli, whom he'd ordained as his physician during their wedding night, to try to pull the tooth with the pliers he provided. She tried. Mr. Napoli held on to the seat of the kitchen chair with both of his hands as though he were flying through space. Maria Napoli bent over her husband, pulled, and twisted with the pliers. Peter Napoli's mouth filled with blood. The rotten tooth, impacted below the gum line, cracked but would not budge. Mr. Napoli never cried out; however, his robust groans carried to the bedroom, terrifying his ten- and eleven-year-old sons, and his twin eight-year-old daughters; the wailing of his children mingled with his powerful groans flew out the open bedroom window, bringing his neighbors to the door. His children ran from the bedroom, fell to their knees on the kitchen floor, and begged their parents to stop. Mr. Napoli had never found it necessary to raise his voice, let alone his hand to discipline his children, and he was appalled that he had frightened them.

Among the neighbors crowding into the Napoli kitchen were Uncle Sol and Aunt Leah. Uncle Sol offered to help. He perceived at once the obstacle of Peter Napoli's fear of dentists. Uncle Sol embarked on a dissertation explaining the efficacy and uses of hypnotism. Peter Napoli dabbed at the blood on his chin with a handkerchief, and sensed in Uncle Sol a tendency to impose on any problem a complexity requiring more patience than he, Mr. Napoli, might muster in a single lifetime. Aunt Leah stepped forward; Mr. Napoli smiled, although smiling caused acute pain in his jaw. Aunt Leah had accumulated more languages than Uncle Sol, and she loved Italian above all others, as she found it the most beautiful. When Mr. Napoli delivered ice to Aunt Leah's kitchen, he and she recited various Cantos of Dante's *Inferno* as comment and benediction for whatever the day's struggle might require. Mr. Napoli respected Aunt Leah as a practical person.

Aunt Leah suggested that the neighbors go home, she said to Mr. Napoli, in Italian, that his reluctance to go to a dentist might have the unintended consequence of dissuading his children of ever availing themselves of the benefits of medical science, cutting them off from the bounty of progress. Mr. Napoli, looking grave, in pain, conceded the possibility. He agreed with Aunt Leah, we live, after all, for our children. Still, in order for Peter Napoli to overcome his fear, it was necessary for Aunt Leah to accompany him to the dentist.

In the dentist's chair, Aunt Leah put him under, and it wasn't necessary for the dentist to use gas; nor did Aunt Leah need the key swaying before Mr. Napoli's eyes. She peered into his eyes, and recited over and over in the most humble and sonorous voice from the Third Canto: "Giustizia mosse il mio alto fattore; fecemi la divina podestate, la somma sapïenza e 'l primo amore.

Dinanzi a me non fuor cose create se non etterne, e io etterna duro. Lasciate ogne speranza, voi ch'intrate'. Queste parole di colore oscuro vid' ïo scritte al sommo d'una porta; per ch'io: «Maestro, il senso lor m'è duro.» Ed elli a me, come persona acorta: «Qui si convien lasciare ogne sospetto; ogne viltà convien che qui sia morta....»

The two, Aunt Leah and Mr. Napoli, went to bed with every syllable. Each voluptuous vowel a habitat for sleep from which neither would ever return entirely; this provided unaccountable nurture to their immune systems, and imposed a longevity for both that addled the distinction between this world and the next. Finally, unspeakably old, and in pain, they wanted to believe in death, but could not.

Aunt Leah refrained from whispering a translation to Doctor Stern, the dentist, until Mr. Napoli lay dreaming, deep, mouth open, sprawled in the chair: "Justice moved my Creator on high, Divine Power created me, Wisdom Supreme, Love Primal. Before me was nothing save the eternal and eternal I endure. Abandon all hope you who enter here. These darkly colored words inscribed above a gate pressed me to ask: 'Master their sense eludes me.' And he answered me as one who knows: 'Shed all fear and cowardice must die'....'" The dentist said, "Thank you," to Aunt Leah, and went to work in Peter Napoli's mouth.

But Uncle Sol continued to astound and confuse me. When he asked what I wanted to be when I grew up, I said a cartoonist. It seemed to me the most wonderful prospect, to draw pictures and tell stories. Uncle Sol looked troubled. As he studied my drawings, he would remind me that the human head was one-eighth the size of the body, and pointing at various distortions in my sketch, he rattled off the parts of human anatomy in Latin. A haunted look came over him, and whether he was lecturing on anatomy, perspective, or figuring the odds for the epochs left in the Spenglerian decline of our civilization, before he speculated on the conceits that would animate the next, he would whisper to me, "Izzy, even if you're able to earn a living as a cartoonist, try to get a civil service job, that way when the next depression comes at least you'll be able to eat."

Uncle Sol said, "We forgot paper," taking the pencil from behind his ear. I said, "I'll get some," and started for the kitchen. He said, "Never mind," and flung the blankets from the bed on to the floor. He tossed the pillows; one landed on a column of books adjacent to the far end of the bed. "Have a seat," Uncle Sol said, gesturing toward a pile of books next to the bed. I built myself a seat out of the volumes of Gibbon's *Decline & Fall of the Roman Empire*. Uncle Sol bent over in a crawling position in the king-sized bed. He touched the point of the pencil to his tongue. He wrote out the problem in simple division on the bed sheet. He worked out the problem, it was easy; then he wrote out a problem in long division. I followed his delight in the destiny of the numbers. Just as I thought I was beginning to get it, he seemed to lose interest. Under my nose the motley of green numbers crawled close to the edge of the sheet. Uncle Sol began to doodle with the number nine, and then with a zero. He said, "Stick out your tongue." I did. He touched the green point of the pencil to my tongue. He said, "Thank you my mouth is dry." I could see that he was excited. The zero dribbled and started to look like oozing sea scum spreading over the bed sheet. The nine became a worm-like mollusk traveling in the oozing sea scum. Uncle Sol pointed behind him at the headboard as though it were a distant horizon, and said, "The Azoic, possibly without life at all."

The numbers that had been the correct answer to the problem in long division became trilobites and sea scorpions of the early Paleozoic. Uncle Sol rubbed his thumb on the bed sheet, under his thumb rose the steamy atmosphere of a swamp forest, ferns, club mosses and conifer-like trees. He twirled the pencil from the green point to the red point and back again. He licked the palm of his hand, scrawled on it, and rubbed his palm on the bed sheet, the abundance of scummy water spread, an insect like a dragon fly hovered in the mist, amphibian-like newts and salamanders moved in the swamp.

The age of the later Paleozoic, the Age of Fishes and Amphibia, passed sometime near lunch, after the bells of the Catholic churches had tolled late Mass. Uncle Sol had covered half the bed sheet, and we were deep in the Mesozoic, the Age of Reptiles. My vision traveled past the soles of Uncle Sol's boat-like feet and his upended backside to study the invasion of the dry land by life. Just beyond the indentation made by Uncle Sol's knee, Tyrannosaurus Rex ambled.

During the Age of Mammals, Aunt Leah brought me a bagel. A herd of long-jawed mastodons wandered near the ancestry of Man. Uncle Sol drew Neanderthal man, a hairy predecessor, and finally Cro-Magnon. They were wonderfully real and labeled and named in his most exquisite calligraphy.

By midafternoon Uncle Sol was on the floor and on his knees, he had rendered the teeming creation of the world to the very last inch of the bed sheet, and he was trying to indicate, by gesturing just beyond the bed, with his hand in the air, where the Bronze Age was and the Iron Age would be. I said, "Yes, okay, I can see it." He sighed and said something about the spreading of the Aryan system of languages between the Bronze and Iron Ages. His hand measuring off air, he said, "Alexander the Great, Julius Caesar," he pointed to the wall and said, "the Christian Era."

I crawled on my belly, hobbled on my knees, pushed with my hands, and struggled up into the cloud of coal dust at the summit of the mountain. The color of shining night, I would knock, once more, on Uncle Sol and Aunt Leah's door.

ANGEL'S STORY

When she started to tell the story again, he noticed that she was limping. They had been walking for a long time and had not seen a cab. She reached out, leaned on his shoulder, and took off her high-heeled shoes. She examined the blister on her small toe. Isaac stared at her brown feet on the moon-white pavement. Laura gave her shoes to Isaac and he stuck them into the wide pockets of his jacket. She took his arm and walked barefoot. After they had gone a little way he saw that she was still limping.

Isaac carried her piggyback. Her thighs were clamped at his sides, his arms hooked behind her knees. She crossed her arms around his shoulders and clasped her hands just below his

Adam's apple. He could feel the cushion of her sex on his spine, riding his lower back. Laura leaned her chin in his hair, his head a pedestal for her head, and he could feel her breath in his eyes. He walked, her weight buoyant and easy, swaying on his sweating back. He was certain he could carry her through the streets of all five boroughs night and day, over the bridge into Manhattan, to his apartment. He thought, "I have the most beautiful ninety-seven pound woman in the world on my back." She said, "My mother needs me to be with her tonight." Isaac looked up. In the alley of sky between rooftops, a cloud shaped like a fish sailed by, and left in its wake a luminous black egg of a moon. He grunted, tilting Laura on his back. "Izzy," she said, "you must be tired; we can take the subway." He shook his head no, boosted her thighs, and felt her belly slide up over several notches of his backbone. He had not really thought about it, but now he believed that if he carried her all the way through Brooklyn, over the bridge into lower Manhattan, and his apartment, their relationship would not end. If he put her down and let her walk, if they took the subway, he would violate something, suffer forfeit, and he would not have made the down payment on his worthiness.

He was breathing a little harder now. She said, "Izzy, please, I can walk." He jiggled her on his back and said he was all right. The street was lined with dead trees and vacant brownstone buildings. All the windows were covered with tin, each tin window had an "X" painted on it. Cats moved in the shadows on the broad steps and ran away as Isaac and Laura passed. She suggested that while she was at her mother's, he could stay at a friend's rather than remain at his apartment alone. He stepped off the curb, tottered, and regained his balance. She gave a little cry, hung on to his neck, and clamped her legs tighter against his haunches. "It's Angel," she said, "Angel's coming home. He gets out this week."

In the horizon, the bottom half of the sky reflected the lights of a busy thoroughfare. Isaac trudged at a steady pace and thought, I have the sister of Angel on my back. Laura had removed her jacket. Her upper body in the billowing blouse was draped like a cowl over his head. She took her cheek from Isaac's wet forehead, reached down, and with the hem of her skirt wiped the sweat from his eyes. When she said her brother's name she pronounced it "An-hell. An-hell is coming home." Isaac's vision was fixed on the pavement. Laura steered him by his ears. Her hands cupped his ears, and Isaac heard Laura's voice under the surf of her breath. On the sidewalk, the moon pulled their shadows after them. She leaned forward and whispered that she was sorry, but it would be best if he stayed away from his apartment for a couple of days, until she had a chance to talk to Angel. Laura said again that Angel was the most wonderful dancer she had ever seen. She missed dancing with her brother. It occurred to Isaac that he had courted Laura with a volume of E.E. Cumming's poetry, and he couldn't dance. Laura's mouth hovered near his ear. She had regaled him with the misadventures of Angel's fate before; this was different. She was pleading. Isaac marveled at the modulations that made Laura's incantation sound like reasonable inquiry. Laura went on and on. Isaac doggedly followed her into Angel's life. She invited Isaac to make a judgment, then dismissed his judgment. She said she had circumscribed Angel's life even while he had her under surveillance; and there was one more crucial thing to be understood, then one more thing, and a mitigating circumstance. "Understand this please, first of all this…"

Abdul fell in love with Angel. At first, from everything Laura could gather from visits and letters, she thought of Angel's cellmate, Abdul, as an ally. Abdul spoke vehemently against drugs, preached to Angel on the wonder and beauty of a clean life, the raptures of lucidity, and the mysteries of reason. Abdul, the inhabiter of many voices, raised the deep resonant baritone of a gospel chant to testify to the compound turnings of syllogism, more miraculous than cocaine. Abdul's pounding, lyrical exhortation thumped up and up, ascending octave by octave to sing in a ravishing coloratura of the glory of sobriety, powerful reason, power that could be Angel's, if he could stay clean, man, clean.

In the jail cell, handsome Abdul sat in a throne-like chair. The back of the chair was shaped like the rising sun. All of Abdul's muscular six-foot body was composed in the sturdy chair intricately made of palm. While in the cell, Abdul wore white satin slippers on his massive, mahogany feet; on his shaven head, a knitted white skullcap patterned with doves. "I qualify to speak and you, Mr. Señor Angel are very, very fortunate I am so inclined," said Abdul, trilling the r's in "very, very." The guard passing the cell turned to Abdul and said, "Good evening, Doctor." The inmates called him Doctor Abdul. He lifted one monumental leg from the hefty law tomes stacked on the floor, serving as a footrest, and with his hoary big toe emerging like a turtle's head from the satin slipper, pushed the carton loaded with legal briefs and petitions he had been writing for the inmates under his bunk. From the adjoining cell came laughter, ricocheting off the metal walls. Abdul roared, "Shut you' fuckin' mouth, nigger." There was silence. "Well, my dear chap," said Abdul to Angel, "I can see that you are an archaic sensibility, an old, old soul living in your sweet brown body. I also perceive that you prefer eternity to the historical continuum, and that has caused some confusion in your life. I understand, I sympathize. I too am inclined to dismiss the minutia of temporal sociology as only incidental to the truth of my life. But of course, this predilection may contribute to the susceptibility for the magical substances. I was once myself a pig for ecstasy. But you can kick baby, you can kick. Freedom is a distinct possibility. You will suffer, of course. Discipline is the beginning of freedom. It behooves you to accept the fact, or it's the end of your mortal ass — cause there ain't no kind of shit you got on the outside that you can't get here — for a price, sweet thing — for a price." Angel said, "My name is Angel."

But it was Abdul's recitation of the "Allegory of the Cave" that made a claim on Angel's spirit. Abdul reached from his chair to the narrow blackboard that stood on stilts and rollers above the cell's metal toilet, and with a piece of chalk scrawled, "Plato, *The Republic — The Problem of Justice.*" As Angel wondered over the aspects of illusion and the shadows on the cave wall, Abdul said that eventually Angel would have to read the *Koran*, the *Sufi Allegories*, and Marx's *Communist Manifesto.* "But for now we will start you with *Thirty Days to a More Powerful Vocabulary.*"

Every day Abdul wrote a new word and its definition on the blackboard. "Du-al-i-ty," he wrote, the white chalk squeaking across the slate. Angel shrugged. Abdul said, "Dual-i-ty," rolling each syllable in his mouth like candy. Angel smiled.

Without love or wonder, Angel accepted Abdul's authority as a teacher. Abdul, down on the cell floor doing one of the six sets of fifty push-ups that were part of his daily routine, said, "That's cool, brother. Detachment is part of the dynamic. You are growing, my man, growing."

Within four months Angel had received his high school equivalency diploma from the prison's educational service. This, Abdul emphasized, was no great feat of learning, but it would earn Angel points toward parole; and, if on the outside Angel chose to, he might attend some center of enlightenment and learn how to be a thief and stay within the law.

Abdul wanted Angel to begin his reading of the *Sufi Allegories* and either Marx's *Communist Manifesto*, or Franz Fanon's *The Wretched of the Earth*. However, Abdul had unwittingly engendered an errant passion. Holding forth on the subject of fear, Abdul had referred to Lucretius' *On the Nature of Things*. He read aloud the passage which elucidated how it was that fear brought gods into the world. Angel entered into this book and did not want to leave. This noble and ultimately reasonable work provoked in Angel a most unreasonable joy. On these occasions, when Abdul had helped Angel gain access to a text that would otherwise have been too difficult for him, Angel felt affectionately disposed toward Abdul. Angel was grateful. He felt himself indebted and wanted to name and define his debt. Abdul congratulated Angel for staying away from drugs and waved his hand, dismissing any notion of indebtedness. The grandness of Abdul's gesture encroached a little on Angel's joy; it was a small discomfit, and it did not make Angel especially uneasy.

Immense Abdul sat in his throne-like chair darning Angel's socks, lovesick for the eternal verities. Among the privileged inmates, Abdul was the most privileged. Only the few were allowed to have an item like a sewing needle; and Abdul's cell was exempt from the periodic searches that were the rule for all other inmates. As far as Angel knew, Abdul was the only inmate allowed out of his cell to roam about and visit other cells.

Abdul stitched the heel of Angel's sock, his enormous hand

and thick fingers gingerly holding the needle. Angel could see the wisp of thread drawing the hole in the heel of his sock closed. Abdul bit off the thread and tossed the sock to Angel; he stood up, took the metal cup from the narrow shelf affixed to the wall above his bunk, and ran the cup across the bars of the cell. The guard appeared, nodded, and stood, like a maître d', as Abdul walked out of the opened cell door. The cell door slid closed. In the morning Abdul returned.

For several days Abdul had been sullen. For about a week he appeared to be sitting on a grand mal seizure of rage. When this happened, he would ring the metal cup across the bars of the cell, and go off visiting. Abdul returned, serene. After Abdul's night of visiting, there was a rumor of an inmate who had disappeared.

Abdul's quiet overflowed. When Abdul was happy, his bounty could make all those who had the sufficient will to call themselves humanity, happy. He gave medical advice, dispensed instruction on diet. In many of the cells gifts of fresh fruit appeared. The legal briefs he had written on behalf of various inmates were delivered. In the recreation yard, Abdul intoned his gospel of Lao Tzu. Angel was entering into Lucretius' *On the Nature of Things* for the third time. He remained untouched by Abdul's cycles of rage and serenity. One day in the laundry room an inmate named Hector de Soto whispered to Angel to be careful. The next time Angel saw Hector, Hector had lost an eye. Hector had pressed into Angel's arms, hidden among the clean, folded sheets and fresh blankets, a ladle that had been made into a shank, a short spear, a little less than half the length of Angel's arm. In the dark of his bunk, Angel fingered the finely honed head of the spear.

The night that Abdul climbed into Angel's bunk, Angel had fallen asleep with the book of Lucretius opened on his chest. As Angel slept the book grew into a great weight. Angel knew that only if he answered Abdul correctly would the mossy boulder be removed from his chest. But Abdul went on speaking, never getting to his question, repeating how a criminal might be redeemed by his crime, how it was necessary for one to honor one's worst acts as one's best, and that theses truisms were mere literature unless one lived them. Angel opened his eyes. Abdul's face was close to his face. In the twilight of sleep Angel thought that Abdul was going to help — he would ask the definitive question and remove the weight from Angel's chest — but the question had been lost on the far side of sleep, and Abdul was saying something else — how love was the basis of pedagogy — as he reached down between Angel's legs.

Angel leapt from the remains of sleep, out of the top bunk to the cell floor. Abdul swung his legs over the side of the bunk and stepped down. Angel was about to remind Abdul of the conversation Abdul had never allowed him to complete — the tacit understanding Abdul had accepted with the wave of his hand. Angel had said, "I ain't that way," referring to Abdul's vast and democratic sexual disposition. Abdul took Angel's face in his two enormous hands and leaned forward to kiss him. Angel was solidly planted on his legs; trying to wrestle against Abdul's strength was useless. He threw the left hook high, at Abdul's nose. Angel's head was tucked in his shoulders. He figured his fist had caught Abdul in the throat. Abdul staggered and gagged, his hands flew up in the air. For an instant Angel felt remorse at the thought that he had maimed Abdul's voice. Abdul's arm came down like a tree. Angel's knees buckled, his head flew back against the bars of the cell; the seam that Geronimo Balducci had put across the top of his skull burned, his vision emptied, and his ears rang. Abdul was tugging at his pants. Angel kicked, reached with one hand, grasped one of the cell's bars, and pulled himself to his feet. Abdul rose above him. Angel ducked under Abdul's arm, and as Abdul turned, Angel reached up under his mattress.

The lights came on along the whole upper tier of cells. Angel squinted, the howls and curses resonating in one bleeding ear; in the other an expirating tin whistle hummed. Six guards in ranks of two were lined up at the cell door. Abdul stood leaning against the wall next to the blackboard, his left hand at the side of his neck, monitoring his pulse. Angel looked from Abdul to the guards and back to Abdul who appeared to have a ladle sticking out of his guts. Abdul's lips shaped Angel's name. His right hand moved the short distance to the waist-high tray of the blackboard. Abdul picked up the piece of chalk and wrote on the blackboard, "Angel. You cannot be forgiven."

Handcuffed and barefoot, Angel shuffled to solitary confinement, and sensed an impending knowledge he did not want; somehow he had provoked the machinations of his fate, and he was six months from his twenty-first year. He remembered that he was a virgin, and it occurred to him that boxing, and then heroin, had each played a part in preserving his chastity.

Standing in front of the isolation cell he felt himself go hard between his legs, blushed and wondered if his flesh rose in defiance of the steel door. One of the guards removed the handcuffs. Angel rubbed his wrists. In the dream that preceded the dream of the boulder on his chest, he had embraced his sister in a shameful way, but since he did not have the power to censor his dreams, he granted himself absolution. The next moment he was inside the iron box of a cell.

He looked down at the concrete floor, away from the abrasive light. Shielding his eyes with his hands, he looked up again.
In the steel door there was a slot through which his meals would
pass and a peek hole the guards could see in but he could not
see out. There was a metal toilet next to a metal cot with a thin
mattress, a gray woolen blanket, and a roll of toilet paper laid
out on the cot; and, he noted, no pillow. If he stood sideways,
facing the cot, he could stretch out his arms full length. In the
ceiling fluorescent tubes buzzed in a chicken-wired cage, filling
the cell with a gleaming white brilliance.

Finally he was convinced that something had gone wrong
with the electrical system and the lights would never go out. He
had yelled and kicked at the door but no one answered. He sat
on the cot, legs crossed in the yogic position Abdul had taught
him, wrapped in the gray blanket. His eyes half shut, he waited
for the dark and tried not to hope for it.

He woke sitting on the cot, his forehead resting against the
wall. His brow smarted and his neck felt stiff. The buzzing of
the fluorescent tubes had stopped, there was a rumbling beyond the wall, the sound of water boiling, and from somewhere
steam pipes hissed. He concluded that he had not gone blind;
the darkness was too absolute for that. He felt his way off the
cot onto the toilet.

The fecund smell of his shit was good. Angel squatted and
told himself the story of his life, carefully avoiding all interpretation; as he reached the limits of his memory and struggled
with an event he partially remembered, he found himself interpreting, and he began again, telling himself that when he finished
this, he would begin again, this time indulging in interpretation.

The event he struggled to remember had happened during
the first week he experimented with heroin. He had been lost

behind his own eyes, intermittently finding himself among a crowd of weeping people and the frantic priest. A policeman had fallen off his horse. Rosita, his youngest sister, had been there, and his mother, but not Laura. There were crowds, police trying to control the crowds, lines of people, and the priest begging everyone to be calm. Newspaper people were taking pictures. Now he could not be sure what he remembered directly and what his mother, Lucia, had told him, so that later his mind invented what he had not actually seen, but definitely, his Uncle Toto had embraced him. Lucia said that Uncle Toto was sober when it happened, which was itself miraculous. His mother had left — she ran from her sewing machine when one of the ladies at the factory told her about it — to take Angel and Rosita to El Barrio where Uncle Toto and Aunt Lydia lived. They had to take two buses. Mama said Aunt Titi was already there. Uncle Toto was the janitor for the building he and his family lived in. He said "superintendent." His wife Lydia and his children called him "El Super."

It happened one day, quite early in the morning, before Uncle Toto had his first drink. He was hauling out the garbage cans and he tripped and fell. Toto got up, cursed, and brushed himself off. The lid had popped off the garbage can; rising in the air and falling to the sidewalk, it chimed and rolled across the pavement, into the gutter and around the corner. On the sidewalk, coffee grounds, eggshells, and beer cans had spilled, and with a terrific clanging from inside the garbage can, echoing throughout the street, the plaster statue of the Madonna had fallen out and stood at his knee. The pigeons roosting on the window ledges and fire escapes fluttered up in a great whooshing sound into the sky. Toto looked up and down the street. He saw no one. Soon the sanitation trucks would come. He had a lot of work to do. Uncle

Toto genuflected. He bent over, and gently, with his fingers, wiped some dirt from the Madonna's face. It was then that he felt the moisture. He got on his knees and peered into the face of the Madonna. From the heavy-lidded, half-closed eyes tiny beads of moisture appeared. On his knees he looked up and down the street. He looked again. Tears were rolling down the face of the Madonna.

The apartment was crammed with people on their knees, praying. On a shelf above the kitchen sink and the leaking faucet was the Madonna with droplets of water glistening under her eyes. Uncle Toto hugged him, his Aunt Lydia and his cousins called out to him from somewhere in the jammed apartment. The harried priest stood between the kitchen and the living room directing traffic. As they had climbed the four flights of stairs leading to the apartment, squeezing between the many bodies carrying lighted candles, a building inspector was yelling that the house was going to catch fire and collapse from the weight of so many people. He was drowned out by boos and the voices of those singing. Although Angel did not know these people, he seemed to recognize everyone, even the wall-eyed adolescent girl with hair sprouting from her chin who called out to the Madonna to make Louie love her. His mother tugged at his arm for him to get down on his knees and pray. Angel believed there was a divine power in the universe, and perhaps even love of a kind; he had been confirmed in the Church, but he was uncertain of the Church's specific descriptions of eternity. Looking out of the kitchen window he could see down into the street. It was more spectacular than Macy's Thanksgiving Day Parade. Policemen on horseback and on foot tried to control the crowds. The sidewalk and gutter were jammed with people. The cops had set up wooden barricades and kids were scrambling over them. Car horns honked, whistles and sirens shrieked, a policeman on horseback galloped after a man who had broken free of the crowd in the gutter and was charging toward the curb, pushing a wheelchair with an old woman tied in it with ropes.

His mother tugged at his arm to kneel and pray. Rosita was on her knees in the attitude of prayer, giggling uncontrollably.

Remembering this, and for no reason he could discern, Angel suddenly felt embarrassed over his infatuation with Lucretius.

The ceiling buzzed and the lights came on, glaring. Angel cupped one hand above his eyes. The slot in the steel door opened into a levered shelf, and on it was a tray with watery scrambled eggs, toast, and a cup of black coffee. Angel took the breakfast tray in one hand, crouched, and peered through the slot into the corridor. A guard stood leaning against the wall sucking his thumb. Angel said hello. The guard jumped, jerked the thumb out of his mouth, and with soft baby hands smoothed the uniform over his huge belly. The guard said, "Hello, I'm not supposed to talk to you." Angel said, "Okay," turned from the door, sat on the cot shrouding himself in the blanket, away from the light, and ate breakfast.

The guard rapped on the door with a nightstick. Angel returned the tray, the spoon, and the metal cup to the shelf-slot in the door. He bent quickly, still covering his head with the blanket, looked through the slot before it closed, and yelled, "Hey." The uniformed guard looked like an enormous infant of indeterminate sex still oily and red from the womb. "What'cha want?" he said, and then answered the question himself in a rhythmic sing-song, "You ain't allowed, you ain't allowed, reading material etc … you are a recalcitrant. Your due process and, uh, medical check are comin.'" The slot in the steel door closed.

Angel did not know why he struggled so long with the idea of scratching a line into the concrete floor with his thumbnail to indicate the passing of a day. He had lost track and wanted to know how long he had been in solitary. But each time he concluded that it would make sense to commence the simple reckoning, it felt like capitulation, and he couldn't bring himself to do it. Instead he speculated in confusion, calculating the passing of light and dark, the number of times his meals had passed through the door, and this arithmetic made his stomach tense. He found some respite in masturbation. He conjured the vision of his cousin, the voluptuous Elena, but in his reverie she became Laura, and although he knew this was wrong the sin excited and distracted him.

He dreamt of Abdul's voice, especially Abdul's voice of lyric exposition; Abdul explaining, and the laughter in his most dire explanations. The tray with food on it came through the slot in the door. Angel put his finger in the soft warm wet of it, stirring the creamed chipped beef, and sucked it off his finger. He put the tray on the floor and crouched under the blanket, away from the piercing light; he bent quickly to the opening in the center of the door. The fact of the soft-looking guard listening to him call out seemed to Angel an extraordinary thing. A human hearing him, listening; it was like touch. Angel squinted through the slot into the dim corridor, and he could make out in the blossoming silhouette that the guard had succumbed to an act of will, ambition. He stood sideways, sucking in his gut, and had a proud military bearing. Angel heard a voice he deduced as his own call out, "Congratulations," absurdly, like a Christmas greeting, or the toast at a wedding. "Salud, dinero y amor," it echoed and rang, repeating, growing faint and insistent until the guard turned; and he was another man. "Your husband's sick," the guard said. Angel was not sure whose voice had spoken; and staring now at the phenomenon of the guard's face, what he had heard became vague. Angel yelled, "What?" The guard hollered, "Shut the fuck up, mambo-lips." Angel blinked, straining to hear, the voice echoing and disintegrating into a ton of nails raining on a tin roof. Angel studied the anomaly of the guard's face. There was the muscular, uniformed body, and the unfinished face. The face, which suggested that the maker had become bored and had abandoned the project, seemed to be made of wet dough; nose, mouth, and eyes, extant and without definition in the lump of head with the military haircut, cohered; the expression of vehemence gave the face coherence, it said something, it was recognizable. "Santa Maria," Angel said, and he knew this was himself exclaiming as he tried to understand the guard's angry shouting. Angel peered through the slot and the guard came closer and closer until all Angel could see was an expanse of breathing khaki, and the slot slammed shut. On the other side of the iron door the howling voice went on and Angel tried to discern what it said. Angel listened closely, trying to decipher the sounds. A silly rhyme he remembered from the streets sang itself in his head. He whacked at his ears trying to dislodge it. "One fine morning in the middle of the night, two dead boys got up to fight, one was blind, the other couldn't see, they chose the devil for the referee." Hooded under the blanket, in his makeshift pocket of dark, Angel pressed himself against the steel door, shielding his face from the sea of blinding milk-white light — the intrusive memory of the limerick further confusing the sound of the voice beyond the door. "Merakay, maricón." Angel could not be sure whether the voice was casting aspersions on his manhood or making a patriotic speech.

It occurred to Angel that the guard was not obliged to listen to him. Still, Angel persuaded himself, it was the guard who had initiated the conversation and it was reasonable for Angel to expect him to clarify what he was saying. Angel kicked at the steel door. The slot opened. The voice howled.

After a time, Angel was able to separate meaning from the raging sound as it rushed through the corridors and vaults, each word shuddering like the clap of cymbals; syllables tripled and flew, the outraged oratory gushing through the slot in his cell door. Angel was willing to study this language as long as necessary. He discerned the sense of words by concentrating and paring away the ringing percussion which seemed to have its own musical logic.

"America was great," the voice raged. Angel agreed. He lost the next few words, but was certain that he had heard the accusation correctly. Angel was ruining America; and not only Angel, but his mother, father, sister, aunts, uncles, cousins, all of his kind. The indictment was so vast, Angel smiled. "Oh man, lighten up, my mother Lucia tells me Jesus dropped the charges. Don' worry man —" And Angel thought, although he could not explain, if Lucretius was right, there is only the grand neutral sleep of eternity — there ain't no damnation except for what we make here. Angel put his mouth to the slot to tell the man, "Nothing to worry, Mister, nothing." The aggrieved voice went on. Angel decided he would tell him a joke, make him laugh. "Hey man, do you know what Washington said when he cross the Delaware?" The voice didn't answer. "George Washington, he says, 'Jesus Christ my balls are freezin'." But now the voice was something else, a fortuneteller, a seer, telling Angel his life, how his father had deserted his mother — that was true, but the rest the voice was saying? The vehement voice went on, telling him his life, and Angel thought, what the voice was saying about his mother, the others of his family, was untrue.

Angel bent his head to the open slot to get another look at the guard. The face, which at every instant seemed at the point of collapse, held together by the enormous effort of the working mouth, was a humid, apoplectic red.

The voice remained angry but took on an ironic and chummy tone; it said it knew what everyone knew, that Angel's pretense of ignorance was only a kind of tropical cunning — his mother was on welfare and driving a Cadillac, his relatives were bankrupting America.

Angel knew that much was wrong; his mother had never been on welfare and she rode the subway. True, Angel thought his incarceration cost the state a significant sum of money, but — Angel reminded the ranting voice — it also provided him, the guard, with gainful employment. But now the guard was going on about the licentiousness of Angel's kind — saying things about Angel's sister, the women of his family.

As Laura related this, her warm breath heating Isaac's ear, she imitated her brother's accent. "That guy," Laura said in her brother's voice, speaking of the guard who had spoken dishonorably of her, "that guy was getting to be a hateful subject to me." "Uh oh," Isaac gasped, with Laura Providencia perched on his back, "uh oh." That's right baby, uh oh, right." Laura said Angel said, "that guy is getting to be a hateful subject to me."

Laura explained how Angel had cajoled from the fat guard several cigarettes and matches. It was an arduous seduction. It had required several days. The guard had wept. Angel was not sure whether the guard wept because he believed his infraction would bring about the collapse of all law, or because he feared he might not survive his tendency for compassion. Angel chewed the cigarette tobacco, spit into the metal toilet, and hoarded the matches.

Angel's bare feet knew the palpable dark. He'd had two sleeps and awoke in the dark. In the first sleep, deformed human creatures threatened and begged. He awoke exhausted. In his second sleep, he slept. Angel moved from his bunk and lifted the narrow thin mattress to his nose; it was made of some synthetic stuff that made his eyes water. He held the mattress at arm's length in one hand, turning his head away from the acrid smell; with his other hand he reached up deep into his ass where he had hidden the two small stick matches wrapped into the thin cylinder he had made from the plastic tag he'd torn from the mattress. He probed his anus and smiled remembering how once, drunken Noel, bragging of siring him, had said, "You know, the cavemen believed that fire came from the woman's vulva." As Angel considered what must have been Noel's desire for his mother, he had the most benign feeling he had ever had for the man who claimed to be his father.

A luminous, saffron-colored mist began to sift under the steel door. The guard Cox sniffed, the smell was reminiscent of the chemical factories near his home. He glanced at his wristwatch. The putrefying mist curled and grew. He stood there not believing what he saw until he thought that the stench itself was a plot, and he raised his club in the air and moved to the steel door.

Inside the cell the smoke was thick, at its center a great flaming egg of orange light which Angel appeared to offer like a garment — and Cox remembered an illustration from a children's

book of Bible stories, Joseph's coat of many colors, offered in
Angel's burning arms. Cox stopped in the open cell doorway.
He gulped air and was surprised by the disappearance of his
resolve. He stood still, his head slightly turned toward the corridor, and took three, and then four, deep breaths. He didn't
want to see any more, willed himself to step back, could not
move, and looked again. Angel held out the smoldering mattress, which burned at the bottom; near his feet, a bouquet of
bright flames inched upward; at the outer edges around the
mattress, a string of fire darted and blinked like a neon light.
Cox heard himself say, "I'm sorry your friend died, they shoulda
taken him outta the prison infirmary to a regular hospital —
peritonitis is what it was." Then he said, "Shit," — shit on his
apology. Through the smoke which had the odor of brass Angel could smell Cox's fear. He knew his own fear, somehow Abdul
had to exist so that Angel might have access to language and
books. Angel had long ago considered how the guards and
prison administrators would mourn the loss of income that
Abdul's enterprises provided, and his own loss was complicated,
too complicated, and he hated it.

Angel made an inviting motion with his head and smiled.
Cox commanded himself forward. Air rushed in from the open
door. The mattress burned brighter, the flames shot up waist-
high. Cox stepped into the center of the cell and stopped; his
powerful body seemed accommodating to Angel, who rushed
him with the burning mattress and pinned him to the wall. For
an instant, the two men with the strip of flame between their
bellies, and flames curling around them shooting like wings
from their backs, looked at one another. The guard remembered that he had dropped his club and looked for it over Angel's
shoulder in the flood of smoke. He could not fathom Angel's

strength. He began to choke. Outside in the corridors and cells the inmates heard animals screaming. Guards and inmate trustees ran with fire extinguishers and a long air-pressured water hose. Angel and Cox, pressed against the wall, struggled with each other at the center of a torch that exploded like a burning Christmas tree. Their illuminated faces were close. Angel sucked air and gasped, "Trouble is you got no fuckin' dignity in your face."

Laura's grief soaked Isaac's neck. She yelled, "Taxi, taxi," her extended arm blinding his right side. He saw her hand in front of his face pointing to the cab parked at the corner. She seemed to have grown out of his back, the two of them one creature, some new, twin-headed, multi-sexed centaur. His head bobbed, he cantered sideways, veering off the curb, snorting, and they rushed over the black asphalt toward the cab. Her head seesawed, their cheeks brushing. She shouted, "Whoa, whoa!"

She separated herself from him, climbed down. He heard a peeling sound coming from his wet back, and said, "Please, don't." "It's Okay," she said, and touched his chest; she had the power to absolve him of his vow. "You don't have to carry me all the way." He stood in the middle of the street, his ribs heaving. She wiped her eyes. "Pay attention, please," she said, "you must understand — what I'splain you," and her perfect English lapsed, and she was speaking in Spanish. All he could understand was that her brother was a man who possessed great danger, and that Isaac should stay away from his apartment for at least a few days. "However," she said, paused for an instant, and regained the most perfectly pronounced English, "he has been reading again: Marx, Malcolm X, Fanon, the diaries of Che, and he has declared himself a revolucionario. If that is the case, we may not have a problem, no matter what my mother told him." Isaac wheezed, "I won't hide from your brother." Laura said, "Please." Isaac shook his head no. She began to cry again. He reached out to caress her and she stepped away from his touch. "The trouble is, Isaac, you want to be a colorful person." She pulled a handkerchief from her sleeve and dabbed at her eyes. She attempted a smile, and she mimicked Angel, the fatalistic clasping of the hands, the voice. "I don' wish to care about this bourgeois shit, a fellow who has dishonored my sister; pero, it's a pity the life is so beautiful, no one wishes for to die, and the solumbombitch been fucking Laura Providencia! It is my privilege to kill him." Isaac regained his wind, his mouth formed a declaration. He had never listened as he listened to her, suppressing and forgetting his own urgent stories in their making; he had never lived as he was living now. He wanted to say in the no-more and not-yet dawn forming in the single tree of that street — he did not know what kind of tree it was, there were two kinds, Christmas trees and other kinds of trees — and the wind not visible in anything else, unfelt by either of them, was furiously shaking the leaves, the small white moon rolling in the branches, fading; he wanted to say that nothing was the same and he suspected he could not use up what he felt for her. She said, "I know, I know," stamping her foot on the pavement, looking from his open mouth to the thrashing tree.

He knew she knew he conspired with it all, the whole dumb show, the moon in the tree, the first light of day shining brighter where she stood. "Give me money for the cab," she said, "Give it to me." She turned to the taxi; the driver was asleep, his head resting on his thick hairy arm in the cab's open window. "Wake up," she yelled, "Wake up." Isaac searched through his pockets.

The cabbie snored. Isaac turned his pockets inside out. He couldn't find any money. Laura grabbed hold of the pocket that hung inside out at his side, like a deflated udder, and thrust it back into his pants. He thrilled to the touch of her hand. Her hand came out of his pocket grasping a ten-dollar bill and three crumpled singles. She gave Isaac the three singles, kept the ten, and hollered at the cabbie, "Levantate, Lázaro." The cabbie's head moved a little on his arm and his eyes fluttered. "Things will work out," Isaac said; Laura said, "Of course," finishing the sentence for him in silence, knowing as his hands gestured at the largess of the sky, the morning light, that he was referring to the unfathomable resource of his love. She danced a little mambo at the curb, singing, "Levantate, Lázaro, levantate —" The cabbie lifted his head from his arm. Isaac was startled by the half-sleeping face. It was Einstein's face with a brute jaw, a Coney Island sea captain's cap on his head, and the stub of an unlit moist cigar jammed in the corner of his mouth. The eyes were all wonder. Laura continued her dance at the curb, wiping her eyes, clapping her hands, and singing, "Levantate, Lázaro." The cabbie stared at her and whispered to his fleeing sleep, "If God thought'a somethin' better'n that He kept it for hisself." He opened his eyes, took off his nautical hat, pointed at Isaac, and said, "Did he make you cry, girlie?" Laura shook her head no. She told the cabbie her mother's address. He said, "Mother of God have mercy on us now," got out of his cab, and opened the door for her.

The cab pulled away from the curb. Laura rolled down the window, waved good-bye, and said something Isaac could not hear over the noise of the engine. He ran alongside the vehicle until it picked up speed and left him standing in a cloud of exhaust in the middle of the street.

Virgins

First light incubating the quiet moment as if the silence were the relic promise of a return to earthly paradise. Beyond the window the street shaped itself out of the blanched dark, the tenements, the pigeons on the windowsill, the plumbing and radiators, were still. I was almost fourteen. Father stumbled into the kitchen and found me at the mirror, stripped to the waist admiring my chest. Barely awake, he came up on me from behind in his underwear, stalking the coffeepot. Entranced by the image of my young body, I forgot the pencil in my hand, the sketchpad on the kitchen table, and a magnificent physique loomed in the mirror, dwarfing me. I heard his bare feet on the floor before I saw his worried face above the shoulders growing beyond the frame of the mirror, and suddenly he was standing behind me. He looked like he'd swallowed something bitter. My face burned. Caught, falling in love with myself, so far gone I'd lost all awareness of the image I'd been trying to depict, betraying that discipline, and exposing myself to his embattled tolerance for my "scribbling" — I heard through an acute listening not dependent on the words he spoke. Fever cooked my head. Alternately dumb and knowing, each breath opened my mouth wider, a gaping megaphone for the entry of his speech. I choked through a stuttering narcolepsy, waking and dreaming, colliding.

I knew he wanted me to understand that that too, and he nodded at the mirror, was no big deal, after all it was only a body, and everyone had one. An impressive physique was probably only a sign that you were not clever enough to earn a living with your brain. Despite his socialist sympathies, and his pride in his capacity for work, he suffered from envy of fat men, the soft flesh a sign that these men were able to provide for their families by using their heads. He would never be able to understand grown men recreating themselves through physical exertion. Sports were for children, and he had no enthusiasm for athletic competition, with the exception of boxing, which was religion. "Time and a half for Saturday," he said, "today I make a real dollar."

He drank a glass of black coffee and reached for his truss, the girdle-like thing draped over the seat of the kitchen chair. He wrapped it around his waist, and said, "Come, be useful." I laced him up tight. "In the icebox is whitefish," he said, "forty cents a pound, eat, before it gets dry." I doubled the knots on the bows running down the front of his truss, threading the cord through the last eye of the girdle, just below his navel. I concentrated on looping and tying off the cord. He stroked my cheek, repeated, something — something a pound. I didn't want to hear the cost. He savored my eating. I swallowed air and gagged.

Out the door, stealthy as a stowaway with my batch of drawings, I fled into Saturday. Surely I could find something in the rich long day greater than my guilt. As the inhabitants appeared, the least the street would offer was forgetting.

I wandered the neighborhood. Sometime between breakfast and lunch I got hungry and buoyant. I set out for Uncle Sol's apartment with the batch of drawings. Uncle Sol had persuaded me not to draw with charcoal so that I couldn't obscure what I was unable to render.

In the apartment next to Uncle Sol, Aunt Leah, and my cousins Daphne and Emily, lived the Levy family. Helene Levy was in the same grade as me, but not in my class. She was the prettiest girl on our block. Many people on our street would, when they overcame the inhibition her passing inspired, whisper, "Beautiful." Her bearing was regal, and she didn't appear to walk, but glide. I saw Nefertiti's profile on her slim, dusky neck long before I learned the Egyptian queen's name. Helene's copper-colored eyes were shaped like fish, which noted the world while never ceasing to be focused inward. Her black hair was so thick, brushing it must have been painful. She wore her hair in one long, heavy braid down her back. When Helene walked her dog Brownie, the guys hanging out on the block muttered to one another, "Watch your language, watch your language." Once, Whitey Costa had been talking dirty as Helene passed and Bummy Birnbaum belted him. Whitey got up from the street, his nose was bleeding. He protested, said he hadn't even seen Helene, and he had been thinking about something else. Bummy said, "Watch what you think, and keep your mouth shut." It was true, there was something in Whitey Costa's glee, a pale malevolence that might soil the discretion which was prerequisite to finer dreaming. Helene had walked by and there was no way to tell whether she'd heard or seen a thing. Doc Plotkin the druggist had seen it all from the window of his store. He ran out with a batch of crushed ice wrapped in cheesecloth, ready to press the remedy to the back of Whitey Costa's neck. Bummy said, "Whitey's all right, I only banged him once." Whitey demonstrated his alertness by walking in circles. Doc Plotkin glanced at Helene as she made her way to her building, and the druggist rubbed the packet of crushed ice over his face.

Toting the batch of drawings I was certain were wonderful, and longing for the praise I knew I wouldn't hear, I headed for the door to Uncle Sol's apartment. All at once I was face to face with Helene Levy. Her dog Brownie was yapping at my feet. It happened suddenly and I hadn't time to turn from the sight of her. We collided and fell into one another's vision. My guts swooped, I think I apologized, and I heard her say, "I'm sorry," and then we were both bent over picking up my drawings.

We sat on the cold steps of the fourth-floor landing and looked at my drawings. She praised my sketches, especially one of the roof, showing a silhouetted figure with a huge baton conducting pigeons in the sky, the Empire State Building was in the background, a cloud skewered by the pointed tip of the skyscraper. Brownie was stretched out on the step just beneath our feet. The dog looked like a dun-colored mop, and as the animal breathed, a sound like a penny whistle played off-key came from the dog's nose. I envied the tolerance Helene showed for Brownie's slovenly love of her. The dog licked her shoe. She patted his head. I was ready to lie down at her feet, next to Brownie. Helene explained without my asking that Brownie had been hit by a truck. Doc Plotkin the druggist wired Brownie's broken jaw, and now as Brownie breathed he whistled through his bent nose. I gave Helene the drawing of the roof, the pigeons, and the Empire State Building to keep as a gift. Again and again I turned from the sight of her, as she looked at me looking at her. There were silences, I noticed that she was having a difficult time too. She studied my drawing. She said that my cousin Daphne was in her cousin Kenny's class. She asked me what I wanted to be when I grew up. I said, "An artist, I think." Somehow that seemed to be the wrong answer. She indulged in a swift and imperious pout. We sat next to one another. I was wearing a short-sleeved polo shirt, she was wearing a short-sleeved blouse. The top parts of our arms were touching. I don't know how long we sat there, it was a long time. A neighbor, Mr. Costello, came up the stairs, and we had to move so he could pass by. We sat down again, and slowly arranged ourselves so that our arms were touching. I had a haze in front of my eyes, I was as out of breath as someone who had played kick-the-can for a hundred years.

It may have been a week, or several days, Helene invited me to her house, and there, we taught one another how to kiss.

Helene introduced me to her mother by stamping her foot, hard, three times on the kitchen floor. Mrs. Levy turned around. She was at the sink washing dishes. She was a pretty woman with skin like cracked porcelain and gray hair. The movement of her hands as she wiped them on her apron was oddly elegant. She regarded me from some inner silence. I found myself bowing, "Pleased to meet you, Mrs. Levy." She answered and I didn't understand. The tone and volume of her voice sounded like the penny whistle in Brownie's nose. She repeated herself. A thin and eerie exhalation of breath was shaped into a meticulous and halting, "How do you do." Helene spoke to her mother, her mouth slowly shaping the sound of each word, which I could read on Helene's lips. I was told to have a seat in the living room. As I walked away, the ethereal sound of Mrs. Levy's voice gave way to a conversation articulated through the most graceful flying of her hands.

The living room was as impersonal as a public waiting room at a depot in a far off, barely inhabited land. The place was ruthlessly clean, it reeked of the same disinfectant my mother used. There were two pieces of furniture in the living room: the threadbare, wheezing couch I sat on, and a console television set with a thirteen-inch screen. There were neither pictures nor photographs on the yellow pockmarked walls. A large bulb threw a light across the blistered ceiling and the waxed gray of the faded linoleum.

Mrs. Levy's haughty and lovely careworn head, pinnacled on a long neck, seemed always to be looking over everyone else's head into the distance, as she waited with dignified forbearance for someone to arrive who would announce that she had only been placed in this life by some error, and in the next the correction would be made, she would assume her rightful place in a heaven tended by a god who had finally become more efficient and had perfect manners. Helene and I sat on the couch. Our arms touched. After a couple of days, on my second or third visit, we brought the sides of our wrists into contact. The couch wheezed, Brownie's paws ticked over the floor, and his nose whistled off-key. Now and again, Helene would shout, "My mother's coming," and my heart would leap as I jumped a distance from Helene. We were supposed to be doing homework together. Mrs. Levy looked upon this with the same weary stoicism she brought to the blank wall above the kitchen sink.

Within a week Helene and I were holding hands. It was necessary to rest from the delirium, and in the intervals she spoke of
her plans to get away, she called it the future. I felt her body
shiver and didn't listen very well. I spoke my dreams and the
narratives varied as I concentrated on trying to keep my voice
from shaking.

Sometimes I slept at my Uncle Sol and Aunt Leah's apartment. I would open the window in Aunt Leah's kitchen and yell
across the alley of clotheslines and flapping laundry that I was
going to sleep at Uncle Sol and Aunt Leah's house. My mother's
shadow would appear in our kitchen window. She'd wave that
it was okay for me to spend the night. If she started to open the
window I knew she was going to holler "Come home."

One night, sleeping on the couch at Uncle Sol and Aunt
Leah's, I dreamt of Abe Lincoln's shovel. I was leafing through
the history textbook I'd had in elementary school. I was looking at the illustrations. I saw the shovel, and the sums young
Abe had scratched on the broad metal tongue of the shovel with
a piece of coal as he practiced his arithmetic. The hovel of light
illuminating Abe from the crude fireplace burst into shining
Eden. Then Abe Lincoln was digging in the ground with the
shovel, and I knew that the empirical aspect of the numbers
scrawled on the shovel's metal, heart-shaped tongue was the
life blooming from the earth. I woke very happy and knew, as
though I'd known all along but had merely forgotten, the wall
above the couch, loaded with bookshelves, was also the wall of
Helene Levy's bedroom.

I took to sleeping at Uncle Sol and Aunt Leah's frequently.
My mother felt bound to honor Uncle Sol's educational function in my life. She rarely objected to my sleeping at Uncle Sol
and Aunt Leah's.

I waited until at last I heard Uncle Sol's voluminous and steady snoring. Emily was afraid of the dark, and a night-light spilled out from Emily and Daphne's bedroom into the living room. With the most gradual movement, I stood in my stocking feet on the couch and parted volumes in the bookshelf to expose the naked wall — on the other side was Helene, awake and waiting. As I waited, every sound, every imagined sound in the sleeping house made me jump. I could make out the titles and author's names on the spines of the books. The books were not organized by subject and alphabetized by author as books were in the public library. Yet, Uncle Sol could always find, without too much difficulty, the book he was searching for. I puzzled over his system. Eventually, years later, I figured it out, I was sure I knew; I was shaving, and the sense of déjà vu, some anarchic dance of time, made me feel I had known all along, as if my longings had been a form of divination. The books in Uncle Sol's library were arranged on the basis of some ever-evolving metaphor in his head. I parted two volumes pressed together, one book was a volume of Spengler's *Decline of the West,* and the other was Flaubert's *Madame Bovary.* At some time Uncle Sol said something about Christianity giving Eros poison to drink. That may have been the key to the arrangement I disrupted. I parted the volumes of Spengler and Flaubert to get to the space of wall, where I would knock, ever so gently, in the code Helene and I had devised. I knocked softly, laboriously, knocked and knocked, "I love you." She knocked back. I counted the knocks, and spelled out "I know."

A week after colliding with Helene we kissed. The tip of my nose brushed within a millimeter of her cheek, she coughed, my head swam several oceanic inches away, then I felt the pressure of her shoulder, a gravitational pull, and I drifted back. My mouth brushed her cheek, I breathed in the nape of her neck, our noses drifted over one another, our mouths touched, we were kissing. Not long after, perhaps another week, Helene's mouth opened while we kissed. We kissed and touched and stroked one another for the next two years. My hands traveled over her body. We gasped, almost fainted. I understood why I could go no further. I honored what she had to keep intact and she honored my honoring it. When I reached under her skirt she yelled "no" and grabbed my wrists. Her mother rested in the bedroom beyond the kitchen, waiting for the world to come. Mrs. Levy looked upon me, when she bothered to look at all, as something of less consequence than the weather.

I brought Helene my ruined face as if it were a gift; it was a spectacle. There was some talk on the street. Whitey Costa had made a remark. I felt honor-bound to edit his speech. When my face healed, my bent nose whistled like Brownie's. Helene was tolerant. I had the feeling I'd done the wrong thing, although I didn't know what the right thing would have been. I was enchanted, she didn't seem to mind, but the look of disdain on Helene's face suggested that I was driven by the wrong imperatives.

I had the feeling of making a mistake again when I met Helene's father. Harry Levy was a big smiling man, and if his wife was unhappy, if his daughter yearned for a life he couldn't provide, he hadn't noticed. Harry was content, jolly, could not believe his own good fortune. He had steady employment in his Uncle Max's printing shop. He worked long hours, arrived home late for supper, and it was always there waiting for him. Harry's big hands, his arms, were black with ink. My aunt Leah, who was a distant cousin to Mrs. Levy, Julia, an orphan, had been born deaf. Harry's hearing was seriously impaired, but he had some residual hearing in his left ear. Ida Nachtgold the matchmaker said to Uncle Max that it was true, Julia couldn't hear, she was stone-deaf. The matchmaker admitted that some people looked on Julia as some kind of lovely idiot. But Ida Nachtgold said, you shouldn't overlook, that Julia, this flower, was only an orphan tucked away all these years in the Jewish Home for the Incurables. Harry's uncle Max made the match. Julia was provided for. Harry woke up every morning next to Julia, looked at her and was amazed. Every week, without fail, Harry handed over to Julia his pay envelope.

Harry had the face of a happy Tartar, the body of a bear. He came home shouting "Hello," delighted to hear his own voice traveling back to him faint and distant. He was always glad to see me. He looked at his daughter's disapproving face as the most glamorous light of a distant star, whose mystery was unfathomable. Mrs. Levy called him with her thin voice and he didn't hear. Mrs. Levy stamped her foot on the kitchen floor, he felt the vibration, cocked his good ear in the direction of the kitchen, and yelled at the top of his lungs his own good name, "Harry, Harry is coming." Mrs. Levy directed him to the sink, where he washed his black arms and hands, which remained black.

From the moment that Mr. Levy arrived home I remained seated. The schoolbooks on my lap tottered on top of the ache that could expose the cloistered something Helene and I wanted to believe belonged to us. There was never enough time. Mr. Levy was a rapid eater. Covered with a textbook, I waited for myself to wane. Helene kept her eyes averted. It ebbed. In the nick of time. The next thing I knew, Helene's father was in the living room, his eyes glazed, rhapsodic, belching his supper.

The couch wheezed. Old Brownie's paws tick-tocked over the linoleum, his nose whistled devotion, my deviated nasal septum breathed its tune. Huge and happy, Mr. Levy boomed, "Hello." The dog, Mr. Levy, and I looked at Helene with such love she didn't know where to run. Mr. Levy turned the television set on, turned the sound up as loud as it would go, and tuned the set into a channel showing a wrestling match. Helene covered her ears and sank back into the couch.

Mr. Levy's great, bald head was cocked in the direction of the television. His eyes squeezed into slits as he was overtaken by his joy. He insisted on showing me wrestling holds. He demonstrated the half nelson, his laughter booming as he bent me over.

Mr. Levy's arms enveloped me, I thought that in his enthusiasm he might squeeze me to a pulp; his voice shouted instructions at my ear. The spectators at the wrestling match on the television screamed and whistled, the volume turned up to the maximum, neighbors banged on the radiator pipes. Brownie barked. Mr. Levy's stubbled chin scuffed my temple, and I looked out from between his arms, relieved that my willingness to offer up my body provided distraction, aided and abetted my clandestine touching of Helene. In the swarm of his powerful body I was creating subterfuge, some small privacy for her and me, a kind of discretion. And Mr. Levy, like any other boy on the street, was showing off for her, entertaining her. She looked mortified. I felt a tension in my neck, as if something were about to crack. The breath squeezed out of me, I was woozy. In some dim way I thought I might be paying for my trespass, my touching having denigrated the bride price; but if I had intruded and dirtied some corner of a sacrament, I paid in decades. Our childish foreplay outstripped the possibilities of consummation, and I would have to learn to put titillation to some other uses, if my heart were not to be worn out with longing.

Harry Levy twisted my arms, bent my neck. Just short of

blacking out, I wrestled him. We were tangled into a mass of limbs, one shuddering, groaning thing. Helene looked at us as the princess looked upon the toad who claimed to be a prince, and croaked love. I knew that her revulsion was only fear. She could be kind. Kiss the reptile and it would turn into a prince, pity the creature, love him and he would turn into something handsome, noble, and graceful. Helene couldn't manage to love it; she did evince some tenderness, first for herself, then for what she saw wriggling on the living room floor. It seemed to be enough.

The voice she heard from the writhing mass said, "Make a wish."

The prince appeared. It took a while. Harry huffed and puffed, through all of his exertions his optimism never faltered. I brought Helene every vision I had. Harry's uncle helped. The same matchmaker, Ida Nachtgold, who had grown very old and quite wealthy, she who had brought Julia to Harry, found Kevin Fine.

Everybody said he was a prince.

Two years of touching. I was almost seventeen. At first she spoke of it as a joke. She said that she didn't know whether her father had initiated the approach to the matchmaker, or her great uncle, her father's uncle Max had done it. But it was ridiculous she said, imagine ancient Ida Nachtgold still alive and in business in this modern age in America.

Then, not more than a month later, things began to happen very fast. For the first time she said she probably loved me. She didn't want me to feel bad. She wanted me to understand that she had doubts about the phenomenon itself; and she said I couldn't kiss her anymore, or hold her hand. She said we could talk. I reached for her and she moved away. Ancient Brownie, who had grown deaf, struggled to his feet and showed me what was left of his teeth.

I knocked at the door. I knocked and knocked. No one answered. Of course, Mrs. Levy couldn't hear me, Brownie couldn't hear me, and Helene wouldn't answer the door. I pounded on the door. I knew she was in there. If only I were inside, and we were close, we would be touching again, because it had its own power. Helene was only hiding. Now she withheld her voice. I talked to the door. I shouted, "I know you're in there." Helene would not relent. The deaf dog wouldn't bark. Mrs. Levy rested in her impregnable silence, waiting for eternity. I begged. I kicked the door. Neighbors passed by in the hallway. I saw pity, mockery, and in all of their faces the conceit that if only I paid attention to them I would learn the thing I needed to know. For as long as I could stand it I hated them all.

I climbed the steps to the next landing and looked down over the banister. I waited. I saw Aunt Leah leave her apartment to go shopping. Uncle Sol was at work. My cousins would be studying.

I knocked at the door. My cousin Daphne answered, reading a book. She didn't ask what I wanted. Daphne stepped aside and I entered. I didn't see Emily. She was probably in her bedroom, drinking milk, eating cookies, and reading. My cousins were budding into young ladies, which was a subject of no apparent interest to them. I went to the living-room wall, removed three books from a shelf, and began to knock on the wall in the code. I knocked and knocked all kinds of messages. There was no answer. Perhaps Helene wasn't in her room, or she was just being obstinate. I remembered that when she told me that I couldn't touch her anymore she also lectured me for being impractical. I had been impatient, annoyed. Perhaps I should have tried to at least look interested in her advice. I rapped volumes against the wall, my knuckles ached. Daphne and Emily took no notice of me or anything I was doing.

I went into Uncle Sol and Aunt Leah's bedroom. I put the books stacked on the windowsill on the floor, opened the window, and climbed out on the fire escape. The well of sky, high above the brick and slate courtyard made by the adjoining tenements, bubbled like lava. The red of twilight dyed the rigging of clotheslines and hanging laundry red. The distance between the fire escape just outside Uncle Sol and Aunt Leah's bedroom, and the fire escape at Helene's bedroom was not too great; but I couldn't just step from one to the other. I was four stories above the street, and I would have to climb out and onto the ladder at the edge of the fire escape, swing out, grab hold of the ladder that extended down from the fire escape at Helene's bedroom window, pull, press, and climb onto the fire escape that surrounded her bedroom window.

I hung from the ladder, kicked my legs, and swung back and forth. I hung there too long, thought too much. I couldn't look up or down. Some fetid weather from the unseen moon fanned my cheeks. I swung back and forth, one time more than necessary. When I let go I dropped. My trousers ballooned with the uprush of air, my legs churned, gravity sucked me down, the red, cloud-veiled sun pinwheeled between the roofs; clawing air, I grappled a crosshatching of metal suspended in nowhere, collided and slashed open my cheek, and had one leg thrust between the rungs of a ladder. I clung there. Shivering.

I hung on, frozen. Finally I urged myself into climbing onto the fire escape before some neighbor saw me and called the fire department to come rescue me.

I stood on Helene Levy's fire escape and wiped the blood

from my cheek. The shade on her bedroom window was drawn all the way down. The window was open a crack at the bottom. Murmuring seeped out from the crack at the bottom of the window. I felt I'd paid for something. I could have been killed; even though I wouldn't tell her about it, she would look at me and know, and she would have to let me touch her, at least hold her hand; and if not, I had my recompense, I was glad to be alive. I could open the window.

I must have made a mistake. I looked through the opened window. The apartment was filled with the whole neighborhood. Looking from the window through the open bedroom door into the living room, I saw Mr. Stevanovitch the janitor. He held in one hand a cord from which a key dangled. In his other hand he held a pair of shoes, and draped over the crook of that arm, several pairs of pants. Mr. Stevanovitch, who was about Mr. Levy's size, was smiling. I sat, straddled on the windowsill looking in. Tillie Blum the grocer's wife was there. She was talking to Mrs. Cheechko. Mrs. Cheechko appeared distracted and reached out toward Mr. Stevanovitch, making a claim on one of the pairs of trousers draped over the janitor's arm. Mr. Costello crossed my line of vision, a loaded pillowcase hung from his hand. Looking at the bedroom told me nothing. It was empty. I scanned the living room wall, it was the pockmarked yellow I remembered, and the peeling ceiling was familiar. There were voices coming from the kitchen. Someone was moving under a mattress toward the door. For years in dreams I would return to this apartment. I would knock at the door and no one would answer. The mattress walked out the door.

Gertie Dresnicky followed, her hair was in curlers and she wore a housecoat and carpet slippers, and she carried a stack of dishes. Mrs. Dresnicky's little girl Pearlie carried the cups.

From the hallway came a great crashing sound of dishes exploding. Everybody in the apartment cheered. Gertie Dresnicky reappeared in the doorway of the apartment, empty-handed, flanked by little Pearlie. They trotted back to the kitchen. The janitor waved to me, invited me in. Now everyone turned to me and cheered.

In the living room I saw that the television set was gone. Tillie Blum called to me in her resounding baritone, "Come boychik, I'll tell you something." Mrs. Cheechko was arguing with the janitor, claiming one of the pairs of pants she was sure would fit her husband. She said, by way of irrefutable justification, that if she hadn't been born dead, her life would have been much more difficult. It was then that I saw, or thought I saw, Whitey Costa. The body streaked by me and out the door, clutching one of the couch pillows. I started after him. Tillie Blum hung on to me. Stevanovitch's hand reached out to hold me in place. "Listen," the grocer's wife said to me, in that extraordinary voice of hers.

One of the bonuses of patronizing the Blum grocery store was that customers who lived on our street could receive telephone calls from the public booth located in the store. Only very few of the well-off had telephones on our street; these were the same people who had refrigerators when most folks still had iceboxes. In any event, when a relative telephoned, Tillie Blum would take the call, say, "Okay just a minute," and go out into the street. Sam Blum leaned on his broom, watching his wife work wearied him. Tillie, out on the sidewalk, set her legs wide, put her hands on her hips, and called up to the fifth story so that she could be heard in the rear of the apartment. "Yetta Berman, your sister's calling from the Bronx." Tillie Blum's cry could blister the hide of a rhinoceros at ten paces. "Listen," Tillie whispered to me in her tenderest voice, and her hot breath began to congeal the cut on my cheek. The janitor and the grocer's wife held on to me. I bobbed my head, dodging Tillie's concussive vibrato hammering at my ear, "It's just as easy to fall in love with a rich boy as a poor boy." Gertie Dresnicky emerged from the kitchen, her arms loaded with pots and pans. "Why not?" she said, nodding in agreement. Gertie Dresnicky looked at me pityingly, and put the pots and pans down at her feet. Little Pearlie stopped and put the lids on the pots on the floor. Gertie reached into the pocket of her housecoat, pulled out a handkerchief, spit into it, and pressed the handkerchief to my split cheek. "Hold that," she said. Tillie nodded. Mr. Stevanovitch the janitor sighed and relinquished one of the pairs of pants draped over his arm to Mrs. Cheechko. Mrs. Cheechko said, "Goodbye, I'm going home to my own troubles." Mr. Costello's two grown sons, Bruno and Frank, came to carry out the couch, which was missing one pillow.

They knew. The whole street knew. I had never seen Kevin Fine. He was a rumor, something I'd heard about. Everybody talked about him, claimed to have seen him, they talked about him like something they almost believed in. They said he was handsome, blond, tall, a prince of a man. Many had seen the car, a chauffeured car. The car was real and the awestruck discussion of the many wonders of the machine validated everything else. Kevin Fine was a prince, heir of his father Maurice, a philanthropist whose picture was often in the newspapers as he presided over various civic occasions; Maurice an heir himself to the fortune made from Fine's Lingerie.

I had been there when it happened and yet I had to be told it happened before I knew, and this seemed a vanity that irritated my neighbors as they explained it all to me with relish.

They also said this was Ida Nachtgold's ultimate and most triumphant arrangement. She instructed the Levys to forget and leave their leavings, as they were to be transported to the kingdom of Westchester to begin a new and other life, and everything needed would be provided. Kevin Fine the prince was in love; moreover, it had been ten years since he had graduated from Yale, and his family had feared his dogmatic bachelorhood, his indifference to the family business, and his predilection for gentile women. All of this was changed, and the Fine family was infinitely grateful.

My mother had finally heard of my infatuation with Helene Levy, and she gave what she saw as my adolescent erotomania the same regard she would have the chicken pox, or if she had thought it more virulent, pneumonia. As far as she was concerned, one's susceptibility to romance was only proof of the generic weakness of the human mind; the whole "love business" was the not so subtle conspiracy of nature, meant to use you up, death being the ultimate capitalist pig.

My unhappiness offended my mother. I moped around. She cursed me in Yiddish. If my translation was correct, she had hissed that the love business had turned my head into a bucket of swill. I skulked around the neighborhood.

I knew Helene was gone. I had seen, I had been told, and still I found myself loitering, sneaking around the hall. I looked to make sure no one would see me. I peeked over my shoulder to be certain no one was coming up or down the stairs. The blood banged in my head. I knocked, softly, on the door, ready to bolt the moment I heard the footstep of a neighbor.

The sound I heard was weary. My guts did all sorts of extraordinary things. I lurched from Helene's door to Uncle Sol and Aunt Leah's door, as though that had been my destination.

The footsteps climbing the stairs were slow. I could charge down the stairs past the slow-moving neighbor, or run up the stairs and not be seen at all, there was time. The sudden enormous shadow of someone, who turned out to be me, made me lunge out on the landing.

I looked down the stairs. At first I didn't recognize him. He looked and didn't know me. He was carrying three fat books, each ascending step a great labor, and he looked confused, as though he'd misplaced the life he knew. "Hello, Uncle Sol!" "You?" Uncle Sol asked. I said, "Yeah." He said, "Don't cry." I said, "I'm not." He studied me, and seemed relieved to see me. He appeared expectant in a way that obscured his resemblance to the Uncle Sol I knew. Nevertheless, the instant I recognized him, climbing, carrying books, my relief bloomed into something wild. My heart felt like an animal that had been beaten, and I stroked at it through my belly and chest. The moment I saw Uncle Sol I was overwhelmed with the feeling that despite the intimate knowledge everyone on my street was sure they had of me, despite family history, despite history, I might invent myself. I wanted Uncle Sol to say something, confirm that. He just stood there. Then the books fell, a look of horror crossed his face. I snatched one, two, out of the air. He sank, falling to his knees — and I flashed on the posture of awestruck grandmothers squatting and frolicking in the Coney Island surf, pulling the bodices of their bathing suits from their necks, and ladling palm fulls of the Atlantic Ocean between their low-slung breasts, groaning ecstatically. Uncle Sol crouched on the steps, he'd caught the third falling book between his knees. He groaned and he sighed. Not one book had touched the floor. The panic faded from his face. He looked sad.

I glanced at the titles of the books I'd rescued from the air.

Uncle Sol blushed. "*The Fundamentals of Phrenology,*" he said, "and, *A Taxonomy of The Terrain of The Human Head*. More," he said, in reference to the volume he removed from between his knees.

He began to explain. I envisioned his large, capable hands fondling a huge, human head that was the world. He looked stunned. I began to know from that instant onward, but didn't know enough, and by the time I could say something that might have been a comfort, offer some small human fellowship, years had passed, and he'd put his mind to coping with a collapsed lung and the ruptured disks at the base of his spine.

The loveliness of the design of the universe had put blisters on his heart, and knocked the wind out of him; but the realization that the most exalted human imagining was an adaptive reflex had taken him to despair. He was reconnoitering, going back, perhaps something had been overlooked; phrenology, palmistry, alchemy, what human longing and kind of knowing was articulated through these, and how could he know unless he explored it himself. The repose he usually resided in while speaking was gone. He appeared uncertain, couldn't be sure that the words he would say could carry the meaning he intended. Everything could be lost in a moment of thought. I watched him struggle to impersonate his old self; the longer he did it, the more he seemed himself. He asked how my father was. But before I could answer, he began to speak, didn't want to hear, might be imperiled by my answer. He mentioned in passing that the captions I'd written under my drawings were more vivid and interesting than the sketches. "Well," he said, "well" as though there had only been the slightest interruption in our talks, and now he was taking up where he'd left off just a short while ago.

The tone and rhythm of Uncle Sol's oratory was perfunctory, the waving of his hands urgent. I may have realized that he wanted me to understand that what he was saying was basic stuff and useful only because of what it would shed light on later. He belabored the obvious as if it were a revelation from heaven — the teacher's priestly function. "Galileo," Uncle Sol said.

I began to dream of ships. He said, "The Inquisition." I looked at him, said, "Don't worry." He still looked Lincolnesque, handsome, very much like my Uncle Sol. I contemplated forgery, and was astounded by the ease I felt, and the sense of possibility. Charlie Lanza had done it. He was far away, out of the neighborhood, on a ship. I was almost seventeen and if I wanted to do it, I would have to forge my father's name. Uncle Sol said, "A traumatic blow to man's narcissim." He reiterated how Galileo had demonstrated, with the help of the telescope he'd improved, the truth of Copernican theory; the earth was not the center of the Universe. "And of course," Uncle Sol said, "Galileo was condemned for heresy." I nodded, of course, of course. Suddenly mighty, puffed up with dreaming, I dreamed I would go away into the world, a place as ignorant of me as I, find and practice the strength to shape the world's dreaming; because she is in it. I remembered; she had stopped to look at the pictures I made. I would make the story; she would know it, and whatever bed she lay in, I would save her from sleeping with the language of strangers.

PROMENADE

One endless August day in the factory, Señora Milagros sat at her sewing machine and waited for the desire to lift her arms. She would reach down, take her street shoes out of her large purse, put the shoes on her feet, and go home. The shooting pain in her back had subsided into an ache, her hands hung at her sides. A brazen twilight blinded the window. She waited; tentatively she moved her neck, sweat tickled her spine, and her eyes burned. She was aware of the women seated in rows beside her, acting out the same slow, repetitious movements in various stages, as if choreographing the locutions of some grand fugue. The air in the factory loft was dense with rainbow tinted textile dust. She stood up on her shaking legs and waited. As she waited she began to suspect that her soul, too, was only mortal. The thought seemed a great act of renunciation. She moved like water out from behind her sewing machine.

As Señora Milagros sat on the plastic-sheathed couch trying to explain it all to Laura Providencia, their shoulders touched, and they sat leaning into one another, their voices, soft and conspiratorial. Laura Providencia couldn't remember her mother ever having been attentive in just this way. They were looking at one another, slightly startled. Laura would remember her mother saying that all this she was trying to tell Laura, she couldn't tell Señora Ramirez. Señora Ramirez wouldn't understand, she only needed to warm herself by identifying the catastrophes of her life in her neighbor, Señora Milagros' life. "However, Laura Providencia possessed understanding." Eventually, Laura would recall that her mother hadn't actually made such a declaration, but that didn't alter the truth of her memory.

Laura waited and felt herself ready to say how she had awakened that morning fatigued and slightly nauseous; as if she had spent the night hostage to enthrallments she could hardly bear, in an all night movie, featuring relentless episodic dreams. Two episodes survived morning, and she could still feel the eyes of the child in her belly peering through the bubbling uterine deeps, and the bright minuscule creatures swimming in her inner water, the infant girl child, the color of coral, laughing bouquets of flowers into the water, and peeking through Laura Providencia's navel out at the hilarious, sad world. In the dream Laura knew this would be the child she and Isaac would make, and in her dream she feared her child's capacity for dreaming, and she was ready to blame Isaac for this, but then she was being questioned by the governor, a woman whose face Laura couldn't quite see. The governor was as remote and featureless as any absolute authority. She returned Laura's passport to her and said the passport was faulty because there was a drawing of God on it, and the drawing was wrong. In the darkest portion of the morning Laura Providencia and her mother, refugees from sleep, discovered one another flopped into corners of the couch, waiting for the first light. Laura prided herself for having protested in her dream, it felt like an accomplishment, something she had willed. She couldn't remember what she had said, but the cost of the protest seemed to her exorbitant as she sat waiting for the day to appear in the living-room window; exhausted, humbled, she wanted to hide, if only she could believe that hiding was possible.

Señora Milagros spoke first, not necessarily to Laura but to empty out the long day in the factory that was recapitulated in the dream that made the day truly endless. After a time the muffled language of trance relinquished its power, and they found they were speaking to one another. Laura's willingness to tell her dream to her mother was almost equal to telling it, as Señora Milagros went on to explain that, as she stood up on her shaking legs and moved out from behind her sewing machine that day, it occurred to her that her soul, too, was something that could die. She became aware for the first time that the weight of the penitential habit she had worn for two years, and had taken off three long years ago, having at last fulfilled her obligation, that extraordinary weight, as powerful as an ocean's undertow dragging her bones and body even when she was naked, bathing in the bathtub, and the garment hung, in the dark closet, now finally, three years after fulfilling her obligation, the weight of the garment no longer oppressed her.

Señora Milagros took Laura Providencia's hand. The last of sleep gave way to the morning light, flushing the dark from the living-room window. The accumulating evidence of the start of day sounded in the walls, the plumbing gurgled, the steam pipes hissed, and the sirens of fire engines, faint, a mile of streets away, wailed toward the day's first arson. Señora Milagros asked Laura if she would like coffee. Laura said, "Oh Mami, I'll make the coffee." Señora Milagros said, "Sit child, I'll make it," and neither moved. They looked at each other and laughed. Señora Milagros let the laughter ride through her chest and throat and jiggle her cheeks; she waited it out, caught her breath, and said that she knew that that day in the factory, which she feared might not have a conclusion, really had ended when she found herself walking in the street toward the subway in her carpet slippers. She remembered then, that she had moved out from behind her sewing machine, forgetting her purse and shoes. She continued walking, determined to go home. As she passed by the newspaper kiosk on the corner of the street of her subway station, she realized that she lacked the subway fare and laughed at herself. People streamed by her and bumped against her as they hurried out of the light and down the steps into the dark of the subway. She heard the stallion neigh, looked up and saw the handsome policeman on horseback smiling at her. The policeman looked down, said something in English she didn't understand, but his voice sounded friendly and kind. The horse blinked its eye, nosed its head toward the curb, and there on the pavement she saw the shining coin. Señora Milagros thanked the horse in Spanish; the horse fluttered its lips, showing his great teeth, sharing with Señora Milagros the joke of fortune's timely charity.

Standing, packed against the other bodies in the subway

car, the floor shuddering, light and dark blinking on and off with every beat, so that the rhythm entered her breathing; Señora Milagros closed her eyes, and in that dark she was able to follow the fugitive thought, nearly annihilated by the train's screaming. Titi worked the late shift at the factory and occupied the same sewing machine. She would find her sister's shoes and bring them home.

Señora Milagros brought the coffee and the plates of suruyos to the couch. Laura Providencia and her mother drank the coffee and ate the cigar-shaped corn fritters. When Señora Milagros began to speak in a voice that was kind beyond all forgiveness, saying that Laura's romance with the white Jew was the first step in the long journey of Laura's desire to eventually be alone, Laura was no longer certain that she hadn't told her mother her dreams of the night before. Laura didn't remember her mother's exact words, but Señora Milagros' description of Isaac's first agony upon realizing that their life together would be only a stage in Laura's evolution, toward an imperial solitude, seemed prescient. The pain of Laura Providencia's and Señora Milagros' previous arguments, the whole issue of dishonor — as Laura spent more of her nights with Isaac, in his apartment, downtown — Señora Milagros mentioned none of this; indeed Laura no longer had to steal herself for an act of defiance, as her mother spoke with the solicitude of a clairvoyant who cannot help knowing Laura was moving into her own life, and the making of a family that would be hers was part of the way to a freedom whose strictures had something to do with the pictures she would paint. Señora Milagros spoke, describing matter of factly, the imminence of what had not yet happened, and paused to complain that Luz Divina, the older sister who hadn't lived long enough for Laura Providencia to know, Luz never came to speak to her mother anymore.

Thin wisps of smoke from a conflagration within walking distance seeped into the living room from the window left open a half-inch crack at the bottom near the sill. The bells of St. Ann's chimed, announcing early Sunday morning Mass. Laura Providencia got up from the couch, walked across the living room, and closed the window on the threads of smoke drifting into the room and floating up to waft beneath the ceiling. Señora Milagros reported, as though she were reiterating the terms of a promising truce, that now that Laura Providencia spent less and less time at home, Titi had taken on more responsibility for the care of Rosita who was almost eleven years old and nearly a señorita, a very dangerous time; but things seemed to be working out well enough. Later, after church, Señora Milagros reminded Laura they would make the long trip upstate to visit Angel. Rosita who rarely walked in her sleep now, but woke slowly, continuing the conversations that had inhabited her sleep, stirred in her bed and chanted gleefully the foul sayings inscribed on the lobby wall of the building. Titi serenaded Rosita toward full waking, and Rosita's language became as demure as her eyes, which had been open all through sleep and were now cleansed of the hectic shadows of dreaming; the skyline of the Bronx formed in the bedroom window. Señora Milagros and Laura Providencia regarded the diminuendo of Rosita's giggling sleep-lathered cries of "shit, shit, shit" and "fuck, fuck, fuck," as they did the floating rivulets of smoke soaking into the ceiling.

Señora Milagros said that, "when Angel returned home," (she never said if, and if there was doubt in her mother's faith, Laura couldn't detect it), "Angel must be allowed to take his place as the man of the house." Laura was not sure that this was a threat on Isaac's life, but the possibility was part of the truce

Laura and her mother had agreed upon without ever having to say the words; and certainly the responsibilities and prerogatives of Angel's life had to be offered if he were to live again, but Laura had asked her mother to never again follow the advice of the espiritista who had prescribed that Señora Milagros take the small photograph that Isaac had given Laura, of himself as a young boy, and freeze it in the ice cube tray of the refrigerator. Laura assumed she had misplaced the photo. When on the warm evening of some months ago Laura had gone to the refrigerator to get some ice cubes for the glasses of ginger ale she had poured for herself and Rosita, she found herself staring into the palm of her hand, where the diminutive twelve-year-old face of Isaac stared up at her, shrouded in a cube of ice. She managed not to scream; but the fear was exacerbated by the most violent feeling against her mother she had ever had. Laura persuaded herself that the spell of arthritic-like pains Isaac had felt in his knees during this time was only coincident with her mother's activity. She did not mention any of this to Isaac until eight years later, when Isaac confessed to an infidelity and stood waiting punishment, and Laura, with a show of great disdain, told him that she had stood between him and damnations he couldn't imagine. Isaac said his problem was what he could imagine, and she punched him in the nose.

Titi, Rosita, Señora Milagros, and Laura Providencia dressed and prepared to leave for church. Señora Milagros trotted down the vestibule between the living room and her bedroom, wrestling herself into a girdle and calling out to remind everyone that after church they were to travel to El Barrio to meet with Uncle Toto, Aunt Lydia, and the others for the long car ride upstate to the hospital to visit Angel. Titi called from the bathroom, where she was bathing Rosita, that she had already prepared the food for the trip. Rosita hummed a bolero, thought of the records she would bring, and lifted her foot out of the water to be soaped. Laura brushed her hair, grooming herself as she would for Easter. The composition of the face in the mirror, which she recognized as her own, was a sufficient distraction, helping her not to think about her duty and desire to help her brother, and her desire to flee.

Señora Milagros reached the end of the narrow hallway at her bedroom door, trussed into her girdle, breathing hard, and holding in her hands, as she would a chalice, a pair of black shining low-heeled shoes with brass buckles on them. As she entered her room, and as she dressed, she speculated out loud on the white Jew, Isaac, who was in love with her daughter, and what that might mean in terms of what the other one, Rosen the lawyer, could achieve, who was also in love with Laura Providencia. Laura smoothed her dress with her hands, listened, and knew that her mother believed that Rosen had the mystical capacity of his people for navigating in the fallen world, and if anyone could find a way to free Angel from the asylum, the Jewish lawyer could do it. Of what use Isaac could be, beyond the general disasters of life and love, Señora Milagros could not imagine. When Laura thought of the bleak severity of Rosen the lawyer's face, she imagined that the monk Savanarola must have had such a face. As far as Laura could tell, all Rosen needed of her was to demonstrate what he could achieve in the world, for Angel, in her behalf. He had of late taken to wearing a beret, along with his customary black vest, and snug pinstriped black suit, starched white collar, and thin slate-gray tie. The beret had the effect of making him appear, not so much bohemian as priestly. On occasion Rosen smiled while looking at Laura, and the phenomenon appeared as an aftershock of moral collapse, causing the lawyer such embarrassment that Laura turned away; but even with his head turning purple Rosen continued to speak, outlining the intricate moves of his legal strategy as if it were a ballad, and as time went on he required more and more conferences with Laura, his need to serenade her with his exposition becoming insatiable; the coda was always the same; Rosen reminding Laura that he was providing his services pro bono after the office of the American Civil Liberties Union had said they could not justify taking on Angel's case, and Rosen said, his usual fee was one hundred dollars an hour.

Señora Milagros sat hunched over on the stool, around which she had sewn a pink taffeta skirt, and huffed and puffed as she brushed her shoe. She called out from the bedroom for everyone to hurry, or they'd be late for Mass, and they also had the subway ride to El Barrio, where Uncle Toto, Aunt Lydia, and the cousins would be waiting. She reminded everyone that the ride upstate was long and the visiting period at the hospital brief. She spit on the toes of her shining shoes, and gently, and vigorously in a circular motion, buffed, with an immaculate white handkerchief, the pointed toes of the shoes. She sighed and said softly, as a confident assertion might annul the fact, her brother Toto was the owner of a new automobile.

Uncle Toto brought candy. Ever since his experience of the weeping Madonna he had not had a drink, and he discovered that he had a monumental sweet tooth. His pockets were full of candy, he consumed quarts of ice cream and devoured cakes. He had also become a Protestant. The Catholic church authorities had not been willing to validate the miracle of the weeping Madonna retrieved from the trash can. The priest had explained that weeping Madonnas, whether statues or portraits, were fairly commonplace, and Toto's statuette could not be officially rec-

ognized as a miracle. Toto imagined miasmas of recondite the-
ology as the church's ruse to conceal its antidemocratic bias.
Why, he wondered, should his miracle be an orphan, nameless,
a bastard? Toto took his religious life elsewhere. He was now
pastor of the Iglesia Pentecostal Nuevo Mundo. In the storefront church he pounded a tambourine, chanted testimony, and
stuffed his mouth with marzipan. Laura barely recognized him.
Tío Toto had gained one hundred pounds with his conversion;
he had become an enormous, little round man. His manic optimism propelled him into a fidgeting dance around the floor
of the facility for the insane, where his nephew was incarcerated, or domiciled for an unspecified length of time, if one could
believe in the redemptive possibilities of the institution's therapies. Señora Milagros' Catholicism was inclusive enough not to
be offended by Toto's religious journey. Aunt Titi however, was
alarmed by Toto's apostasy, but even if he had been a leper, a
condition she would consider less serious than his straying from
the church, Toto was family and not to be excluded from the
Sunday afternoon visits with Angel.

Uncle Toto licked the chocolate from his lips and drove in
circles for a time trying to find a space in the crowded parking
lot. His little daughter Nilsa, who was a year old and about the
size of a well-fed and nimble house cat, had climbed across his
shoulders, and fallen asleep. He knew she was asleep when the
drool from the child's open mouth trickled down his neck, and
her thin arm hung down his chest. He had driven the last several miles of the journey this way, his little daughter's perfect
cat-like balance, weighted across his shoulders, her slight whistling snore in his ear, and the drool trickling down his neck
filling him with happiness. The child slept through his singing
"See the USA in your Chevrolet."

Finally he found a parking space. Looking out of the rolled-down window on the driver's side, Toto viewed the bars on the windows of the institution, and the high chain-mail fence, and to reassure his sister Milagros, said softly and emphatically, "We have arrived, at the hospital."

It was festive. Aunt Lydia shook out the long tablecloth she had purchased in Chinatown. The iridescent cloth was patterned with the three-dimensional effect of a hologram; the flowers in the glowing pasture swayed momentarily over the heads of the family gathered around the long table, a sheaf of pastoral vision Aunt Lydia flung in a space of air, surrounded by the greater cavernous space of the visiting room, an angel's wing, seen and gone, falling like manna onto the table as Aunt Lydia bent over and smoothed out the table cloth with caressing hands. Señora Milagros placed the two large pots of rice and chicken at the center of the table. Aunt Lydia turned and put out the three-tiered cake. Titi, dipping into the bottomless shopping bag at her feet, while balancing Lydia's five-month-old daughter Esperanza, whining on her hip, managed to set out the plastic containers of codfish cakes and pasteles. Rosita, budding in a dress of exploding pink, distributed the paper plates, plastic forks and spoons, and bottles of soda around the table. Cousin Elena, the mulata whose most restrained strolling provoked prurient naked dreaming in almost all male creatures, including, Aunt Titi had said, genuflecting, dogs and cats — this motley of street animals on two legs and four legs, with and without tails, followed in Elena's wake — barking, meowing, whistling and howling, and Elena yawned behind her lilac-colored fingernails. In Aunt Titi's cautionary fables of male bestiality, told for the edification of Laura Providencia, and then Rosita, Titi prophesied, in this case accurately, Elena's invincible allure would last three years, from the ages of fourteen to seventeen, after which she would balloon into a two-hundred pound Sybil and have a profitable career advising brides on the vicissitudes of marriage. Aunt Titi, in collusion with Aunt Lydia, and to save the world from anarchy during the three dangerous years of Elena's rampant erotic power, arranged the marriage of the fourteen-year-old Elena to Eduardo. Eduardo the groom was seventeen years old, and in the second week of his marriage, still on his honeymoon. He had the bearing of an exquisitely wrought, androgynous mannequin. Eduardo wore candy-striped, bell-bottomed trousers, and a swashbuckling pirate's shirt with ballooned sleeves, a ruffled front, and an open neck, displaying an array of gold chains. During the week Eduardo was employed piloting, in a hussar's uniform, a golden cage of an elevator up and down in a luxurious and venerable apartment house on the Upper East Side. Eduardo was in a union, his employment paid well, and during the day's gliding up and down, the tides of his blood wooshing in unison, he dreamed of Elena and the coming night, up and down, and Eduardo gainfully employed, up and down, tumescent beneath his brocaded hussar's tunic, considered that his life was a gift.

Eduardo smiled a smile of perfect teeth and followed after Elena wearing her new sheath outfit of bright green. The couple searched for an outlet to plug in the phonograph set up on the far end of the dining table. Rosita set a record on the turntable and scooped little Esperanza from the table. The child had been crawling in the direction of the cake. Rosita handed the baby back to Aunt Titi, from whose arms Esperanza had wriggled free.

Rosen the lawyer sat just to the right of the head of the table. He lifted his eyes from the plate of unkosher food he could not bring himself to eat, and moved the muscles in his face in what he hoped was an agreeable expression and said, "Thank you," to Señora Milagros, who had set the food in front of him. He looked around the long table. Toto had tossed him an orange, which Rosen had caught like a blow in the center of his chest. Rosen placed the orange in the attaché case holding the secret he'd wanted to share with Laura Providencia for weeks. Toto, shouting "Hallelujah" with a wedge of cake in his hand, skipped off into the din of the crowded room in the direction of a face he had glimpsed that seemed to him susceptible to the glory of what Toto knew to be God's word.

Rosen thought, once again, the afternoon would not afford him the opportunity to reveal his secret to Laura Providencia. Somehow the circumstances were never right, and he told himself that he wasn't waiting for the optimum conditions, but again he hesitated, and the delay suggested terminal paralysis. The previous night, at least he thought it was the previous night, it might have been several nights before, in any event, the event was recent; Rosen had been catapulted out of bed by a dream of falling into an innumerable hour, in which he was illuminated by the giddy notion that Laura Providencia should address him forevermore as "Rosie." It seemed to Rosen a pleasant notion. He padded around the dark bedroom, looked down the length of his lean body, where his cherubic feet, the most voluptuous part of him, shined like lamps; and as he was agreeable to the name change he was able to return to sleep, and in the morning the idea no longer had the force of necessity.

The attaché case resting lightly on Rosen's knees accrued a weight in his head that made his temples throb. His fingers fumbled at the little tumbler, keeping the attaché case locked on his lap, the combination having absconded from memory;

this lapse, quite aside from his aching head, seemed an illicit joy. There was a kind of hushed ranting in his head "Rosie, Rosie, Rosie" as his fingers found the configuration of numbers, and the lid of the attaché case sprung open on his lap. Discreetly, he held the lid down, but did not snap it shut. The attaché case held his secret first attempt at watercolors, the orange Toto had tossed to him, and the glassine envelope of what Laura had said her brother needed most. Rosie noted that Rosen the attorney was only shocked by his not being shocked by his breach of the law, smuggling the marijuana into the institution taking him beyond the pale of any fiduciary privilege he could claim. But never had Rosen experienced a longing so excruciating as his need to show Laura his watercolor rendering of the water-filled milk bottle and daisies; postponing, never finding the time really appropriate, as the display of this first attempt at watercolors could reveal some alluvial depth of soul requiring just one more reprieve, so he might prepare himself for something he couldn't imagine.

Rosen looked up and around the visiting room. What he saw seemed to him the fleshing out of his father's admonition, the consequences of Rosen's need to adventure in the gentile world, and he thought too of the reproduction he had seen in the art supply store where he purchased his paints; the print, in a spectrum of reds, all the colors of blood, an ancient advertisement for a Barnum & Bailey freak show, foreshadowing the world around him, read, *Peerless Prodigies of Natural Phenomena.*

The next voice he heard was enough like his Uncle Irving's to rebuke what Rosen identified as his own bigotry. The man had the large leafy ears of an elephant, his nose and lips were borrowed from an anti-Semitic cartoon, he shuffled forward quaking from the hilarity of some joke from which he would never recover. He was energetic, slight, and the incongruous dome of his considerable gut was parbuckled by suspenders and belt. He moved between two white-uniformed male attendants, and didn't speak to them, but through them, broadcasting to the world. "Do you know," he said, looking toward one attendant, and proclaiming to all, "do you know how to make a Romanian omelet? Huh? First you steal the eggs." The little man's gut slung in the network of belt and suspenders, he moved with surprising grace. He scanned the crowd with the intimate and knowing eye of a family member who knows everyone's secrets, winked to reassure everyone that he wouldn't tell, his telepathic scrutiny coming to rest briefly on Rosen, who could hear the erratic rhythm of his own heart. The little man pantomimed the Statue of Liberty, mimed the statue's fall into the posture of a minstrel singer on his knees, arms out flung, his mouth shaping the word, "Mammy"; the silence weighted on his red visible tongue grew heavy, ballooning his cheeks and he crooned, "It's us, ma, the wretched refuse of your teeming shores."

The two stout, white-suited male attendants lifted the little man by his armpits to his feet. They appeared to scold him, each speaking into one of his leafy ears. The little old man scanned the crowd frantically trying to locate the family member he hoped was there, lost among the many, trying to find him. Finally one of the attendants flanking the little man yelled, "Nobody, Brodsky, nobody's come to see you again." Brodsky blew a kiss to a little girl of perhaps ten, wearing a pink crinolined dress, skipping toward the outstretched arms of an uncle or father. The two attendants exchanged a significant glance, and quickly and efficiently scooped Brodsky up by the arms and legs. The old man struggled and they dropped him once. The little girl in the puffed crinolined dress watched bemused, as the old man threw a tantrum.

Rosita was the first to see him. She pointed past the two attendants carrying the struggling old man toward the door, held open by someone in a dark corridor. "Look there," she said, "there!" and clapped her hands. Angel followed after the nattily dressed physician. The doctor wore dark sunglasses, a stethoscope dangled from his neck. When the doctor paused to light a cigarette, Angel paused. Angel seemed ready to sit down and join the family seated at the nearest table, until the doctor took his elbow and led him on. Laura Providencia watched their progress. Her brother followed the doctor, staring, surprised. Laura turned away. The windows in the side walls were barred, the glass cross-hatched with wire was dim; in the ceiling forty feet up, three large turret windows revealed the floating blue floor of heaven. Three columns of light fell to the floor, spotlighting Angel's slow treading after the doctor, a family weeping on the far side of the room, and Johnny Ferris the hydrocephalic. Seeing and hearing Johnny Ferris again, Laura felt the dread that she identified as her due for the weekly visit. Johnny's huge melon of a head breathed, his blood-red temples, gills, the head trembled on the stem of his neck in the falling sunlight, and Laura couldn't help thinking of this patient inmate as the Humpty-Dumpty oracle, a nemesis of mocking ill-will. Humpty-Dumpty perched in a large cushioned chair was flanked by a huge male orderly who looked like a professional wrestler, and a tiny mother or aunt, dabbing at her eyes with a handkerchief.

Ferris' enormous head simmering in the falling light howled his customary greeting across the room at Angel, "Ay, ay, hello how do you like it now Spanish Willie?" Laura in that moment tried to respond as she imagined Isaac responded to so much of life happening to him; it was a story, even as it was happening, an act of memory, an experience viewed from a promising critical future that could make something more and other of it. But as Ferris yelled, "Say hello Spanish Willie, lots of doom and gloom going round and round," Laura winced and saw her brother wave to Ferris, a befuddled look on Angel's face. When on a previous visit Angel had remembered and explained, Laura thought she understood, to some extent, her brother's fascination. Beyond Ferris' misdemeanors and felonies was Ferris' ambitious attempt to eat the living arm of his aging father. Angel had no idea of what Johnny Ferris may have suffered at the hands of his father, if anything; but Angel was especially fascinated by the process of shunting, the draining of the sodden planet of Johnny's head, as if in so doing Johnny could be relieved of the desire to devour his father.

Laura didn't like herself for hating the stranger, one of God's odder creations; she preferred not to think about it, and she had no desire to explore why she had felt relieved at the news Angel had conveyed during the last visit: "Humpty-Dumpty got no teeth," he'd said. Evidently the doctors had concluded that the socialization of Johnny Boy Ferris required the removal of his teeth. Now the great moon of him breathed, and the wet red membranes glistened from his palpitating gill-like temples as Johnny leered at the world, and bawled, "Ay, ay Spanish Willie, fuck 'em where they breathe, Willie, they don't know whether to shit or go blind."

The shouted profanity had done it, the mammoth orderly, squatting and straining, lifted Ferris up, not as Atlas had supported the world on his shoulders, but in the manner of a workman hauling a keg of beer. The old aunt or mother followed wiping her eyes. The great egg of Johnny traveled steadily on the broad shoulder of the orderly, howling, "Fuck them where they breath Spanish Willie," his yelling diminishing and melding into the general roar as he was carried out. Cousin Elena and Eduardo were dancing. Rosita turned up the volume on the phonograph and clapped her hands in rhythm to the guitars and bongos. Aunt Lydia served cake to the children. On the other side of the room Uncle Toto shouted "Hallelujah!" Angel sat at the head of the table saying what he was instructed to say: "Hello, I'm glad to see you, I'm fine."

Doctor Lawton, impeccable, ageless, and eyeless, for all anyone could tell, from the large dark sunglasses that made his face as neutral and impervious as his voice, had delivered Angel and proffered a polite "hello" to all those gathered around the table. The doctor conferred briefly and inaudibly off to the side with the attorney. Doctor Lawton departed as usual, with a mandarin nod and a smile; and as usual, Laura questioned Rosen about what the doctor had said.

"Nothing new," Rosen whispered. "Be patient, soon, the doctor said, soon," Rosen said, and quickly palmed the envelope of marijuana to Laura clasping her hands reassuringly, and she slipped the envelope into her blouse.

Laura on this occasion did not press Rosen for what "soon" meant. When she had, during the last visit, he had responded with anger that had shocked her, and seemed so disproportionate to the tone and specificity of her question, she had felt bludgeoned by everything that might have ever hurt or injured Rosen. Now she decided to wait for good news, or at least hopeful news. Rosen seemed remorseful, anticipatory, on the verge of saying something he couldn't say, very different from last week's visit when Laura for some reason was especially in need of reassurance, and had asked if this was really the only way, the only strategy. Then Rosen's contorted face turned away, his strangled voice became exacting, ironic. He delivered rhetorical questions, precise body blows, "and what do you suggest as an alternative to a life sentence now that your brother Angel is no longer eternal?" Laura flinched. The shrinks, Rosen had explained, his eyes fixed on the black attaché case resting on his lap, the shrinks were sufficiently taken with their mumbo-jumbo to sometimes declare something akin to a cure and release a patient out into the larger mad world. There was a risk of course, of being committed for a lifetime, but if the patient and patient's family seemed to honor the doctor's therapies, there was chance of release. As a lifer at a maximum security prison, Angel would have no chance at all.

Then as now, Angel sat benignly at the head of the table, his white-gloved hands creatures at rest on the table he vaguely recalled. He sensed that the talk concerned him. Laura stared at the scrolled flesh of Angel's throat, the fire had swirled that flesh like the eddies of an incoming tide. On Titi's lap, the two youngest children, Esperanza and Nilsa, wriggled and ate cake. Nilsa hung head down from Titi's lap, her mouth smeared with white frosting, her tiny fingers exploring the width of Titi's broad knee. Señora Milagros sat at the opposite head of the table staring into Angel's eyes. She reminded Angel that his name was not "Spanish Willie," he was Angel. Angel was agreeable, yes he nodded, yes. Aunt Lydia winced and laughed as the new life in her womb kicked. Rosita changed the record on the phonograph. Eduardo and Elena danced a bolero, humming in one another's ears. Nearby, a patient inmate, a man with the reddest hair in the world, who could have robbed banks with his face, was finger spelling and signing, shaping a desperate declaration in the air as his relatives stayed several arm-lengths beyond his reach, nodding enthusiastically. The man with the terrifying face watched Elena's moving hips, pointed at his mouth and groaned. Elena took in the red-haired man's glance and gesture as she turned in Eduardo's arms, reached to the table, and tossed him a roasted chicken wing. The man chewed the wing, flesh and bone, swallowed it all, the wedge of his Adam's apple riding up and down in his throat, and wiped his mouth with his sleeve. Elena stood still and applauded. Eduardo stroked the ruffles on the front of his shirt and stared defiantly into the eyes of the red-haired man. People applauded. Rosita turned up the volume on the phonograph. Applause boomed on the far side of the cavernous visiting room, rippled and grew thunderous. The red-haired man smiled. His relatives stepped back, giving him more ground, and joined the applause.

Angel clapped his white-gloved hands. He looked, Laura his sister, they had been introduced. "This," Titi had said, "is your sister, Laura Providencia." "Encantado," he said. He remembered her from the last time. The beautiful one. A miracle that she was kind. The table with all the food looked pretty, but he wasn't hungry.

Again they strolled arm and arm alongside the high, olive drab walls that went on and on, past the barred windows, around and around. She told him that in their hometown in Puerto Rico, young couples who were courting strolled like this in the plaza around a fountain. Angel and Laura strolled. She told him the stories of his life. He laughed. They were wonderful stories. He decided he would try to believe her. She described the three-tiered fountain, the splashing water, the tiled pavement, and light tread of the decorous couples walking around and around the fountain. The white-tiled pavement gave back the colored lights of the lanterns, and the moon multiplied into shadows of dozens of little moons jumping underfoot like frogs. There was guitar music of course, she said, and the white cement houses smoking with the last of the day's terrific heat, washing the blue night with a faint sheen of rose, the red-faced moon's reminder of the sun's sovereignty. "What else?" he asked, "What else?" They strolled. He remembered mud. She said when they were very little they followed after the parade of lovers mocking them, mimicking the way the couples gazed into one another's eyes, murmuring with serious intention, "Corazón, mi vida." "Truly?" he asked." "Yes," she said, "without a doubt." Someone screamed. From the north corner of the room there was weeping, a kind of gulping sound, someone drowning. Somebody called, "Spanish Willie." He said he didn't know why or how he had been named Spanish Willie in this place. She said he didn't have to apologize. They strolled. She held his arm. He thought he remembered part of last Sunday, pieces of previous days. On one of the Sundays she had told him that he was a fancier of coconut. "Truly?" he asked. "Oh yes," she had said, and the next time she brought him a coconut. It was true, the taste of it was a great pleasure. He never forgot her entirely. From week to week they were introduced. She was always there, and always beyond memory, and in spite of what he did or didn't retain of her recitations of what she said was his life. He begged her for the reefer until she said, stop please stop, telling him he didn't have to beg; and then she was weeping, the force of it yanking her upper body back and forth, she willed control of her legs. They promenaded, her racked upper body bending toward him; from a distance she might have appeared to be laughing, and she slipped the envelope of reefer into his shirt. "Mujer!" he pleaded, commanded. She stifled her crying, swallowed. Only Rosen the lawyer, watching, knew. He was thrilled with knowing. He was sharing an unlawful act with her. He brought the reefer into the facility in his attaché case, he was holding it at his side as he consulted with the doctors, and Rosen knew from studying juries and judges, the doctors were affronted by Angel's ingenuous eyes. Angel managed; sometimes he smoked it, sometimes he ate it, but always he was stoned on his way to the electric shock therapy. The doctors were not certain how much therapy was needed, but they were confident they could get at the criminal tendency, blasting and scorching those hemispheres of mind where it lived.

On the promenades during the first month of Sundays, Angel tried to explain to Laura why he needed the marijuana. Finally she thought she understood, although often he lost the intention of a sentence he had begun, retrieved words in Spanish and English to other conversations with himself, others, forgot her, and found this beautiful young woman on his arm, speaking.

She spoke, she presented him with his life, and it was vivid, glorious. He smiled. She faltered. She wondered, did he know somehow what she had left out, and how what she had left out frightened her?

At last she explained what she thought he had been trying to say about why he needed the reefer. "Si, exactamente," that was it, he concurred, the marijuana made him hungry everywhere at once, even on the way to the next electric shock treatment his hungers still existed, he desired. Even up to the moment when they strapped him down, put the rubber bit in his mouth, and told him to clamp down on it — it was reminiscent, bite down, salve on his temples. The next day, days after, he ached everywhere, inside and out, he didn't want to blow his nose, it might cause his eyes to swell shut. He would reach behind to wipe himself, slowly, slowly. She told him he fought one draw, he had never lost. He said he remembered some of that, and suddenly he remembered too, getting something out of books, but he couldn't remember what.

The gong went off. Every human sound that preceded the invention of speech hummed in the air. Laura reminded Angel that visiting day would end in fifteen minutes. Angel began to pat at the midriff of his shirt. "It is there, there," Laura reassured him, jabbing more roughly than she had intended at his stomach. She felt a little sick. Closing her eyes she saw her mother wave, to come, the movement of her arm strenuous, trying to sift silence into the drone of barking, yowling, laughing, and weeping; with her eyes nearly shut Laura saw Titi step into a column of light, her arms raised, tilted little Esperanza sitting on top of her head. A nurse in a white smock passed through Laura's vision, obscuring Titi. Laura heard Uncle Toto shout, "Hallelujah!" She opened her eyes. Esperanza was perched on Titi's head; Titi clutched one dimpled thigh, Esperanza wriggled out of her diaper. Angel said, "Amiga, mujer, hermana," and finding her name, "Laura Providencia, cojelo suave, be cool sister, por favor." She reassured him she would return the following Sunday, and the following Sunday too would happen.

THE TRIP

The college set in the Garden of Eden. The nude volleyball players drenched in twilight. Adam and Eve buoyant in the amber air float among the butterflies and the
sublime bodies. The radiant pubic hair, heliotropic bouquets,
tug them aloft, where the young men and women drift near the
green net, their supple bodies shaped like the clef notes of music only they can hear.

How did I get here? I was inspired. I was talking. They gave
me drink as long as I kept talking. I talked about books I loved.
One young man leaned over the bar and wrote down the things
I was saying. A young woman next to him laughed and applauded. She hugged me. I forgot what I was going to say next.

Another bought me a drink. I gulped it down and asked for a chaser. They didn't seem to mind. One of the young men shouted to the bartender, "Another beer please." I couldn't find the thread of what I'd been saying. The young man who had called for the bartender handed me the beer and said, "Lawrence and Dostoyevsky," I took a swallow of beer and continued to speak. That was in the city, four, no five years ago; my daughter Maria was not yet born.

Now they pay me for it. Talking about books. Fantastic employment.

Exaltation rests. I wonder: are the students infatuated by my words, or infatuated by the spectacle of my infatuation? A pied piper susceptible as the children in his wake. They surround me. Demand the secrets of my heart laid bare. I remember when my wife Laura suggested that I get the necessary credentials that would allow an institution of higher learning to recompense me with a salary. I recall the day we talked about it, in the city. The newspapers, the television, and the radio were full of the news of the day. Dozens of young people had gone to the floor of the stock exchange and set money on fire. They touched burning matches to currency, danced and exhorted the herd of stunned traders to join them in the dancing and torching of money.

Now the young people I speak to have become sweetly adamant. When I first arrived from the city, lugging my suitcase across the meadow, and stumbled onto the nude volleyball game, I momentarily had a vision out of H.G. Wells' *Time Machine*. The nude college students floating in the paradisal dusk were the lovely and hapless Eloi, and at any moment, the Morlocks, the devolved industrial masses, some of the kin I fled, would emerge out of a smoking trench and carry off the beautiful people and make a meal of them. But it's not like that at all. I, who first presented subjects to them, have become the subject. It is possible, they insist, to bring about a world ruled by love rather than money, and my participation requires a confession.

They believe in spontaneity. I don't remember everything. They visit our home at odd hours, as they are moved, still interested in my talk. The various accounts of what they say I did conform to the parts I can remember and the evidence on my body. Rainbow Schwartz, the one who looks like a goofy John the Baptist in his loin cloth with bare reptilian feet, offers an exhausted smile; he's barely survived the ravages of his laughter. Laura, my beautiful wife, whose face also precipitates intoxication from which I continue to recover, smiles. She is generous. Her capacity for happiness is a mystery she doesn't attend to in any special way I can see. She can paint or not paint, make pots or not make pots. She whispers in my ear, still smiling, "I can't go on living like this, and where were you? You've been gone three days, all weekend." She turns to the rotund, evangelical, bald Bible salesman who, in his green suit, white shirt, and red bow tie looks like a defrocked and shorn Santa Claus. Laura points to the front door and says, "Go. Now!" Santa, rosy and beside himself with joy, had been recounting how the "Israelites smote the Arabs in the Six Day War," which meant, he said, "soon the graves will give up their dead, the sky rain blood, and Jesus will come on a cloud." Maria, my five-year-old daughter, who had opened the door for beaming Santa bearing lollipops and a suit case of black Bibles, is sitting on the floor building a large vessel out of blocks. "Noah's Ark?" Santa asked. "A spaceship," said Maria, "so the extraterrestrials and my other cousins can go someplace nice." Laura says to Santa,

"Walk, the door is that way," and Santa waddles, the momentum of the swollen suitcase of Bibles propelling him to the door.

I want to tell Laura that I agree, we should move out of the village, find a place we can rent if need be, a house not so close to campus, a home that cannot be confused as part of the college. She has been more than hospitable to all the gifted and variously troubled students who have found their way to our door at all hours. Although it all began as something festive, a celebration of some auspicious inaugural we will understand some day, or so the students have intimated. Bernard Tummelman, the brilliant English major and former piano and mathematics prodigy, cannot abide Rainbow Schwartz. Tummelman — tall, pale, and tubercular looking — is costumed in a white shirt, blue wool moth-eaten tie, and a tweed jacket. He regards Rainbow in his loincloth with contempt. Bernard, on the first day of the semester, during the first minute of the first hour, dismissed Rainbow as a mere life stylist, and he considers the attention I give Rainbow evidence of a serious weakness of my character, the requirements of my vocation notwithstanding; moreover, Rainbow Schwartz is taking up Bernard's valuable time. Bernard takes Rainbow in obliquely and keeps at least three yards distant; were he any closer, Bernard would be in danger of contagion from whatever orthodoxy animates Rainbow's life. Bernard has come to discuss the one-act play he has written in verse. Just before Laura banished Santa Claus, (Bernard a compulsive explainer who must be weaned from the endless explanations that encumber his work) had begun to explain his play. Two commercial travelers, Kafka's Gregor Samsa, a dung beetle who has finally given up trying to get a conventional two-legged pair of trousers onto his many wriggling legs, has learned how to whistle a blues riff, and Arthur

Miller's Willie Loman, who sustains a coherent lament through convulsive sighs, commiserate with one another in some tolerable suburb of Hell.

Ms. Kim, as she prefers to be addressed, is also waiting. It seems that our class discussion of Tolstoy's *Death of Ivan Ilych* has precipitated a family crisis. She had begun her undergraduate career as an engineering major. The literature course she happened to take with me became the great illicit thing in her life. Enormously gifted, Ms. Kim's success as an engineer was meant to liberate her mother, father, and two sisters from servitude in the family grocery store in Bed-Sty Brooklyn. Even before the family's flight from Korea, Ms. Kim's father had dreamed of the glory and wealth this eloquent child, a wizard with sums, would bring to the family. Now her father promised to die of heartbreak. But it was Ms. Kim's contemplation of Ivan Ilych's long death as the single richest and most urgent opportunity for true thought that led Ms. Kim to the damning judgment of her father's life of obedience and drudgery and ordained her escape — and that escape entailed changing her major to Comparative Literature and the study of the Russian language, so that someday she might render Tolstoy and Dostoyevsky into English prose truer to the originals than the nineteenth-century euphemisms or anglophile absurdities that characterize the translations now available.

What Ms. Kim wants from me, she explained to Laura before I arrived and has now repeated, is that I telephone or write to her father and try to dissuade him from coming to the college where he hopes to entreat the president to revoke his daughter's scholarship if she persists in abandoning her responsibility to the family. Ms. Kim repeats, and I don't doubt her, that she wants to devote her life to writing. I'm tempted to say to her, as I would to her father, trying to exonerate myself, that I don't recruit for the ranks of the damned. But she is tearful, close to begging, and I say, "Yes, of course, I'll do what I can, I'll write, telephone if I must."

Meanwhile, Rainbow Schwartz has attempted to return the conversation back to Dostoyevsky, but his curiosity is loaded with messianic concern, which drives Bernard Tummelman over the edge. And, as happens frequently when Bernard is out of patience, he throws a tantrum, gushing passages from Lewis Carroll's *Alice's Adventures in Wonderland and Through The Looking Glass*. Effortlessly he memorized all this, and what he has memorized has taken dominion over some portion of his mind, and as Rainbow says "So Prince Myshkin ..." Bernard lapses into a seizure, shakes and fumes:

> *Twas brillig, and the slithy toves*
> *Did gyre and gimble in the wabe;*
> *All mimsy were the borogoves,*
> *And the mome raths outgrabe.*
> *Beware the Jabberwock, my son!*
> *The jaws that bite, the claws that catch!*

Rainbow raises his voice to speak above Bernard's recitation. He says we had been speaking of Prince Myshkin. Rainbow tries to persuade me that I might be that kind of idiot, and reminds me that I'd noted how, in the clumsy presence of Dostoyevsky's prince, everyone, all of Russia, is stripped to some nub of conscience. Laura's glance makes Rainbow's voice quaver, but he is tenacious in his own way. He is insistent and wants me to describe again how in *The Idiot*, Prince Myshkin's truth-telling wrecks the known world. This is a paradigm of a necessary destruction that Rainbow Schwartz believes must come before the new world can be created.

Laura says, "Wait, what I want to know is how he got this," and she pulls the sweatshirt up from my waist and leaves it gathered around my head. A cool breeze feathers the hair on my stomach. I'm draped in darkness. Her fingertips tickle as they run over the scabs outlining the palm tree on my chest, her name, palimpsest among the gnarled roots around my left nipple in the vicinity of my heart. It is quiet for a moment. I feel them studying me. I'm the evidence of something. I remember myself as the man who wanted to say yes. "Well?" Laura insists. Rainbow says, "He's a trip." Bernard says, "*Why, if a fish came to me, and told me he was going on a journey, I should say with what porpoise?*" My daughter Maria looks at Bernard and places her forefinger across her lips. Bernard makes a show of his momentary silence by an exaggerated pursing of his lips. "This," Laura says, jabbing her finger under my heart, "who did this?" Bernard blurts, "*You might just as well say that I breathe when I sleep is the same thing as I sleep when I breathe!*" Laura quiets Bernard by looking at him, and asks again, "Where did he get the tattoo?"

I remember that Chancy Lonegan, Rainbow's pal and fellow apostle, Chancy who rarely said more than "Wow," except for fortnightly torrential mutterings during which he speculated, trying to find, he said, his true self, drove the VW bus. He had, a week before, dropped out of my course on the American short story after I'd explained, during our conference, that I didn't know how to evaluate invisible work. I didn't challenge his claim of greater self-knowledge, nor that he'd reconciled the different warring beliefs within himself. And although I tried, I couldn't understand what those beliefs were, his "Wow" proliferating into an avalanche of superlatives, a coda of rhapsodic thanks, for what, I wasn't sure, but he was radiant with the peace that passeth understanding.

Peter Julius, the Botany instructor and Lonegan's academic advisor, had told me that Chancy, who was on academic probation, was flunking all of his courses and was likely to be suspended from the college. The moon drooled purple over the office window. I reminded Chancy that he would lose his student deferment and very quickly become subject to the draft. He said something that I took to be an offer of forgiveness — to me, his instructors, the dean, the college, and the world at large. His face was swamped with such tolerance and love he could say nothing more to make his message plainer to those not yet capable of understanding. It had been a long day. It was getting dark, usually at that hour I was home. Chancy looked at me as Jesus must have looked at Pontius Pilate; he was ready to die for my sins. I asked him if he wanted to wind up in Vietnam and get his ass shot off. He shrugged and showed me the palms of his hands. I resisted the impulse to punch the light out of his martyred eyes and reached for the bottle in the bottom drawer of my desk.

I must have said something justifying my right to a drink at the close of day, something I'd earned if anything can be earned, and I thought I heard Chancy mumble. "Do your own thing." He looked sadder, even if the general largess of his gaze didn't falter. When he reached into the burlap sack at his feet to offer me the wizened mushroom as an alternative to the bourbon I was partial to, offering it as a sacrament, nearly frowning at the bottle in my hand, almost disapproving — if he could disapprove of anything — I'd already begun to tell him the story of *The Procurator of Judea*. After several sweet sips, a warmth that started in my chest eddied out, and I had my own largess to offer; the desire to grab Chancy and shake him passed. I told him the story. I told him why I was telling him the story. I sipped the bourbon and argued against martyrdom. It was (I said) unnecessary, a form of violence. Consider, Chancy, how humanity is enchanted by the varieties of sanctimonious slaughter. Anatole France's story of Pontius Pilate offers a cynical perspective, built on a piddling irony, of course, but...

Chancy interrupted, silently offering the mushroom, wearily insistent as a mother spoon-feeding a child who refuses to eat. I washed it down with the bourbon.

Consider this Chancy: here is Pontius Pilate, back in Italy, returned from his administrative duties in Judea. Pilate is being borne by litter bearers in a coach-like contrivance. He is on his way to a spa where he hopes the healing mineral waters will alleviate his gout, fatigue, and ennui. At a juncture on the road where there is a tavern, he gives the order to his slaves to stop. He will dine and rest at the tavern. There he recognizes an old friend, a comrade and soldier who did service for the empire in Judea. Pilate is overjoyed to see his old friend.

They talk, drink wine, and reminisce; comrades and patriots who endured a pestilential place for the good of their country. They're veterans who share special knowledge that cannot really be communicated to those who haven't been there. They reiterate, remembering, amazed once more by the backwardness of the place, the stubborn, fanatical people, resistant to any rational improvement. Pilate recalls how his plan to install a hygienic plumbing system, a far-reaching construction of aqueducts that would have done much for the health and civic life of the inhabitants, was resisted by the suspicious natives.

And Pilate, as in the days when they were both young men, begins to chide his friend and former comrade for his impulsiveness. He reminds the old soldier that he could have gone far but for his recklessness, his abandonment of duty to pursue romantic adventures. The old soldier agrees, without rancor, and concedes that he did, by his own action, undermine a promising career. Pilate counters by saying, "What might have been a brilliant career." Pilate's tone is contrite, as though he were seeking pardon from his old comrade, "But that last episode," Pilate says, "that dereliction of duty," when his friend had disappeared to chase after the Jewess, who was after all little more than a prostitute, that last incident was looked upon at the highest echelon as too grievous to be mitigated by anything he (Pilate) could say in favor of his friend.

The old soldier's monumental head looks like something already memorialized in stone, his face and the prominent nose cast beyond stoicism, a primary virtue, merely noted, there is about the old soldier a resignation that is not defeat. He shifts his weight at the table like an elephant grazing. His hand holding the goblet of wine slowly makes a salutary gesture, much to Pilate's relief. Pilate no longer feels the need to elaborate on the futility of coming to his friend's aid to rescue a career that could not be rescued. He thinks he can read the ruminating thought laboriously working its way to the soldier's tongue, and Pilate agrees, the soldier's delinquent adventures were no more foolish than his own attempts to govern anarchy. Slowly, words come to the soldier's mouth. He does not object to anything Pilate is saying; anything either of them says has no more significance than the wind; nevertheless he would like to clarify his own specific history. Mary Magdalene, the Jewess. It could be said that she was a woman of easy virtue. He had heard from comrades whose word he would not dispute that she had sold her favors; but when he knew her she was dancing in the taverns. It was also true, the old soldier says, that he was mad for the woman; never before, or since, has he been so obsessed. For a short time she favored him, and then lost interest. He followed her from tavern to tavern, place to place. His career, his dignity, his very self seemed superfluous, and it was when he had finally reached this state that she once more seemed to care for him, for a time, as if at last he'd shed the accouterments of the world, and could aspire to enter into an equality with her — it was then she disappeared.

The old soldier says that he lost his mind entirely, he was capable of only one thought, finding her again. Even now, he says, after the passing of years, for which he is grateful, and the infirmities of age, all of this, he fears, insufficient protection from the desire to see her again, if only once; but she'd vanished, and he had followed the rumors. It seems she became a follower of a preacher from Nazareth, followed him and his ragged band of peasant believers wherever they went. "For a while it seemed I always arrived just a little too late to some remote hamlet or strangely hushed bazaar or tavern, a pathetic oasis barely worthy of the name, soon to succumb to the encroaching desert, where always the mordant Jewish peasant lingered, barely able to hide his contempt, ready to tell me, yes tribune, they left a little while ago, to the north, south, east or west. I followed her. She followed this Jesus. Pilate, do you remember him?"

And Pontius Pilate, who wants to empathize with his old comrade, can, in an intellectual sense, understand the old soldier's obsession. He tries to remember, as if the recollection of this detail could assuage his friend's pain. "Jesus," Pilate says, but he can't recall, and although he doesn't want his friend to think him indifferent, he cannot muster the energy to lie. "Jesus,"

Pilate says again, pausing, searching his memory, "no, really, I don't remember him."

Chancy said "Wow" and asked for another story. I might have been Aesop, only in the telling I'd lost sight of the lesson the story was supposed to tell — something to do with keeping this boy out of Vietnam and getting him to write a term paper. We were out of doors by then, standing in front of Stokes Dormitory, where my office was located, the dormitory named for the benefactor who had contributed considerable sums of money to the college. The grass covering the tantalizing swell of hill on which I stood was an impossible blue. The sky veiling God's face, lavender, speckled with stars, in one instant winking and blinking invitingly, and in the next cold, brilliant, and remote. Rainbow Schwartz appeared in his loincloth, his tentacle feet gripping the earth, impervious to frostbite, shivering like a tuning fork, he came closer, smiling. From the corrugated strip of his belly the wiry thatch of antenna-hair sprung upright. I thought I heard him burp, a sound like a frog singing, but it was not the season of frogs. I imagined him dining on locusts and honey.

I blinked my eyes and Chancy was standing on Rainbow's shoulders, the two stood like circus acrobats. Rainbow, all hair and sinew in his dingy diaper, hands on his hips, the shadow on the ground between his wide-spread legs as tremulous as a large reptile egg about to burst with wriggling life. Chancy stood knees bent, balancing himself on Rainbow, his bare feet treading gently, nimble and steady as though he were crushing grapes on Rainbow's shoulders. Chancy, reaching up, was wearing a loose fitting tunic and balloon trousers, some sort of boudoir pajamas. I looked up above them and saw the turbulent, tumbling clouds and sensed the invisible sky God emptying the entrails of fate in a motion like my mother flapping a bed sheet, hurly-burly falling down, some last binge before the end of days, love and every kind of folly in contention, the promised land every-where just beyond sight, and I saw Chancy spired up on Rain-bow, his outstretched hand choking a serpent. The laughter and cheers of young women from the surrounding dormitories rang in a dark as bright as day. The Volkswagen bus the color of an orange lollipop lay on the horizon, the sun that wouldn't go down. I thought then that I might tell Chancy and Rainbow the story of the serpent winding its body around Buddha seven times, and unable to crush him, turning into a youth, bowing before Gautama. Glimpsing Chancy's strenuous effort on Rainbow's shoulders, his swaying back and forth, maybe the story of baby Hercules strangling in his cradle the two serpents sent by Hera to destroy him would be more helpful. What was their effort all about? I wanted to ask Chancy and Rainbow again, maybe if I listened more closely I'd understand. The two piled one upon another, were they attempting to reach up and touch the divine so that at last they might become truly human? I wasn't sure whether I'd just thought the story of Buddha and the serpent or told it, opened my lips to ask and swallowed a mouthful of night. Like a kid at the water fountain, water up my nose, in my throat, choking and laughing, there was laugh-ter all around me. Chancy, swaying on Rainbow's shoulders, was laughing, in his hand the serpent had turned into the letter S, which he'd removed from the lintel above the door. The dor-mitory formally known as "Stokes" was now named "Tokes." The night was filled with applause.

Laura put Maria to bed. She still wanted to know what had happened. I said I wasn't keeping secrets and that was the truth. Ms. Kim said that this was a good time for me to telephone her father. Laura said, "Wait," pointed to my chest, and asked Rainbow, "were you there when he got this?"

What I remember: I don't remember getting into the bus. The person who handed back my half-finished fifth of bourbon was introduced to me as "Dude." He appeared to be a frontiersman, cowboy, or brigand. He wore a jacket the color of an aged bison hide, with leather fringes hanging from the shoulders and sleeves, tight blue denim trousers, a large brass belt buckle with an eye of God etched on it shone from his lean middle, and he stood in knee-length tan cowboy boots, intricate vines, cactus, and prairie flowers carved in the leather. On his head a nobly battered ten-gallon hat, one pearl earring dangled from a pink fleshy lobe, and a thick braid of gold around his neck, from which hung the sun, planets and stars of our solar system. When he moved bells tinkled. I didn't recognize Dude as a student enrolled or hanging out at the college; he appeared older than Rainbow and Chancy, although he might have been their contemporary. His face — gap-toothed when he smiled, blonde, blue-eyed — might have once been perfect for a Hollywood casting of the sweetest and most sentimental Huck Finn; now like Huck too long on the river, his face was neutral, his skin tougher than the cracked leather of his boots, weathered by the desolate and punishing climates of the wild west, or somewhere, an American orphan; and his costume was what he offered in lieu of conversation; he no longer required or offered an explanation for anything.

I studied Dude's face, his eyes in shadow under the brim of his ten-gallon hat. In spite of my first vision, which I couldn't repudiate entirely, I was rattled by the sudden resemblance to my brother — the laconic version of my brother's face, Jacob as a cowboy. That too. Why not? Lord knows Jacob had wandered the most unfathomable wide-open spaces. Was Dude my brother? My brother may have well been Dude, as well as everyone else he had been and would be. Jacob, now living in the supervised group home, can't keep track of his stories, and so he is sometimes furtive and mysterious; assuming an identity that subsumes all the previous ones, he finds himself incredulous at the person he once might have been, as best as he can remember. But at least he's no longer out on the street selling his blood for cigarettes and other necessities.

The bus rolled, the inside as commodious as a Bedouin prince's tent, hanging madras sheets a softly breathing enclosure, under me a mattress and cushions. I could see through the draped labial folds part of the back of Chancy's head; he was driving, and next to him Rainbow's shoulder-length hair, full of twigs and bits of dried leaves. A soup of night and stars splashed though the vapor on the oblong of windshield in front of them.

Rainbow's oracular voice was soft over the humming of the tires. He said, quoting Bambino, the eleven-year-old Perfect Master and Bodhisattva, that the higher power gave humanity the unperfected world so that we would all have meaningful work. Chancy drove confidently and at great speed through the thick mist rising up over the unseen country road and said "Wow!" I couldn't hear clearly the next thing Rainbow said because he was laughing, but I thought he was saying something about the large, olive drab duffle bag serving as Dude's pillow; inside was the stuff that when disseminated would reveal everyone's hidden desires and secret practices, so that nothing ever again need be hidden or secret.

Dude stretched out, rested his head on the duffle bag. He smiled, yawned and looked me over. I was a mild curiosity. We passed the bottle back and forth. Chancy's "Wow" took up residence in my head and secreted the fuming odor of reefer, my head a censer filled the air with smoke. It occurred to me that the mushroom I ate had not only turned the dark into neon, which I experienced as some sort of confirmation of democracy, but a surfeit of conviction, what I thought and saw, unhobbled by doubt, left me as humble and excited as a virgin groom on his wedding night. But then, why was I crying? Dude handed me a can of beer and a joint. I sipped the beer and took long tokes on the joint. I'd learned that marijuana would allow me to drink a long time without getting sick. Dude was stretched out like a cowboy on the prairie. Beyond his regalia he gave off an air of adventure that was not an affectation, a sense of adventure that originated in being abandoned, as only the truest adventures must begin. I thought of Moses, Hansel and Gretel, and my brother Jacob. I could not ask Dude to tell me his story. The celestial blue of his eyes stared through me and miles beyond. He was distinctly Dude and not Jacob in that moment; to ask for his story would be a violation of the code of the West. As long as I didn't ask we could share an eloquent and necessary silence, a camaraderie that might serve the idea of brotherhood so long as no one uttered the word.

Suddenly I felt the need to apologize to Rainbow and Chancy for having condescended to them. My heart whispered "brothers." The prophetic dark was waiting on us, but the journey had neither a song nor a story to accompany it. Dude was snoring. His body crunched into a ball, his knees pulled up to his chest, the bracelet bells on his wrists tinkled, I thought I heard him moan "Fuckin' Nam." His eyes flickered open, and closed again. The tongue that lives in my head began to babble and I thought even if I'm talking to myself, anything thought

will eventually be heard in the world. The road whooshed beneath us. The shadow of my brother leaked from the vapors
streaming from the dimly lit censer of my head.

Like Cain I'm the first-born. Like Abel I'm the favored son.
And I, like Abel who maimed Cain's life because he couldn't
resist finding favor in his father's eyes, needing, and wallowing
in being father's favorite, betrayed his brother, did not love him
enough. Cain cast out, reputed to be the founder of cities, wan-
ders as I wander trying to find the human sympathetic intelligence with which I will converse (and charm), so that I can
secure the judgment of my innocence; and getting it, never able
to believe it, because it is what I contrived to get.

Dude's face, eyes closed, asleep, becomes one of my brother's
faces, the dreaming cowboy. In a burst of candor I tell Jacob
that among my students' favorite authors is a British psychiatrist who characterizes schizophrenia as a smorgasbord of spiri-
tual possibility. I say to Jacob, "I hate that book," and offer this
hatred as a token of my good faith. Dude's face succumbing to
the ideogram that is my brother's face tells me not to worry, all
he requires of me (he tells me once more) is that I believe him;
this, he says, is the basic requirement of his presence, or else he
will disappear again, and I can wonder and worry where he is.
I've struggled many years to achieve this faith. But for now I
only want to take my brother in my arms and hug him, ask him
how he is, what's new. And as Jacob begins to tell me, in a world-
weary voice that sounds like Humphrey Bogart in *Casablanca*,
he confides that recently, when he was rescuing a beautiful young
woman from Mafia thugs who were about to sell the woman, a
girl really, he says, into a life of white slavery, it occurred to him
that also he should cut down on his drinking. As he tells the
story of the rescue, the girl he describes bears an uncanny re-

semblance to my wife, Laura. Once again, I anticipate hearing some aspect of my life come back to me as something fantastical. I'm used to this or should be, have come to expect Jacob's appropriation of those parts of my life that he may need. He also appropriates the adventures of various movie heroes and portions of the biographies of the people who attend his group-therapy meetings, and books; the actual events of his life intricately braided and lost as they become the always urgent tale he is making, which is his life forever being born.

Jacob's diary, a library of tremendous weight, is an oral narrative which he recites while engaged in his various odysseys; the enormous epic he is authoring is essentially a primer, cohering into one question — how can he be worthy of existing in God's fabulous world?

I'm left to wonder whose predilection for fiction is the madder, my own mechanisms for coping in the world just a little more adept than my brother's. The year before Laura, I, and Maria, who was just a baby, moved from New York to Vermont, the psychiatric social worker assigned to my brother's case telephoned to let me know that she had found my brother. He'd disappeared for a little over a month, and I had no idea where he was, whether he was dead or alive.

My brother had been living in a subsidized hotel apartment owned by Catholic Charities, his SSI check, along with what I and my mother sent on a monthly basis, should have been sufficient. But when my mother came to visit him with her plan to apprentice Jacob to a distant cousin who would make Jacob a diamond cutter, thus insuring Jacob's material future, and a photograph of Henrietta, a "girl" at least a decade Jacob's senior, who "schlepped a leg a little" Momma said, but owned a co-op apartment in Queens, a Laundromat, and was a self-employed accountant, Jacob disappeared, taking refuge beneath a subway station to live with a colony of street drunks in an abandoned excavation. Once he was settled again in his apartment after a hospital stay, he'd been pissing blood and had had a concussion, we talked. At first I didn't get the reprise of the James Bond story of his rescue of the girl about to be sold into a life of prostitution, told in his Bogart voice. I got another story. A tale that holds me hostage still. I'd been advised by various shrinks not to challenge my brother's stories, but to inquire surreptitiously and with great tact, and then I might garner some useful clues that could shed light on what might serve Jacob's real needs. If I betrayed a trace of skepticism, he'd tell me nothing and prepare his next getaway, first raving and denouncing God for his sloppy work.

On that occasion, Jacob, aware of my drinking problem and my initial dalliance with the AA program, "shared" with me how he had reached bottom and finally given up drinking. I had mentioned to him that I thought I might need help with my booze problem and that under the influence I sometimes found myself in places I didn't want to be. As I spoke I saw my brother's eyes grow wide, a zany avidity set the whole face in motion, eyes and mouth agape. I cautioned myself. Be careful what romances you may allow to take root in Jacob's head. He'd taken a fearsome beating. I could only conjecture about what might have happened to him. Jacob and I embraced and cast one shadow. We were overtaken by the laughter that began its rampage when we were children; it shook us, inside out, the horrific particulars of the world incomprehensible and hilarious. The gut-aching laughter worked us over until our faces were hammered dumb as Adam, wondering in his most simple heart why he should be deprived of Eden, because, since eating the apple he knew no more than he did before the first bite. "So what happened?" I asked when I was able to speak again. He said that he had been walking a dog, a poodle, for a rich lady who lived on West End Avenue. Every time he walked the dog she threw him a ten or twenty, whatever came to her hand first. One day she gave him a c-note and invited him to a party. At the party, said Jacob, he had too much to drink. He woke up hung over and seasick in a gurgling waterbed somewhere around Central Park West. What he found in bed next to him caused him to give up drink. He had, he said, hit bottom. "What?" I said, "who?" "Zsa Zsa Gabor," he said, "no shit, and she is older than anybody imagined." He went on to describe a crone aging by the second, a creature resembling H. Rider Haggard's "She" dissolving in flames, her teeth in a water glass on a nightstand beside the undulating waterbed where her blonde wig thrashed like a drowning cat. I was allowed to laugh since Jacob appreciated how humor can allow access to what might otherwise be unspeakable, but my laughter could not suggest the slightest hint of anything that might subvert the veracity of what he related. "Jesus," I said. "Yeah," he said and shrugged, heavy with terrible knowledge, Odysseus finally come to terms with the fate of his faithful and drowned shipmates — not quite so fit as he to wrestle with and survive defying the gods.

He escaped into the subway. Riding the trains for the better part of the night, he considered the dangers of drunkenness, the risks of ecstasy. He explained that this was a little while before he took up residence beneath the Canal Street subway stop, and he wanted me to grasp his special, if eccentric, robust fitness, an earned pedigree that made him always welcome in the infernal regions. All this a prelude to his rescue of the virgin immigrant girl who would have become a sex slave to monsters.

I thought I recognized elements of a story my mother had told. In the immigrant ghetto where she was a girl, it was not unheard of for girls and young women to have disappeared, chloroformed and kidnapped (in one notorious case a girl was abducted from a movie theatre while the audience roared at Charlie Chaplin in *The Gold Rush*, famished, eating a shoe). There were sufficient instances of real disappearances (while the police turned a blind eye) for my grandmother to make a cautionary tale, so that my mother and her five sisters never strayed far from home.

I wondered what arrangements, if any, had been made for a follow-up medical check for Jacob. Whatever had actually happened, which I might glean over the years, he had also lost some teeth, but he was no longer complaining of headaches and it had been two days since he last pissed blood. I wanted to discuss this with Jacob and accompany him to the doctor. He was regaling me with his dark night, what happened after he climbed out of the subway into a dangerous neighborhood in his flight from the crone, Zsa Zsa Gabor.

Jacob claimed to have learned something, the yield of weariness, a revelation he would share with me. As he told the story, I recognized — knew what my brother would say next. I'd hear the state of my mind, when, during one of my seasonal leaps of faith, and knowing that I must bring more to my brother than money and groceries, I confided in him, believing it is imperative to believe, that I must, without restraint or equivocation, tell him of the meaningful happenings in my life, and this act of trust, among others, could allow Jacob to imagine his own life, always nearly within reach — help him gain access to the actual occurrences, or at the very least enable him to trust me in his times of crisis. Jacob may not have been able to distinguish between what was true and what he wanted to be true, but he had a connoisseur's ear for what was real in the experiences of others, whatever he would make of it later.

I'd told him how, during the time Laura was pregnant with Maria, things were tough financially. We'd found an inexpensive apartment in the South Bronx and I'd taken on a second job. The eighty-hour workweek was to provide, beyond household and medical expenses for the baby that was coming, money to be put aside so that we could move to a more desirable neighborhood. One night, sometime after two in the morning, I staggered out of the subway, my pay in my pocket, the checks from each job converted to cash. All transactions in the neighborhood required cash or postal money orders, and I walked aching and red-eyed through the dead streets toward home. I walked the same streets that remained strange every night, desolation keeping everything new. That moon-bright night I heard the shadows arguing behind me. The tone as soft as prayer, a liturgical sigh polished the sound of the words, meaning sulking several reluctant heartbeats behind articulation, all utterance an excruciating effort they could barely abide. "You diddy bop jive ass mother fucker, you the one supposed to cop." "Uh oh, uh oh, I gotta lissen to this shit, they's a drout, you know? Hard times? I the one tryin' to cope, alls you do is piss and moan."

The two junkies, their eyes needle-points, bundled in topcoats despite the balmy night, robbed me at knife-point, looking as though they might collapse under the weight of the moonlight. But they were armed and I was not. Swaying, they were focused, one blade trembling under my eye, the other at my back.

I was never robbed again. Deep in the night-long year of little sleep, gritty eyed, numb, I acclimated to the exhaustion that found me, sometimes in a spasm of thin sleep, standing up, clenching the pole in the subway car. The booming scream and shudder of the wheels on the tracks blasted up through the shivering floor, my legs and spine trembled. I rode the convulsions, eyes opened or closed, an accomplished dreamer of infallible balance. Awake or asleep, the other hand not grasping the pole, anchored deep in my pocket where the money was, fingers alert, holding the pushbutton switchblade.

The one that tried me the next time must have been watching from the street looking though the window of the bodega as I got my change from the grocer. He wore a New York Yankees baseball cap, warm-up jacket, sweatpants and sneakers. His smile was pleasant and business-like. His movement agile, confident, he appeared quite fit except for the deeply jaundiced yellow of his face, glistening with sweat.

The Bronx Third Avenue El roared above us. On the street it was impossible to speak and be heard. The man who wanted to rob me, and I, communicated through miming. It was all clear enough. He had his blade out. He pointed at my pocket. People on the street walked by, giving us room, no one stopped or stared, after one discreet glance everyone hurried on about their business. I took a couple of quick steps back, carefully placing the grocery bag with the container of milk, box of rice, and can of coffee on the pavement. I circled to gain a precious few seconds, he followed after me and looked grave, as though I'd committed a breach of faith that now required that he end my life. But I had my knife out, extended in my right hand like a southpaw, set to jab, comfortable at that angle, despite being a novice with the blade, my unfettered willingness to kill this man present in my face, body, beyond doubt or an act of will was clear to both of us. He shrugged and walked away.

And what I felt then but was only able to explain to my brother a couple of years later, was that neither machismo nor courage had anything to do with my sudden readiness to kill. It was weariness, profound fatigue, an inability to bear, cope with one more thing. I'm tired, don't fuck with me, watch out.

In my brother's version he cut the would-be mugger who ran off clutching his gut. Jacob was left to wonder if he had inflicted a mortal wound, taken a life, was now a killer. His upper lip did the Bogart twitch. He spoke. His voice remote, disembodied, a voice-over replicating the most haunting echo of film noir; the voice narrated, and he contemplated the meaning of an experience, the truth of which only tough-guy stoicism could keep from the corrupting influences of hypocrisy and illusion. All I could do was listen. He wiped his lips with the back of his hand; his eyes fixed on me in a challenging stare (could I possibly understand, appreciate,) since it was so difficult for him to keep the integrity of what he related. But I was an audience, the world, he might as well talk to me. His tone, the shrug of his shoulders, suggested his awareness of something noble, if futile, in his effort.

He wanted me to understand that he made no claim of courage. It was only that he was weary, profoundly tired. The barbarity of the world wearied him.

I looked at his battered face, felt sick again at the thought of the beating that could have cost him his life, and thought: it's true, he is someone who has survived a battle. The laconic, contemplative tone of his voice, which he is voicing from some deep cavern of himself, a place he's not obliged to know, says that he is making the effort to discover some coherence, which he may forget, the event that gave rise to meaning the most ephemeral, because his life is crowded with adventure.

He said he walked the streets full of remorse and couldn't imagine an act of reparation that might allow his conscience to grant him a recess from self-disgust. His voice, as he described trudging the blighted city during the darkest part of the night, changed. It was no longer world-weary Bogart, but in Jacob's interminable narrative became a low-pitched obbligato, a rabbinical singsong, the voice of a soul that finds itself will-less, living in allegory. If not the singsong locution, then the thought of the ineffable suffering of the innocent of this world produced an immediate curvature of his spine. He talked with his hands. Tugged at my heartstrings, although not for the reasons he might have imagined.

I considered what I once believed, perhaps still believe my brother learned early. The world of the street is predatory, hurtful, inimical to him. Home is a battleground at least as dangerous as the street. Outside and inside the same punishing place. The only world that Jacob can trust is the one he invents, an enterprise nevertheless fraught with too many possibilities, endless imponderables, and perils. He leaves a wake of half-finished worlds, fabulous and botched, which he quickly forgets, and I and the psychiatrist, and or the psychiatric social worker, follow as stunned explorers. Jacob, whatever his confusions, is always current and adept in his display of the psychiatric zeitgeist, the most contemporary plague, whatever the fashion and language of "mental illness" throughout the decades, he will provide the doctors gainful employment.

He said, tired, exhausted, he found himself in a freight yard. The first hint of morning lightened the night sky. The line of boxcars and the engine train seemed abandoned. He was standing at some center where all the tracks abruptly ended. Pyramids of rusting sheet metal, small mountains of buckets and tin cans, piles of crumbling bricks and industrial debris of every kind flanked the tracks, shiny as black ice, that went on beyond sight heading south. He followed the tracks, bending to free his right ankle from the sheet of newspaper that the wind again and again wrapped around his leg. He refused to read the news, he knew what the paper said and now he only wanted to rest, sleep for a while. He'd been thinking of the great disparity between man's technological genius and moral stupidity. If the weapons we were allowed had to be commensurate with our moral development, mankind could not justify the slingshot, let alone the bow and arrow. Jacob said no more about his horror at having possibly taken a life. I didn't know whether that was forgotten. For an instant he paused, a Talmudist lost between worlds. Then he was present, the singsong rabbinical tunefulness a whistling past the graveyard, his terrifying vulnerability and sympathy for all living things a provocation to the wrath of rednecks everywhere. Jacob said he climbed into a boxcar and went to sleep.

He awoke in the dark boxcar, locked in, traveling somewhere. Alone, he was overwhelmed by the stink of living things that had been transported to slaughter. He was thirsty, alternately cold and suffocating. Sweating and shivering, in a fever, he found a corner to shit. After a time he was no longer hungry but still thirsty. He felt his way, his hands on the walls of the roaring boxcar, willing to trust whatever he could make out in the dark. He couldn't find a way out, a lever, a sliding door that would open. He collapsed on the rumbling floor(covered with hay) and closed his eyes, and tried to hide from what he was thinking. But, said Jacob, it occurred to him that his destination in the locked freight car was not Auschwitz.

During what was, he said, probably the second day, the train pausing but never stopping, he slipped in and out of consciousness, and his life passed before his eyes. He felt a kind of disappointment and resignation at the thought that he would die of thirst, fever, or hypothermia before he learned his whole story.

And I thought, if Jacob imagines his death he may die, the power of his story-making taking him to places beyond the will of his imagination; he'd begun to describe for me his neighbors when he lived underground beneath the subway; there was Rudy the Aqua Velva man, named for the aftershave lotion which was his favorite drink, and Andrew O'Leary who was occasionally overtaken by some paternal impulse and cooked beans for everyone over a flaming can of sterno; one of O'Leary's eyes was locked in peripheral vision, the other a blister, his voice box fried from drinking too much King Kong, a Puerto Rican moonshine, and once a week O'Leary rasped, "Suppertime, come and get it."

I wasn't going to ask Jacob who among his neighbors beat him and left him for dead; besides he wasn't going to tell me, and I needed to confess, tell Jacob about the fire. There we were in his kitchen like two lunatic Greek choruses going at once, neither hearing the other. But I could hear myself, or perhaps the words so long in my mind, hounding me in a whisper, were only audible in my own shameful dark. "Jacob, remember? I started the fire, fed the flames paper bags, wooden clothespins and a newspaper."

Obeisant, in worship of the flames leaping up out of the bathtub in the kitchen, I was seven, Jacob five; supplicants, transfixed, we crouched at the side of the white enamel tub where the flames danced. It was a Sunday morning. Momma and Poppa were sleeping later than usual.

The smoke curling through the apartment brought

Momma running in her nightgown, screaming. Poppa was charging, naked, his face something terrible. Immediately I turned on the faucet in the bathtub, made my face into a precocious replica of adult alarm, repudiating the majesty of fire; I was the one putting out the flames and I blamed my brother. Poppa grabbed Jacob, swung him in the air, shook him, bellowed in his face, whacked him hard on the ass, once, twice, and again, and on the thighs and shook and shook him. Momma screamed, "Stop, Abe, for God's sake stop, you'll kill him." Jacob was howling and pissing, Poppa's face twisted in disgust and he dropped the unclean thing into Momma's arms.

If I'm not my brother's keeper I may well be the instrument of the trauma that tumbled my bother's mind, bleeding together into one anomalous tissue, a consciousness in such a turmoil of flux that the mystery is total; there is never a tranquil moment in which the most astute physician (although they never tire of trying) can chart a probable geography; this is the conscious, and that the unconscious mind; it is all in constant motion, the essential heart of the mind/minds always hidden.

Or maybe it's not my fault. Maybe I'm absolved after all. The latest theory suggests that environment is of secondary significance. My brother is as God made him, inheritance is nearly everything, an anarchic something lives in the blood chemistry of the mind that may only be domesticated by the right pill — understanding, the talking cure useful to the extent that it reinforces the regimen of the corrective chemistry.

Jacob said the train stalled and slowed. I thought how finally we come to respect what we call our inner lives as one respects a resourceful opponent.

I tried to arm my brother. Teach him how to box. We were boys. He was thirteen and had come out of a long silence. He

moved toward me and seemed to want to be in the world. It
would be another year before the first of his many hospitaliza-
tions. It was difficult to teach Jacob: "Jake stick out your left,
like this." I demonstrated the stance as my uncle Max, who had
been a professional, instructed me. But Jacob mistook the task
as an issue of identity, or is it that with every other heartbeat he
traveled to another universe? He was willing, but it took him
years to take offense at anything. He was perpetually amazed. I
tried to share with him a practical epiphany: "and also Jakie
you can get a lead pipe. An equalizer. If you make it cost there's
a lot of trouble you won't have."

Came a day when a kid named Anunziato Messina pushed
Jacob off the stoop. Nunzio pointed to the step where Jacob had
been sitting and said, "That's my spot. Me, Anunziato Messina,"
Nunzio said, as if the slow saying of all the throaty vowels bond-
ing his name could measure the time my brother had left to
live. Jacob looked up at me for a sign. He wanted to do the right
thing, what was expected of him. I was just across the street
standing in a yard of rubble where me and my pals had been
busy ransacking the plumbing and wall fixtures from an abandoned tenement where there had been a fire. We tore out radiators, sinks, whatever was worth money and could be sold to the
junkyard. Jacob tried to put on a ferocious face and pointed it
at Nunzio. Nunzio was confused, not knowing what the silly
face was trying to say; he concluded that the gaping mug was
meant as an insult and let go a roundhouse right as Jacob stood
watching, fascinated. The blood streamed from Jacob's nose over
his mouth, chin, soaked his shirt. I took off after Nunzio with a
brick.

Jacob wouldn't stop bleeding. A doctor had to be called to
the house to cauterize Jacob's nose, long gauze ribbons with

some burning chemical inserted in my brother's nostrils with swab sticks finally scorched the tissue and stopped the bleeding. Every time Jacob got hit he bled like that.

The train had stopped. The boxcar door was unlocked. Jacob said he lay in a dark corner until the voices of the men outside went away.

He crawled out blind, not able to see in the glare of light after what he figured to be two days or more in the dark. He made his way on all fours squinting. As his cheek brushed the upper part of his arm he realized that he had the substantial start of a beard. When he was able to stand and walk he opened his eyes, shading them with his hand. He said he thought he might be in Oklahoma, Texas, or Arkansas. The stunted street that emerged out of the boiling dust-laden glare was made up of a gas station, general store, towering silo, storefront church, and a bar. The wind blew tumbleweed through the town's one street. The earth was flat and went on forever, empty in all directions. The enormous enveloping sky squat on the horizon, a fuming red conflagration hugging the earth. He walked toward the general store in hope of water, something to drink.

Jacob said that the first Indian he saw was a middle-aged man walking slowly with great formal dignity, wearing a suit, bone necklace, featherless headband, and long black braids. The man's nose was bleeding. Jacob stopped and stared. The Indian's eyes acknowledged Jacob in a noncommittal way, unperturbed, and he walked on. Jacob said the next two Indian men he saw were younger and they too moved with the same inexorable grace, their walking, wherever they were walking to, suggesting dance and ritual, a purpose which would not be diverted by anything, and their noses were bleeding. Before I could ask Jacob anything or interrupt with something as mundane as my need to confess the fire and beg his forgiveness, he said that he'd wandered into "a Choc-taw pogrom," all the drunken cowboys of the town commemorating something that required that they break the noses of every Indian man foolish enough to venture into town on that Saturday evening. Jacob saw more Indian men all with bloody noses, and drunken, laughing cowboys, spilling out of the bar, shooting pistols in the air.

Jacob said he looked around him and knew he was too frightened to be whatever it was he was meant to be, his soul something he needed to take back to incubate in the dark, and he started to run and didn't stop until he reached the freight yard. There he fell on his hands and knees on to the parched ground, and drank the clearest and most delicious water he'd ever tasted from a horse's hoofprint before climbing into the freight car for the journey he had to make to get home.

My eyes adjusted as the lamplight fell warming the sweatshirt wrapped around my head. I peered through the warp and woof of the fabric and smelled the salt odor of my self. As Rainbow told it and I remembered more I wanted to explain certain things to Laura myself. She didn't argue with Rainbow, but did dispute his characterization of Dude as the apostle of a new faith, a missionary Johnny Appleseed sowing the means of revelation. Laura said, "He sells dope." Rainbow said, "Yeah but," and tried to offer what he considered a moral complexity worthy of serious consideration. "Dude served in Vietnam, he's trying to live down the nightmare; he was one of the vets who joined the March on Washington." "And now," Laura said, "he's a dope dealer." I pulled the sweatshirt down to my waist. Rubbed my eyes. Laura was about to show Rainbow the door. He took another tack. "It was Dude who did the tattoo. Isaac asked for it. He said your anniversary was coming up. He wanted to surprise you."

I remembered it happened somewhere in Maine, at the commune. Part of Dude's itinerary. The danger had passed. The hunters were gone. There was a lot of pot, hashish, and homemade beer available. Dude had rendered a string of roses around the ankle of a lovely young woman who had cooked a vat of lentil soup. If I got the chance I could, to a certain extent, explain it to Laura, because the enchantment hadn't passed. I needed to do something irrevocable. Her name, intaglio carved in my flesh, a tribute to my love and the sunlit island that was her birth. That's why I asked for the palm tree and her name etched in the roots on my chest. I had a sense of a necessary transgression as prerequisite of a larger embrace. As a vestigial Jew I felt myself challenging some hoary edict concerning graven images. A powerful impulse of a new faith claimed me; I didn't have to understand, but obey. There were moments when I became aware of something scary, and hung over, sober, or partially sober I marveled at my survival. It seems that at a certain point between the fifth and eighth drink I had to obey the command resonating in my head, a voice of true religious authority, righteous, like the voice coming from the burning bush. I was pretty sure that is how I came to be standing with Dude in front of the commune's barn, the two of us leveling rifles at the hunters from New Jersey.

The day before Dude and I arrived, one of the hunters had stumbled upon Deborah, one of the founding members of the commune, at work in the pottery shed. The hunter, Deborah said, reeked of alcohol. He and the other hunters must have been very frustrated. It was an unseasonably warm November and a heavy rain had washed away the little snow cover; it was impossible for the New Jersey hunters to track deer. Deborah as always was friendly, even though she disapproved of hunting, would not eat meat, and she offered the hunter a cup of herbal tea. The sad hunter separated from his companions had been rambling about all the things in life that ought to be free and uncomplicated. Deborah agreed that in an acquisitive, materialistic society we become slaves to false necessities. Deborah said she didn't become frightened until he started to touch her, and even as he tugged at her blouse and she struggled to fight him off he continued to mumble his grievance; he was convinced that the impossibility of hunting and his stumbling into the place where free love reigned was portentous, and the hunter couldn't understand why she would single him out for rejection. She screamed and struggled, others from the commune came running at about the same time that the hunter's companions found him. The three, drunk, laughing, drove up in a new red Ford station wagon. They carried their struggling friend away trying to mollify him, "After all," one explained, "who said that life was supposed to be fair?"

That evening the station wagon returned. The hunters didn't leave the vehicle but remained parked on the narrow dirt road adjacent to the pottery shed. They shouted invitations to the women of the commune from the open windows of the station wagon. The plaintive yodel, "I need a woman," soon became an angry screaming description of erotic possibilities. The members of the commune stayed inside and held a meeting. The obscene screaming from the drunken men outside continued. In the communal kitchen some suggested inviting the hunters in and engaging them in dialogue as the necessary first step to raising their consciousness. One young man suggested calling the sheriff or town constable. There was a loud collective groan and the young man was reminded that the sheriff, the town constable, the law were antagonistic to the commune, and the quantities of grass and hashish on the premises could get them busted, and even if they hid the stuff, the discovery of some seeds, whatever, would be a sufficient pretext to arrest them all. One young woman said that they ought to consult the I Ching before they decided on any action. Deborah began to cry and confessed that her most powerful desire was to do the hunters violence. A half-dozen of the young men and women surrounded and hugged her.

Eventually the hunters drove off screaming, "Pussy, pussy, pussy," at the moon. In the large, kerosene- and candlelit kitchen the members of the commune, ardent believers in participatory democracy, hadn't been able to reach consensus.

The four hunters, wearing iridescent orange jackets and caps, returned the next day. They got out of the new, red station wagon and started to walk toward the barn. Two carried rifles over their shoulders like soldiers on a parade. One clenched a bouquet of weeds with the mock seriousness of a man courting. Another waved a box of chocolates. The one carrying the bunch of weeds laughed, winked at his friend with the box of chocolates, and said, "candy is dandy but liquor is quicker." Dude handed me the rifle; he carried a shotgun. I followed him as he closed the distance between us and the hunters.

The burning bush was talking to me, and when I fired I believed that I was giving a lesson in empathy as I blew out the headlight on the new, red Ford station wagon, clearly the most beloved possession of the creep marching with the rifle on his shoulder. He crumpled up with grief. Dude raised the barrel of his shotgun into the face of the other who was armed and said,

"Please go, or there will be some new faces in Hell shortly."

Dude and I, Chancy, and Rainbow were part of the celebration at the commune. I smoked the pipes that were passed around. Drank beer. Desired bourbon. The moon of somebody's dream, a vanilla pie with a slice missing shone in the window of the large communal kitchen. All around us candles in the shape of gnomes, flowers, unicorns, rainbow-colored vulvas and phalluses melted and drooled, glowed and freckled the faces of Buddha and Che Guevara on the wall. I felt absolved of any need to reconcile contradictions. The stereo blared "All You Need Is Love." The goodwill of the simple melody chanted, giggled, and shrieked by the leaping dancers grew thunderous. The thumping feet made the floor buck and the hundred little bellies of flame danced. Then they played "Blowin' In the Wind." I would have preferred Gerry Mulligan, and the Dylan that had moved my life hadn't played the guitar. Then I remembered what the roly-poly Welsh poet had said at one of his readings: "If every hermaphrodite were a schizophrene, which half would you take?" But it was all all right. The mushroom I had eaten — was it only a day ago — was producing its own beneficent weather. Boredom had never been my problem, but now I felt immune to it forever, and I had a quantity of ease too good to last but I wasn't worried. Incense filled the air with the scent of lilacs. Rainbow said, "Far out, Professor Isaac, he's a trip, like the Gunfight at the OK Corral." A couple dancing close- by cheered. One young man, dancing alone, throbbing and waving the great fan of his hair, wheezed, "Bad Karma, bad." Dude working at the tattoo on my chest by the light of a kerosene lamp blushed and said, "Honkies messin' with my clientele is unacceptable man; I won't have it."

That was all he had to say on the subject. Dude guided the

electric stylus that gnawed at my chest; he dabbed the blood away with a clean cloth and I watched the palm tree with my wife's name take form in my skin. I admired Dude's art. I could see Dude was Dude, not Jacob nor anyone else. Whatever the contentious nightmare of Vietnam, within and without he could only experience interpretation and history as a violation of his being. Dude was and would be whatever he was doing, and to explore meaning would be antithetical to his ability to draw breath. In his transparency I could see whomever I might, that was my business. Huck Finn, my brother, Billy the Kid or Dude among the most endearing and innocent of American killers. Still I wanted to reassure the young man who'd said "bad Karma," and any of the others who saw me as a symptom of the world's bad news, after all I was over thirty, although not by much. I reminded everyone of the fortuitous thing. Chancy had decided to go to Canada with his new friend Morty the Candlemaker. Morty, a transient resident of the commune, was also in flight from military service. Many of the commune believed this concurrence of events was a mix of Jungian synchronicity and Marxist dialectic, the prophetic hodge-podge confirmed by the Tarot deck and the alignment of the stars. Who was I to argue? After all, these young people, however privileged, whatever their giddy tantrum, were seriously opposing the war, and they might succeed in unleashing those forces in American life that would at last bring a halt to the slaughter. Aside from what I found silly this was also a glorious moment for American democracy.

Polly, the commune's favorite interpreter of the I Ching, a diminutive girl who appeared little more than a child, wearing large horn-rimmed glasses, concentrated her face in a serious look, someone engaged in strenuous study; she read the Tarot deck and said it augured well.

Morty and Chancy, the dreamers running away to dream, would be sustained by the candle business which Morty would teach Chancy. Best of all, the stars pointed north, away from the hell of carnage. Chancy's father, a veteran of WWII and a believer of doing one's duty without question, would eventually, Polly said, reconcile with his son; and Morty could count on continued financial support from his parents as long as he kept a distance from home. I longed for home.

Bernard Tummelman left a copy of his manuscript for me to read and started the short walk back to campus an hour before the others considered going. At the door, Ms. Kim reiterated the arguments I should make to her father and again asked for reassurance that I would speak to the president of the college. I promised I would and said that I doubted that her scholarship would be revoked because of her father's complaint. Rainbow Schwartz said goodnight, offering his smile as an endowment, lest we forget the many delights of this world.

Rainbow and Ms. Kim lingered at the door for just a moment, anticipating the invitation to Thanksgiving dinner that Laura usually offered to those students who for reasons of their own were not going home for the Thanksgiving break. When the invitation was not forthcoming they said, "Goodnight."

Laura was distant. It seemed false to offer a perfunctory apology for my absence. I imagined I'd consummated something important on the journey that I was bringing home, and thought again that until I married Laura I'd never had a home I wanted to come home to. She stood close to me but the distance between us was inviolable. What I had wanted to say before I perceived the futility of saying it was that although I wasn't sure whether I had actually recited Dylan Thomas's "In My Craft Or Sullen Art" while I was being tattooed, it was the last two lines of the first stanza, 'But for the common wages / Of their most secret heart' that spoke to me of my happy acceptance of the terms of life, and this was intrinsic to my love for Laura, and I couldn't wait to get home and tell her the news. I could recite the poem in the hope of greater understanding, but then I would be making the poem part of an argument. But perhaps I wouldn't lose my conviction of the tattoo as a sacramental act if I recited the poem silently, to myself:

In my craft or sullen art
Exercised in the still night
When only the moon rages
And the lovers lie abed
With all their griefs in their arms,
I labour by singing light
Not for ambition or bread
Or the strut and trade of charms
On the ivory stages
But for the common wages
Of their most secret heart.

Not for the proud man apart
From the raging moon I write
On these spindrift pages
Nor for the towering dead
With their nightingales and psalms
But for the lovers, their arms
Round the griefs of the ages,
Who pay no praise or wages
Nor heed my craft or art.

Laura said, "You're not quite sober." As far as I could tell I hadn't had anything for about eight hours. I had difficulty restraining myself from asserting that during my little odyssey I wasn't merely stealing and gorging pleasure. Laura said she slept poorly and was worried sick during the three days I was away. Suddenly she seemed angry with herself for saying it. I apologized then and meant it. I mentioned Thanksgiving, which was less than a week away, and she explained why we wouldn't be having Thanksgiving together.

Laura said that she had joined an organization. The purpose of the organization, which was a peer-counseling group, was to offer support and guidance to the families of alcoholics. Wives, husbands, sons, daughters, brothers and sisters, anyone whose life was affected by an alcoholic, was welcome to join. She said she and Maria would be having Thanksgiving dinner with their group and that she had attended her first meeting while I was away.

The moment before I was able to speak again was far longer than my recent journey. Although I'd seen her exasperation I'd assumed that our love was as inexhaustible as my delight each morning to open my eyes and see her.

Finally I said that I had never lost a day of work because of drinking and never lost a job. She said, "Not yet." She also said that I was in the binge stage of my drinking career, I hadn't yet hit bottom.

The thought of our life together as an item for therapeutic gossip, the meaning of our marriage matriculating through psychobabble, was a betrayal and degradation I had never imagined as a disaster that could happen to me.

Laura anticipated what I would say next and told me, "You can't be here anyway. Your mother called three times while you were away. I expected you home on Friday and I told her I'd give you the message as soon as you got here. After her second call late Friday night I concocted an excuse, which is something I'll never do again. No more excuses for you. That's over. Anyway I said that I was sorry, that I'd forgotten that you had to attend a conference out of town. She didn't believe me and was certain that I was preventing you, somehow, from answering the telephone. When she called back the third time early Saturday morning, she said that people who dig graves for others often fell in themselves, and before hanging up, ranted in Yiddish, cursing me in ways I'd rather not have translated." I said, "Darling, I'm sorry." Laura said, "She is a frightened old woman. And your uncle Sol called. He said your mother's behavior is becoming very strange and that you should come to New York at once and try to comfort her. Despite the hell that was her marriage she has never recovered from your father's death. She doesn't cope very well on her own. And yes, your uncle said your brother seems to be doing well enough in the group home, no crisis there, for now. It seems your mother had some spots or discolorations on her back that her doctor diagnosed as benign. However, she is certain she is going to die. Uncle Sol said that you are the only one who might be able to persuade her otherwise. And there are other complications. Your Uncle Sol and your Aunt Tessie could not reach your mother at home. They tried phoning and then went to see her. They knocked and no one answered the door. She has been away for a little more than a week, and although she telephoned Sol, Tessie, and tried to reach you here, no one has any idea where she was calling from. Your Uncle Sol, who helps her balance her checking account, says that she's withdrawn all her savings. Sol called again to say she returned to her apartment yesterday but she is giving away all her belongings to neighbors. He says you had better get there as soon as possible. Your mother now refuses to talk to Sol, or even her sister Tessie. She won't let either of them into her apartment. Sol said that in his last conversation with her she cursed and dismissed him in Yiddish, which he translated for me as 'onions should grow from your navel.'"

During the eight-hour bus ride to New York I comforted myself with the thought that finally somewhere near three A.M. Laura and I, unable to sleep in estrangement, had to touch, hold one another to find rest, and the touching took us to lovemaking. But after, before first light, everything she said was tinged with something that made me think that the lovemaking had the quality of a parting gift. Still, after lovemaking, our quiet talk of practical things had a repose that neither of us had willed. The inexplicable that made sweet reason sweet. "You'll have to take the bus," she said. I asked, "Why?" "The car needs brake work," she said, "and I'd rather not think of you driving." I remembered that not long ago under the influence, I'd parked the car somewhere and it took several days to find it again. I promised that I'd cut down on my drinking. Laura said, holding me close, that was not an option for me, that I lacked the gift for moderation. Then I remembered and asked her how she was going to get her three paintings to the group show in Boston. She said she'd arrange something on her own. We drifted off, sleeping deeply for about three hours. When we woke, Maria, hugging her large, tattered cloth doll, was sleeping sandwiched between us.

On the street beneath the elevated train, some five blocks from my mother's apartment, the inhabitants of my mother's neighborhood, mostly aged people, were able to make themselves heard, although the sound of the Atlantic Ocean, only one block to my right, was drowned out by the thunder of the trains overhead. My parents had moved to Brighton Beach, also known as Little Odessa, a short while after Laura and I had married. The incredible lungpower of the old folks seemed a natural endowment, requiring no special effort. The wonderful aroma of baked goods and smoked meat drifted out of the shops and delicatessens lining the street and mixed with the scent of the ocean. The movement of the people in the street seemed urgent and happy. The congested traffic in the shadow beneath the elevated trains screeched; the expert near misses between cars, taxis, and buses in no way inhibiting the choreography of the pedestrians, young or old, nimble or staggering, dodging the vehicles they cursed. There seemed something more festive than usual about the older inhabitants especially. They lurched, dazed, giddy to the point of hysteria. I stood holding the compact overnight bag that held the *AA Big Book* Laura had packed with my things. I'd promised her that I would get around to reading it. The tide of street traffic had swept me between two clusters of old folks. Buffeted gently among the old bodies I looked over their heads. In the window of the delicatessen a roasting chicken, dripping its juices, turned on a rotisserie, and the old people before the window moaned like erotic maniacs at a burlesque show. I squeezed myself out of this group and was working my way toward the easier flow of traffic, but was momentarily stuck, caught in another knot of old folks standing before a newspaper kiosk. "Did you hear?" someone in the crowd called, "We're innocent!" "Oh yeah," another answered, "of what are we innocent?" "We didn't," the chorus chimed, "kill Gott." "You don't say?" another said, convulsed with joy. "I do say." I craned my neck and maneuvered to get a little closer to the kiosk. I glimpsed the newspaper on the counter and was able to make out the beginning of an article about a meeting at the Vatican that had concluded that the Jewish people should not be declared guilty of deicide. Then I was bumped out of position by an old gentleman with a cane. The proprietor of the kiosk, chewing on an unlit cigar, was considerably younger than his customers. He pointed at me with the stub of his cigar and bawled, "Sonny boy, this ain't a library, you wanna read you gotta spend a dime." Someone yelled at him, "Schnorrer." Several were waving the newspapers overhead like flags. Another to my left, creating space for himself with his elbows, read and reported that in France there were priests who objected to the Vatican's decree. The call and response from the east and west of the crowd was "Let them wallow in Hell — in their bones." I wondered, is it possible with Buddhist monks setting themselves on fire, and kids rioting in New York and Paris, that the cry from the streets had reached Rome? "So, nu?" a voice from the heart of the crowd demanded, "if we didn't kill God, who did?" After a brief pause, someone answered, "Maybe the Puerto Ricans."

I worked my way free of the crowd and before turning left on Brighton Sixth Street to walk the four blocks to my mother's house, stopped at a candy store to buy a pack of cigarettes.

I asked for a pack of Luckies. The wizened old guy behind the counter slapped down the pack of cigarettes, blew his nose into a hankie, and said, "You heard? We didn't do it. So who did it?" I said, I didn't know. He said, "Probably the Hungarians," and trembled from head to toe.

I knocked on my mother's door. No one answered, not a sound from her apartment. I knocked, waited, and called "Ma." The old woman coming slowly toward me dipped and rose resting on her chrome walker. She was wrapped in a great quilted bathrobe. Her gaunt head was topped with a cone of pinkish hair that looked like cotton candy. "A mother," she called down the narrow hallway, "can wait forever." I said, "I'm sorry." She said, "Everybody is sorry." She paused and rested midway down the corridor. A plastic bag of trash tied with a string hung from her walker. "Come," she commanded, "do a mitzvah."

She handed me the bag of garbage and pointed to the in- cinerator drop at the other end of the hall. As I dropped the neatly tied bag down the chute she said, "Your mother's walk- ing on the boardwalk. Such a nice day you should take advan- tage, nu, go." As I pushed the elevator button and waited, the old woman laughed and said, "So you heard the news?" And before she could take me through the paces of the joke, I said, "They say we didn't kill God, maybe it was the Ukrainians." "Oy," she said, "such a sage. Go, go find your mother."

The benches in the Brighton Beach section of the board- walk were loaded with old folks bundled in topcoats sunning themselves. Some held reflectors under their chins. I unbut- toned my coat as I walked, it was quite warm. I studied the benches looking for my mother. Above, the clouds gyrated, the seagulls hung like kites, and the ocean lay calm. The tide was out and the surf gurgled on the shore. I passed a group of four men seated around a card table playing pinochle. A little fur- ther on I walked past an old guy in a fur cap singing "Romania, Romania" to an audience of two fur-coated old women seated on a bench, holding parasols above their heads. I walked on past an old guy strolling and serenading himself with a balalaika. It occurred to me that I was lucky that my grandfather had been a draft dodger from the czar's army; and then I wondered what urgent business my mother's fear of death had precipitated, and how I could persuade her that she wasn't about to die. Perhaps she could no longer live alone, unassisted.

By the time I passed the parachute jump ride, and the Cyclone, Coney Island's notorious roller coaster, both closed for the season, there weren't many strollers on the boardwalk. Despite my casual stride I'd examined all the benches carefully and mistaken one old woman for my mother; she nevertheless had been ready to embrace me even as I backed away and said, "Oh, excuse me." I thought that before trying to convince my mother of anything I should show her Maria's latest drawing — which I carried in my inside breast pocket — and tell Momma how well her granddaughter was doing in kindergarten. The child could already read, "kinehora." Every utterance of her granddaughter was received as pure genius, and was the only proof of the miraculous in the otherwise benighted world. Yes, before venturing any other topic, it would be wise to speak of Momma's granddaughter.

I was thirsty. I remembered that unlike past occasions, before I left, Laura hadn't extracted the promise that I wouldn't drink. This restraint was probably an aspect of the new program she'd committed herself to as a member of the self-help group. I felt both relieved and threatened; this was, perhaps, the beginning of something final. But I reasoned that if I had a couple of beers, no hard stuff, that wasn't really drinking. I turned right, descended a ramp from the boardwalk into the Coney Island streets, and after walking two blocks found Clancy's Bar and Grill. I would have two, perhaps three beers at most, and then search the boardwalk again; this time walking in the direction of Brighton Beach, and if I didn't see my mother I'd try her apartment again.

Clancy's Bar and Grill was an oblong burrowed out of perpetual dusk. The neon beacons in the opaque window said Rheingold and Budweiser. The smell of frying onions drifted up over the narrow grill attended by a tall man in a white smock who appeared to function in a trance. There were three patrons seated at the bar. I pulled up a stool and sat down. The bartender, a huge woman with one of the most beautiful and tranquil faces I've ever seen, glided with the grace of a whale and came to rest standing above me; she looked down, smiled, and said, "What will it be?" Looking up at her I had the sensation of sitting too close to a movie screen where my vision traversed the larger-than-life head of unbelievable beauty. I said, "Beer." She tilted the glass expertly under the spigot, lowered the beer to me, and rolled as though on coasters to the far end of the bar where a male patron had called in a tender voice, "Maureen." At that distance and at that angle she appeared more than Rubenesque in her proportions, and a little less in scale than a Sumo wrestler. "Jimmy," she said in a voice that was not loud, but distinct, "you've had enough now, it's time to go home"; and pushing back the change he'd left on the bar, said, "and you hang on to that, don't spend it on playing the number; use it to pay your insurance premium." Jimmy nodded. "You promise," she said. Jimmy said, "I promise," and made his way to the door with the deliberate gait of a man who must concentrate not to fall.

She studied for a moment another patron sipping a mixed drink from a tall glass. The man was dressed in a business suit, shirt and tie. He was not young. "Barney," she said, "you should think about having a sandwich before you continue on your rounds, and don't forget your briefcase."

Maureen served my second beer just before I was about to ask for it and moved on to the one woman patron at the bar. The woman, wearing a checkered cloth coat and a kerchief

round her head covering a nest of wire curlers, smoked a cigarette and studied the glass of sherry set in front of her. She sat
in a cloud of cigarette smoke. I lit one up. She said, "Maureen,
he's lost interest. I know we've been married ten years, there's
the three kids, and he works the night shift and all. But he's so
damned polite, like I'm someone he's just been introduced to
and he ain't terribly interested." Maureen asked, "And who's with
the kids now?" "Oh, the mother-in-law." I drank my second beer
and signaled with the empty glass for a third. Maureen served
me and said, "It won't hurt to slow down fella," and she returned to the woman customer sitting in the cloud of blue cigarette smoke. I thought, Maureen a subversive maenad, no longer
in the employ of Dionysus, domesticated and grown huge in
her good works. "Now Fay," Maureen said, "Your Charlie is devoted to you and the kids. He's a steady provider. Many would
consider you a lucky woman." "That," said Fay, "ain't the issue." And tilted over the bar and whispered something into the
white expanse of Maureen's aproned bosom. "Well certainly,"
Maureen said, "you could try that. After all you've got a marriage license, and if you feel the need to confess you can do it
here." "But," said Fay, "he doesn't find me attractive anymore.
It's the weight I think, after all I'm barely five feet tall and I
weigh a hundred and thirty pounds." "Oh darlin'," said Maureen,
"what's to worry, my cunt weighs a hundred and thirty pounds."

I guessed that there was less than an hour of daylight left.
The sky above the ocean was violet, on the horizon a horizontal
seam of silver glimmered on the blue black sea. The boardwalk
was almost deserted. To my left, here and there lights went on
in apartment windows. The wind had picked up a little, but it
was more refreshing than cold. In Vermont, weather this moderate in November would bring snow. The air smelled of rain. I

found myself rehashing some of the things I should have said to Laura before I'd left. She'd said with uncharacteristic bitterness that I was sober on the mornings that I preserved for writing, but did not grant my relationship to her the same importance. I'd had no answer but to protest my love.

When I reached the Brighton Beach area of the boardwalk the only people left were the four resolute pinochle players still at the table, and one old guy in a folding chair, under a large brimmed slouch hat; he was wrapped in a blanket, snoring, while from the portable radio in his lap a mellifluous voice crooned "Embraceable You." I stopped, rested for a moment, and touched the inside jacket pocket that held my daughter's drawing. I would present this right off to the first woman in my life, who, according to my uncle's reports, was preparing for her imminent death. I tried to light a cigarette. Even with my hands cupped to protect the tiny flame, the breeze extinguished the bit of fire before I could light up. One of the pinochle players, without rising or looking away from his cards, handed me a smoking cigar and I lit my cigarette from the burning end of the cigar, returned it, and said, "Thanks." The pinochle player grunted. The four card players bundled in their coats and hats around the table seemed impervious to the weather, the season, the time of day. Their profound meditation on the cards might have been an esoteric reckoning with which they hoped to fathom God's aliases. From the lap of the sleeping man the portable radio played and I recognized the voice of the young Frank Sinatra. The card players' hands moved, their lips moved, and their eyes moved occasionally, as when some intrusion of the given world threatened to impose itself, as I had, and an efficient response was necessary to keep any distraction to a minimum. They rarely spoke. Kibitzers would not be tolerated.

I inhaled, taking smoke into my lungs; it tasted good, and I was ready to move on.

The one who had given me his cigar to light my cigarette, cocked his eye toward the street side of the boardwalk and moaned, "Oy, it's Irving's Shirley." Another set of eyes surfaced above the rim of the cards he was holding and said, "Who?" "Shirley, Shirley," the other growled, "She ain't coming for me." The third card player, emerging from his meditation, but alert to his surroundings, said, "That ain't Shirley." The fourth card player slid his bifocals up and down his nose. The woman marching toward the card table had her arms spread wide; she was wearing a silver-colored fur coat, or some synthetic that looked like fur, her banana-yellow hair was done up in pageboy fashion, popular I think during World War II, and as she bore down on the table she called, "Yoo-hoo darling, suppertime," and the pinochle players looked at one another accusingly.

She blundered into me. The powerful aroma of lilac enveloped us and I wasn't certain whether it was the woman's perfume, or the scent unleashed by the mushroom I'd eaten several days before still inhabiting my senses, that journey insinuating itself into this one. The woman's arms moved to embrace me. Before, I had backed away from the woman I'd mistaken for my mother, just as she was about to hug me; now I felt that maybe if I overcame my squeamishness, was a bit more generous and embraced this woman, surely someone's bereft mother, my own would appear. Her face had the tooled perfection of a doll. Sumptuous, lacquered eyelashes, blue mascara, but under the rouge of both cheeks, beneath her eyes, there were large bruises. We were in each other's arms. She moaned, "Oy, mein kind." I held her at arm's length and said, "Mrs...." She said, "Come to supper. I'll make you potato latkes." I said, "Sorry, really I don't have time." She said, "Since when don't you have time for potato latkes?" One of the pinochle players mumbled, "Go, go eat the potato latkes." "Did you," she said, "call your brother? Blood is thicker than water, and Jacob hangs on your every word." "Ma?" "Yeah, me," she said. "What have you done?" "My nose I done. And don't worry, the doctor said the bruises will go away in a little while. And I look like Ginger Rogers, no? And the blond hair is also pretty?" I thought I must find a telephone booth and call Laura, tell her everything so that I can believe it's happening. This day nearly as eternal as childhood. "Your brother, he's a poor eater, a boy with problems. If he had a trade, the right girl. But you, you're an eater," she said smiling. I knew the voice. It was my mother's voice coming from the waxworks Ginger Rogers. She was holding my hands, smiling. I tried to smile. Why, I asked myself rhetorically, did she mutilate herself. I thought of noses and how medical quacks had attached leeches to Gogol's nose as he lay on his death bed. I remembered my mother's rapture over my daughter's pert nose as the most notable accomplishment of my life.

The pinochle mavens hunched over their cards barely glanced at us, in their improvised, monastic retreat, hiding from their mates, they slapped their cards down with the vehemence of children. The sleeper in the folding chair snored, and from the portable radio in his lap Sinatra sang the refrain of "Embraceable You." Momma said, "Come Izzy, like Fred and Ginger, I'll let you lead." The moon was visible although it was not yet night. We waltzed around the table of the card players . The dance as much as I would ever be able to do to convince my mother she is beautiful.

Courting Laura Providencia

The day Laura Providencia deflowered Isaac was accommodating, providing the silver-tinged dark of a full, moonlit night. Despite the first impression of impending rain, which Isaac quickly forgot on his way to work that morning, the weather was self-effacing and the street seemed as hospitable as his own somnolent, tick-tocking kitchen.

He'd arranged with the manager of the bookstore to work only from eight to noon on this particular Saturday. The four hours passed slowly. Finally he was walking in the proximity of time he'd thought would never arrive, toward the door and the street where Laura was waiting. He passed by the tables and shelves of books and knew he coveted too many, and he had no idea of what he would need as he felt himself living through the earliest and most primitive stages of some archaic religion. Still, what was happening was an unimaginable inheritance, a destiny richer and wilder than any flaw or grandeur in his character.

Again, he'd spent too much of his pay on books. The pockets of his sports jacket and pants were bursting, and as pendulous as udders, with books. He moved dazzled, feeling the life of the words hanging about him, a many-breasted beast, weighted down with language breathing on him, as he breathed the words running riot in his blood-gorged head. He placed one foot in front of the other and continued toward her, waiting outside on the corner in the world.

The sky withholding the flood leaked a luminous silver light on the city. The walkers on the street hurried, but cautiously, a hint of something tentative in the movement of the people on the pavement, confused by the richness of the light. The crowd moved in the direction of where Laura stood, parting, moving around her, men and women, startled, turning their heads to glance back, to take another look, reaffirming what they saw as they crossed the street. Laura, assiduously not seeing the people gawking at her, spotted Isaac weaving his way through the crowd. Isaac's terrific effort, the crawling pace of a dreamer unable to learn the lesson of his dream, appeared to struggle in place, as though on a treadmill, and Laura had the sense that she had forever to make up her mind, whether to stay or go.

It seemed to Isaac that the time required to walk the hundred yards from under the bookstore canopy to the corner where Laura stood was equal to the passing of the entire morning, which had not yet passed; and then the books were falling around his feet, and he winced as they hit the pavement. He bent to pick them up, not stopping his excruciatingly slow progress forward. The spine of one book was injured, another lay open on the street, the wind rampaging the fluttering pages. Isaac scooped the books up from under the pedestrians' feet. He hugged the books to his chest and stumbled forward. The most discreet, silent thunder shot a bolt of yellow across the silver sky. Isaac saw Laura in her peach-colored dress, her hair blowing about her shoulders, and at last he was standing there, in front of her. The procession of people continued to flow around them, turning their heads to look at Laura, once, and then twice, before continuing on. Beneath his belt buckle he felt the rumble radiate deep down through his groin, some manner of sudden photosynthesis, and his sex stiff as a tree ballooned and pinnacled the trousers below his waist like the apex of a circus tent. People walking around them saw. Laura saw. She said, "You're disgusting." Isaac burst into tears. But the sex of him just stood there, swelling and casting a shadow on the pavement that enveloped his feet. He cried, tears ran down his cheeks. He said, "I'm sorry, really, I'm sorry." He opened and passed a book in front of him, down there, like a kabuki dancer flashing a fan. His face said he was blameless, and he knew this was untoward, something happening quite aside from anything he might wish. He stood there, petulant as a child who had been done an injustice, sobbing. He tried to fig-leaf himself, placing the open copy of Kierkegaard's *Fear & Trembling* in front of his thighs. He had hoped, in a long-ago hour of the morning, that the most melancholy Dane, now providing purdah, might provide some light on the inexplicable and limitless requirements of faith and love.

Laura watched him weep for half a moment, studied his dumb face, beautiful in its own particular way; she took out her handkerchief and wiped his wet cheeks; she brought the handkerchief to his nose and said, "Blow." He honked his nose.

She laughed. He laughed too. His laughter sounded somewhere between a horse's neigh and a mule's bray. Laura wiped his nose with the handkerchief and looked at the protuberance. She had stepped to the side to wipe his face, and it occurred to her that his swelling was a stigmata, the bruising manifestation of his wonder. When she thought this she was also listening to his grotesque laughter, and somehow she knew that the child that they would have would be burdened with making such an ungainly sound when she laughed, and the absurd animal laughter would be one of several notable inconveniences of the child's wondrous capacities. Laura borrowed from the tenderness she would feel for her child, and took Isaac by the hand and led him down the street.

Isaac, like a capsizing vessel whose mast is reaching nine o'clock and nearly parallel with the horizon, let Laura tug him around the corner to the bus stop. For the sake of modesty he had taken off his sports jacket and draped it in front of him.

Seated on the bus next to Laura, Isaac veiled his blooming lap with his jacket. On top of the jacket he stacked the paperback editions he'd excavated from his torn, misshapen pockets. Kierkegaard's *Fear & Trembling*, Gogol's *Overcoat*, Chekhov's *Lady With A Lapdog*, and Buber's two-volume *Tales of the Hasidim* made the trembling dwelling on his lap, levered by his sex, as secure as an earthquake-proof skyscraper. The miraculous balance of the swaying books on his lap was also aided by the slightly elevated angle of the right cheek of his buttocks; he'd neglected to remove the paperback with the crippled spine from his back pocket, and so, tipped up slightly at a right angle, he sat on Jung's *Modern Man In Search of A Soul*.

Isaac looked through his inflamed eyes out the bus window at the noonday street, soaked in the phosphorescent night-white of some further galaxy's heaven. Laura took hold of his hand and he turned to her. He felt her shoulder press his. Something like thought began to cohere in his mind. He remembered that earlier in the morning, as he had been shelving books in the store, he had opened, at random, one of the volumes of Buber's *Tales of the Hasidim*, and read that King David had prayed to the Lord with the same fervor that he had gone to Bathsheba, and the Lord had forgiven David on the moment. Isaac thought that if he'd had the presence of mind, he might have explained himself to Laura that way. But he was not yet able to speak, and now he didn't want to sully the great wealth of her smile with justifications.

The doors of the bus hissed closed and the vehicle began to move. He felt the evanescent presence of the other passengers.

Seated on the slowly moving bus, she clasped his hand tightly, and he couldn't turn his face from her. His breathing was slow, deep, and labored as one who had been running so long he'd lost the realization of the fact in his headlong flight to run out of himself; the sickening fear that had assailed him in some prehistoric moment of childhood, never to cease but to become subterfuge in something that wasn't quite forgetting. He was incarcerated in his own body, had never known, seen, touched, through any mind, eyes, skin other than his, and he couldn't outrun the suffocating limitation, or say it, only run, terrified. His first-grade teacher looking into his mute, anguished face had hinted to his mother of his probable impairment; and when the suffocation of being in himself was more than he could bear, he began to run, and ran finding himself still locked in himself on strange streets; and he ran and ran. Now, beyond the oblivion of the great effort, through light and dark, he was aware the womb-wet marathon, creeping and running, had from the first forgotten thump thumping of his small heart's time, left him staggering into this minute, when, inexplicably, he found himself riding, seated next to her, pressed against his shoulder; and he glimpsed a whole world sliding by, in repose, in the window, and at last he caught his breath. His left cheek still smarted from the red salvo of his mother's hand booming across his burning ear, illuming his head in heat. He remembered that he couldn't assuage his mother's grief, or remember why he had disappeared. She screamed, "Again! Again?" She grabbed the hair on his head and dragged him around the room. She pulled at his hair and he commiserated with her tears, and her effort; if she pulled hard enough, she could tear the hair out of his head and read from the roots, his mind; and she would know the mystery of her little boy's repeated disappearances, the flights which he yearned to explain, if only he knew. He knew his mother suffered terribly, and he would have comforted her if he could. But he was, he remembered, baffled by more than her suffering. The policeman who had found him wandering late at night near the beer breweries had asked him his name and address. He told the policeman his name, and the name of his street, and declared that he was almost seven years old. The policeman said, "Your mother gave me this." The policeman crouched down and showed Isaac a photograph of a little boy wearing a conical hat topped by a fuzzy berry. The little boy in the funny hat and puffy sweater sat on a forlorn pony, the pony was as hairy as a dog, and the boy's face was a smear of rapture that Isaac found unsettling. The policeman said, "See, this is you." Isaac said, "OK."

And Isaac marveled at how he came to rest, here, in the wheezing coach rolling down a great avenue, next to her, smiling at him. Stunned, in the presence of such beauty, which would have to be expendable to be human, Isaac found himself suddenly in happy collusion with God's antinomies. His cock was at rest, under the books, dozing on his thigh. Beyond Laura, facing him, Isaac glimpsed a plain, stout woman seated with a little girl of about six or seven. Isaac imagined that for some brief span of time someone must have desired this woman. The woman fondled various brand-new acquisitions lying in her lap: a plastic gold-flecked soap dish, a glass flower vase in the shape of a rabbit, and the butterfly barrettes she had purchased for her little daughter sitting next to her, smiling. For a moment Isaac thought that even if the woman on the bus was the world at large in all of its prejudices, he could find a way to love her. In Laura's presence he could believe such things. Laura reached up to pull the cord and signal their stop. Isaac heard the buzzing. Laura said, "We've gone a couple of blocks past our stop." Isaac said, "Oh," and saw the passengers on the bus in a blur as he rose, bundling the books in his arms. Laura took the two most cumbersome paperback volumes, which had split Isaac's jacket pockets so that they were half-gone and lay like elephant ears at his hips. The passengers on the bus said in chorus, "Good luck, good luck," and Isaac blushed and said, "Thank you." The bus driver, whom Isaac hadn't taken any notice of at all, said in a sweet voice at Isaac's back, "Congratulations," as Isaac and Laura stepped down, getting off the bus. Isaac turned to say thanks, but the bus was already pulling away from the curb.

The silver sky took on a sun-suffused blue. They crossed the street and turned a corner. The flock of pigeons that had accompanied them for two blocks, wheeling overhead in the strip of cloud between rooftops, ascended, shrank, and scattered, exclamatory specks threading through the white coil of cloud, pursued by the howls of the boys in the street below, playing punchball. The kids in the street dodged traffic and chased the pink ball that bounced off the roof of a slow moving car. The players' screams echoed up in the canyon of street.

The driver of the car, and the driver of the moving van directly behind the car, craned their dazed, apoplectic faces out of the driver's side windows, honked their horns, and cursed the kids. The boy who had punched the line drive ran from the steaming manhole cover, speeding over the black gutter and up on to the pavement, landing and riding, teetering on first base, a garbage can lid screeching over the sidewalk for a two-yard ride, and then the runner, finding his footing, leapt and ran back across the gutter, threading between the car and truck toward the hunk of linoleum that was second base, as the shortstop behind the car caught the ball bouncing off the fender of the car and rifled it too late to the first baseman, who was chasing first base as it rolled, clattering down the street. Isaac and Laura cheered the punchball players. Neither the players nor the traffic stopped, the vehicles moving at a stately pace, the drivers honking their horns and cursing, and the ball players, running, darting, realigning their positions.

On the opposite pavement, two very young boys harnessed with clotheslines pulled a black lacquered baby carriage, grand as a Spanish galleon, loaded with a bounty of stray cats and empty milk bottles. The canopy of the carriage was gone, the wind played something atonal in the necks of the bottles, the cargo of cats meowed, and Isaac, assaying the light playing off the clinking and fluting milk bottles, wondered if his week of cleaning his apartment was sufficient. He had also painted the apartment off-white, and he had placed candles and flowers everywhere, and purchased a madras bedspread for his mattress on the floor.

The next hitter stepped up to home plate, the steam rising from the manhole cover curling about the hitter's knees. The hitter threw the ball up, as a tennis player would toss a tennis ball up, positioning himself for a powerful serve. The hitter swung overhand, his right arm arching above his head, bringing his fist to the ball in the instant the ball dropped in the air, launching the pink Spaulding off his knuckles up and up. The ball sailed a parabola between rooftops, spinning beneath a long white cloud, and descended into the network of fire escapes jutting out of the factory building on the street opposite where Laura and Isaac walked. The ball fell and bounced down the ladders and cages, suspended between heaven and earth. Below on the pavement the left fielder danced, circled, his face parallel with the sky, his mouth gaping, sucking air, he studied devoutly the floating, bouncing descent of the ball.

If the ball hit the street before the left fielder could catch it, and bounced off the pavement once, it was a single; if it bounced twice, a double, three times a triple, and four times a scored run. The traffic stopped. The punchball players were still watching. The left fielder moved, his arms stroking the air as though he were swimming under water, beneath the shadow of the fire escapes and ladders, funneling up, up, his scrutiny of the ball returning to earth, wrapt. The ball, two stories up, bounced and hung in the air. The two little boys harnessed with clotheslines and hauling the baby coach loaded with cats and empty, tinkling milk bottles, trudged past the left fielder, floating in the dense shadow. Across the street Laura and Isaac continued to walk, watching the sky. Isaac had taken off the belt holding up his pants, and as he walked the fluid motion of his legs conspired with heaven's gravity to hold up his pants. He'd used his belt to bundle the books he carried dangling over one shoulder, and with his other hand grasped Laura's hand as she led him toward his building, although she'd never been there.

The left fielder sank into an obeisant posture, arms extended, palms up, as the ball's descending trajectory accelerated, his knees hammered the pavement, and the ball found his upturned hands.

The stoop was not littered with inhabitants. One old man, bent and overdressed for the mild day in a gray topcoat and wearing an ancient black derby hat, felt his way with a cane down the stoop steps. The old man's eyes could not be seen under his puffed, hooded lids, and the rest of the face was a collapsed blur of flesh, returning to the formlessness of its earliest life. As Laura and Isaac passed the old man, he began to rise, straightening his bent back, eyes emerged in the face, and with the hand not grasping the cane, he reached into his coat pocket and put a set of dazzling teeth in his mouth, smiled at Laura, and tipped his hat, making his way down the remaining three steps with a deliberate, upright posture. Laura smiled and said, "Good afternoon."

The dim hallway and the three steep flights of stairs leading up to Isaac's apartment were as quiet as in some predawn hour. Isaac, grateful and surprised, felt that his week-long labor of scrubbing and painting the apartment had in some way contributed to the making of the silence, and now that quiet seemed to have extended itself. The hallway's scent of paprika and garlic was not unpleasant. All the way up Isaac followed Laura. By the time they had reached the second double-tiered flight of stairs, Isaac had forgotten the old man who had furnished the gaping hole of his mouth with teeth to smile at Laura.

They reached the third-floor landing and stood, leaning on the banister, breathing hard. Isaac pointed at his door.

He fumbled with the key, turning it in the lock, and forced the door with his shoulder.

The apartment had the stark good cheer of a monk's cell. The flowers on the table and window sill had the introverted beauty of cave-dwelling things. Isaac moved to each of the four orange-crate bookcases and lit the long white candles he'd placed there. Startled, he looked around his apartment, and helped Laura take off her jacket. He offered her a chair.

They sat, side by side, in the straight-backed kitchen chairs. The ceiling caught the light trickling in from a scratch at the top of the window. Isaac had been able to scrub away many, but not all the layers of grime. The magnified reflection, the size and shape of a bed pillow rolled across the bellied-out ceiling, as though kicked by the footfalls of the children running across the floor overhead. Laura laughed into her cupped hands. Isaac stifled his laughter as one might repress a sneeze, his ears ringing, most of the silence preserved, he sat and trembled. He remembered that he had wine, cheese, and fruit in the refrigerator, but was not that moment able to get up on his feet or speak. Laura Providencia was sitting next to him. He looked at her, saw her. She was there. The sweet orderliness, the speckled candlelight, the crepuscular blue of the air made of the railroad flat an abode Isaac recalled as a longing, something unattainable, a place where he had wanted to live, always, desired so that he could barely keep it in memory.

He would not remember who had initiated touching. He assumed it must have been Laura. He hadn't been able to move except for the trembling feeling, which he hoped wasn't a spectacle. He recollected the first touching and tumbling into the tangled struggle of disrobing each other. Each solicitous, helpful stumbling. Then when he saw her naked, he was struck dumb and might have remained in paralyzed worship, but she handled him, and he became aware that she was trembling too, and then all at once there was the reprieve from all that entered through the eyes, and they rode the dark and it rode them, and when they saw again they were on the floor under the kitchen table and they had only overturned one kitchen chair. Emerging in the air they lay still for a bit and breathed, breathing was lovely. Without speaking, moved by the nascent telepathic capacity that moved their bodies, they lumbered across the floor on all fours toward the mattress on the floor in the further room, the mattress draped in the madras coverlet of red and green arabesques appeared as inviting as a lush garden, fortuitous, and sprang to life that moment for them.

The candles were half-gone, the small dish of light each provided taking on the preeminence of glowing planets in the dark. The deep blue of the window rippled with the shadows of humming traffic, the sound a little more audible than their breathing; the cars moved beyond, on the overarching Williamsburg Bridge, unseen except for the streams of head-lights scattering like meteor showers, gleaming and gone against the blue black glass of the window.

Naked, Isaac stretched out, kicked the walnut shells off the periphery of their little island. Laura had made a small mound of apple and pear cores near the pillow where her head rested. When Isaac reached from the mattress to the floor for the bottle of wine, she said, really it was time for her to go, and that he needn't accompany her home. Her voice sounded sweet, and to his ear, furtive. He didn't know and didn't calculate how many times they had made love, but as he turned to her again it seemed to him wrong to stop; it would declare its own surcease when the time came. To stop now, to exercise such will would be a blasphemy. But, she said, it was dark, her mother was waiting, she had to go really, she'd see him later. He heard a reluctance to go back to the far place they had been and felt a grief so deep and pervasive he lay like a statue. She spoke to him as though he were a child, reassuring him that indeed Christmas would come again. He felt alternately rage and sadness, so complete he knew nothing at all and lay like a stone; that was when, for the first time, she told him about Sal and his Packard that was really a Buick. She left hours later, they didn't make love again that night, and aching for her and it, he was nevertheless taken deeply enough by her story to wonder about its possible meanings well past the years of his climacteric.

A police siren wailed in the street. She tickled his stomach. She whispered in his ear, "Muchacho, I took your cherry," and laughed. Her voice was balm. The void in his gut filled with laughter. Her hand rested on his stomach. Never had he been moved from despair to joy with such rapidity, and to orient himself he listened very closely, in the dark, to her every word.

He thought maybe she had been moved to confess how she had lost her virginity, or perhaps the need wasn't so much to tell him, as to tell him and study his reaction to what he'd been told. "Sal D'Blasio," she said. *Kiss Of Death*, she said, "did you see it?" "Sure," he said, "it's an old movie, I saw it on television, years ago." "Well, Sal D'Blasio looked like Victor Mature." "Really?" "Really, he was very handsome. My cousin Elena who saw him first said, you should see him, this Italian guy, muy guapo, he looks just like Victor Machuga, I think maybe he's a gangster too."

Isaac, half-sitting, his raised head resting in the palm of his hand, his right elbow propped on a pillow, hoped that his face remained neutral as Laura spoke of handsome Sal D'Blasio. He wasn't sure what the story meant, but he felt that he was being tested. His face was close to Laura's face. He hoped that if his face showed anything, it was only sympathy and interest. Laura paused, studied him, a splash of light from the window made his nose iridescent and his eyes hot coals. She laughed, patted his hand, and said that her cousin Elena had been right, and it was true, Sal D'Blasio was movie-star handsome; but Laura said, engaging Isaac's eyes, "Not all that smart."

Isaac started to ask, and she anticipated his question. It wasn't, Laura explained, that Sal was stupid. Sal, she said, wore a weary look, as if he knew something dark and bitter; and was wise because he knew the most terrible something about human beings that most human beings couldn't know, because they couldn't bear it. Laura said from the very beginning, even before he chauffeured her in the great car, she suspected that his acceptance of the most terrible things human beings were capable of was the result of his participation in much of the worst. She saw, she said, when she found herself closer to him than she had ever wanted to be.

Isaac said, "Wait, when? when was this?" Laura, momentarily stumped, searched the dark room and the aureole of light blooming around each candle flame, "Oh," she said, and laughed, "oh, I was a sophomore at Music and Art High School."

She clasped Isaac's knee, looked at him expectantly. The good will of his open-mouthed bafflement made her laugh. She put her fingers over his lips. He closed his mouth. He could barely keep himself from asking, not why, but what had happened.

She admitted she had been excited. She'd said, "I admit..." Isaac was tempted to say, I absolve you, but couldn't bring himself to risk joking.

Heavy footsteps thumped across the ceiling from the apartment overhead and made the candle flames squat.

She said she couldn't sort out whether it was the danger, or Sal's conceit, the mask of melancholy pride he wore as expertly as his expensively tailored clothes. "All of that had something to do with it. I was attracted," she said, "Oh yes, definitely."

She said it was the car she noticed first, the grand gleaming thing with white tires made her stop and look. No one was in the car. On her way to school she stopped and stood still, clutching her books. Usually she avoided this street; it was an Italian block, with the exception of one building on the corner infiltrated by Puerto Ricans, some her second or third cousins. There had been some serious fights with the Italians. A number of the Italian families began to move to Queens and New Jersey, but Laura's subway station was also on the street, and she descended early in the morning and climbed up in the early evening, after her day at Music and Art High School. Walking seven blocks out of her way to the next subway station would have reminded her with each passing street, and at the day's end when she was tired, how, and how much she had capitulated to fear. Seven long blocks to avoid this street would be a humiliation. She couldn't go out of her way and she would use the most convenient subway stop.

There was a large man in a belted camelhair overcoat, and a slouch hat the same color as the coat, in a telephone booth near the curb, a short distance from the parked car. The man's back was turned to her. His shoulders filled the breadth of the booth, he could not have closed the folding door of the booth. At the time she hadn't realized she'd seen him, it was only later that she remembered, or thought she remembered, when she knew Sal received his orders from this telephone booth, on this street, the car and the telephone booth his outpost.

She stood balancing the textbooks in her arms and felt a

vague guilt looking at the car. She had seen the great car, unoc-
cupied, before, and had been a party to appropriating it. She
and her cousins, Elena and Papo, and Aunt Lydia and her mother
and Uncle Toto, before he dreamed he'd ever own an automobile, took a photo of the family in front of the car as if it were
theirs; they were all dressed up. It was Easter. The street was
deserted. Uncle Toto hurriedly arranged the family members
around the car for the photograph and placed Laura's hand on
the car door's handle, as though she were about to enter, and
Uncle Toto said, worshipfully, "Un Packard." Laura learned later
that all large prestigious automobiles were called "Packards,"
Pontiacs, Cadillacs, and Buicks were "Packards."

"This Packard," Sal would inform her that day in autumn,
when they first spoke, and Laura didn't know what else to say,
and so she made some complimentary statement about the car,
referring to it as a "Packard" in her still Spanish-accented English. "This Packard," Sal said, "is a customized Buick."

Sal waved for her to come closer. Laura approached the car,
clasping the large text of Jansen's *History of Art* across her bosom. Sal leaned out of the car window and said, "I don't bite."

Isaac thought, Sal D'Blasio said, "I don't bite." Laura told it.
Isaac saw the street vividly, saw Laura, as she described herself,
coming closer to the curb, slowly, clutching her textbooks as
shields, as she did on crowded subway trains, covering her bosom and abdomen, and, she said, she was frightened. Handsome Sal sat behind the wheel, smiling, waiting; and "yes" Laura
said, as she passed the palm of her hand over Isaac's forehead as
a mother might feel a child's brow for fever, and yes, she conceded years later in an argument with herself, at that distance
there was also the glamour of terrible knowledge.

Laura hesitated a short distance from the car. Sal leaned

out of the window on the driver's side, stared at Laura, and surprised by his surprise, said, "I ain't the big bad wolf you know, I may be, all right, yeah, worser." He laughed the high-pitched laughter of a child. He glanced up and down the street, he patted his forehead with a white handkerchief, and his face composed itself again into impregnable handsomeness. Now his voice was deep, sure, melodic; it was his prerogative to coax reason since anything he wanted was reasonable, because he wanted it. "No," he said, "I ain't the big bad wolf," and he leaned over and opened the door on the passenger side next to him, and said, "get in, I'll drive you to school, kid."

Laura got into the car and sat next to him as though it were foreordained. She didn't have to think about it. This part of whatever would happen was not her responsibility.

She had the feeling, she told Isaac, that Sal's surprised declaration that he was worse than the big bad wolf, was a bit of intelligence distilled from the stories he knew he'd never be able to tell anyone, not even a priest, and the bile of that oblivion had begun to jaundice and puff little pockets of flesh under his eyes.

Laura's eyes adjusted to the dark. If Sal was opaque, needing the abstraction of darkness, Isaac was transparent in his naked nakedness, fathomless in a light more trackless than the dark, and she found herself leery, and sometimes irritated by his stumbling. She knew, although she questioned the use of the knowledge, she knew and couldn't help gleaning parts of Isaac's waking dreams from the sound of his breathing. "All right," she said, "of course, sure; Little Red Riding Hood, a.k.a. Little Red Cap. Please Isaac pass the wine."

Isaac reached from the mattress to the floor for the bottle and Laura leaned over him, her breasts sweeping his side; she reached, and drank straight from the bottle. She handed him the bottle. Isaac swallowed, still seeing Laura drinking from the bottle, which was now in his trembling hand, and he wondered how even Laura's drinking from the bottle had appeared graceful. His hand shook and he spilled some of the burgundy on his stomach and thighs.

Isaac removed the pillowcase from the pillow behind his head, and used it to wipe the red wine from his stomach and thighs; he dabbed at the red that had trickled into his pubic hair. Laura stared at his red-drenched thighs and laughed. She gave him a loud, wet kiss on the cheek.

He'd started to say, "Little Red Riding Hood, also known as Little Red Cap," paused and lowered his voice, which seemed enormous to him in the visible dark. "Little Red Cap was carrying wine and cakes through the woods for grandma." "All right," Laura said, with a patience that clearly required effort, but she was still patient; "Little Red Riding Hood was carrying wine and cakes through the woods for grandma, and she didn't know enough to be afraid. Finally, she was instructed by fear; I was afraid to begin with, and it didn't change a thing."

"Yes," Isaac said, "and the wolf ate her, and grandma, and when the hunter came, he didn't shoot the creature, but cut the wolf open with shears, and Little Red Riding Hood and Grandma popped out, and Little Red Riding Hood said it had been dark inside the wolf, and she and Grandma finished the beast off by filling his emptied gut with stones."

"Well, yes, yes," Laura said, "I know, but Sal D'Blasio drove me all the way up Convent Avenue, parked the car, got out, and opened the door for me; and he stared at the school as though it were the dark kingdom. He said, 'I heard of this place, it's infested with communists.'

"I laughed at Sal D'Blasio. He was shocked. I watched his angry face change quickly to forbearance, but not so quickly that I wasn't awed by the show. He'd concluded, I suppose, that my ignorance made me a danger to myself, and that my ignorance was an aspect of my virginity. Sal thought, I should for a time, at least, be granted some kind of dispensation."

Isaac listened in a silence that opened a chamber of space within him that he could not have dreamed into existence. He listened and saw, at the vanishing point of the converging lines of the distant perspective, that autumn, the flagrant beauty of dying leaves in the park Laura walked through as she went from Sal's car, passing through the park to the school; and he smelled the acute autumn air she breathed, inflaming what she knew beyond doubt was forbidden. The exhilaration of the dalliance with downfall and shame was only a part of it, although the shame her mother would feel, and her mother and Titi's concomitant sense of damning failure was a nearly obliterating pain; but she, Laura Providencia, had to walk and move in a life that was her own, and maybe the oblivion of shame was the first entrance she must transgress.

For nearly all of the autumn Sal D'Blasio drove her to Music and Art High School. In the streets of the neighborhood, where despite certain governing and obligatory silences, nothing remained hidden, Laura felt that the audacity of her entering into Sal's car had rendered her invisible; no one who knew her, who saw it, would believe what they saw.

She was never late for school, and through all of September he never touched her. He drove. She sat next to him. Most of the time he was silent. One morning he turned the car radio on to an FM station and classical music. She asked him if he liked that kind of music. He said no, but it was important that she improve herself. She almost smiled, but said nothing, sensing a wound in him so deep and beyond healing that to receive his offer with any expressed irony would have required a capacity for cruelty she could only imagine. But about a week later, when he turned the car radio on to the FM station with classical music as he drove and ignored the red lights, Laura having been slow to get herself started that morning, and Sal was determined to get her to school on time, again he spoke of self-improvement, the importance of education, and he said Laura should go to college. "See," he said, pounding the car horn as a pedestrian scrambled out of the path of the speeding car, "see," Sal said, and laughed, "'cause if you married me, I'd pull down all the venetian blinds on the windows and take away your shoes." She said, "I'd never marry you!" "Oh yeah," he said, "I could make you do all kinds of things you think you don't wanna do."

Twice in late September, and once in October in early morning, as she moved beyond the last of sleep and she approached the car clasping her textbooks and sketchpad, she blundered into the tail end of what appeared to be serious conferences. The fragments of the negotiations she overheard in the startling early morning light struck her as the wishes proffered in the scariest of fairy tales by goblins and witches whose pedagogy was not benign, infatuating wishes that were disguised warnings, the terminal cautions before the abyss of pain and remorse, forever.

Sal D'Blasio sat behind the wheel of the parked car as on a throne, the tawny yellow of his camelhair coat mantled about his shoulders. The window was down and he dispensed advice to the young man who stood at the curb. As Laura came closer, she saw the look of perplexity on Sal's face and Sal's large, square hand swooning in the air, the gleaming, manicured fingertips of the forefinger and pinkie-ringed pinkie, pinnacled above the knuckles of the middling closed fingers, the spired forefinger and pinkie swooping up, and languishing down, indicating the infinite, below. The effeminate movement of Sal's robust, hairy hand astonished Laura always, and the look on Sal's face that pleaded, don't make me do it, look what you're going to make me do, chastened the young man at the curb. The young man stood there, apologizing, understanding that he bore the brunt of causing Sal to commit an act that could damn Sal to one of the deeper regions of hell. The words Laura caught as she came closer to the car concerned the efficacy of seeing-eye dogs, and the young man, head bowed, studied the pavement and relinquished his vision to try on a dumb, blind look as an object lesson.

Sal looked up and saw Laura. "Get in the car," he said, "you're gonna be late for school," and to the young man, "Do me a favor, Tomaso, run across the street to Lena's candy store and get the kid here, a light coffee, three sugars, and a sweet roll — three sugars right?" Sal asked, turning to Laura. She nodded. Sal said, "Please hurry, Tomaso, and thanks."

The morning in October Laura found herself standing in the drizzling rain at the curb covering her head with her *Elements of Biology* text, Sal sat in his vehicle, sunk so deep in disbelief that Laura's presence was as incomprehensible as what he had just heard from the lovely and theatrically defiant Anita Palmisano. Laura looked at the beautiful young Italian woman who had achieved notable celebrity in the neighborhood as the winner of several beauty contests and was now appearing as Juliet in an off-off Broadway production of *Romeo and Juliet*. Laura said, "Good morning," and sneezed. Anita, soaked to the skin, said good morning to Laura as though granting the favor of a brief audience, and handed Laura a handkerchief. Laura recognized Anita from a photo in the newspaper, and a giant full-faced photograph in the window of the shoe repair shop Laura passed each day on this street on the way to Sal and the Buick. Laura was certain that she had once passed Anita Palmisano on the steps in the apartment house on the corner, where Laura's cousin Paco lived. It was Anita's mother, Maria Palmisano, a widow, who owned the building where Laura's relatives lived, and it was Mrs. Palmisano who had rented to the Puerto Rican families in defiance of the wishes of Sal D'Blasio and his overseeing colleagues, and of the more remote authority which could not concern itself with this level of detail.

Sal lamented, "Oh Anita." He didn't look at her, but stared at the patterns of rain dripping down the windshield. He mourned what he hoped was not the irrevocable loss of circumspection. Gravely he turned his face to Anita Palmisano, "You," he said, "should think what you're doing, use your head. You wanna be an actress, make a living with your face, and you open a big mouth to me! Are you a crazy person?" Then all at once he saw Laura. "Jesus! What are you doin', standin' in the rain?" Laura went around to the passenger side and got in. The car lurched, screeching away from the curb. Laura thrust out her hands against the dashboard to keep her head from colliding with the windshield.

The rain poured. Sal drove. The avenue dribbled and swelled, awash against the windshield, the wipers clicking back and forth, providing brief glimpses of a recognizable thoroughfare. Sal didn't speak. Laura didn't recognize the part of the city they drove through. If they were on the way to school this was a route she couldn't make sense of. She said, "Sal," and he didn't answer.

Finally he slowed the car down as they approached a red light. Laura understood that Sal had not suddenly recognized the authority of traffic lights, and he hadn't recovered from Anita Palmisano's defiance. There were, evidently, forms of reckless unreason in the world for which there was no remedy. Sal guided the car into the desolate street. He stared ahead, contemplating the folly of unreason. Laura looked out the side window through sheets of rain the color of sewer water. The street glided by. The dark, falling water appeared to melt the buildings piled above the pavement.

Sal pulled the car to the curb. Slowly the moving street came to rest. The dark holes of windows in the deserted factory sucked in the rain. Next to the abandoned factory was a burnt-down tenement; one wall completely collapsed, exposed a bathroom three stories up, the bathtub, and white toilet bowl suspended in the wet murk of air, above a wraith of smoke upon which a pigeon perched, tucking its head beneath a wing. Next to the factory another tenement leaned out towards the curb, the gray, fossilized bricks oozing dirty water, one elderly inhabitant becoming extinct in a rain-shrouded window.

Laura decided that she didn't want to go to school that day anyway. What she would like, what she longed for, was to see the Flemish paintings again at the Metropolitan, to revel in that light, and to see again Cezanne's baffling dominion over the color blue. She tried the car door handle. The door was locked. She pressed against the door. "Sal," she said, "please, let me out. Sal, please?" She knew there was a button somewhere under the dashboard near the steering wheel, or perhaps under the driver's seat that would open the door. "Sal, I want to go, I'll take the subway, open the door, please."

"What?" Sal glanced at the street. "It's pouring rain," he said,

the rising inflection of his voice in the vicinity of a scream, identifying Laura as another specimen of the irrationality that would
doom the human race. "Let me out!" "What?" Sal's face went
from incredulity to a tolerance that was saintly. "Do me a favor,
will you?" "What favor?" He reached under the driver's seat and
removed an oxblood-colored briefcase. The odor of the leather
was rich. He zipped the briefcase open, placed it on his lap, and
removed the white towel. "You're soakin' wet, drippin'. Wipe
yourself for god's sake. You trying to catch pneumonia?"

Laura wiped her hair and rubbed the back of her neck with
the towel. She tried not to stare at the open briefcase on Sal's lap.

In the briefcase, from which Sal had whisked the snow-white
towel, was a handkerchief, a notebook, a handgun, and a paperback book with a glossy cover depicting an iridescent star-laden
heaven.

Sal took out the math book and the small notebook, zipped
the briefcase closed, and put it back under the seat. From under
the same seat he removed a small laundry bag with drawstrings
at its neck. "Put the damp towel in here," he said.

Neatly, Sal folded the laundry bag with the damp towel in
it, and placed it under the seat. "Look at this," he said, handing
Laura the book, "look at this."

The title of the book, *Mathematical Mysteries*, was rendered
as a celestial light falling from a black hole in space. "It calms
me," he said. Laura sat with *Mathematical Mysteries* on her lap.
Sal pressed the opened notebook into her hand. The rain
drummed on the roof of the car. She brought the notebook
close to her face; the page was dense with Sal D'Blasio's equa-
tions. He was saying something about the etymology of the word
"algebra" and the Arabic root, which referred to the reunion of
broken parts.

Laura burrowed into the appearance of close study of the page. She might have been deciphering the codex from the cave wall of the first human heart's utterance. The letters and numbers swam before her eyes. She squinted her face into a mask of observing, hoping that her fear, which had become repugnance of him, wasn't evident. She nodded as though she were really listening, and he went on and on about how certain mathematical formulas revealed secret and unheard of relationships, the shape of some fundamental plot of the universe, and it was "therapy for him," he said, "good for his nerves, better than love even — which makes you worry in the long run — and all that worry makes some people think they're good, but they're only worried."

The effort was too much. She couldn't go on, and then she hated her concern for his fragile dignity. She turned and let him see her face.

He flinched and held his breath, tried to remain stoic. The blood in his face fled to his brain. He turned the color of marble.

She wanted to say "I'm sorry." She remembered that only a week ago, as Sal was driving her to school, he mentioned seeing her cousin Elena walking on the street. "Mama mia, what a body," he'd exclaimed. Laura had felt heartsore all that day. She couldn't bear the thought of his touching her, and still she wanted him to desire her only. It was very confusing, as when she had walked past the marquee of the Loew's movie theatre. The glowing red letters on the marquee read, *Samson & Delilah.* A cool breeze and a candyish scent wafted from the lobby of the theatre. There were life-size posters of the actor Victor Mature, shorn of gangster raiment for the role of Samson, wearing only a diaper, the hulk of his glistening body straining as he pushed apart the pillars upon which the Temple of Dagon the agricultural God rested. The face of the actor, impersonating blind adoration, was Sal's face. In spite of herself she was thrilled and embarrassed. She had told herself that she was too smart for these feelings, and yet she was fearful of losing this susceptibility, as she would be of becoming afflicted with color blindness and losing the sight of a primary color.

But now she needed to go to the Metropolitan, to see the Rembrandt, Vermeer, and she needed to travel there alone. She couldn't allow Sal to drive her to the museum. Her anticipation of what she would see was part of her seeing, an extension of the composition and color before and after she stood before the paintings; her thinking and dreaming extending the presence of her vision, like time itself, every which way as intimate and more profound than touch, and she could not have Sal be any part of it.

She said, "Please." He said, "Say it like you mean it." She said, "I mean it." "You," he said, "have to learn to be patient," and he put his arm around her shoulder; she froze, his knuckles brushed the side of her breast. Immediately he removed his arm and moved away. He said, "Excuse me." She said nothing, knowing that her status as a virgin made something in him hesitate. "Partly that was an accident," he said. "If I want to really touch you, it won't be no accident." "Can I go?" "Like I said, you have to be patient."

The rain continued. He got out of the car, bent over and said, "You promised to wait." Laura didn't remember promising. "How long?" "Something I gotta do, as long as it takes."

He walked off. Laura noted that he hadn't locked the doors of the car.

He was gone for about a half-hour. First she felt like she had to pee, and then that went away.

Laura thought of Ruthie Berkowitz in school. Ruthie was trying to become her friend. In the school cafeteria, one day, Ruthie had asked Laura if she had a boyfriend. Laura found herself saying, "Oh yes, his name is Sal, he doesn't go to this school." "Where," Ruthie asked, "does he go?" Laura said, "Oh, he's a little older, he works," and later at home, when she was listening to music on the radio, she wondered if she had spoken the truth to Ruthie Berkowitz. Maybe Sal D'Blasio really was her boyfriend.

Laura thought of leaving, of just getting out of the car and walking away. Then she would have to avoid the street she walked through each early morning, where Sal was parked, waiting. And she recalled how his face had gone from marble-white to the waxy-white resembling a mortician's art, and then his face was alive and itself again, and he was smiling.

He was smiling now as he opened the car door, the rim of his slouch hat beaded with rain. He bent at the waist in the most courtly manner, his face claiming that everything that had happened was part of a plan he had, an exercise to nourish some aspect of his being that he couldn't begin to explain to her. He smiled, and his smile was as broad and winning as the actor he resembled, preparing for a swashbuckling role, some rogue that God himself could not help loving. "Here," he said, "is the umbrella. I'm sorry the only color the store had was black. Do you have subway fare?" He pressed money into her hand. "The subway's three blocks from here, turn left at the corner. You'll have to change trains at 59th Street for uptown."

Laura walked sheltered under the broad black umbrella. The muffled cantillation of the rain thumping on the tent-like roof above her, aiding the sense that she carried within her her own portable refuge. The fashionable coat she wore, her mother

had made from the sketch Laura provided. The coat was snug
and warm. She walked down the seeping wreckage of the street
and held the umbrella over her head. Sal followed, driving very
slowly, a little behind her and parallel with the curb. He surveyed the street. She walked, canopied under the great black
umbrella, and he followed in the glistening car, gliding in the
surf of gutter water all the way to the steps of the subway entrance.

That was Friday. On Monday morning Laura woke, shuffled
to the kitchen, and heated some milk in a saucepan on the gas
range for Rosita. Rosita sat at the table and complained that
there was skin in the milk. Laura began to cry. She wiped her
eyes with the sleeve of her bathrobe and looked out the kitchen
window. The October sky promised winter, and testified that
Brueghel had gotten it right; the magnificent sky vindicating
the sixteenth century painter's art brought more tears to Laura's
eyes. Rosita hurried past her sister, out of the kitchen, and called,
"Mami, Titi."

Laura realized that everything was making her weep,
laughed, and wept some more. She wiped her eyes and nose
with a dishtowel. She remembered that when she had stepped
out of Sal's car, and he had held the opened umbrella over her
head, and then handed her the umbrella, she'd left her schoolbooks behind.

She looked at the membrane of burnt milk in the saucepan
and hiccupped. Sobs pummeled her chest. She put her hands
on her hips and recalled that she'd taken her sketchpad and the
small box of charcoal; but she couldn't carry the textbooks, box
of charcoal, sketchpad and the umbrella, and so she had left her
books on the back seat of Sal D'Blasio's car.

The fact of her books lying in Sal's car made her cry. The
thought of it depressed her even as she reasoned that she hadn't

needed to study for a test, and she wasn't behind in her home-work.

Puzzled, she blew her nose into the dishtowel. Finally all she could figure out was that she was uneasy about what mean-ing might accrue to her leaving her books in Sal's car, not the meaning that might grow in his mind, but wherever it is that meaning is first made.

Her mother, Titi, and Rosita crowded into the kitchen. Señora Milagros put her lips to Laura's forehead. She held her daughter still for the space of a half-minute, her lips pressed against the center of Laura's forehead. Señora Milagros stepped back, and with her fingers pried the lids of Laura's eyes wider, and asked Laura to move her eyes. Laura moved her eyes, avoid-ing a direct gaze into her mother's eyes, fearful of what knowl-edge was accumulating in her mother's heavy breathing reti-cence. Her mother announced to Titi, who was crouched be-neath her, Titi's ear pressed to Laura's stomach, that Laura didn't have a fever. Titi, with her eyes closed, kept her ear to Laura's stomach and listened closely to the rhythm of things flowing in her niece's stomach. Laura's mother asked Laura to stick out her tongue. Titi rose out of her crouching position and she and Señora Milagros took turns examining Laura's tongue.

They concurred — Laura had her period — and as Titi prepared a large quantity of the special tea, which she laced generously with paregoric, Laura felt the first of the cramps and her blood began to flow.

Her mother and Titi hurried. They were both working the same shift in the factory that day. Titi would first accompany Rosita to school.

But before they left they prepared Laura's bed with fresh sheets, blankets, and extra pillows. Laura drank a full glass of the tea. She lay in bed, her body wrapped in the blankets, a poultice fragrant as a rain forest damp against her forehead, and bound about her head by a strip of satin. Titi rubbed her stomach gently in circular motions and chanted softly, "Sane que sane, culito de rana." Señora Milagros moved from one side of the bed to the other, crouched, and blew a cool stream of breath against Laura's temples.

She was not aware of their departure. Still, lying there, alone in the apartment, she felt the drops from the sweet-scented poultice drip over her eyelids. Her mother's cooling breath lingered about her temples, and the shadow of Titi's hand continued its circular caress of her stomach. On the nightstand next to the bed was a pitcher of the special tea and a glass. Laura could, as needed, sip and feed her sleep. On the floor, next to the bed, within arm's reach, was the bedpan.

When she awoke from the interval that was not quite sleeping, she realized that the white-humped arches she had been staring at were neither the backsides of laboring pack animals, nor the mountains they climbed. Laura looked at the pile of upside down soup bowls, and the deep dish with the remnants of white rice, and the tiny lake of milk at the center of the plate, and she couldn't remember eating. Slowly she sat up in bed. Titi, wearing her coat and her floral kerchief wrapped around her head and knotted under her chin, brought Laura a cup of coffee. Laura sat in the bed and drank the coffee. "What time is it?" she asked. Titi said, "Miercoles." Laura sipped the coffee and said, "Oh, I've missed two days of school." Titi shrugged. Laura's mother came into the bedroom and exchanged a significant glance with Titi. She was dressed for work and called out to Rosita to button her coat, and she crouched at the side of the bed and retrieved the lidded chamber pot Laura remembered using in a remote past. Señora Milagros rose with the chamber pot in her hands and carried it off to the bathroom, and Laura thought she saw something brewing beneath the far range of her mother's inscrutability.

Laura heard the toilet bowl flush. She heard water running, heard her mother washing out the chamber pot. She wondered what her mother might know.

At the front door, her mother called, "Despues," Titi shrilled, "Cuidado," and Rosita giggled. The door slammed, and quiet rolled back and filled the apartment.

Slowly, Laura got out of bed. Barefoot, she padded to the far corner of the bedroom, and there on the dresser was the clock, whose loud ticking she heard the moment she remembered the instrument's existence. The clock said six-forty. She would have to hurry. On the dresser counter with the clock, hair brush, and jars of ointment, was the studio photograph of the little girl in the white communion dress, kneeling, with her hands clasped in prayer. A corrugated stream of heavenly light fell, upon which three angels squatted. The stream of light supporting the weight of the angels flowed down and burst into an aureole of petaled light about the girl's unctuous face; Laura recognized the child and recoiled, turned her eyes away, and up, and saw the young woman in the dresser mirror who was wearing a white nightgown and progressing slowly as someone rowing a boat against the tide, and the young woman was also herself.

She started for the bathroom, paused at the bedroom door, and looked back into the room where she had been dormant for two days. She wondered whether she had betrayed herself. In her sleep she could not have maintained the vigilance of her secret; perhaps her mother and Titi knew; perhaps they had taken some action.

Under the shower she told herself it was only anxiety, the residue of the sleep that would have to be measured in its useful aspect as simply two days of rest.

Laura dressed. She sat down at the kitchen table and wrote a note, excusing her absence because of illness, and signed her mother's name. She went to the closet, put on her coat, and looked for her books. At the moment when she realized she would be late for school, certainly missing the homeroom taking of attendance, and perhaps arriving after the first class had begun, she remembered that she'd left her books in Sal's car. She picked up her sketch pad and the box of charcoal from the floor of the closet, and promised herself that after school she would restore the closet to order, having ransacked it in the search for her schoolbooks.

The day was not especially cold and the air smelled like winter. The sky was gray and rain seemed imminent. Laura walked down the street, passed the shoe repair shop with Anita Palmisano's picture in the window, and in the distance she could see Sal's car.

As she came closer to the car Laura saw two early morning petitioners, a middle-aged man and his wife, hovering near the car, arguing in whispers; they glanced at Sal, who appeared unaware of their presence as he chewed at his upper lip. The man took two steps in Sal's direction and his wife tugged at his elbow, pulling him back. The man look relieved.

Laura noted that the couple had decided to consult with Sal on another occasion; they turned and walked back into the tenement that was only a few steps from the curb where Sal was parked.

She stood next to the window on the driver's side, and said, "Good morning." He turned and his face didn't reveal any sign that he knew her. "Yeah?" "Good morning Sal." "I can see it's morning." She peered into the car and saw her books piled on the back seat, nestled on the lining of his camelhair coat. His slouch hat rested on the back seat next to the books. The great, imposing bulk of him, formal, barely contained in the shiny blue pinstriped suit, his hand drifted up to compass the exact location of the knot of his white tie. "Those are my books," she said. "You think so girlie? oh wait, yeah, I remember you, you must be Laura Providencia. I thought maybe you went back to Puerto Rico or something. The way you people go hopping back and forth, I don't know what." "Those are my books. I need them for school, Sal. I want my books." "Oh! you askin' me or you telling me?" Laura sighed, "I'm asking you." "Well, at least you learnt somethin'. Get in the car."

Sal maneuvered the car out of the parking space. Laura sat next to him. He looked aggrieved, and for a moment she considered showing him the note she had written for school, explaining that she had been ill. But the absurdity of such a gesture was too much. Sal negotiated the car through the narrow street. Laura turned and started to reach for her books on the back seat. He slammed his foot on the gas, she fell back and bounced against the backrest of the front passenger seat, and her face hit the side window.

She dabbed at the bit of blood on her lip with the hem of her skirt. She couldn't keep her legs from trembling. The car barreled crazily through the streets. The throbbing subsided in her cheek. She was able to make out, from the wobbly reflection in the windshield that she wasn't marked.

She'd almost yelled, I want to go to school, couldn't allow herself to cry anything so childish, and heard herself scream, "You almost hit those people." He thumped the steering wheel with the palms of his hands, beating a conga rhythm counterpointing the pauses in Laura's intake of breath as she screamed, and the car sped through the streets.

Neighborhoods, the garment center, Chinatown, flew by dizzily in the car windows — she closed her eyes. His voice rose, taking on a pedantic air. "I try my best not to do nothing by accident. I can only try, that's human, right?"

She kept her eyes closed as she had when she rode the Cyclone roller coaster in Coney Island, with Angel. At last the car slowed and the queasiness in her stomach subsided, but her legs were still trembling. She decided that she would open her eyes. If she felt sick again, she would close her eyes.

He appeared calmer, light-fingered, he maneuvered the steering wheel.

Slowly they rode past a rubble-strewn lot. In the lot was a hut, wide and low as an igloo. A stovepipe leaned out of a tarpaulin roof. The walls of the structure were made of tin and linoleum and several hexing moons of hubcaps.

An inhabitant crawled out of the hut, unfurled into a standing position, and staggered forward like a man languidly drowning, across the curb into the gutter, nearly hitting the car broadside.

For an instant the man swayed at the window. He wore a woman's coat with a fur collar and a baseball cap. His face seemed made of discarded flesh, the eyes mucousy puddles, possessing, Laura thought, some kind of amphibian sight. The man thrashed backwards and sideways, out of sight. The car had almost hit him. Sal glanced at the side window with a faint look of distaste, unable to recognize a form of life as human that couldn't be threatened. Laura had cried out as the car had almost sideswiped the street drunk. Sal looked confused, wondering what had caused Laura's alarm, and he turned the car around the corner.

They were parked. Through the front windshield she saw two great sand dunes, and beyond, the East River. He was talking. She'd let him talk, finish. Then he'd let her go. The car doors were locked. She couldn't get out, and she couldn't keep her legs from shaking. He was talking about her brother. She didn't want to hear it.

"You know he started out a kind of stand-up kid. He crippled Geronimo Balducci, that's practically a relative of mine. Listen, I don't hold no grudge, don't get me wrong, that's just the way it is, kids rumbling."

She studied the composition. In the foreground, at the base of the two sloping, story-high sand dunes, a row of barrels the color of old pennies, and wheelbarrows, and two long metal troughs, and rising above it all, above the graceful uppermost slopes of the dunes, the skeletal steel frame of a gigantic building, the abstract frame of the towering structure measuring off vast squared vistas of gray sky, the East River, and sea gulls swooping in the framed sky above the river, Brooklyn smoldering across the river on the far horizon.

"No workers here today, nobody, they're on strike. Anyways, like I said, you gotta be realistic, your brother that they put away, he's a punk and a junkie, and all his friends are punks and junkies. That whole bunch didn't last out on the street. They're noddin' out, falling down, in the joint, or on their way to Kentucky to get clean and rehabbed. A waste of taxpayers' money. The ones still in the neighborhood, you think they can look out for you? You gonna look to them? They'll have you peddlin' your ass in the street to support their habit."

A large cloud shaped like a furry cow floated into the framed panorama of sky, the falling shadow of the cow's udder tethered to a tug boat, hauling the tiny vessel across the horizon.

"Look at me when I talk to you!" She looked at him. What he saw made his face awful. First he whined, "I know you think you think things I could never think." Then he ranted, "Princess! superior person! her piss could etch glass and she shits ice cream. You think you're too good for me!"

She wanted to answer, reassure him, say that whatever it was he saw in her face she hadn't meant to offend him, but in spite of the trembling in her legs that had spread to her stomach, she knew she was incapable of apologizing to him; and if her inability to apologize was an offense, it wasn't an offense against him, but perhaps something else, something other, and he was, after all, incidental.

His hand moved to his crotch and rested there. She had seen the gesture before, it wasn't so much sexual as comforting, like patting a baby's back to dispel a burp, the large hand, with the glossy manicured fingernails, the ruby pinkie ring resting there between his legs, and his voice became muted; still angry, he would not be the object of his own rage. His hand lay there, as over a puppy snuggled in his lap, and he said, "Yeah, the body's the temple of the spirit, I believe that. And you think you're so special with your private place where I can't go and there's only you. But I go where I want, and you'll remember me forever. Like Mario Lanza sings, 'Come primo,' that's me, primo, which is first and remains always."

She wanted to say please, please let me go, she even felt willing to try to lie and apologize, but the trembling had moved into her voice, and she thought then of the Pegasus pin she wore on her blouse, at the nape of her throat. She could slip the pin off when he held her close, and she could stab the needle into his eye. But he studied her and said, in the most calm and sensible way, "You think you're gonna fight me physically, resist me. I'm gonna hurt you only a little bit, and what's the fucking tragedy that you ain't gonna bring a virgin pussy to your wedding night? You're hanging out with them communists and Jews at the Music and Art School that'll teach you to live like a whore anyway. Why shouldn't I have it first? We're gonna do it."

"Our Father who art in Heaven, hallowed be thy name, Thy kingdom come, on earth as it is in Heaven —"

She didn't know she would say it, and the words were warped although recognizable, like a record played at the wrong speed, the awful trembling of her voice widening the vibrato, the vowels nearly drowned in her throat, and the prayer spilled like vomit from her mouth; gagging, the words came out, and he said, "Just get the fuck out, OK." He pressed a button, leaned across her, and pushed the door open. "Get the fuck out."

He tossed the books after her, and her pad, and the box of charcoal that spilled all over the street.

Isaac helped her search for her shoe. The candles had burned down to flickering nubs, and Isaac was ready to relent and turn the lights on when he found the shoe on the floor beneath the kitchen sink. She was dressed, ready to leave, and lacked only the shoe. She still insisted on going home alone, but she would allow him to help her find a cab.

Isaac finished dressing, pulled a sweatshirt over his head, and put his shoes on. He took a jar full of coins from a cabinet above the sink and emptied the coins into Laura's purse, "For cab fare," he said. She nodded.

He opened the door of the apartment. They went about

the room and blew out the candles, and moved from the dark of the apartment to the dimness of the hallway.

"That's right," she said to Isaac, answering the question he couldn't bring himself to ask. "Sal didn't," she said. "The prayer came out of me, hypocritical maybe, but it just came out of me, and he didn't touch me. He let me go. There was only that next to last time when I was with him, and his hand brushed the side of my breast and he apologized. And he never taught me to drive either, and he'd promised."

They didn't have to walk very far to find a taxi. Once more he asked if he could ride with her to the Bronx, he'd take the subway back. She insisted again that she ride home alone; she said that she needed that, but she kissed him, held him before getting into the cab, and he had the sense that he was not in the world the same way he had been before they had made love. He walked back to his apartment, tired, oddly at rest, and more at home in the street and the night than ever before. He stopped at the corner bar and had three dime beers before going home to sleep.

A week later in the first hour of dark, they made love standing up against a tree in Central Park.

They had been walking on Fifth Avenue lost in conversation, and wandered into the park. He noticed, interrupted Laura, and questioned the wisdom of walking in the park at night; she said something acknowledging the risk and went on talking. She had been telling him that for a long time, or what felt like a long time, a month or better, she had avoided the street where Sal parked. She walked the circuitous eight blocks to the next subway stop to avoid seeing him. When finally her anger at her humiliation became too much, she determined that she would not go out of her way. Sal might presume to own the street, but she wouldn't inconvenience herself, she'd walk where she pleased and take the subway station closest to home.

The Buick was parked in the usual place. The large photograph of Anita Palmisano's beautiful face, calm and impervious, was still in the window of the shoe repair shop, casting its aura over a portion of the sidewalk. Laura walked past Sal's car and the man she saw presiding at the wheel resembled a cat as much as a human could resemble a cat and remain human. His small wrinkled face with its wisp of mustache looked disdainfully at the world. The middle-aged couple who had been fearful and reluctant to talk to Sal were walking away from the car towards their building, looking tranquil. Laura maintained her pace as she walked by, but couldn't keep herself from staring at the couple and the man who looked like a cat. He looked back from the window of Sal's car, taking Laura in, indifferent; she signified nothing more than any other human stuff making its way down the street. She stopped, turned around, and forced herself to take a few steps in the direction of the car and the nattily dressed catman sitting behind the wheel. "Where," she called, "is Sal?" The man behind the wheel twitched his whiskered upper lip and waved for Laura to come closer. He would not speak if he had to raise his voice. Laura took several steps closer to the car, but kept her distance from the curb. "Sal," she said, "where's Sal D'Blasio?"

The man behind the wheel said, "There ain't no Sal D'Blasio, there's me, Mr. Leonelli, and anyway your home ain't in this street"; and the tips of the fingers of his small hand, half-drowned in the wide, white cuff of his shirtsleeve, wiggled dismissal.

The next day Laura gathered up her nerve, and on her way to the subway stopped in the shoe repair shop and asked Anita Palmisano's uncle where Sal D'Blasio was. The uncle, who clearly understood English, shrugged, and said, "Who?" Laura thought that Mr. Luigi Palmisano, the shoe repair man, looked a lot like Fat, from Fat and Skinny in the movies. Like Oliver Hardy, Mr. Palmisano's round face was cast in blustering exasperation, perpetually about to burst into complaint, but all the man said and repeated when Laura asked about Sal D'Blasio was, "Who?" Looking very much put out, Mr. Palmisano turned his face from Laura and continued pounding with a hammer on the heel of a shoe.

Two days later Laura inquired in the candy store on the far corner next to the subway entrance. The old woman behind the soda fountain smiled and said in Italian that she knew no one by the name of Sal D'Blasio. Laura would have sworn that she heard the old woman purr.

Day after day as Laura walked by the shoe repair shop, past the phone booth, and the Buick parked at the curb, the catman sitting in the car conducting what had been Sal's business, nothing on the street changed, except that Sal's existence seemed annulled.

One Saturday morning, not long after she had made her inquiry in the candy store, Laura, returning from the bodega with a quart of milk, a box of white rice, a small jar of capers, and two pork chops, encountered Ponce de Leon in the lobby of her building. She shifted the bag of groceries in her arms.

Usually, if she could, she avoided Ponce. She had never wanted to hurt his feelings. He continued to bring her, from time to time, gifts, which he had stolen and most of which she refused. He had offered during the past two years, tubes of oil paint, brushes, costume jewelry, perfume, a small portable television set, a vacuum cleaner, and a handful of tiny baby turtles with the Empire State building painted on their shells. Most of the gifts she politely refused. She had taken the paints, brushes, two of the tiny turtles, which she gave to Rosita, and she did take a bottle of Chanel Nº 5, although she asked him to stop offering these gifts since she knew how he got them. But she knew he wouldn't stop.

Ponce, always with the utmost respect, and matter of factly, announced that he loved Laura and accepted that she did not, could not return his feeling. Laura had long ago given up speculating what else Ponce's fidelity to unrequited love might require of him. Laura thought Ponce's anomalous intelligence made of him truly something strange. Thin, smiling, nevertheless mournful looking, Ponce lacking certain warrior's virtues, had become by default, but not entirely without his own true aspiration, chronicler of the Bishops and the street; the housing project's walking talking Homer, knowledgeable, street-wise, a talented shoplifter and thief, responding to various moral dictates of his soul too arcane for him to question. Around Thanksgiving he stole frozen turkeys and hams and dispensed them to families who had become accustomed to receiving the holiday foodstuff. He confessed his love to Laura without hope, or sign of hopelessness, as he confessed that he was one of the two former Bishops (Carlitos being the other, and Carlitos would become a narcotics cop) who had not become a junkie.

On this occasion he apologized for not having a suitable gift, his eyelids at half-mast, swooning, his body and mind re-enacting a junkie's devastation as recompense, and his lack of a gift for Laura made him moan at the juncture of such an uncool fate, "Oh man."

Laura, suddenly full of resolve, and mindful that later she would have to respond to an obligation she had up to the present, avoided, or rationalize the forgiveness of such a debt, would name the gift she wanted. Swaying, stuffed with more information than any one human head should house regarding the life of the street, gangs, and the status of who's who, Ponce couldn't claim not to know, not to have some idea. "What," Laura asked, calmly and clearly, "happened to Sal D'Blasio?" Ponce's half-lidded dark eyes sunk to nearly all white, his knees bent and his upper body tilted backwards, his arms floating like the arms of a shirt buffeted by the wind on a clothesline.

He answered at length. His articulation swooping and sinking, words chasing the noise his mouth made of a car tire's screeching; key nouns were replaced by various sound effects, the sound of a gun firing, feet thudding on the pavement, a woman's stifled cry. He crouched, ape-like, let his arms hang loose, his knuckles swept the floor, and his arms swung up, his hands clamped his ears, then his eyes, then his mouth. Laura thought, the three proverbial monkeys would tell her nothing. Ponce, whispering, conceded a little to the spoken word, "everybody, they don' hear, see, speak no evil, like they don' know nuttin." He didn't say anything more as his body swooned into a death fall, one hand clapping his chest after the impact of the bullet opened his mouth wide in astonished silence. Laura struggled to retrieve meaning from the performance. She knew he didn't lack for words; he was not impoverished of language, but always he was contemporary, his style the up-to-the-minute latest thing, so that his new eloquence employed the sound of the person, place, or thing the noun would have named; many verbs were replaced by the word "like" as an introduction to endless unnamed analogies partially acted out in a pantomime, and partially spoken — "like, like, like," and Laura lost patience and scolded him in Spanish, and asked him to speak plainly.

"Oh," Ponce gasped, "like wow!" The extraordinary request

tripping him up, he answered, confused, not quite sure what was being asked of him, and a little incredulous that his recitation would not suffice to tell what Laura wanted to know. He let his next words fall as inert information, as if he were a recording, an emphatic mechanical pause between each word. "Sal D'Blasio — the guinea — made some kind — ah — mistake — he — gone — it — dint — have — nut-ting — to — do — wit — you."

Laura repeated, "Nothing to do with me?" and Ponce, unable to resist extrapolating, caught in the power of his new narrative means, began to act out his extended commentary: his arms flew, his body danced, his mouth made the various noises of the city, and here and there, studded in the performance, a few parsimonious words, shining and isolated, embraced by his song and dance, and she wished he might be a little more generous with nouns.

She attended closely, asked him to repeat certain things she wasn't sure she saw-heard correctly, and then as she watched Ponce's body replicate her Aunt Titi's bouncing walk and her mother's dignified floating march, she heard and saw, after two repetitions, and Ponce was nodding yes to signal yes, she had got it right — her mother, Aunt Titi, and the Italian lady who worked at the factory with them, who could speak Spanish as well as Italian and English, had spoken to Sal. The Italian lady had served as interpreter. And then Laura wasn't sure. She felt lightheaded; that there could have been collusion between her mother, Aunt Titi and Sal wasn't something she could ask Ponce to repeat, clarify, and she felt ill.

She leaned against the wall in the lobby and hung on to the bag of groceries. Ponce ran to a neighbor's door and returned with a glass of water. Ponce took the bag of groceries out of her arms and handed her the glass of water. Laura sipped the water. She looked at Ponce, returned the glass of water, thanked him, took her groceries back, and couldn't ask again whether she had heard him correctly; nor could she bring herself, ever, to ask her mother or Titi.

Off the avenue, into the park, the last of dusk illumined the trees and path, and Laura explained "It" was among the questions she could never ask. Soon, she said, she began to question what she'd actually heard from Ponce. She told herself that surely Ponce could be misunderstood. When this rationalizing seemed like weakness to her she tended to the harshest interpretation.

They walked and talked. Isaac listened. Laura concluded that Sal had assumed from his meeting with her mother and Titi implicit permission to teach her a lesson. Isaac suggested that Laura not build too much into a shared point of view between Sal, her mother, and Titi. Laura agreed. It got dark. They walked. Laura found that as she continued to speak the subject of what had happened to her became a thing in itself, and it was, among other things, funny. They walked in the dark and laughed. He reminded her that hours ago he had begun to tell her the fragment of a dream he'd had the previous night. He was aboard a ship, and he was told he couldn't go ashore because Columbus was seasick, and he, Isaac, would have to stay on the ship and take care of Columbus. "That's all I remember," he said. Laura laughed, "Pobre Isaac," she said, "pobre Columbus."

They held hands and wandered deeper into the park. Neither knew the hour, "but it must be getting late," he said. He suggested that they find their way back, out of the park, to Fifth Avenue. She agreed, and they kissed. Then they were against the tree, fumbling with each other's clothes. He started to say, "wait, we shouldn't here … foolish, even dangerous." He saw her eyes looking at him, smiling, her hand unbuckling his pants, touching him, and then she said, "wait, maybe we shouldn't," and he stopped his slow slide down the tree trunk rasping his back, but she was unbuttoning his shirt again, touching again, and what he felt coming from her was a striving that wasn't sexual, and for an instant he was confused and sad, the sadness like a scent borne on the wind, and gone; but they were slipping down from the tree onto the ground, his face in her hair, and they were making love and that was all there was.

After, sitting on the park bench, buttoning themselves up, smoothing out their clothing, laughing, they picked leaves and twigs out of one another's hair. She asked if he had a comb. He said he hadn't. She found a comb in the bottom of her purse; she combed her hair. He watched. The sadness he'd felt at something he couldn't quite define, only he'd had the sense that she hadn't been moved by desire, all this he forgot. He watched her comb her hair.

Laura after making love was surprised by what else she was remembering; and he, the Jewish boy, recently a virgin, seemed in some way an agent of the memory. The comb fell out of her hand. He bent down from the bench to retrieve it from the ground, but she held him now with real tenderness and he just listened.

She was astonished and laughed at the little girl's survival, and flourishing, that had been her. She said she thought she couldn't have been much more than five. Noel, the man who was her father, had begun to be a scarce presence. Her mother was young and cried a lot. Titi was there taking care of household things, and Angel was in the backyard. Now Laura said she could think of how her father's first inevitable infidelity, his life taking him from infatuation to infatuation — his manly prerogatives burned among the wounds of her mother's young life. Laura said she was five, and her mother had relapsed into grieving over the loss of Luz Divina, Laura's older sister who had spent a scant week on earth before departing; Noel's defection must have mocked her pain and her daily efforts to cope. The teachings of the Church, and Titi's proffered wisdom, a form of penance for sins the young woman didn't really believe she committed, except for perhaps desire, and she was absolved of that, after all, having been married in the Church; and moreover the raw new desire for some kind of justice must have seemed impossible, and bitter, and the notion of acceptance insinuated by Titi, another kind of punishment, all provoking rage, and Laura remembered her mother weeping and weeping. Her mother's unhappiness, powerful as hatred, was a creeping devastation, and Laura needed to keep her distance from it, and she could by going deep and far into the pattern of sunlight on the floor where she played with her doll. The brilliant colors swimming through the flawed glass of the window and creating on the floor, between her legs, a dancing blob of light, warming her knees and upper legs, and the warmth and pattern of light making a way within her where she could be quite content. With her fingers and hands Laura could change the worlds of shadow and light on the floor, and she could raise her hand and have the streams of light coming through the window play through her fingers. Her mother was sitting at the edge of the bed. She had stopped crying and sat slumped and hanging downward, her arms dangling toward the floor. Titi called her name from the kitchen as though it were a reprimand. "Lucia." Laura Providencia sat on the floor, playing with the light, her hand shaping shadows on the window and walls, the great pool of rippling sunlight on the floor an ocean, between herself and her mother. Still she could smell the odor of her mother's unhappiness, and the only refuge from the smell was deeper into herself where she focused on the colors and shapes her fingers made dance on the shimmering window.

When her mother called, "Laura, Laura Providencia come to me," Laura sat pretending she hadn't heard. Her mother called again, "Laura, ven aca, por favor." Laura sat stiffly within herself. Her mother called again, louder, pleading. Laura turned to her mother. Her mother held out her arms. "Come," she called, "come, please, give me a kiss." Laura didn't move. She sat there and looked at her mother. Her mother said, "come." Laura couldn't move. Her mother said, "Come, give me a kiss or I'll die." Her mother sat there, her arms outstretched. Laura sat rooted to the light. Her mother's eyes rolled back in her head, her body fell backwards, and her arms flayed on the mattress; her shuddering legs extended off the bed, the heels of her feet thudding on the floor.

Laura was screaming, tugging at her mother's leg and screaming. The body lay there, inert. Titi scrambled in from the kitchen, scooping Laura into her arms. Her aunt was trying to shout above Laura's screaming, her sister's name, "Lucia, Lucia," and to Laura, "It's only a game, she's playing," Titi called, as if she had the power to call her sister back from the dead. Laura's mother sat up on the bed, the oddest smile on her face that Laura had ever seen, and Laura's aunt and mother embraced her.

On the park bench, in the dark, Isaac embraced Laura, and without knowing what he would do, or why, he sang to her. The melody was from "Finiculi, Finicula," the alternative lyric, his boyhood friend Charlie Lanza had taught him: Isaac sang at the top of his lungs, "Christopher Columbus whatta ya think of that, a big a fat a lady, she sat upon my hat — uh — Christopher Columbo, whatta ya think of that."

Laura knew the song, and despite not having the benefit of Isaac's friend Charlie to teach her, she knew the lyrics and joined Isaac in the song.

They sat on the park bench in the dark recovering from the exertion of singing and their laughter. The edge of their hands, the side of his jaw against her temple, always touching, and they remained quiet. He had picked up her comb from the ground and put it in her purse. Her purse lay next to her on the bench.

The night sky was bright. From beyond the park the sound of automobiles rolling over asphalt was hushed, and the car horns sounded distant. Opposite them, beyond the gravel path in the wash of dark, was a hedge wet with moonlight, sprawling and damp as bulrushes. Isaac thought he saw a child's smiling face among the leaves. He wasn't sure but he smiled. The hedge trembled and laughed back. The laughter sounded to Isaac like the giggling of the Munchkins from the land of Oz. Laura moved away from him. Her skin and breath suddenly gone away from his face. She whispered, "Be still." The kid squeezed himself out of the hedge, two more followed, and then many, multiplying out of the dark, surrounding the bench.

The one who snatched Laura's purse from the bench appeared to be the oldest, he was, perhaps, thirteen. Laura said again, "Isaac, don't move." He'd started to stand up. The kid standing behind the bench holding the blade to the side of Isaac's neck may have been eleven, and he was smiling, waiting for something hilarious, which might happen any second. Isaac sat still, feeling absurd, knowing the boy would cut him, still Isaac had to repress the impulse to grab the kid and lay him across his knees. Isaac figured there to be about twenty of them. The leader, the one who grabbed Laura's purse, had a judicious manner, every movement of his body elegant, serious, an improvised art too accomplished and habitual to be self-conscious. Isaac thought the kid was beautiful. They were all beautiful children. The leader, pert as an angel in his army-surplus fatigue jacket, Jesus and a black ebony hand hanging from cord necklaces about his beige throat, the boy counted the money he'd taken from Laura's purse, the gesture of his hands more like plucking the petals from a daisy — she loves me, she loves me not — than counting money, and he sighed. Isaac sat on the park bench. The two kids standing in front of him almost reached his shoulder. One boy held a large bread knife at Isaac's stomach, and the other boy had a car aerial poised on his shoulder. The two looked serious, determined, and neutral. They would do whatever was necessary, without prejudice. All the other boys surrounded the bench in a circle. Laura began to talk to them quietly, calmly, in Spanish.

Isaac didn't understand. Laura continued to speak calmly and at length, but intensely and too rapidly for Isaac to be able to translate the small store of words he might have otherwise understood.

Some kind of parliamentary process was taking place. They had taken a vote. The leader was counting raised hands. It was very orderly. Isaac sat there, one knife blade at the side of his neck, the other pointed above his navel. "Si, OK, yeah," said the leader. It was unanimous; a great celebratory cheer went up. Once, twice, and again they cheered. The leader raised his hand to indicate that there had been sufficient cheering. He returned the money he had taken to Laura's purse, and bowing from the waist, handed her the purse. Sir Walter Raleigh laying his cape across the puddle for the queen's royal foot could not have been more graceful. "Por favor, lo siento mucho," he said and, "this way, please." The pint-sized lieutenants holding the blades at Isaac's throat and stomach put their weapons away, and the boys formed two neat ranks beside Laura and Isaac, an orderly phalanx, one to each side, the way before them clear.

The children escorted them to the edge of the park. Laura and Isaac walked in the center, between the two files of boys, the leader in his army fatigue jacket marching at a leisurely pace just in front of them. In all the negotiations Isaac had not heard him offer his name. He turned his head to them and looked up, speaking to them both, but his eyes sought Isaac's attention in particular. "Man, you care for this girl? You did a foolish thing. You shouldn't be here, it's too dangerous." The others marching along answered, emphasizing the wisdom of the leader, "You got to be crazy or somethin'," the one who had held the blade to Isaac's neck said. "Jesus," another said in the dark, commiserating with the victims of the slaughter that had nearly happened.

The leader stopped for a moment. Everybody stopped. From where they stood on the path they could see the traffic on Fifth Avenue. The leader spoke directly to Isaac, "You lucky, we just jitterbuggin'. The next bunch comin' through here, they a black gang, serious. They think the park is they turf. Belong to them. No conversation. Nothin'. They just kill you for real." The leader said, "Understan'?"

Isaac thanked the boy for the advice and said, "Adios," and in the next instant, they were gone, running beyond sight and hearing into the darkness of the park, their disappearance swift and complete as an act of magic.

They walked on Fifth Avenue towards the subway, amazed. Laura saw what Isaac was thinking and she was baffled too. What had happened in the park had been so quick, complete, they hadn't had time to be afraid. Even now, like tourists, they took in the actuality of the danger as if it were an idea, and they were alien, other, and everything they had known, still knew, as real inhabitants of the city, they could no longer use, being under a spell, and that seemed truly dangerous. They were tender with one another, solicitous, did not feel themselves to be reckless, and enjoyed the night keenly. They held hands and walked on the avenue, looking at everything, the lights, the grand buildings, people moving toward home, and entertainments. It was Saturday night. "What," Isaac asked Laura, "did you say to them?" "Oh," Laura said, "I told them that the money they took from my purse was from my mother's welfare check. That's a lie of course. We have never been on welfare."

Laura told Isaac how she collaborated with her mother and Aunt Titi in establishing the agenda Angel would address to Isaac now that Isaac had finally been accepted, at least implicitly, as a serious suitor. First and foremost, honor and respect for the house, the family, Laura Providencia herself. All of this part of the reclamation of Angel's life, he now, man of the house; there were things he could remember and retrieve. In the process of recovering himself, he was open to the persuasive themes his mother, Aunt Titi, and Laura presented to him. These too would be him. He could not become entirely his own creation, nor something books instigated, nor the world's history, nor the family's history, nor the street. Laura had suggested that they move out of the neighborhood, away from the South Bronx, but Señora Milagros said they couldn't afford that, and whatever Laura's unease regarding her improvisations, her perhaps blasphemous collaboration in the remaking of her brother, she had watched, with relief, Angel's eyes come back to life. "Safeguarding the family's honor would require Angel's vigilance," Laura had emphasized, taking hold of Angel's scorched hands, which had the texture of the pads of a street dog's paws, "and to be capable of maintaining such responsibility," Laura reiterated, while her eyes brimmed, "Angel would have to stay clean."

Angel raised the glass of rum to indicate that this salutary drink, on the ceremonial occasion, was enough for him; he could live without heroin.

And Isaac felt himself contributing to the enterprise. He lay in the dark of the living room and watched the heavy rain beyond the windows. He had been invited to spend the night, for the second time. Señora Milagros commented that the young man seemed always to arrive with a torment of weather, laughed and shuffled off towards sleep. Isaac smiled in the dark and considered how he, nested, lying and breathing there, provided verisimilitude to the project of Angel's reconstitution.

Isaac, cozy and warm in the bed that extended out of the convertible couch, studied the ambiance of light flowing from the dimension of wet night beyond the window, to the drowned grotto where he lay, the Caribbean blue of the enormous lighted tropical fish tank eddying its tides of light to the glowing cave walls, where the huge, tapestried face of President Kennedy seemed to provide some deep sea nurture to the shadows, and the velvet Last Supper on the adjacent wall particularized Jesus and the Apostles into a glowing garden of fungi.

Angel's thunderous and precocious old-man's snoring chugged-chugged through the dark, from the bedroom down the length of the vestibule to the living room. Isaac thought of the grand patriarchal mustache Laura and her mother had encouraged Angel to grow on the rugged and handsome ruin of his face. When Angel had spoken to Isaac, late that afternoon, Laura Providencia, Señora Milagros, and Rosita were cloistered in the bedroom. Aunt Titi, satisfied that her counsel had been heeded, was able to go downtown, where she would spend the night administering to Uncle Toto's sick gall bladder.

Titi stopped for a moment under the arched opening of the living room. She surveyed the two young men. The bottom of the shopping bag she carried at her side nearly touched the floor. In the shopping bag she carried the provisions for her journey: a thermos of café con leche, four saltine crackers, three codfish cakes, and a canteen of water. The trip from the Bronx to El Barrio should have taken a half-hour. But Titi, who would not ask instruction from even those who might speak to her in Spanish, had charted her own route which took her through Queens and part of Brooklyn, so that she traveled seven hours or more. But she was constant. Always and at last she arrived at her destination. Titi lingered for an instant, satisfied that the conference she had ordained, with some reservations, was happening. She hefted the shopping bag, smiled, said, "Adios," and, "Angel, portate bien."

Angel and Isaac sat in the living room. They sipped the rum and smoked the cigars Isaac had provided.

Angel paused often, to find or weigh a word, or phrase, he had chosen. If he discarded some choice of language, he did it silently as he puffed or sipped; he never retracted a spoken word. Isaac, taut and joyous, just short of delirious, whatever the terms of his new life, saw with an acuity that felt supernatural. He, Angel, that was his name, which he had never forgotten and repeated like a mantra. He felt a delight in the novelty of his being as he threatened Isaac, smiling; both young men could not keep from smiling, beyond surfeit with dangerous joy, the threat a promise of a future.

"You serious about my sister, you ain't foolin' around?" "Absolutely." "Absolutely? You understand I got obligations here. Nobody likes for to have tragedy in their life. Families to live with such terrible things forever. Nobody wants that," and Angel shifted his shoulders, the weight of potential tragedy heavy on his neck.

As fascinated as those about to fall in love, they could not take their gaze from one another. Angel remembered an inquiry he was instructed to make, refilled Isaac's glass and his own, and asked again, "What kind of work do you do?" Isaac smiling, noted Angel's confusion, sipped rum, tasted the air heavy with cigar smoke, and tried once more to explain. Quite aside from any information Isaac provided, it was difficult to dislodge the notion that he was wealthy. As Angel seemed to accept the novelty of the idea that Isaac wasn't rich, he also appeared to be evaluating the whimsical recalcitrance by which Isaac resisted becoming wealthy, because surely Isaac could be wealthy if he didn't resist his intrinsic capacities.

"I'm working in a bookstore," Isaac said, "I may be offered the position of assistant manager." "I heard about that," said Angel, "the store in Greenwich Village, right?" "Right." Angel studied Isaac's happiness. Isaac studied Angel studying him. Angel, smiling, scrutinized Isaac's smile. The moment he felt his willingness to end the young man's life he sensed the veracity of the role his mother and aunt said was his, and anticipated with surprise and pleasure the other parts that might also be himself. "Some guys," Angel said, "got an attitude. These kind of white guys, they think Spanish girls are easy. Know what I mean? Guys who think they're slick." "Slick?" "Yeah, slick, and it's a shame to die for such ignorance, finished, no more time to get smarter." "Slick," Isaac said, smiling and puzzled, moving the word from the roof of his mouth with the tip of his tongue. Slick. Slow too, he returned from the distant vantage point where he had been watching the young Angel and Laura Providencia during their first day in the United States, drinking the powdered white milk and eating the thin slices of pound cake Señora Milagros said would have to last two days. On the third day she had found the job at the blouse factory and brought home a bag of groceries.

Isaac watched them, in that first apartment, before they moved into the housing project. Laura Providencia and Angel eating cake, looking up through the window from the rear of the basement apartment; what they could see of sky and light sluicing down through the dense geometry of fire escapes, windows and bricks, carried the echoes of the most raucous and anarchic screaming of children they had ever heard. They were thrilled and frightened. Isaac was there, belated, but maintaining his vigil, watching what had unfolded in Laura's and Angel's life as Laura had told it, and as it lived thereafter in him, the distillation of meaning as he remembered and knew it, seeping backward to reshape the event as they would all remember it.

Angel stared at the open, incomprehensible face. He didn't see a trace of mockery, but an attentiveness so vivid and strange that it appeared as the chaos of idiocy.

"You understand what I'm telling you, Man? It's for your own good too. There's other important things my mother and aunt think I should talk to you about. But I think it's too soon yet. We got to wait and see. We watching you, to see what kind of person. In the meantime…" and Angel paused. Isaac watched him search in silence the language close to his heart. "In the meantime, like Titi says, portate bien, you know, Comport yourself well, like, take care, respect."

Señora Milagros, Laura Providencia, and Rosita paraded into the living room. They crowded Angel and embraced him. Laura's hand brushed Isaac's, hanging at his side; he was standing now, sipping rum, and he couldn't tell whether Laura's touch was a surreptitious caress, or the accidental touch of passing. Her smile, beaming momentarily on him, passed, and it was not just for him, but for everyone, and herself, and the auspicious day. The rain had stopped. The sun was out. Señora Milagros, round, wide, and smiling, coasted in her slippers towards the kitchen to brew coffee.

Isaac would have guessed that he'd heard the flute notes first. Hot, lyrical, the guitars and congas accenting the second and fourth beats. The trumpets joyous, celebratory, formal. The radio, somebody's radio, might as well have been playing in the apartment. The music sifted through the walls, clear and bright. Rosita's female adolescence camouflaged and plumed in the bright yellow and pink tulle of the dress her mother had made— Rosita pursed her lips, not saying, but tasting the word, mambo. Laura's body began to move of its own volition. And Isaac didn't know, couldn't tell whether Laura moved to the music, or her movement carried the music. Her brother Angel, whatever the punishments of prison, the devastations of the electric shock treatments, his mind housing the pell-mell wreckage that could be a coherent past, through his and the collaborative art of his sister, mother, aunt; but his body hadn't forgotten. He danced with his sister. Rosita stood near the music-soaked wall, the pink and yellow puff of her fibrillating like some spring bug about to burst into glory. Señora Milagros, round as a planet, radiant, glided back into the living room, her extended arm offering Isaac the cup of coffee, and her belly, hips, shoulder, barely moving,

danced, the swell and flow of music gravitating in the vicinity
of her monumental thighs. Her children were dancing. She
danced. Something more profound than a smile on her face.
Angel and Laura joined, one form in the light, turning, and
Isaac wondered whether music was the invention of experiment-
ing with sound, the experience of hearing, or perhaps movement
of such grace as Angel and Laura provoked inevitable music.

   Isaac backed away from the dancing family. His back hit
the wall, and he looked over his shoulder. His shoulder rubbed
against the velvet tapestry, buckling the table of the Apostles at
the Last Supper, the ancient cousins frozen and static as he. His
back thumped the wall, knocking the breath out of him; his
vision jumped, and he watched Laura and Angel, fluid, moving, and he considered how language might be a compensation
for not being able to dance. Rosita reached out a hand to him
and said, "Try." He couldn't move. The cup and saucer in his
hand tipped and the coffee spilled on his pants. Rosita laughed
and said, "Try," again, her voice tolerant and cajoling. The fumes
of rum in his nostrils and brain promised a willingness to try
on some other occasion, and he watched Angel and Laura sweep
in a dip. Isaac's hearing altered, saw the music, grateful, daunted.
His back pressed against the huddle of Apostles.

Moist, he ebbed out of her, coasting in the dark where he began
to distinguish shapes that were him, her. Dream gasps floated
from the far bedroom, muted, calm, regular as the refrigerator's
intervals of humming, and the basso profundo of Angel's snore,
audible again in the dark. It was her hair brushing over his face,
and the face making itself out of the illumined dark was Laura
grinning, a child challenging him to the most serious game,

goading him toward a ritual of the utmost importance, the consequences of which he must accept without knowing. And oh, she was beautiful, and he remembered being angry, a rage quenched in the scent, sight, and touch of her. But when Laura had first appeared at the side of the bed in her nightgown, smiling as though she were about to pick a fight, he wondered if she was testing his courage, and then he thought maybe it was a requirement of her machismo, something she had to do for herself; whatever it was, it was not desire he felt coming from her, but some manner of self-assertion, and he surrendered to that prurient possibility, and after came out the other side breathing heavy, and at last they were tender with one another, and he remembered his anger as a bruising theme in a former life. He felt the ache of it still, and for all he could tell, Angel, Rosita, and Señora Milagros had slept through it all. Laura left the bed and he was able to find sleep again after he had balled up and held to his chest the damp placental sheets upon which they had made love.

AND HOMAGE FOR
ELEANOR ROOSEVELT

I search through the pockets of Momma's coats trying to find her teeth. In the dark the pockets spawn pockets. Drowning in the weighted air my fingers feel inside the tissues of dark, probe fissures in stiff fabric, and the soft folds of lining, the warm, moist interior of a rabbit-eared slipper.

This morning I rescued her from sleep. She was moaning. I stood at the bedside, shook her shoulder and called, trying to breach the nightmare. Her eyes popped open. She sniffed the air, choked and whimpered, "The smoke, the smoke." I sat down at the edge of the bed, stroked her hand and called, "Ma, it's okay Ma." Her vision penetrated through to me. She was glad to see a familiar face in the flames. Then she screamed. I held her in my arms.

She sat up in bed and I put the peeled orange in her hand. She examined the wondrous thing. "I thought I died," she said. "Did I die?" "No Ma, you're alive." "For real? You wouldn't kid me?" "I wouldn't kid you Ma, you're alive." She laughed and laughed. "I thought I died and was burning in Gehenna."

Awake, at the breakfast table, she is unaware that my wife, Laura, is gone, forgets that she had ever been here. Laura is away helping her mother and aunt get resettled in their hometown in Puerto Rico. Life in the South Bronx has become too dangerous. Crack addicts stalk the old. When a stray bullet crashed through the living-room window of a neighbor's apartment, Laura's mother and aunt decided it was time to return to Puerto Rico, and the two old women agreed that it was the recently arrived Santo Dominicans who had destroyed civility and made life unlivable in the Bronx.

Neither will my daughter Maria come home again. She is in her sophomore year at college and refuses to come back during the mid-semester or Easter breaks. Her refusal is not an act of defiance. She says she just can't bear to be near "it" anymore. When she came home for Christmas vacation my mother whispered to her granddaughter that her mother, Laura, was an evil woman, someone who ought to be feared. When Maria wept, Mother took her tears as confirmation of Maria's realization of the terrible truth. Maria says she prefers to remember the good times when she was a little girl and a trip to grandma's was a journey into the most lavish love, and grandma's apartment in Brooklyn a Babylon where toys and candy could be found under the couch pillows, beneath the kitchen sink cabinet, and in the large bed where she would sleep with grandma, the two finally exhausted from laughter since everything the child Maria said was wise and funny. Mother's granddaughter and daughter-in-law have disappeared from her consciousness; they could be miraculously resurrected, but it is impossible to predict. For now my wife and daughter have vanished from Mother's mind as if they had never existed.

A week ago my mother accused my wife of trying to poison her. She directed her remarks to me although Laura stood close-by. Momma's posture and tone suggested that she had concluded, without having to think about it too much, that the best way to deal with an assassin was to remain alert but snub her existence. Momma said, "Listen boychik, I don't sleep under your bed, maybe you're having a good time and I don't begrudge you, but the shiksa you married will murder me if I don't watch out." Then she ranted for an hour, enumerating her sacrifices, until her screaming carried her to sleep. Now like a nightmare passed, a dream realized, my wife is nullified for Momma, never existed, not a trace to trouble her memory.

My mother-in-law telephoned from Puerto Rico on the evening of the day when my mother accused my wife of attempting to poison her. Laura's mother said, her voice sad and heavy with acceptance and knowledge of the cost of getting wisdom, that she knew a woman of the street, a woman who had never worked in a factory to provide for her children, a woman who frequented bars and this woman's grown children were nevertheless grateful; they gave significant sums of money to their mother and visited her every Sunday, while she (Laura's mother) could only hope that she would see her children before she died. When Laura reminded her mother that less than three months had passed since her last visit, and her sister Rosita had visited within the month, and Laura was helping with money on a regular monthly basis, as was Rosita, her mother answered by saying that her pacemaker had to be replaced. She spoke of the device as a homunculus enthroned above her heart, a tyrant who must be appeased, "He doesn't like the light that goes on when I open the refrigerator door, then he blows gas into my chest and makes my legs shake. And when my neighbor plays loud music, he kicks me in my heart." But Laura's mother said not to worry, Aunt Titi was fine. In spite of her cataracts Aunt Titi was able to make her way through the mile of barely discernible shapes to Mass each day, although she wasn't inclined to stop for traffic; cars, trucks, and horses stopped for her.

Laura said, "Mami, I'll come to Puerto Rico and accompany you to the hospital and stay with you while the doctor adjusts or replaces the pacemaker, and of course I'll rent a car and drive Titi to Mass," which is what Laura knew her mother wanted to hear. I miss Laura; our life together seems a memory I'm not sure I can trust.

In the brilliant interval of the autumn morning Momma was calm, clear and beyond all praise or blame, opera banished from her rhetoric. She put her glass of tea down on the table and simply asked me to help her kill herself before she reached the stage when she'd have to depend on a stranger to change her diaper. She said she was sorry but there wasn't anyone else she could ask. Doctor Maier had said that this was a subject he couldn't discuss. "So, Izzy," she said, "I ask you."

Again, I find myself wanting. Whatever the virtue, the strength necessary for such kindness, I don't have it.

I stagger out of the closet, handkerchief to my nose, eyes tearing, gagging on the camphorated air. She is looking through a pile of handbags and singing, "We're in the money, the sky is sunny." Momma finds it soothing to handle her shoes, builds mounds of them. She looks down at the piles of shoes and handbags surrounding her, moans in a way she knows is unseemly for a woman of her years, and says, "So sue me," to the deity she is sure eavesdrops in her room. There is no point in my asking her again if she remembers which coat she might have been wearing the day she lost her dentures. She won't remember that any more than she remembers her hunting and gathering of garments and shoes at various church bazaars, charity organizations, and lawn sales. She is delighted with the sudden presence of abundance. "Oh," she says again, "how did I ever accumulate so much?" She is happy now, and I'm grateful. She doesn't have to know what day it is. She can recognize the season in the window, the last of autumn spitting snow.

The last time Doctor Maier administered the test to monitor Momma's condition, he asked her what year it was. She smiled, thought for a moment, and said, "I give up." Doctor Maier said, "Try, guess, Sarah." Momma likes Doctor Maier. She says he's handsome. She flirted with him. Held his hand. "Try," the doctor said. Momma closed her eyes, concentrated and said, with only the slightest inflection in her voice suggesting that she might not be entirely accurate, "Well," she said, "Oh yes, nineteen thirty-five."

Of course she is right. It has been nineteen thirty-five since nineteen thirty-five. There is no getting through that year. She has lived there ever since and always, even before the onset of Alzheimer's.

"Sarah," Doctor Maier asked, "Do you remember how old you are?" "Well," she said, "not a kid anymore, I turned already fifty." Doctor Maier said, "Your son is fifty-four." Momma laughed, looked at me and said, "Wow! This kid here?" "That's right," Doctor Maier said, "Your son is fifty-four." She laughed and laughed, doubled over in her chair.

She looked at the doctor, looked at me. Okay, the doctor wouldn't lie to her, but this whole business of aging seemed a joke someone had begun to tell her many years ago, an unkind joke describing how some old party is betrayed by her own body and mind, all of it faulty, breaking down, and Sarah is a young person listening and laughing, anticipating the punch line hidden in a shaggy dog narrative as protracted as the always imminent coming of the Messiah; the punch line, unbearably hilarious, beginning to articulate itself with the labored wind of her own breathing, is the news she is the old party.

"Sarah," the doctor said, "you're seventy years old." "Wow," she said, "Jeepers creepers, what am I going to do? I can't fight City Hall." And suddenly she wasn't laughing. Her eyes narrowed. She glared at Doctor Maier. The doctor, an agent of sorcery, rendered her, abracadabra, seventy years old.

Momma's accusatory stare would not waver from Doctor Maier's face, but finally she smiled at him and said, "Cutie, life is shit." Doctor Maier, hunkered down behind his impregnable compassion, said, "Sometimes," and continued to make notes. "You want to help me, Doctor, maybe you can give me a new head?"

"Sarah, we can give serious consideration to a new hip, and this medicine will help you feel less anxious." It's okay Doctor, I'm just kidding you because you're such a sweetheart." "Thank you, Sarah. Just a couple of more questions. Sarah, can you tell me your address?" Her eyes scanned the office walls, paused for a moment on Doctor Maier's degree from the Albert Einstein School of Medicine. She sighed. The name was familiar to her, she said, "Albert Einstein." The sound was reassuring, some vague memory of a Jewish wunderkind. "Sorry Doctor, they made from me such a world traveler now I can't keep track where I am." "Okay Sarah, can you recall how long you have been living in Vermont?" "Vermont? Oh yeah." And she stared out the large picture window above the doctor's desk at the hills and the pine trees cresting the horizon of mountains, and the panorama of clear, brilliant sky. "Yeah, beautiful," she said, "so beautiful, looks like on the stage in Radio City Music Hall." "Do you like living in Vermont?" "Like it? I feel like I'm in a movie."

"There were reasons, Sarah, for your move to Vermont," said Doctor Maier, his most kindly voice insinuating that help and care were being offered, and that life might not be entirely shit.

"Yeah sure," she conceded, "Brooklyn got terrible. Dangerous. Twice my apartment was robbed. They broke in when I was out shopping. They took the television, the vacuum cleaner, the rug, the few dollars I had in the house. Why they came the second time, I can't figure. What could they steal, my troubles? And you know it reached a point I was afraid even to go out of the door of my apartment, to go down the hall to the incinerator drop to get rid of the garbage. A prisoner I was. In the street I got mugged. Believe me, they study, they watch, the bastards."

"Yes Sarah, that is why your son moved you to Vermont. You have been able to stroll around town and shop in the stores without clutching your purse. You have commented on many occasions on how safe you feel here, and how polite people are." "Yeah true, Doctor. Only I feel like I'm in that movie and any minute I'm gonna meet little Mickey Rooney and Judy Garland coming down the street with Judge Hardy, and they're gonna say, 'Let's put on a show,' and they're gonna expect me to sing and dance. And I started out just to look for a kosher butcher, which I can't find and I might as well be on the moon."

Doctor Maier cleared his throat. He told Momma that she wore her years well and that she didn't look her age. Momma

cried, "Such a stunt he pulled on me!" "Who Sarah?" "His father," she said, looking at me, aggrieved. "His father, some stunt
he pulled, how could such a horse die? Never a sick day. A regular ox, made of iron. Then one day, poof, he's gone, go figure. I
went to work then in the barbershop as a manicurist."

"This was in Brooklyn?" the doctor said, "After your husband died, you remember all this?" Oh yeah, how can I forget,
Scheckie's Barbershop in Brooklyn. They tried to make me a
criminal. You know, a woman alone they take advantage. At the
end of the week when I get my pay, Scheckie, he's giving me
Turkish numbers, cheating me out of hours. I'm so confused I
can't argue. All right, bad enough. So he pays me. Cash. I go to
the bank to deposit the money and the teller says it's funny
money, counterfeit, and where did I get it? I'm not a fool. I say
I don't remember. I quit Scheckie's. Believe me, if my husband
was alive they don't try such tricks on me. He was no bargain,
my man, crazy he was, but for some kinds of trouble he was
very good."

She is singing, "So let's have another cup of coffee, and let's
eat another piece of pie. Izzy, sing, how come you don't sing?"
"My throat feels a bit sore, I had to lecture today." "Lecture?
What lecture? You don't work by Joey Scheinfield's, you quit?
Joey wouldn't fire you." "Momma that was a long time ago,
years." "Oh," she says, "so you're not in the factory no more, so
sing." She sings, "So let's have another cup of coffee — oh yeah,
I remember, you worked for Joey from before?" "That's right
Ma, a long time ago." "Yeah, so what do you do for a living now?"
"I teach, Momma, at a college." "Oh yeah, right, how nice, I
remember, and you write stories. But from that you can't make
a living." "True." "Oh boychik, have I got stories for you! So let's
have another cup of coffee, and let's eat another piece of pie.

You know that song Izzy." I whistle the refrain. "Doctor Maier," she says, "what a doll! A real mensch." "Yes," I say, "he's very dedicated, a fine man." "A doll," she says, "a mensch."

I repeat, in response to Mother's astonished declaration, every second or third minute, "Yes Momma, we're lucky to have such a caring physician." Momma becomes quiet. I milk the incantation, "Doctor Maier the mensch," to extend the cheery affect, the positive outlook. Almost five minutes. Silence like balm. She turns her face from the window. Startled, she stares at me, her eyes emptying of all recognition, except for the alertness to an immediate threat. She glances out the window again and turns her face to me. The dark is a conspiracy and I'm part of it. I still bear a resemblance to someone she knows, I'm as familiar as bad news, but I might be a kidnapper. "You know," she says, "I'm a fighter, in this life you learn." "Ma," I plead. She looks out the window and screams, "Where am I? This is a wilderness!" I chant the catechism, "Ma, the rent is paid, there's food in the refrigerator." She responds by rote, "and the electric?" "The electric is paid Ma. You don't owe anyone a penny." She circles me, backing away toward the dresser. She spits on the floor near my feet. I might be a scam artist, a hustler of the Diaspora, ready to deposit her in a ghetto, without steam heat, where the residents subsist on the memory of food.

She lifts the scissors from the dresser top and wields the sharp point in front of my face. Five, perhaps seven seconds go by; she shrugs, points the tip of the scissors at her throat, and then, like a conductor launching the downbeat of a symphony, slices the air and shrieks, "Esther, you take me to my sister. I'll live with Esther. Go call a cab." "Ma." "Pay attention, boychik." "Momma, it's a ten-hour drive to Brooklyn, and last year we went to Aunt Esther's funeral. Remember? We went on an airplane." "Ach," she says, as my words are almost heard, become something else. "Esther never calls, not a telephone call, a lousy dime it costs, such miserly traits she wasn't born with. That she picked up from living all those years with that husband, Irving Pisher the Schnorer. But she's a widow now and," "Momma, Aunt Esther passed away last year. We went to the funeral. We flew on that little airplane and you said, 'What is this, Barney Google airlines?'" "Yeah," she says, "I'm a world traveler, a refugee." She puts the scissors down.

I try humming, "Let's Have Another Cup of Coffee and Let's Eat Another Piece of Pie," and "We're in the Money, the Sky is Sunny," but sustaining these melodies must make my face look unfriendly, and Momma looks frightened; she might start to cry. Quickly I begin to talk about our grand project. Why didn't I think of it before? "Oh Ma, I nearly forgot, we should fill out the absentee ballot. You're going to vote, Ma." "Vote?" "Yes, Ma. Remember all the talk with the other ladies at the Senior Citizen's Center? You said you wanted to show them that you're a citizen. You said you wanted to vote. This will be your first time." "Oh yeah," she says. "The fancy yentas. That one she thinks she's a duchess. They looked on me like I was a freak when I said I never voted. Really it wasn't her business, and I was a fool to expose myself. What I'm going to explain, why do they have to know?"

And again I reassure Momma, no questions about why she didn't attend school. "Sure," she says, "I'm going to explain to them that Esther got the shoes and so she went to school?"

"Right," I say, and now I know I've got something going. "Right, but you were born in this country, Momma, it was Esther who was born in Russia." "Right!" she says, "right! I'm the Yankee! Esther, she's a greenhorn. But Esther got the shoes, so she went to school." "Ma," I assure her, "No one will ask any questions about schooling. We have the absentee ballot, I'll help you fill it out."

I reiterate that she was born here, she is a citizen, there is no penalty for never having voted, and she can't be deported. She says, "Are you sure?" I say, "I'm sure." "Well," she says, "I better vote just to be on the safe side."

She studies my face. "You know, you don't really look very much like your father, more like my brother Yussie. Let's telephone him." "Ma, Uncle Yussie passed away. You and Aunt Tessie are the youngest, born in this country, the real Yankees, and the only ones left, the others have passed on." "Schlimazel! And Tessie had a stroke, right?" "Right Ma, she lives with her daughter now."

I make one more foray into the closet. No luck. I can't find Momma's dentures. She has turned on the television set. A political advertisement is declaring some candidate a family man, a veteran, and a protector of the interests of ordinary citizens. Momma must not like the candidate's face. She has begun to curse the office seeker in Yiddish. For starters, she wishes cholera on him, and then builds the maledictions into a complex of catastrophes and plagues culminating in a toothache, which will reside forever in the candidate's one remaining tooth. "Filth," she says, "Connivers, the best of them. Who am I going to vote for, Izzy? They dray mine Kup, finagle, I'm dizzy already." I call from the closet, "I'll help you Momma. We'll look at the ballot sheet together." "Never mind," she yells at the television, and to me, "Listen Izzy, I got it, I want to vote for Eleanor Roosevelt. She's a real human being." "Ma, Eleanor Roosevelt passed away, and when she was alive, she never ran for office." "Oh yeah, I forgot."

Standing in the meager floor space between the gold-colored couch, heaped with pink-tasseled pillows, and the large, plush, plum-red French Provincial chair, I survey the flock of winged, rosy-bottomed cherubim nailed to the wall. In an attempt to make Momma as at home as possible, I had moved the Brooklyn rococo splendor from her one-room efficiency apartment in Brooklyn to the largest room in our old Vermont farmhouse. Momma's room is a little larger than her old apartment. Still, with the couch, the large French Provincial chair, and her screened off queen-size bed, dresser, two coffee tables, television and radio in the red-lacquered entertainment center, the room is crowded; although Momma says it's cozy. I stand, one foot in front of the other, as though traversing a tightrope.

"Look what I found," Momma sings out from under the bed. I weave my way between two candy-green, waist-high pedestals; on one a plaster of Paris bust of Beethoven's brooding mug, the saturnine visage etherealized in milky white; Momma has touched up Ludwig's lips with a little pink, and his eyes she has dabbed the same periwinkle blue as Snow White's frock; the glass figurines of Snow White and the Seven Dwarves, suspended in the most fetching attitudes of gamboling on the pedestal alongside and a foot away. The splashes of color Momma has lent to the monumental head of Beethoven, staring at Snow White and the Seven Dwarves — she has also rouged his cheeks, just a little — seem to have given the composer's face a grimace of perpetual sweetness. Carefully I turn and squeeze between the two pedestals.

On the glass coffee table an electric candelabra illuminates the wall where the three-winged cherubim are nailed, and above, a colored photograph, a triptych in a gold-leafed frame of the wailing wall in Jerusalem.

I wonder how many times I've moved the furniture, pictures, knick knacks, Momma often finding sufficient delight in
each new arrangement to stave off what she glimpses in the
abyss, and can't say. When now, more and more, her synapses
sputter and she loses words, they fall, flee, abscond with meaning, and she screams, excoriating her own blood; her scream
opens up to the last redoubt, the ranks of words thinned out,
the "schrei" has led her to that ranting, where she knows the
yearning for justice that has made love and sanity impossible.
The scream is coherent; it dumps and empties memory, history, that less scrupulous form of fiction, a deluge, these pennies from heaven, shocking. My Momma, of that tribe of maximum expressiveness, veins and nerves wired so she and they
were (I thought) incapable of censoring anything, and I grow
up longing for the refinements of repression, and aspire to a
life of quiet desperation, and now I find as her soul empties
itself of its stories that there are unexpurgated versions. Momma
too, after all, liberated from her subjugation to art.

Momma is crawling around under her bed, laughing.
"Look," she says, "look what I found." I get down on all fours,
and there under the bed, are three cans of sardines and a five-
pound bag of flour. Loaves and fishes under the bed.

She is surprisingly agile as she creeps out from under the
bed; in one hand she clutches an umbrella, which she hands to
me, "Don't open it in the house," she cautions, and winks; and
at the end of the still shapely leg, what seems grafted on, a misshapen, bunioned foot, pushes a photo album along the floor.
"I thought I lost it," she says, rising and making her way to the
coffee table. "Come Izzy," she calls, "We'll peek, take a look." I
glance under the bed one more time before joining Momma at
the coffee table. All I can see in the shadow under the bed are

the cans of sardines, the bag of flour, one mateless slipper, and two, I think, aspirins. I didn't really expect to find the dentures but I can't help hoping. The shadowed space under the bed breathes the musk of another time into my face. The dank air of refuge where a boy could wait for the human storm to pass. Just lay there, underneath, not wanting to hear anything more, and the tide in my gut turning, chasing me out of myself in a great ache to know another way of knowing.

I sit at the table with Momma. She is delighted as a child learning to say the names of the things in the world on the morning of the day when the universe was six days old. The candelabra rains down a miniature aurora borealis on the black pages of the photo album. Mother points at a photograph and, one by one, calls out the names of her sisters and brothers, "Molly and Esther, Lily and Leah and Tessie, Yussie and Max and Rosie." She pauses between the saying of each name to look at me so I may smile in praise. The edenic epoch lasts another five minutes. Then, as if the rampant naming, the hubris of words summoning her sisters and brothers breached some alluvial wreckage, churning memory, she cries, "Rosie! my sister Rose, TB took her, twenty she was, dead." Momma enraged, trembles. If I don't interrupt with something, perhaps the business of voting, which was an urgent and fascinating matter to her for several days, I will hear the gospel narrative, the same story again and again, each version more bitter and vituperative than the last. The permutations of the story turning in its grief, and beseeching, the assigning of blame imperative to the making of any moral understanding. This story, part of the parcel of stories that fascinated me, and which I turned into fiction, and now I pay for the conceit, the stories return, turned again through the long dark gestation of Momma's gauntlet to oblivion.

I reach for the absentee ballot sheet near the edge of the table. But Momma is looking at me, smiling, and puzzled. "Is anything wrong?" she asks. "Wrong?" I say, "of course not." Momma's anguish of a moment before has slipped down the memory hole, gone, the serendipitous bounty of the disease, somewhere between subject and predicate the tale precipitously flushed down into dark limbo. I needn't be anxious about what kind of telling this will be. The struggling, insistent words strangling Momma, as the story's denouement cooks up her blood pressure, and I fear a stroke, and we have to rush to the emergency room, where I and the nurses restraining her, will be denounced as traitors; and Momma knows that the doctor approaching her with the hypodermic wants to put her out, to deprive her of the opportunity to indict God for crimes against humanity. But now, this time, all is whimsy, sweet melancholy.

Momma points to a sepia-tinted photograph in the album, "Him," she says, "He came from a well-off family, the father was a druggist. They moved from the neighborhood to live with the other allrightniks in the Bronx. His name — his name was," "Sammy," I say. "Sammy, right, a fine boy, serious, quiet. He wanted to marry me. Your father threatened him, scared him away. If I'd married Sammy we would've lived on the Grand Concourse. Big, wide streets. A peaceful life boychik. You would've had beautiful red hair."

Momma goes on and on, rhapsodically, about how I would have been if only she had altered the genetic recipe a little, stirring a dollop of sweet Sammy into her womb. A man, any man, but my father in particular, may have been an imperative, but not quintessential ingredient in my making. Flavored with Sammy I would still be me, only better, with curly red hair.

It is almost time for Momma to take her evening medications. The vials of pills clink in my jacket pocket as I shift my weight on the chair. Momma has launched herself into a sentence she cannot complete. Open-mouthed, she searches the air, my face, she's anxious, not yet desperate; the theme is not entirely lost to her, but will be, if I don't complete her thought. And I do. I know the story. When I jump-start the stalled narrative I'm sometimes rewarded with what had been the hidden version, previously shared only with Momma's sister, my Aunt Tessie. I retrieve Momma's lost words, insinuate myself into her language just enough to shade meaning away from screaming grief. I have become a totalitarian regime, establishing my dominion over the meaning of Momma's stories.

Last month, before the new antidepressant was prescribed, she told me the story of the honeymoon again, and this time I learned that I was present, splashing around in the amniotic tide, nauseating Momma on her wedding night. I started to apologize. She didn't hear me. "And oh," she said, "the street knew and I couldn't hold my head up. The disgrace!" That night as I tucked Momma in I regaled her with glorious and funny tales of untimely births, bastards; "Think of Gimpy Sarah Bernhardt, Momma, the poor girl had to make her limp look like dance, think of all the illegitimates who had in the course of time achieved spectacular things in the world, bestowing upon their mothers 'nachus'; 'kvelling' such bragging rights — the last word and the last laugh forever after Momma, cannot be rescinded."

As I fluffed up Momma's pillow I included Moses in the honor roll, and managed to croon a lullaby, "And the old Pharaoh's daughter, she fished him, she said, from the stream."

"Did you say something, boychik?" "Would you like me to tell you what I know about the candidates, Ma?" And I slide the

absentee ballot sheet a little closer on the glass surface of the
table. Momma says, "Wait, look at this." She is pointing at a
photograph in the album of herself and my father. In the picture they are walking in a street, wearing their best, unaware of
the photographer. Momma looks frightened. She is hanging
on to Father's arm. He is dressed up in his George Raft suit,
shoulder pads like the wings of a Mafia torpedo, his slouch hat
tilted at a rakish angle. He bought me the same outfit, cut to
size, for my bar mitzvah. I went up to read from the Torah looking like a midget effigy from Murder Incorporated out on an
assassination contract. Momma says the picture of her and my
father was taken by a street photographer, and I'm surprised by
the details she can retrieve from her long-term memory. "Your
father," she says, "bought me a corsage and the hat, the shoes,
and the coat. My momma made the dress. Your father took me
to Radio City Music Hall. It was new, a palace. I couldn't catch
my breath."

She is telling me about her honeymoon again. I know the
story. The many versions. Hers and mine. She is telling it, eyes
closed. I try to figure how I can reconcile the facts, recently revealed, when Momma was ranting in the hospital emergency
room, during a heart attack that wasn't, how can I use this new
information to see the way it probably happened.

In one of Momma's earliest versions, a declamatory rendering I salvaged from her shrieking denunciation of God for
having invented the male race, a vision. I saw them on their
nuptial night. "Remember," she said, "I was a girl, almost fifteen."
I calculate, then Father was sixteen. She said she pleaded. He
tore off his clothes, yelled, begged. She said she'd never traveled
on the subway alone. She said, "Wait, please. Not yet." I see him,
the sixteen-year-old groom, naked, rabid as King Saul, climb

out on the window ledge. She said he threatened to jump. "With him, you never knew. He might do anything. Naked he was, half out the window. I should have said, jump." Momma paused and aimed the question at my eyes, "Was that a man or an animal?"

Once upon a time I heard this telling and I was newly armed with the desire to see the story as a story. I knew my fear. I was cursed, as my father was cursed, because any man so passionately hated by a woman was surely cursed, and I am my father's son. When my fear of my mother's curse subsided, a fear I'd felt more acutely than my father's capacity for violence, I saw it this way: Mother, like Minerva who was wombed in the head of Jupiter, a virginal goddess of reason, grabs the hair on Father's head, and he, like the centaur, had his head raised toward the light. She lifts the centaur's head by his unruly hair up, up, beyond his bestial lower parts, confounding his blood by the broader scope of his vision.

But wait — in the recent account she said she couldn't lift her head up. Couldn't bear the disgrace. On the wedding night I was already there, gurgling around inside, making her queasy. So maybe the nuptial night wasn't a night. It could have been a day. Night or day. I believe, yes, he would have threatened to throw himself out of the window. But they both may have been virgins. And Radio City Music Hall would have been after, after things had been smoothed out a bit. Father wouldn't have wanted to be in trouble with Momma's brothers, Max and Yussie, and anyway, he wanted to marry Momma, had been courting her, would court her in his way for the better part of his life. And of course he was cuckolded by me. Even if he had been the wisest and sweetest, he was too far from the first birth.

I'm related to his wife by blood, he is not.

But I was his pal for a long time, while I was there, and he said, "Put in a good word for me kid." I tried. He said, "Clarence Darrow for the defense. Twelve years he is and he got such words. Darling," he said to Mother, "Heart of my heart, talk to my lawyer." "Momma," I said, "He's not a bad guy." "A whore-master," she said, "a man who brings social disease into the house, sleeps with his socks on." "He works very hard. Two hernias he's got." "Socks is all he's wearing to bed. He has the habits of an animal." "He's generous, Ma." "To the world he's generous. He once beat his own mother."

Sunny Sunday morning. The wind whistles in the great funnel between tenements. Through the kitchen window I can see the bed sheets popping on clotheslines like the sails of ancient galleons. The kitchen table is resplendent with golden whitefish, black bread, cream cheese, and halvah. Father, in his undershorts and socks, his muscular body crouched on the stool in the posture of Rodin's *Thinker*, one hand holding the fish to his mouth, his ear pressed against the speaker of the phonograph, listens to Borra Minivitch and the Harmonica Rascals play, "Chinatown, My Chinatown," and his tongue explores the soft inside of the fish's gill. "Where's your brother?" says Ma, "You're the older. You're supposed to keep an eye." "Nothing to worry, he's up on the roof helping Mickey Callandrillo with the pigeons." "You gave him to eat?" "Yeah Ma." She looks at me skeptically, turns the skeptical look at my father, and the skin on her forehead roils like boiling water, her face clenches with revulsion. "A whore's rags and perfume," she says, standing over the kitchen sink, "I put aside nickels and dimes for your bar mitzvah, and your father steals the money to dress me in nightgowns you can see through." I hope Father hasn't heard the word "steal." He still has his ear pressed to the speaker of the phonograph; he is tapping his foot to the rhythm of "Chinatown, My Chinatown," the skeleton of the whitefish hangs from his hand, the golden smoked head of the fish swinging back and forth.

Momma says again, "Where's your brother?" and "You're the older. You're supposed to keep an eye." I repeat, "He's up on the roof helping Mickey Callandrillo with the pigeons," although I can't be sure. He may be in the vacant apartment on the top floor, adjacent to the roof, where he is housing and feeding the stray dogs he's collected. The janitor knows about it, but he won't complain to Father until the look on Father's face changes. It has been a tense week. Almost two. At night something bunched tight in my stomach measures the silence. My brother and I sleep in the same bed. He has one ear pressed to the pillow, his eyes closed. I cover his other ear with my hand. I can't tell whether he is really sleeping. He is almost ten now and the story he is making to live in is so elaborate that the plot has become incomprehensible to him; he will be lost and endlessly inventive, and the physicians who will try to help him escape the story can look forward to a mystery impervious to science. My father, endorsing the idea of brotherly love, will say again and again, "so your brudder is skitsofrantic, he is still your brudder." But through the two weeks of nights I keep my hand over Jacob's ear so he will not hear Father begging, "Sarah, a word, a touch." Momma's nighttime voice, not quite a whisper, says, "Lay one finger on me, and I promise, when you close your eyes you won't wake up."

Last Sunday Father chose exile. I went with him as Momma testified to the white icebox enumerating Father's crimes, his body grew tense, his tapping foot lost the beat of "Chinatown, My Chinatown." We left for the Turkish Baths. First we stopped at a bar. Father had a boilermaker. I had a soda. Father had two boilermakers. A man in oil-stained, dark blue overalls sitting at the bar next to Father, sipped beer and glanced down at the newspaper under Father's elbow. "That," the man said with indignation, "is a commie newspaper." Father said, "What?" and turned his head slowly toward the man. I was sitting on Father's left side, the man on his right. I said, "Pa, take it easy." The man to Father's right seemed put out; there was something in his voice and manner that said that Father was violating the protocol of some fundamental hospitality. "That," the man repeated more emphatically, "is a commie newspaper."

The bartender, a large man with a red, patient-looking-face, served a customer at the far end of the bar and moved quickly in our direction. Father, incredulous, was looking into the face of the man seated beside him. The man said, "This is America." Father said, "Yeah?" The man didn't say anything else for the moment, satisfied that he'd made the definitive statement. I put my hand on Father's shoulder, and said, "Come on Pa, finish your drink, let's go to the baths." "Mister," Father said to the man, "You shouldn't aggravate me. I'm a very emotional person." The man, looking in Father's face, saw something, began to perceive that maybe he'd made a serious mistake, still he couldn't stop himself from saying, "Well, if you don't like it here you should go live in Russia." I said, "Pa, please." He sucked in his breath for the last that he could say to the man, and in his most tender and solicitous voice, once more astonished, asked, "So you want to get crippled?" Then the bartender was in front of us pouring Father one on the house. The bartender filled the shot glass to the rim. "Easy does it," he said, tilting the larger glass with the beer chaser under the spigot. "Eddie," the bartender said to the man sitting next to Father, "Eddie keep your trap shut."

Father and I, naked, move around in the steam. He is standing. I crawl around on my hands and knees, on the bottom where it is a little cooler. Looking up through the shifting clouds, I have various views of him. He has forgotten the incident in the bar. All that will linger is his fear of losing his temper. His hawkish face, eyes closed, dreams in a mist. Vapor veils his face. I can hear his voice, encouraging, "Come on boy, on your feet, stand up." I start to rise, get another glimpse of him, wet and shining in a great white cloud of steam. His torso is tilted, an upended slab of marble about to topple into the billows of steam. I know that his radical list is an illusion abetted by his right shoulder, which is almost three inches lower than his left shoulder, from all the lifting and hauling. I rise and the wreaths of steam drift from his groin. I can see the two deep trenches of his hernias. He is holding my hand. My hand feels small in his. The texture of his hand is moist and rough as the bark of a tree. I am standing, and it is good. It occurs to me that the weather of Paradise is what is unusually attributed to Hell. He says, "Wait," lets go of my hand and begins to climb the mist. I see the rhomboid block of him climbing up over the bleachers and through the boiling clouds. At the top, a smoky horizon evaporates, and three heads, two bald, one with sinewy reddish vegetation standing on end, appear: The features of the faces, simmering and liquid, could be mimicking everything that can be said at once, while the drooling flesh remains dumb. Father reaches the summit. The clouds shift and I can't see what's happening up there.

I can hear Father talking to the men in Yiddish. Then in Russian. Down where I stand a body moves by me in a drenched toga, the folds wet and heavy as sculpted stone. That figure, like a statue huddled in grief, passes through a yellow cave-like mouth and vanishes as the mouth itself is swallowed in a bloom of smoke. The old gnome who has appeared at my side, standing on his toes so he can reach my ear, is Yitzhak the schvitz attendant. The old man smiling his toothless smile is wearing a white sailor's cap with the brim turned down, and a g-string fastened to a white oilcloth codpiece. "Listen to me, please," he whispers, "you should keep Poppa calm, okay?" And Yitzhak reaches into the boiling mist and upends a bucket of water over his head. The beads of water gleam from Yitzhak's lean body, as densely and intricately muscled as braided rope. He moans ecstatically. From up above, more rhapsodic moans. I say, "I'm gonna try my best, Yitzhak." "More than that I wouldn't ask," he whispers and returns to his duties. I can hear Yitzhak working. He is dousing the earthen stone walls with buckets of water. The walls hiss and burst clouds of steam. When we entered Father announced, "Jeezus it's freezin' in her, Yitzhak, please how about some real heat." He promised Yitzhak the usual tip if he could furnish the "real heat." The Russian room emptied except for the several devotees melting blissfully on the top shelf. Yitzhak's other service is to provide massages, platzers, on the topmost shelf of the Russian room. The massage consists of kneading and pounding with soap-soaked oak leaves, and intermittent dumping of buckets of cold water over the prone body; miraculously, Yitzhak, the perpetual motion machine, can keep the buckets full and moving on an assembly line of his own devising. He moves between two constantly running faucets with buckets beneath them, and moves the buckets forward on a slithery board. His movement in the fog of steam is swift and graceful. Periodically he dumps a bucket of water over his head, the motion of his hand flipping the bucket as deft as a magician's. Yitzhak appears to be emptying a waterfall from a top hat, and he shudders with pleasure under the shower.

I can hear Father above, tumbling through three languages. He wants the three men to sing. They are reluctant. I don't understand most of the words, but I can follow the pattern of Father's cajoling and threatening, by the intonation of his voice; the timbre of his enthusiasm indicates that things haven't reached a crisis point. Yitzhak's large, pink ears, succulent, water lily-shaped clusters, drip, and are fine-tuned to the dialogue gurgling through the aquatic mists. Yitzhak hollers up, offering Father a massage, "A platzer for free, gratis and for nothing, 'til the revolution. Abe come." Father doesn't answer. He is caught up in the urgency of his effort to make the men sing. One man says, "I'm in infant wear," indicating the nature of the business by which he earns his livelihood, and the assertion is also meant to stand as an explanation for the man's inability to sing. I remember that Momma said of Father, "You can't say no to him," and that the hard-won triumph of her life is that she has said "no" to him, continues to say "no." Her life is built on this "no." Yitzhak whispers, "Do something." I reassure him, "Nobody's going to get hurt," and I think I begin to understand a little the powers in the world. There is much that remains mysterious. Father's rage makes him appear fearless. The unrelenting aggression of his every expression, love or animus, all sound like a threat; the mode of his communication resembles the style of James Cagney and John Garfield in the movies. Life may imitate art, but Father is truly afraid of losing his temper. Beyond any self-consciousness, he can never know what the world will look like after he loses control. But now, in the delicious heat, even as I hear the uncertain voices above begin to sing the Russian Cavalry song, "Meadowland," which the men claim not to know, and Father, who hasn't any notion that he is bullying, only that it is such a beautiful melody he will not allow these men to deprive their souls of the experience of the melody; even as I hear the song I become aware of what I have always known. My father, like all the men I have ever seen, is subdued when in the presence of my uncles Yussie and Max. I haven't thought about it before, barely noticed, because it seemed part of the natural order of things. It has always been that way. Men are deferential if not subservient around Momma's brothers. Uncle Max is a devout capitalist, and very patriotic. When Mother and Father argue, berating one another's side of the family, and Father refers to the disappearances of Uncle Max's business competitors, Mother begins to yell about Uncle Max's statesman-like qualities. It is true — Uncle Max can settle all kinds of problems in the neighborhood by making a couple of telephone calls. I've heard relatives and other people who live on our street say that the police sometimes call Uncle Max to smooth out a difficult problem. And Uncle Yussie used to fight pro, and when he forgets and hits some regular citizen, because, Momma says, her brother Yussie tends to be temperamental, then Uncle Yussie is liable to felony charges because he was once a professional fighter. Momma says that it often takes all of Uncle Max's statesman-like qualities to keep Uncle Yussie out of jail. I've heard my father say that Uncle Yussie beat people up for money in and out of the ring. Quite aside from the defamations Mother and Father heap on one another's side of the family, the legends of my uncles are preeminent in the neighborhood, and I begin to appreciate the realpolitik of the street. It is not enough to be a "Schtarker."

Not that Father has any talent for discretion, or can discern for the part of valor that can be called wisdom. But my parents grew up on the same street. My guess is that while Father was a boy, his first and primal learning established his relationship to Momma's brothers — as many others also got out of the way, as the young Max and Yussie, several years Poppa's seniors, began to lay the foundation for power and principalities, in what is, after all, the land of opportunity.

Uncle Max's and Uncle Yussie's hegemony over large portions of the neighborhood persists, although they live in what seems to me a kingdom as mythic and grand as Camelot — Rego Park, Long Island. When on rare occasions they find the time from their ceaseless and arcane business affairs, they visit the old neighborhood. All along our street the visit has the aura of potentates descending from the realm where the secrets of plenty flourish. The presence of my uncles is salutary, the inhabitants of our street move with greater vigor, as in the presence of living promise, and this display is necessary to be worthy of good fortune. I too am overtaken by the glamour of it all. My giddiness feels a little like the betrayal of my father and his crowd of lefties. However, they too are deferential around my uncles, withholding the full measure of their irony for later, when they let me know that my uncles exemplify the gaudy ascendancy of America's true and primitive religion — capitalism. Usually, after a visit from my uncles, my father's comrades will recite to me the fate of the Scottsboro boys, or the story of Sacco and Vanzetti, as a kind of biblical instruction and corrective to the infatuation that has tainted me.

Nevertheless, when Uncle Yussie and Uncle Max come to visit, I will be standing at the curb with all the other kids on my block, near to swooning at the sight of Uncle Yussie's new Packard and Uncle Max's new Oldsmobile, the shining vehicles parked one behind the other in front of the building where I live.

Maybe too Uncle Yussie will ask me again if I want to go to the Friday night fights at Madison Square Garden. He took me once. Sitting at ringside, just before the main event, men kept coming up to Uncle Yussie to shake his hand and pay their respects. Uncle Yussie introduced me to Mr. Whitey Bimstein and Mr. Blinky Palermo. Uncle Yussie said, "This is my sister's boy, the kid's alright." I felt as though I'd been knighted.

Yitzhak drifts out of the steam and whispers the most plaintive, "Please, my clients." I can hear Father berating the reluctant caroler; it sounds like Poppa is getting angry. "Please," says Yitzhak, "talk to your father." What to do? I remember the smell of frying onions and garlic as we had walked through the small restaurant on the floor above, just past the dormitory of cots, and I have an inspiration. "Poppa," I cry, "I want a steak." My father climbs down out of the clouds, eyes shining, and takes my hand.

On a Sunday evening, when Poppa was listening to "Chinatown, My Chinatown," the inevitable happened. After three weeks of enforced abstinence, Momma has also imposed silence. She serves his meals in silence, slamming the plates on the table. Father scoops the mashed potatoes from the tabletop with his thick forefinger and brings it to his mouth. He devours the food. Momma watches him eat. Her face screws up with disgust. Although Momma will not speak to Father, she will testify to the icebox, the sink, or me, the expression on her face when she is orating in my direction not different from the face she wears when she's talking to the sink. She lists Father's crimes and misdemeanors, his animal habits, and, speculating out loud on the cursed and damaged genetic inheritance that made Father, she describes his parents as "two simple Mocky dwarves." "What," Father says, rising from the table, "I'm a playboy or a workingman," and he opens his pants displaying one of his hernias. "Ah," Momma shouts, "time for Tomashevsky and drama."

My kid brother is considering making a dash for the door, so that he can return to the roof and hang out with the pigeons until all this passes. But it's too late. He doesn't want to chance getting too close to Poppa's swinging arms, and Poppa has torn the kitchen door from the hinges and flung it across the room; the door crashes into the cupboard toppling it, and dishes and cups smash and scatter over the floor. With the kitchen door torn away I can see the inhabitants of our building hurrying by in the hallway, eyes averted, ducking pieces of chair. The furniture is airborne. Mr. Blum the portly grocer waddles by as fast as he can, and the grocer can't resist one quick glance into the exploding kitchen, where on New Year's Eve, when Mr. Blum and several neighbors visited, Poppa, who was only happy, lifted the grocer up and chipped the loose paint from the ceiling with the grocer's bald head, which tap-tapped against the ceiling with a fluid and seemingly effortless upward thrust. At that time Momma had come up to Poppa and scolded, "Abe, put him down, your hernia's going to pop." I know that the janitor, who has various custodial responsibilities, will not intervene either. The janitor, as the landlord's agent, had tried to scrimp on heat, as per his employer's instruction. Tenants in the building complained to Father. Momma just let it happen. Father went into the janitor's apartment. There was, of course, a confrontation between Poppa and the janitor, Mr. Stevanovitch. I'm not sure exactly what happened, but Poppa came out of the janitor's

apartment carrying pieces of smashed furniture which he carried down to the basement and burned in the furnace. Ever
since, the janitor has been as subdued in Poppa's presence as
Poppa is when he is around Uncle Yussie and Uncle Max.

   Poppa is punching craters into the kitchen wall. Momma
moves gingerly between the smashed chairs, the upside down
kitchen table, the four legs up in the air, which I and my brother
touch, as if we were playing tag; we're ready to run. Momma,
on tiptoe, moves about the wreckage of broken dishes and cups
scattered over the floor. Two lamb chops, a bottle of milk, and a
cake of ice fall to the floor as Poppa lifts the icebox and throws
it against the far kitchen wall. My brother and I duck even
though the icebox comes nowhere near us. My brother imitates
the sounds of exploding bombs, like we were watching a war
movie, and he makes a dash for the bedroom where he will take
refuge under the bed. I'm about to follow him. Poppa is crying
and smashing out the kitchen window with a frying pan.
Momma appears oddly calm as she moves about the flying glass,
the raining debris, all of this wreckage in the air, which she gestures at with her outstretched hands, is the empirical evidence
she has sought in her speculation of the means of Poppa's nativity.

   From under my bed, my brother and I watch Poppa move
from the kitchen to the living room, where he ransacks the
couch. Momma follows after him, they move out of sight, and
along with the sound of things being smashed, I can hear
Momma talking in Yiddish. I can't understand all of it, but the
gist of it is about Poppa's mother and father. And then, very
loud, the sound of one hand clapping.

Momma sounds surprised, surprised she is remembering, or surprised she is remembering without rancor, simply recalling a life that happened to be hers. It is dark outside. The candelabra showers light over the glass surface of the table and the family photo album. She is holding the absentee ballot sheet, an official and puzzling document that must be explained to be neutralized of any possible threat. I have explained it. I will explain it again. She is calm, and finds her calm wondrous. The absentee ballot sheet, which was an item of fascination to her, now is an official paper representing the dangers of the world, which she is facing philosophically. She is speaking to herself and addressing claims and threats in the text of the paper in her hand; her voice is serene. She is talking about hunger, and how, as a child, she tried to fill up on water and a penny pretzel and felt sick. I remember that the doctor at the memory clinic in the university hospital described the attenuation of memory in Alzheimer's like a frayed and dying electrical connection. The wire is almost gone. Sometimes the current of memory makes it through the thread, sometimes not. Midway through the career of the disease, one suffering from Alzheimer's may have moments of clarity, and recall, said the doctor. But I'm tired. I think I might be able to sleep tonight. I want to give Momma her evening medication, tuck her in. Momma says, "See, see." I see the photograph she is pointing to, but I don't see, can't follow the connection, the leap of Momma's exposition. "Look, look at them, they're your grandparents too."

In the brownish photograph the faces of my paternal grandparents are blurred. I can see that they're smiling. They are old people. My grandfather is wearing a derby hat and a stiff dark suit that seems to stand a fraction of an inch before him. My grandmother is wearing a babushka's kerchief and a man's overcoat. They are standing with their hands at their sides like soldiers at attention, in front of a tenement, smiling. I don't remember them very well. They died when I was not quite five years old. Momma says that my cousins enjoyed measuring themselves against my grandparents because even the younger children were never much smaller than Bobbe and Zayde. I have a vague recollection of this. Momma claps her hands and laughs, she says that for these grandparents of mine, "America was truly the land where dreams come true. "She," Momma says of her long gone mother-in-law, "she couldn't conceive. No matter what she tried, how she prayed, nothing. Who knows, maybe that little vantz of a husband was shooting blanks. He looked like a toy anyway. And she with a womb like a teacup, maybe a turnip could live in there. In the old country she went to rabbis, spiritualists, even a priest. She tried potions, ate roots and grass, bathed in animal dung, nothing worked. She pleaded, called on God, on the dark powers, begged, was ready to make any kind of deal with whatever and whoever in the universe. Nothing. Everything in creation was deaf to her, except for your little Zayde who wept and apologized even when she cursed and beat him. When they came to this country they were no longer young. Your grandmother was well past childbearing age, at an age really when a woman can expect to become a grandmother. She had given up hope, and she lived her life like she was in mourning. Your grandfather apologized constantly — to his wife, and to everyone for everything. And then, the first year in this country, old people they are already, they hit the jackpot, go figure. Who knows how or why? The how remains the same for all human people, but to look at them, you wouldn't believe it."

"Your father," says Momma, "as you know was an only child. And to say that they treated him like they gave birth to Jesus

Christ is no exaggeration. Only he was dictator, this little Messiah. But no matter what, your grandparents were happy. A word of English they never learned. Happy they were, and lost. Your father, even when he is a little, little boy, he is taking care of everything, without him they can't go or do anything. He's in charge. If he is served a meal he doesn't like he's throwing the plates, screaming. They tremble in front of him, but no matter what, they're happy, he's a miracle."

I listen to Momma and think of my father and his parents. He must have appeared to them as a giant, an American giant. I see my paternal grandparents as I have dreamed them, two doll-like Eastern European dwarves, enraptured and witless; they are subject, as Hansel and Gretel were subject to their father, stepmother, and the witch. In this tale the wee parents are the orphaned children lost in the forest of the world. The world is America, and tyranny is imposed by a child.

Momma says that my grandparent's love seemed to drive my father to greater and greater fury. It is true, she acknowledges, that without Father, his parents, "living hand to mouth" and with hard times giving way to even harder times, would have starved; that it was the enterprise of the raving boy that put food on the table seemed to the tiny and perpetually bewildered parents further proof of the miraculous in their life.

He was only a boy when somehow he got hold of a pushcart, a scale, and a quantity of onions and potatoes.

My father, the boy, and his wee father pushed the pushcart through the streets. "Your father's voice carried, you know," says Momma. He cried out, up to the windows of the tenements. They sold onions and potatoes. "Your father ordered his father around, and your grandfather looked always befuddled, and like he was about to weep with relief or joy. Every minute of his existence was a reprieve. With every bag of onions or potatoes, the old man, in Yiddish or Russian, thanked the customer and apologized for using up oxygen when there were other people who needed it."

When the potato and onion business didn't earn enough, Father got hold of an old horse, a wagon, and a cowbell. They rode the streets. Grandfather banged on the cowbell with a stick. Father hollered, and they bought and sold old rags and used clothes. Most of the time, Momma says, thanks to Father, they managed to eat. But at home or at work, Momma says always Father was hollering. Sometimes when he lost his temper he smashed up the apartment. His parents trembled. Once, Momma says, Father, in a rage, took his mother by the back of the neck and threw her to the floor. Then he cried, and begged forgiveness. He scooped up his mother and father in his arms and embraced them. His mother stroked his head, said that everything was okay, and that they loved him. Mother says, "When I met them for the first time I was already expecting you. Your father tried to behave, but every time he looked at his parents, he was ashamed. Then angry. Your grandmother was a very good cook and she made a special meal for the occasion. Your father wanted everything to be perfect, and his parents shivered. By that time your father wasn't any more with a horse and wagon. He was working in the scrap iron yards. But every week he brought his parents money so they had with what to live. Your grandmother served the soup. It smelled delicious, but I didn't have much of an appetite. You were in my belly making me a little sick. Your grandmother kept a very clean house, but the poor woman was confused. I don't know whether she was confused because of her suffering, or her suffering was because of her confusion; maybe crossing the Atlantic Ocean in steerage, she got so "farchadat" she could never get anything straight again. The house she kept clean. But nothing had a fixed place. She might put something anywhere. So always she was searching. Anyway, she served the soup, and then she couldn't find the spoons. She looked and looked. The bowls of soup sat on the table, smoking, getting cold. Your grandfather helped her search for the spoons. They trembled and searched. Your grandfather found one big ladle, which he displayed like a sign of hope. I was about to suggest that I go to a neighbor's house and borrow some spoons. But it was too late, that was first time I saw the flying furniture.

"At your grandmother's funeral, oy, did your father cry. He carried on so everybody at the ceremony forgot about the person they were putting into the ground and watched him. He made such a show with his grief. I'm telling you he could have been on the stage. A regular Tomashevsky, better even; nobody could take their eyes away from your father. He was spectacular. I don't have to tell you. You ought to know. And again such a show when his father passed."

Momma's hand hovers over the absentee ballot sheet lying on the table as though it were giving off heat. She appears calm. She is looking into my eyes, wants to be sure she has my attention. She is instructing, giving a valuable lesson to her son. She is poised and earnest, reclaiming authority. A mother. She has forgotten that she has ever forgotten. "You know boychik, your father begged me. He pleaded, begged me not to tell my brothers. I was going to. Then I thought of you and your brother. How would I take care of you? Did I have a way to earn money? I was never out of the house. Never traveled on the subway until I was married. Years later, when your father died and my brothers also had already passed away, my sister Tessie, she taught me how to manicure. I was able then to do fingernails in the barbershop and earn a little. But before that, what could I do? I had to think of you and your brother. If I was a widow how could I feed my children? Trust charity? Such a fool I'm not. I had to be responsible. So I didn't tell my brothers. But your father, boy did he beg. He pleaded. He carried on almost as good as he did at his mother's funeral. And I let him sweat, not like at the schvitz, where he enjoys it. In a manner of speaking, you, and your brother too, saved your father's life. I had to do the responsible thing."

She runs her tongue over her gums. "And teeth, I need teeth. I can't live on bananas." She is waving the absentee ballot sheet in my face. I think I understand, she has assumed some sort of connection between the absentee ballot sheet and acquiring a new set of dentures. "Nothing to worry, Momma," I assure her, "I'll call the dentist in the morning and make all the arrangements." "I can't live on baby food and ice cream, and this," she says, "what are we gonna do about this? I'm gonna be in trouble?" I take the absentee ballot sheet from her hand. "Really Ma, not to worry. You're just going to vote. Be a real citizanya, a Yankee." "No kidding? So for which of the connivers should I vote? All of them are *dreck*, no?" I look at the sheet and try to explain which candidates are likely to protect Social Security. This was the issue that seemed to concern her most when we had first talked about Mama voting.

"But wait, I'll make another look," she says, and she is off to search through her box of costume jewelry again in search of her teeth. "So, tell me professor," she calls, "for which one should I vote?" I continue with my summary of the candidates' records and try to explain that even if we are forced to vote for the lesser of the evils she should vote. Momma sings out, "You don't say?

Very interesting. Listen boychik, I want to vote for Eleanor Roosevelt, she's a good woman. The only one I trust!" "Momma," I say, "she was a fine woman, but she's passed away." "Really?" she says, "Oh yeah, that's right."

I take Momma's evening medication, a glass of water, and the absentee ballot sheet to her. She puts the two pills on the back of her tongue, takes the glass of water from my hand, and brings the glass to her lips. She throws back her head and swallows. "What a week it was," she says, "Terrible." I wonder which week she is referring to, but I won't ask. She says, "Awful," and brings her fingers up to her cheekbone, "I got sunglasses boychik, like I was a movie star in disguise, a regular Lana Turner. All week I avoided my sisters. If they saw and told my brothers that would have been the end of your father. Outside I wore the sunglasses and covered up the bruise with powder and makeup. And that was the week the landlord found out about the stray dogs your brother was keeping in the empty apartment, near the roof. Your father for once in his life was quiet like a ghost. I had to take the dogs to the ASPCA. Mangy, sad looking things. They put them to sleep. Of course, who would want them? All week your brother cried. Also, this was the time you picked to get crazy in the street. You ruined your looks." "Momma, I'm sorry." She shrugs, "Before the fighting you had such a pretty profile. Even Aunt Tessie said you could have been in the movies." "Momma," I say, "it is almost your bedtime, why don't we take care of this? And I lay out the ballot sheet on the dresser, take the pencil from behind my ear, and review, once more, the particulars concerning the candidates I think Momma will find least objectionable. She listens patiently. "Boychik, I'm telling you, Eleanor Roosevelt is an honest woman, she has 'rachmones,' her we can trust." "Momma," I say, "I think you're right," and on the absentee ballot sheet, in the space provided for a write-in candidate, I scrawl in a cursive script as earnest as my initial attempt in second grade *Eleanor Roosevelt*.

THE LONG WAY HOME

SABBATICAL

Isaac is on sabbatical. His pockets are full of candy. He considers that his salvation depends on his ability to endure the clichés. He can hear the voice of Charley McDougal, survivor of the Battan death march, his sponsor, reminding him, "an alcoholic is someone who cannot drink in safety. Think the drink through. Eat the candy. Telephone your sponsor." Isaac stuffs his mouth with chocolate kisses. He thinks of calling Charley to complain that he can't remember the last time he got more than an hour of sleep. But he knows old Charley will only repeat, "it ain't lack of sleep that will kill ya," and Isaac, "should cultivate an attitude of gratitude, take it one day at a time, one hour at a time, when necessary, one minute at a time."

Isaac is grateful for longing. The shrink at detox had explained that he was grieving, mourning for the loss of the great
wild love of his life, drinking. It seemed to Isaac that huge Dr.
Morris Konig, regal and smiling, whom all the drunks referred
to affectionately as Dr. Moe, appeared, despite the long white
hair mantled about his shoulders, a youthful and zany Moses.
Perhaps it was Dr. Moe's evangelical good cheer, an enthusiasm
beyond all reason; but maybe such a capacity is required to res-
urrect a life from wreckage; the enterprise itself is not reasonable. Isaac wanted to believe in Dr. Moe's optimistic assessment
of his chances for recovery, and Isaac, whatever his doubts, didn't
begrudge the obvious pleasure the doctor felt when articulating his theories regarding Isaac. Isaac could only hope that Dr.
Moe was right.

There were aspects of Isaac's doubt that he had tried to keep
to himself. At last he divulged his sense of the eccentric economy
that hoarded perhaps the most glorious possibilities of his life.
He felt at once ridiculous, and as though he were betraying himself, surrendering; but he was compelled to speak because he
couldn't be certain he was alive.

The anecdote he'd read somewhere may have been apocry-
phal but its meaning for Isaac grew powerful. When, sometime
during the protracted hangover of the first days in detox Isaac
blurted the name of the poet, as though he were coughing up a
piece of his lungs, Dr. Moe smiled and shrugged, and said that
he had never heard of Rilke. The story, Isaac said, seemed to
him one of the analects whose imperious truth governed his
speech and his silence. Dr. Moe sighed and sustained a kindly
smile. Isaac plunged into the story.

When Rilke was dying, a Russian admirer, a poet herself,
Marina Tsvetayeva, wrote to Rilke to say, "You are not the poet

I love the most, you are poetry itself." But many years before, when Rilke was prolific and tortured, he relented, thinking that the excess of his suffering was unnecessary. He approached one of the granddaddies of the psychoanalytic movement and confessed he was harried by demons. However, Rilke never returned to the analyst, and that good doctor, certain of the new precepts that could light up the inner dark, and old enough to esteem poetry, wrote to Herr Rilke inquiring why the poet did not avail himself of the means of making his existence less painful. Rilke responded by writing to say yes, it was true that he'd wanted to be freed from his demons, but then he was afraid that his angels would flee as well.

The look of forbearance on Dr. Moe's face modulated his smile from robust good cheer to whimsy. Quickly Isaac had tried to explain that his primary concern was that somehow by accepting the terms of Dr. Moe's discussion he would be subverting, cashing in the vital substance of a vocabulary that might he his. Isaac could not keep himself from trembling when he said this.

Dr. Moe's benign smile didn't fade as he said, "Well Isaac, you're free to leave the program and we'll willingly refund your misery." Isaac considered leaving and also suspected that he had become addicted to Dr. Moe's reassurances.

It had taken Isaac a week or longer (he couldn't be sure, the reckoning of mortal time seemed a provisional and dubious invention) to speak of the other pervasive haunting shrouding his life, if indeed he were alive.

For the better part of a year, or could it have been six months? — he tried to remember, desperate as a child being tested in the most unforgiving school, and stunned before the greater mystery implied by numbers, computing this sum correctly might be the secret means of returning to life.

"A year," he said to Dr. Moe, "six months, no it had to be longer than that, a long time anyway," his skin had seemed a deadening mesh, muting all feeling, sensation during lovemaking a remote throbbing within him.

Isaac was attentive and surrendered to a kind of faith. After all, as he had to rely on others, often strangers, to tell him what happened and what he had done during some event that he recalled vaguely or not at all, then he might be wise to at least consider the ideas of Dr. Morris Konig, a mosaic shaman looming gigantic out of a straight-backed kitchen chair, radiant with good will and concern for Isaac's life.

"You," Dr. Moe said, building on the language he'd borrowed from his associate, old Charley McDougal, who had survived the most savage fighting in the Pacific, endured the unspeakable as a POW, and then very nearly perished from the fatal glass of beer offered to him as a war hero, "you," Dr. Moe said, like other alkies might die from terminal individuality. What applies to humanity is not supposed to apply to you and what you hoped to find in oblivion is the exception to be made in your case."

Isaac listened, he surmised from the many repetitions that the recitation of his conceits was part of the healing and a form of prayer meant to restore him. "Remember," Dr. Moe said, "you're not sober yet, only dry. And you're fortunate, really. Whatever the economic uncertainties, the career you've ruined, Laura is willing to try this one last time, provided you never pick up a drink again, and she means it. She can't live through another one of your disappearances. You have a family to return to. You should be grateful." Isaac could not say he was grateful and Dr. Moe didn't require that he say it.

Dr. Moe studied Isaac's struggle. Isaac stammered. Dr. Moe reminded Isaac that his struggle, even his feeling of humiliation were signs of life. Finally Dr. Moe said what he knew Isaac wanted to hear. Dr. Moe turned away as he spoke, discreet as a man giving alms, and now Isaac was grateful. Even the stilted clinical vocabulary seemed to Isaac a kindness, describing a universal malady and not particularly his own shameful demise. The doctor reiterated: The diminution of sensation that Isaac had experienced during lovemaking was not uncommon for the bereaved and deeply depressed. The loss of sensation was also a symptom of shock, a kind of death in life that would pass like a fever.

"And Isaac," Dr. Moe said, again looking straight in his eyes, "you need to think about your infidelities, one of the privileges granted to you by boozing. After a certain number of drinks you were free to adventure beyond good and evil. At least that was your own description, or were you only bragging? Think about it."

Isaac thought about it. He had been told by various friends, acquaintances, and strangers that the trajectory of his drunkenness went from charming, endearing, foolish, sloppy, to violent. Whether the booze stripped the artifice of civilized inhibition to liberate the creature of rage incarcerated in the deep dark of his psyche or the booze itself turned him into a nut for its own purposes, he couldn't determine. Charley McDougal and Dr. Moe, as well as other recovering drunks in the program, worked hard to persuade Isaac of the urgent practicality of not delving into such what came first, the chicken or the egg conundrums; it was not necessary to journey and search forever round and round the mystigogic circle of origins. All he needed to do was not pick up a drink and the anguishing riddle

would cease to matter. But when Laura had insisted on knowing where he had been, he couldn't say for sure. The left side of
his face, swollen from his eyebrow to upper lip, was the color of
port wine. She managed not to cry, clenched her fists, and asked,
"Well, do you know how you got that?"

He remembered coming to in a cavernous underground
garage, crapped out in the back of an empty bus. It took him a
long time to figure out how to open the front door of the bus
and longer still to find his way out of the labyrinthian dark of
the underground municipal parking facility without a single
human attendant in sight. Blood-red exit signs blinked and
beckoned and he hiked through the interminable time in darkness, listening to the dumb thumping of his heart. He emerged
into a bright street that wasn't New York, the only city he knew.
He recalled that recently walking in the village in Vermont, where
he now lived, he'd had the powerful desire to eat lobster and
spaghetti with oil and garlic at Gene's in Sheepshead Bay, Brooklyn. He walked through several streets tempted to ask passersby
what city he was in but couldn't bring himself to ask. He looked
at the cityscape and speculated, Chicago? Philadelphia?

"Did you hurt anyone?" Laura asked. "No," he said, "I don't
think so," and hid his right hand, too swollen to hold a pencil,
behind his back.

He remembered suddenly, vividly, and began to tell Laura because there was an element in all this she could empathize with.

He turned the corner into a street and there crowds of young
people were marching and singing "Give peace a chance." Some
skipped, some danced, some appeared to be ice-skating over
the asphalt in their sandals. Several lovely young women in
granny gowns gliding like sleepwalkers gave flowers to the police who were hemming in the hostile crowd at the curb. The

policemen receiving the flowers looked confused and then angry, certain the bouquets were an expression of mockery. Isaac moving along in the throng thought, yes, there is that too; he could hear tinkling bells, smelled incense and marijuana. Just past the three graces floating down the avenue strewing flowers, Pan — shaggy and human in bell-bottomed trousers, his pointed ears attuned to the sensual music in the general racket — played his pipes, rolled his eyes, and didn't duck the empty beer cans lobbed from the sidewalk, raining down all around him. Someone handed Isaac a joint. He inhaled deeply, held his breath, longed for a beer to top off the smoke, and thought, if history were a nightmare from which he could not awake, this at least was another dream. Strolling along in the gleeful bedlam, Isaac found himself walking beside the Calendar Christ at an inauspicious moment. He, the Christ, was young and very pretty. His long blond hair fell about his shoulders. He wore a garment that looked like pajamas, a penitential washed-out gray, and his pale feet in sandals tread gently and tentative as the most humble visitor to the planet. His dazzling, wet blue eyes were drenched with a tolerance that nevertheless seemed to be importuning, like the most tenacious beggar, something from each individual that one could give at only the greatest cost to oneself. In the instant that Isaac overcame the repugnance he felt for the presumption of the Calendar Christ, whose eyes locked on his and seemed to be asking, no, demanding some kind of ultimate nakedness, Isaac remembered that in spite of his promise to Laura, after one month he'd picked up a drink again; and it occurred to him that this happened because he lacked the necessary minimum of self-knowledge to live without the illusion of freedom that booze offered. The Calendar Christ batted his eyes in agreement.

The beer cans and a couple of bricks bounced off the pavement. An exploding bag of garbage splattered coffee grounds, fragments of eggshells, and damp noodles on Isaac's legs. As he bent over to wipe the mess from his pants he became aware of the aggrieved sound of a group of six or seven construction workers growling just to his right. A policeman who'd failed to keep the group confined to the curb, and had been swept into the milling center, argued sympathetically with the men and tried to restrain them. One of the workers, with the grace and skill of a gifted quarterback, threw his coffee thermos, spiraling true and swift, at a protestor's head. Another, with close-cropped gray hair, squat, powerfully built, leaned on the head of a pickaxe as though supporting himself with a cane, nodded approval at the accurate throw of his younger colleague and howled, "They fuck like rabbits." The complaint confused Isaac. The older worker's outcry sounded like a man who had just discovered that his pocket had been picked. On the opposite curb a couple of teenage boys had broken through the police cordon and they were punching a demonstrator who had his arms raised over his face. Three solemn looking policemen had decided to punish the protestors for failing not to provoke the angry onlookers, and the cops clubbed the protestors. Isaac, at the quiet center of an estrangement that felt like objectivity, the contemplative sense, a bit of the ephemeral bounty of booze, Isaac thought, and for which he knew he would pay, as to any usurer, the vigorish here incalculable; still he would not forgo the pleasure of figuring it all out. First the construction workers had seemed outraged patriots. Many of the young protestors, the workers would think, the most pampered and privileged creatures on Earth, enjoying college deferments from military service and having all the time in the world, could afford to squander time, protesting, betraying their country, while others fought and died in their place. But also there were the men screaming "whore" and "they fuck like rabbits" at the young women dispensing flowers and singing "Give Peace a Chance." Isaac wondered whether these dedicated family men had been traumatized because the young people seemed able to fornicate with a greater ease of conscience than they, abstaining or traditional adulterers, could imagine. Turning, Isaac noticed a pretty young woman with red Valentine hearts painted on her plump cheeks reaching into the crowd of construction workers. She handed her last daisy to a handsome bewildered young worker of draft age, smiled, and said, "girls say yes to boys who say no."

As if on cue, the young men demonstrating against the war, parading behind the pretty young woman with the glowing red Valentine hearts on her cheeks, set matches and cigarette lighters to their draft cards; they raised their arms in a gesture of triumph, bits of flame and smoke ignited from their fingertips, and Isaac thought of the girl who might never be lovelier than she was this moment, employing Lysistrata's gambit without a clue of the danger; only a moment before he had dallied with the hunch that the workingmen, whose earnings and time were strictly apportioned, feared that there was a finite amount of pleasure in the world, and these kids were going to use it all up. As the notion became a conviction, Isaac was tempted to say something, try to explain. Alarmed, he wanted to warn the men that such resentment would annihilate the possibility of anything noble in their lives. But Isaac couldn't speak, not even to the powerful looking older worker who resembled his father.

In a trance snug as a womb, Isaac saw it all and came out swinging. Whether the celebratory raving of the construction workers as they lifted and pitched the young co-worker, still looking bewildered and holding the daisy, into the girl who'd promised "girls say yes to boys who say no," or the narrative force of his dreaming reaching a conclusion flushed him out, Isaac couldn't say. He was in the thick of it. The girl went down hard, the boy on top of her. She was hurt. The construction workers cheered. Isaac caught a glimpse of the Calendar Christ looking heartsore, staring, demanding something. Someone yelled, "Give Jesus a haircut and put him in the army." Isaac couldn't see anymore. Close, intimate, his face resting on the chest of the man in front of him, the man's face resting on Isaac's chest, in the posture of drowsers propping one another up, they punched into one another's body digging deep.

He would lay claim to remembering that much. The effort not to cry made Laura angry. When she began to cry she became very angry. Isaac thought that what he had told wasn't an altogether sad story, not hopeless. But he saw Laura staring, as if his face were a magic mirror, reflecting the horrors of the world. "I'm me" he wanted to say, invoking again one of the strands of the longstanding marital argument, feeling violated he needed to say, distinguish, that he-they, Isaac and Laura, were something apart from the world, distinct, even if a part of it. Still, seeing what she saw in his face, she appeared so hurt that he was sure that arguing would only make matters worse.

Her sobs frightened him. He argued in his own behalf to himself. Mitigating circumstances, like destiny. It didn't help, Isaac thought, that superficially the pattern of some of his experiences resembled the fate of her brother Angel, a heroin addict. Isaac saw she was tired, exhausted by Angel's endless innocence. Her brother's career as a junkie, revolutionary, and now the saint of Sing Sing, guru to the damned, had cost her dearly. The monstrous process of Angel's sainthood, the most dreadful means to an end, Isaac concluded, left his wife, the Catholic girl, still lighting candles, bereft, pitying the feeble inventions of human reason and morality, and thinking how her brother had become the Mother Theresa of Sing Sing made her as ill as chewing on the carnal wafer of sublimity.

Isaac reviewed all this discreetly and tried to hug Laura, comfort her as she moved away, crying, studying him. He cautioned himself; it was rare for Laura not to know what he was thinking, if not precisely at least in essence; he felt helpless before this and a little thrilled remembering the attribute as an aspect of the odd wealth they shared, an immediacy that had been theirs from the beginning.

He remembered his attempt to write Angel's story and his belated judgment of failure, following Laura's judgment of his failure. He'd been too worshipful of the mythic possibilities of the facts, and this spawned an unwieldy chronicle, as Isaac was unable to sacrifice anything because it was all, all fantastically true. He'd been obsessed with Angel the casual patricide. In one of the stories, the one that also prevailed in court and resulted in the judgment of involuntary manslaughter and a plea-bargained sentence that turned out to be three years and eight months with time off for good behavior: Angel — finally visiting the man who occasionally bragged he was Angel's father, the paternal acknowledgement an item in the celebration of the man's virility — had pushed his father off the roof. Noel, the erstwhile father of Laura and Angel, vain and worshipful of the prerogatives that lived beneath his belt buckle, had fathered children in three of the five boroughs of New York, and an old wife, a contemporary of Laura and Angel's mother, more steadfast than Penelope, still waited in Puerto Rico for Noel's return and sat on their son, a Telemachus ripening into a prodigious arsonist.

Laura had responded to Noel as a rumor who occasionally appeared to take a bow. She was grateful that he was one male presence that made no claim on her, nothing for her to negotiate, finesse, escape. But Angel had been engaged in some way she would theorize about for years.

Noel invited Angel to attend the picnic on the roof and Angel surprised himself, and Noel, when he found himself there. Noel welcomed him with laughter. He said, "Hello, how are you? And how is your sister?" Angel shrugged his shoulders to the first question, then said, "A Jew wants to marry her." Noel said, "I may marry her myself," and laughed again. For a long time Angel thought he'd dismissed what he'd heard in the laughter, but later he recognized that he felt responsible for teaching Noel that such laughter could not be given with impunity. Patria, Noel's woman, was polite and fearful. Noel and Patria's three young children seemed content. Oranges and plates of chicken and rice were spread out on a blanket. A large styrofoam cooler with cans of iced beer and soda and a portable radio were set in the shade, beneath an abandoned pigeon coop. The pretty twin five-year-old girls played with their dolls as Patria watched them. The boy, about seven, fiddled with the dial on the radio. It was a muggy day, the sky becoming overcast; some fetid breezes from the East River doused the tenement roof.

Angel and Noel had been drinking but were not drunk. What the argument was about no one remembered. It didn't seem serious. Who gave the first shove no one recalled, but it was Noel who tumbled from the roof, and that, Patria would testify, weeping, appeared to be an accident. For a time before Angel was arrested, during Patria's grieving, she became Angel's lover.

Angel, while he was still talking, and Laura still religiously listening, tried to explain the feeling of passing through many deaths as he watched his father fall, Angel on his way to selflessness. Laura tried to hide her fear and revulsion as she thought there was no conflict, no suffering, and no crime that Angel would not live through, and she didn't want to hear anymore.

But when Angel managed to kick, cold turkey, and was clean, after an ordeal that left some portion of Laura's soul numb, she felt obliged to listen to her brother's wonderstruck whispering. He spoke, and Laura, stunned, saw that he bore no resemblance to the thrashing, vomiting thing that she, Aunt Titi, and her mother had tied to the bed with ropes, piling their bodies on him to quell and comfort his trembling as he screamed and begged, cursed them and all women with such inventive and scorching vehemence that Laura would forever after have to muster the greatest self-control not to flinch when she overheard even the ingenuous misogynist jokes that some boorish stranger thought funny.

Although Laura was fearful of hope, when Angel was still clean after seven months she couldn't help hoping, and this hoping began to wear away her heart. She listened as Angel spoke of his reading. He needed her to listen and she willed a presence of mind while she fended off her dread of Angel's relapse, and the near delirium when she found herself believing in his recovery. She noted peripherally his Marxist theorizing, the Che Guevara beret he had taken to wearing, the latest invention of himself, a symptom and a sign of returning health like his complexion blooming and human, no longer the jaundiced yellow of a junkie.

Angel lived at home with Laura, Rosita, Aunt Titi, and his mother. He helped coach the Golden Glove hopefuls at the

YMCA. Laura listening to Angel, watchful, gathered evidence to support her belief in Angel's recovery, which day by day was miraculous, real, and exhausting. She could dismiss her uneasiness when Angel spoke in the most gentle voice of his contempt for being merely an aggregate of progressive political opinion. She was quick to remind him of his good work in the community, his coaching of the boxing team, and his mentoring in the reading program at the public library, organized for the children of the neighborhood. Years later while explaining to Isaac why his novella based on Angel's life didn't work, she became very upset when Isaac attempted to explain that the Angel in his story had to become a hero before he became a saint, and Laura found herself remembering the night it all crashed and Angel shot the cop who died four days later.

Angel's sidekick and shadow, diminutive Indio, with his straight blue black hair and copper-colored skin, resembled a princely Aztec child. Indio was always smiling, silent, and armed. He'd never been affiliated with a gang and had been allowed to go his own way. If, as was rumored, he supported himself, widowed mother, and two sisters by armed robbery, whatever his trade, he kept his activity far from the home barrio. On occasion Indio stated his guiding belief. "You don't shit where you eat." Polite and believed to be lethal, amazingly Indio had reached his twentieth year. Chaste as a monk he did not drink, smoke, or use drugs. Laura thought but had no way of proving that Indio's devotion to Angel was based upon some not thought out and implicit sense of meaning accruing to Indio from proximity to Angel's words and life, and by Indio's unspoken dedication to Angel.

There were conflicting stories. The facts availed themselves to the several versions of the truth. One policeman was dead, another left paralyzed, and Indio was dead. The prosecuting attorney maintained that in the shootout the police had been ambushed by Angel and Indio, who fancied themselves revolutionary guerillas, "liberating the neighborhood from the oppressor pigs." Some residents of the building testified that the policemen, responding to a complaint of domestic disturbance, crashed through the door of the wrong apartment and beat into a coma a man who had not been battering his wife, but embracing her, happy and boisterous. Neither the recent immigrant from Santo Domingo nor his wife could speak English, and the police didn't understand Spanish. When the cops dragged the man into the hallway they had their guns drawn. One ancient black woman of formidable dignity, who spoke English and Spanish fluently, testified that she was much too old and too tired to be threatened by anything this side of the grave, and she understood why her neighbors were intimidated. The confusion surrounding the incident of the alleged domestic disturbance had taken place earlier in the evening. The two policemen who were shot were plainclothes detectives, bagmen (known to the people of the community) who were there to collect their monthly take of the dope business.

The old woman, Señora Cortez, admitted that her eyesight was failing but insisted that her hearing was acute. She recognized the voice of Rodrigo, the chief dope dealer of the barrio, and his second in command Joey Ramos. There had been a business disagreement, a breakdown in negotiations; before, when she had entered her apartment carrying groceries, she had seen in the hallway two shadows that might have been Indio and Angel. She had assumed they were there to score dope. The bagmen cops and Rodrigo and Joey Ramos hadn't arrived yet. Señora Cortez went into her apartment and locked the door. A

little later she heard the argument and the shots. Three stray
bullets crashed through the wall of her kitchen. Her refrigerator was destroyed and a pot of African Violets shattered. She
was able to save the African Violets and repot them.

Joey Ramos was dead, Rodrigo escaped and disappeared.

When Angel testified, trying to support the claim of self-
defense, he said he and Indio were caught in the crossfire and
had to defend themselves from assassination since they found
themselves at the wrong place at the wrong time. Indignantly
he added that he happened to be in the building where he lived
and was on his way home. Under cross-examination he admitted that as a convicted felon he had no right to carry a firearm,
and Indio had provided him with the revolver. Despite the advice of his attorney, and Angel's assurances, when Angel testified
he couldn't refrain from calling the police "pigs," and venturing
the opinion that the pigs, complicit in the dope business, and
profiting from it, as well as Joey Ramos and Rodrigo, who were
destroying their own people, all deserved to die.

Angel was convicted of second-degree murder and received
a sentence of life imprisonment. The remorse he felt was for
Laura and the closest he came to an apology was his confession
to her, during one of Laura's visits to jail before he was sen-
tenced, that he had begun to use again. The night of the shootout
he was in the hallway because he hoped to cop. Worshipful Indio
had pressed on Angel a confession that required several days of
stops and starts, until finally, purging himself, Indio admitted
his phobia of needles; it was only this dread that prevented him
from shooting up. Indio had no way of articulating what it was
he hoped to emulate from Angel's life, but around Angel he
enacted (not only the aroused revolutionist) but humbly and
without irony, a heroin addicts somnambulistic nodding out,

and the dream locutions of such speech while remaining supremely alert.

Angel told Laura that he hadn't been using long at the time of the shooting and that he regarded her vigilance, which he had to be resourceful to circumvent, as an expression of her caring. She shouldn't, he pleaded, think of his trouble as her failure. But now he needed to confide, wanted her to understand that he'd only wanted to taste again the high that was the closest a human could get to paradise: transcending all human need for food, sex, justice, a foretaste or theft of religious accomplishment he might not otherwise know or guess. That he'd been able to convince himself that he could have this once in a while was a seduction, he didn't have to be prompted to acknowledge, and damnation was palpable.

Isaac couldn't think of anything he could say that might comfort Laura. First he saw her reproach herself. Then he felt her assessing their life together. What was wonder had become incredulity as she tried to understand what fate was trying to teach her; fate conspiring with what character flaw allowed her to marry an alcoholic after having loved a brother who was a heroin addict. What deep predisposition, like the genes that carry the secret code of the body's destruction, made her susceptible to Isaac?

Not then, but in the next ten or twenty minutes after the shock of no thought and no feeling, reviving after the blow, Isaac was aware that he was dead. Laura no longer loved him. He heard himself breathing mechanically, loud. He watched her marshaling her resources to get beyond him as another of life's interesting follies. His heart became a dead weight in his chest, as an interior monologue went off in his head like the light traveling from a dead star. He considered the rudiments of the way the dead talk to themselves.

But first she had cried. A torrent of Spanish came at him. The isolated words and phases he understood weren't enough to reveal what she was saying to him or declaring to the universe.

She grabbed the lapels of his jacket, yanked him close to her, and said clearly, slowly, and in English, "Isaac, the Vietnam War, the protests, all that has been over for four, almost five years. You've been gone a week."

Laura began to tell him what she knew about what had happened, and he was certain of the memory of his attempt to appear to be drinking moderately. He'd had a plan. His effort to appear a social drinker required that he drink his hidden pint of whiskey at home before leaving for the faculty Christmas party. This strategy would enable him to sip slowly one or two martinis, and with the foundation and ballast of the whiskey he could be a successful social drinker for the space of an hour, which was as long as he intended to stay.

Isaac didn't dispute Laura's account of what had happened. For all of his caution she'd seen him sneaking his pint from the drum of the broken washing machine in the bathroom alcove. Now she told him that was why she'd refused to attend the party with him. It was Peter Julius, Laura said, who brought Isaac home. Isaac said he remembered that. Laura said that Peter Julius saw to it that Isaac got home safely on at least two other occasions. Isaac hadn't any recollection of the previous occasions, although he had a distinct sense of Peter Julius, as well as others, including Laura, once she heard the stories, describing his misadventure at the Christmas party.

They all agreed and he wasn't in a position to challenge the veracity of his colleagues' and wife's version of the incident. He may have had his arm around Dean Hemshaw's shoulders, but he didn't have any recollection of choking him. A month before, during Thanksgiving dinner, Isaac admitted to Laura that the unfortunate resemblance of the dean to former President Richard Nixon worked as a provocation that he'd successfully resisted on several occasions. True, Isaac had communicated to the academic dean his dismay over the decimation of the humanities program, and the dean's acquiescence and or sponsorship for the dropping of various philosophy and literature courses. Yet it all seemed so outrageous to Isaac that his indiscreet language struck him as meek. He'd proclaimed to his colleagues and the dean his grief at having Aristotle and Dostoyevsky disappear to make way for new courses on the art and science of money grubbing. "Yes," Laura said, "but you tipped over the table of hors d'oeuvres and Peter Julius and what's his name from the history department had to pry your arms loose from the headlock you had on Hemshaw. They said the poor man was gagging and you were dragging him toward the door." Under the circumstances the suggestion of a sabbatical rather than a demand for his immediate resignation seemed generous to Isaac.

He apologized. Dean Hemshaw nodded his head and said that Isaac's relationship to the college would be reevaluated at the conclusion of his sabbatical. Isaac apologized again. The dean said he assumed that Isaac would seek the appropriate professional help he needed to overcome his problem. Isaac, truly contrite and ashamed of jeopardizing the well-being of his family, said he was sorry again, truly sorry, and that he'd already taken steps to deal with his problem. Dean Hemshaw looked sad, however, thought Isaac, the dean always looked sad, and tired. Isaac couldn't remember how he knew; Dean Hemshaw was his contemporary, about forty-two years old, but

Hemshaw looked much older. Bundled in thick tweeds, he maintained his dignity while his inflamed, sweat-glazed skin suggested the symptoms of malaria. For a moment Isaac empathized with the dean and considered the administrative burdens that may have been destroying the man.

Isaac stood up to go and held out his hand. The dean hesitated and then shook Isaac's hand. Isaac stood there clasping Hemshaw's hand and thought of Laura's recounting of the Christmas faculty party as he would his long ago reading of the *Epic of Gilgamesh*.

The house he occupied felt like a memory, a place emptied out by the purposes of his dream, which he couldn't fathom and feared he would forget. The bookcase swollen with former loves was now an archive of puzzles, his wife and daughter were not present and in their absence even the furniture seemed ghostly. The six by eleven painting, Laura's work in progress, turned the living-room wall into an explosion of light and color, a panorama of what Isaac had taken to calling the Big Bang, the dawn's dawn of creation. Much of the floor was covered by the city Maria, his ten-year-old daughter had made. Dwellings made out of cartons, the interiors visible, each box was set on its side, the inhabitants were made of pipe cleaners, the walls brilliant collages cut and pasted from magazines, lakes made of clay, papier-mâché trees, the kingdom stretched along the floor from wall to wall, and Isaac thought how having this child had humbled him. It was his child's beauty that confirmed that his life hadn't merely arisen from his mind. He remembered, Maria was not quite three when she began to talk. Isaac couldn't remember anything he could call baby talk. It was very disconcerting. Maria at three might have addressed the United Nations. There was about the child a certain repose, a dignity that convinced Isaac early on that he should assume he knew nothing and that he would have to learn to love his daughter in the manner she indicated through the years. She was his great friend, a joy, and he would rather listen to her genealogy of the creation than talk to his colleagues. Often he thought he should take notes, write down what she was saying, but he was too rapt to move.

Isaac waited. Laura said she and Maria would return that day. The day was half gone. Perhaps Laura's unfinished painting was a sign that she hadn't meant to leave him for good. Isaac knew Laura didn't indulge in ploys; he hoped she hadn't been swayed by second thoughts, doubts.

He waited. He didn't desire a drink, but he did desire what a drink would do to waiting. He ate a chocolate kiss. He ate three chocolate kisses. He considered for a moment taking a walk. But the house in the village was too close to the campus. Whenever he encountered a colleague averting his or her face, making believe he or she hadn't seen him, Isaac didn't know whether he should apologize, he couldn't remember what he might have done and he too averted his face. He decided to stay put, wait. Laura said she was going to return, and although she had often kept him waiting she had never stood him up. He tried to hold on to that thought.

Isaac couldn't help admiring the oak cabinets, built by Peter Julius on the wall facing Laura's painting. The cabinets were new. Laura stored her art supplies there. Peter had also repaired the broken washing machine. Isaac had thought of his former colleague, Peter Julius, as the silent botanist. Dr. Julius, professor of the natural sciences, despite his frugal speech, which was always accurate and accessible, was, like Isaac, a popular teacher. Isaac had admired the gifted teacher's ability to inspire, and imagined Peter Julius, the only native Vermonter on the faculty of the small liberal arts college in the northeast corner of Vermont, as a facilitator of the earth's wonders who did not speak of wonder. Modestly Professor Julius presented and shaped the sequence of information so that his students inferred the germane idea. Peter Julius also rescued and repaired injured birds. Isaac had long been aware and in awe of the array of Peter Julius' competencies. He was an accomplished carpenter, plumber, stonemason, and gardener. Their professional relationship had always been cordial and Isaac hadn't any inkling that Julius had been courting Laura. It was Laura who had told Isaac just before his last binge that during his previous disappearance she had invited Peter into her bed. When Isaac thought of the extensive repairs Peter Julius administered to the house, roof, plumbing, and foundation, repairs that Isaac didn't know how to do, nor could he afford to hire people for the work, he wanted to move from the house or burn it down.

He considered setting the place on fire, but first he would have to rescue his daughter's bowl of goldfish and his wife's painting. The logistics of salvaging the goldfish and the painting, and his reluctance to pick up a drink, subverted his passion for fire. Laura had arranged with a neighbor to come in and feed the goldfish while she was away. For reasons Maria refused to say, she had insisted on leaving the goldfish behind during the three months she and her mother lived with Peter Julius. Now for reasons Laura didn't care to explore, she was returning to Isaac, and Peter Julius had resigned from the college and was on his way to Alaska.

Isaac thought of his wife's lover. He resembled certain actors of an older generation, youthful in spite of his white hair, his handsomeness unostentatious, the effect of the persona somewhere between Jimmy Stewart and Gary Cooper. Peter Julius radiated an archaic wholesomeness and male innocence. Isaac wondered, in the austerities of Peter Julius' speech, had he heard a fitness, the disposition of a love that had a greater and more legitimate claim to his wife's affections. Peter's reticence would find expression in what he could build and provide for Laura; but now the peerless bachelor was on his way to Alaska; Laura, as Dr. Moe had pointed out, had chosen Isaac. At last Isaac was grateful, but he wasn't sure he could bear to look at Laura's reasons for returning to him.

Sitting there, watching winter disappear in the window, Isaac preferred to recall Laura's characterization of her first lover, the young man who had taken her virginity. Laura told Isaac shortly before they were married. She put on a comic lugubrious face as she told it, and he began dreaming her dreams. She laughed so violently at first that it seemed she wouldn't be able to tell it.

Isaac waited. Laura commenced with a conclusion derived from the story she hadn't told yet, but the thought allowed her to breath while her eyes continued to laugh. Her discovery that her mother and aunt's science (and magic) was not, after all (her terror and pity) sufficient to detect the loss of her virginity relieved and disappointed her. Maybe it was only that she had grown beyond them into a skepticism in pursuit of a life that would be hers, but the loss, despite the comfort and novelty of privacy, would be hers too. She spoke of handsome Harry Walters as incidental to all of this. Isaac had heard of Harry Walters but never met him. After just one semester at City College, during which he played the young suitor in the drama department production of *The Glass Menagerie*, he dropped out to pursue study at the Actors Studio. Laura said Harry took a one-room apartment in Greenwich Village. There were no windows in the apartment. The rough stucco walls were ocher. On one wall of eddying deep yellow was a bullfight poster. The matador on tiptoe balletically avoiding the powerful mass of bull-rushing death. On the opposite wall, a reproduction of a French impressionist master, working in shadow, tromp l'oeil, a window opened to a lovely sun-filled garden, a tantalizing bucolic stupor leaking into the sun-colored chamber. In a corner, two wooden kitchen chairs and a round table, on which an empty straw encased Chianti bottle with a single lit candle sticking out of the neck burned, dripping baubles of wax. Below the illusion of the sun-filled window, a long, fat, dun-colored couch. A stereo system tucked in the dark of a functionless dumbwaiter emitted Bach's suite No.1 in G major for unaccompanied cello. Laura said she visited Harry twice, and she thought him a very gifted actor, someone born for the Stanislavsky method. He never spoke of his parents or where he had lived. The actor seemed to have no ancestry, came from nowhere, all the energy of his consciousness compelled to inhabit the persona he was performing; and aside from a handsomeness reminiscent of Angel, Laura wondered where he might have learned Angel's mannerisms, and the peculiar soft purr of Angel's speech. Harry entertained Laura. He assumed the identities of several of the instructors he and Laura had taken classes with at City College. He performed for Laura scenes from the plays of Sean O'Casey and Tennessee Williams. Upon request he became James Dean.

Eventually Laura would remember that during class discussion, or for that matter talking to her, Harry never really expressed an idea, but provided the emotional affect of an idea expressed by someone else, the fluent instrument of his body and face adhering to someone else's words to create an aura seemingly as substantial as the idea itself, but far more glamorous in the guise he presented.

Isaac maintained that on at least two occasions Laura had mentioned Harry's uncanny resemblance to Angel. Angel, before drug addiction and battles in and out of the ring, hammered his face into something blunt and peculiarly eloquent. Later, Laura denied ever making such a statement and Isaac didn't insist, even though he was certain that that was what he heard, but in Laura's repeated tellings she was consistent in all the other essentials.

Sex for the actor of possible genius involved a blind intake of breath before the assumption of another mask, that would after due effort take on the luster and texture of transcendence, the enactment of passion. What surprised her, Laura said, was that she had long since given up going to confession in preparation for something unknown and momentous, something she had to do.

She was sympathetic to Harry's performance and returned to his pad one more time. She hadn't taken precautions and the risk lent the act verisimilitude, confirmed by the anxiety when her period was late. Then in the great relief to find she wasn't pregnant, she thought about it all again. The accretions of her understanding through the years making it difficult for her to say what she believed for certain, when; but for a long time now she maintained with some confidence that somehow she knew that the prerequisite to a life she might call her own required that she rid herself of virginity, the arbitrary thing of supreme value she was to bring to a husband, if she were not to be looked upon as soiled goods, while the husband, before and during marriage, if he were a real man, was expected to satisfy the demands of his virility (sometimes at home and) in the wide world whose yielding would provide a song for him alone. Laura's choice would be, like her mother's, operatic lament or providing stability to a home through her noble, melancholic, and silent forbearance.

It isn't, she told Isaac, that she'd thought this all out back then, but she was compelled by an instinctive act of will to partake of a ritual that shadowed the possibility of her own real choice.

Isaac hoping and awaiting rebirth felt the need to get beyond the conclusion, his own damning judgment that the botanist, Peter Julius, could be a better husband to Laura than he; and Laura, not a promiscuous person, had loved Peter, perhaps still had feelings for him. Death then, was not a way station at which one's moral shortcomings guaranteed rebirth for continued education, but final darkness, and the only light and hope was Isaac's memory of their first night together, a night in which the primary city of the world in all its workings was stopped for them.

The Vesuvius

I t began with her mercy. He was aware that she was aware of the professor's infatuation with her, every male in the class aware of her, the weight of the air in the classroom charged with the gravitational pull of all the young men performing for her, whatever else they might have been trying to accomplish at the same time, so that she felt that inadvertently she had contributed to his public humiliation.

He would never forget it, Speech 101. His oral presentation was based on Santayana's *Sense of Beauty*. As he spoke he made an effort not to look at Laura but knew he was speaking to her, the other thirty or more students in the classroom were bystanders, overhearing what seemed to Isaac a song, a theme that had chosen him. At the conclusion he was soaked with sweat, near collapse, and certain he was at the pinnacle of something new in his life, ordained by the way clamoring language found its way in him. Primo Landolfi, his dear friend the philosophy major, who described himself as a fugitive from the Jesuits (the most beautiful fat man Isaac had ever seen, Primo may have been the one male at City College who could turn his unencumbered gaze on Laura because he loved too much to ever be in love), Primo at the conclusion of Isaac's presentation was standing and applauding. Then suddenly Isaac heard, and his ears burned, "X-cape" and "Poyg-nent," his speech clanging like garbage can lids bouncing off the pavement. Professor Dearborne's mimicry was expert, cruel, and to Isaac's burning ear, accurate. Isaac, hearing the sound of his voice debasing anything he might think, the deepest aspirations of his heart revealed, an absurdity.

The professor appeared to be reading from the moon in the window to the tired night school students; "Although a Midwestern bray might be tolerable and a southern accent sometimes acceptable, a New York accent is substandard."

Isaac's undoing had been signaled by his pronunciation of "poignant" and "escape." Primo, who would be drawn back to his priestly calling and one day disappear in a Peruvian rainforest, was destined to repeat Speech 101 when Professor Dearborne heard Primo pronounce "oil" as "earl."

Isaac fled, hurried away from the reassurances he knew Primo would offer; he needed space and time to come to terms with the truth of his life. He sat in a corner of Finley Hall lounge drinking a cup of coffee and smoking a cigarette. The raucous sound of the voice, which he'd recognized as his own for the first time, echoed in his ears. After the third cigarette and the second cup of coffee it occurred to him that the sound that came from his mouth, and demeaned the possibilities of poetry and intelligence, could be obscured, silenced on the page. He consoled himself, inhaled, filling his lungs with smoke, and began to believe. He was not lost.

He looked up expecting to see Primo, who often offered Isaac, Isaac's own most optimistic notions before Isaac laboriously thought himself there; but it was Laura Providencia standing in front of him, introducing herself. Although she was in his Speech class, Philosophy class, and Comparative Lit class, they had never spoken. All the purposes of the imponderable hello accumulating in him for three months making him dumb, he made some sound of greeting. She said she had enjoyed his presentation and quoting him said that she wanted to hear more about how, "the natural desire to contemplate beauty creates morality, art, and religion." She was waiting. No matter how much he feared the barbarity of his accent it was necessary for him to speak. His invitation for her to sit was inaudible. He gestured toward the chair opposite him. She sat down, laughed, and changed the subject. She said that before City College she had gone to school across the street, at the High School of Music and Art, where she learned to explode her "t's" and "d's" and was divested of her Spanish accent; she said all this enunciating in the most impeccable patrician tone and then was overtaken by laughter that made her shake so that Isaac brought a glass of water to her lips.

Soon after they would walk all over the city. They talked incessantly. At first the talk was respite between and after lovemaking. They had an inkling of the ways in which their stories would live in one another, something akin to but more profound than sympathy — a transmutation of history precipitated in delight and recognition that couldn't be accounted for by their appreciation (these avid students) of psychology or sociology; he was her and she was his amanuensis in their telling and finding the stories that would be their undiscovered life.

Isaac sat there, willed and conjured the memory, the event cocooned in the city's most ferocious winter night ever; the snow in twenty-four hours as good as forever after, better than the legend of the flood, and it was not "the fire next time," but snow, the deluged metropolis called "the Apple" by the giddier sinners, some of whom felt compelled to count — quantify the immeasurable — how much had fallen from heaven from midday to early evening, all the suddenly privileged inhabitants of the city, relieved and grateful to be subject to some other primacy than their own crazed coming and going. Isaac and Laura wandered through miles of snow-drowned streets, the city disappearing beneath the blossoming mounds of endlessly falling white. Their evening had begun as the rest of the world was on the way home from work. The subway trains were delayed but still running. Bundled together as chastely as some archaic New England couple, courting through the dividing plank in a crib, where only sleep may serve as touch, Laura Providencia and Isaac rocked in the grinding train, all of exhausted humanity pressing in on them. The train lurched to a stop. They separated themselves from the bodies packed against them. Parting, but still linked by holding hands, they wriggled and squeezed out of the train. They moved through the tunnel and climbed up the steps, and up a second tier of steps; out of the belabored roar of the subway thundering below their feet, they climbed up into the dense falling snow. The little they could see was reduced to the length of a single stride, and what they saw bobbed forward a small distance, as from the prow of a skiff on a fog-bound ocean. The known geography of the streets became obsolete as they walked slowly, found their way, and arrived by some precursor to faith, and entered the restaurant. It was warm.

The maître d' glided up to them out of the amber light, the tilting of his body suggesting the sweetest deference, so articulate and expert, that Isaac and Laura, surprised and shy, were precluded from wondering whether they were worthy of such homage. The maître d's utterance was a discreet species of silence. The snow on their shoulders became water. He seated them. It was, he said, "a slow night." Solicitously, and with a sense of grave responsibility, the maître d' brought their attention to the weather, nodding his head toward the restaurant's frosted window. The maître d' noted that the few remaining patrons lived in the neighborhood and did not have far to travel. "Although please," he said, "you are most welcome." Behind the maître d' an elderly waiter bowed in creaking shoes, the weight of the tower of his sculpted white hair pulling him forward. He bowed from the waist, and offered two warm white towels. Isaac's hands nested in the warmth of the towel, he looked from the white of the towel to Laura Providencia, wiping her wet, black hair and he went blank for a moment.

The maître d' introduced the waiter who collected the towels as Antonio, and apologized for the weather and for leaving them; his duties required that he be present for the remainder of the evening in the private dining room in the rear of the restaurant. The maître d' said he was sure Antonio would serve them well. Antonio's torso rose slowly to an upright position, the pinnacle of his silvery pompadour shivered, the damp towels draped over his extended arm. The maître d' in his black tux receded toward the rear of the restaurant, and vanished in a door which closed and became part of a latticed façade festooned with plastic grapes and vines; two lanterns hung, glowing, where the door had been. Isaac turned to the sound of the waiter's creaking shoes padding off to the right, where behind the bar there was a fresco of spewing Vesuvius, the bar itself, studded with ruby-red neon lights. The young bartender smiled at Isaac as though acknowledging an old friend he hadn't seen in a long time.

During dinner Isaac drank two bottles of Chianti. He needed, he told himself, to blunt his inhibitions, and the inhibitions and confusion Laura's presence inspired; he needed some balance, some equivalent to poise. She laughed a lot during dinner.

She said the food was delicious, suggested that Isaac should eat, and, she said, he talked like a book. He wondered about that. He was aware of a formal effort, he chose his words carefully; he wanted to be absolutely honest, and he hadn't meant to impose on her a kind of shriving, as he told everything, in the throes of inspiration, which was work. Isaac was compelled by the sudden conviction that only God might love truly and keep secrets at the same time. But at least Laura Providencia was smiling. He assumed that the sound of his speech as revealed by Professor Dearborne, (the droll clanging from his voice box straining through his nasal passages, a sound not unlike a Jew's harp to rhapsodize beauty and truth) had neither offended nor distracted Laura. She was still listening, interested. They had been talking about the paper he had written for philosophy class. Laura reminded Isaac that Professor Sloan had read the paper to the class, and said that it was the funniest and perhaps the most brilliant paper he had ever given a failing grade. Isaac remembered that the assignment had been an analysis of

Kant's preface to the *Metaphysics of Morals*. He said that under the influence of Henry Miller he had titled the paper "A Prolegomenon To All Future Rides On The Ovarian Trolley." He was quick to add that the phrase "ride on the ovarian trolley" he had borrowed from Miller's autobiographical opus. Laura shrugged the small confession away. "Why," she wanted to know, did Isaac write a paper that he knew would receive a failing grade. She said that Isaac had never struck her as the type who needed to distinguish himself as the class clown. Isaac said he wasn't sure, but he had felt swindled by the convolutions of the German philosopher's language; when he had finally figured it out he felt himself once more confronted by his mother's homey wisdoms. "And," Laura asked, "what's wrong with your mother's homey wisdoms?"

Isaac looked around at the half-dozen patrons in the room eating serenely in the amber-colored silence. The old waiter hovered not too far from their table, tucked in the shadow of the Vesuvius fresco, the red neon bulbs of the bar flashed from the tops of his shiny black shoes. Isaac breathed in the aroma of the shrimps and clams fra diavolo wafting up from the plate. He set to, devouring the food on the plate so swiftly that Laura found herself more amazed than appalled; the issue of table manners seemed irrelevant, Isaac's dining appeared a blissful rampaging in which the food disappeared in the space of two ransacked minutes. Isaac's eyes focused again. The wine he drank slowly, sipping, and rolling the liquid in his mouth and swallowing in little, quiet gulps. Laura Providencia smiled, and asked once more, "And what's wrong with your mother's homey wisdoms?"

Isaac was still trying to explain when the waiter brought dessert. Laura listened, and smiled, and laughed; she nodded, her ironic comments and questions, Isaac thought, testaments of her sympathetic understanding. Isaac was greatly moved and propelled to say more, tell and explain. He had said that what hurt most was his inevitable betrayal of his parents. "Why betrayal?" she asked. Laura had winced at the word, looked stricken. He filled her glass with wine. She sipped the wine. "Because," Isaac said, "he could not live to vindicate his parents' lives no matter how complete their sacrifice, no matter that the sacrifice was predicated on the expectations of his accomplishments in the world, 'nachus' honor he would bring home because of his achievements." "What sort of achievement?" "I should be," Isaac said, "a doctor, a lawyer, at the very least, a dentist and a respectable member of the community." Laura was laughing again, "A dentist," she said, "Isaac the dentist…"

The elderly waiter with the elaborately coifed, white wavy hair didn't stray far from their table. With a red cloth napkin draped over his arm like a matador's cape, he removed dishes from Isaac and Laura's table, served dessert, turned from Laura, and genuflected. Laura picked up the dessertspoon, the shadow beneath the bowl of the spoon a little larger than a postage stamp, coalesced into the small face of a woman frozen in a valiant effort to smile. Laura jumped in her chair, her hand holding a cloth napkin shot up from her lap to her mouth. Isaac looked down at the whiteness of the tablecloth, and there next to the dish of pastry was the sepia-tinted photograph of a woman's face. Isaac and Laura looked up from the table at the elderly waiter. The waiter said something in Italian. Laura translated, "He says, it's his wife, no longer in this world." The waiter reached to the table, retrieved the small photograph, and returned it to his wallet. The old waiter stared at Laura. "The same face," he said, in a hushed, Italian-accented English. Isaac thought that when he had glanced at the postage stamp-sized severe face of the woman he hadn't seen any resemblance to Laura Providencia at all. The old waiter looked toward Laura, the angle of his vision askew, not so much as one struck blind, but bludgeoned by a kind of agnosia, the scorching splendor of what he thought he saw rendering his eyes sacerdotal holes, blank and milky, nailed through by some idea that made it impossible to make ordinary sense of the world. But when the waiter turned his face away from Laura Providencia, no longer scoured by rapture, he saw what he saw like everyone else, the impassive blankness that had fallen from his dumbstruck eyes dissipated, and he only looked foolish. The old waiter looked at Isaac, laying claim to some sort of kinship.

The bartender, an impossibly handsome boy, posted under the panorama of exploding Vesuvius, stood in a posture of militant languor, poured a martini from a beaker into a glass, and called, "Antonio, Antonio." The palm of Laura Providencia's hand brushed over the tablecloth where the face of the dead woman had appeared. The waiter excused himself and shuffled to the bar. The pretty young bartender scolded the old waiter in a rasping whisper that carried about the room. Isaac thought the young bartender looked pleased, reassured by the brutal sound of his voice. The old waiter looked with studied and obvious irony around the nearly deserted dining room, and answered in Italian. Laura leaned to Isaac and translated. The waiter, she said, was asserting that he hadn't violated protocol, and he had been attentive to the needs of all the patrons.

The expensively dressed, middle-aged bohemian couple seated near Isaac and Laura watched as the old waiter was reprimanded. The man, wearing a beret, peered into the bronzed gloom through dark sunglasses. He held a cigarette holder with a cigarette half gone to ash in the air. The woman wore sunglasses also, and a man's tweed double-breasted suit, her white hair was braided in two long pigtails that hung down to her shoulders, and she was smoking a cigar. Simultaneously, and without consultation, they removed their sunglasses, exposing their naked faces in the dimness, two great boiled eggs etched with special knowing, they frowned at the handsome young bartender. The bartender was given pause; he shot the elderly waiter a hateful glance that promised the old man that he would pay for the look of disapproval he had received.

From the rear of the restaurant a rectangle of dark opened in the latticed façade of grapes and vines, and out of the dark a tenor yowled, "Mala Femenina." The old waiter winced at the sound. The maître d' stepped out, closed the door on the song, and the gleaming vines and grapes trembled. It was quiet again.

The maître d' collected the handsome bartender for duty in the private dining room in the rear of the restaurant. The old waiter, and a younger colleague standing in shadow against the opposite wall, would be responsible for mixing and serving alcoholic beverages in the sparsely populated main dining room.

The elderly waiter shuffled to Isaac and Laura's table. He stood there, hands clasped behind his back, red-faced. No one spoke. Isaac was tempted to ask the old man to sit down, but knew that in spite of the light requirements of the quiet night in the restaurant, the old waiter could not sit down. Isaac glanced sympathetically at the old man. The elderly waiter sighed, turned to Isaac, and said his colleague, the bartender, was a petty man, concerned with trivialities. Laura said to the waiter that she wouldn't want him to lose his job. The waiter averted his eyes, tilted his head toward Laura, but was careful not to look at her, and said, that yes, he could be fired, it was a possibility, although the brute bartender, who was his immediate supervisor, was also his nephew. "However," he said, bowing to Laura, "it's a small thing, the job, in spite of the humiliating necessity of money."

Isaac could see that beyond the gallant bow the waiter was suffering; the imposition of his old blood flushing his face was unseemly, and the waiter knew it. His hands trembled as he polished the dessertspoon Laura had dropped on the floor, and the tremolo of his voice, when he had said, "it is a small thing, the job," cracked. "Antipasto," he gasped, and swept the plates loaded with the monumental pastry and ice cream confection from the table and hurried on shaky legs to the kitchen.

The old waiter careened toward their table under the large salad tray. He swayed above the table, the salad tray at his shoulder. He confessed that he had forgotten to serve the antipasto; this lapse so overwhelmed the old man that he appeared close to weeping. Laura whispered to him in her Spanish-accented Italian. "Antonio," he said, "Si," giving his name as something he might be called, now that he offered the word that was his name. Laura and Isaac introduced themselves. Laura explained that the fact that their dinner would be prolonged over the belated antipasto, and through dessert, coffee, and liqueur was a distinct pleasure.

Isaac and Laura, sotto voce, included Antonio in their conversation as he came and went from the kitchen. Antonio acclimated himself to looking at Laura obliquely; his velvety brown downcast eyes veered from dreaming to dream, taking her in, in a series of small, hurried glances. Antonio assumed the air of independence of one utterly condemned.

Isaac resumed his narrative. He intended to answer Laura's questions and respond to what she had told. On the way to the restaurant, which Primo had recommended as one of the best in the city, Laura told Isaac how when she was fourteen, on her very first day in the United States, she heard the bearded, black-garbed inhabitants speaking a language that sounded as though they were all choking, trying to clear their throats in a ferocious and desperate effort at articulation, a language in her ear that signaled the unrelenting strife of the new world.

She said to Isaac that she remembered, like interplanetary travel, the migration from Puerto Rico to the Lower East Side of New York.

On that first day she saw the young Jewish boys she identified as "los Americanos," shrouded in dark gabardine, each head topped with a small saucer of knitted color, the unshorn earringlet hair flapping at their pale cheeks. Stooped, they trod up the steps of a school building and Laura worried that her brother Angel would have to wear the costume, grow the sideburn locks, and constrain himself to some piety of learning that would also make him precociously old.

Laura said her mother rented a three-room railroad flat on Broome Street. As Laura and Isaac had trekked through the snowbound streets exchanging history, both finding affinity in the discovery that some things are difficult to exaggerate, he telling everything because beauty is truth and truth beauty, now in the restaurant he confessed that although he'd lived not very far away, and they didn't meet until Speech 101, it was possible that he might have strolled by her when he was not quite fifteen. The three virgins — he, Jo-Jo Pizzaro, and Bummy Birnbaum were on their way to the whorehouse located near the corner of Broome Street. Laura said, "Yes," her family lived on Broome Street then, and it would be another two years before they moved to the Bronx, but her mother had made her promise on her knees, before the Virgin, that she would never walk on that side of the street.

Isaac said the gray Madam's voice was hard and punctilious, and her Medussan stare froze him, Bummy, and Jo-Jo to the floor in the vestibule. She assessed them and they couldn't move. Contemptuously she told each, in turn, how much money was in his pocket, and she was accurate within pennies. Then she said that the three would have to pool their money so one could go inside and the other two beat it out to the street. Izzy and Jo-Jo gave their money to Bummy who was sixteen, the oldest, and in all things the most audacious.

Izzy and Jo-Jo stepped outside, closed the door on the perfumed air the Madam had stood in, and walked down the stoop steps. Isaac felt then that the mystery he believed to be beyond price had been given a price, and this was the principle the Gorgon Madam maintained in behalf of the world.

Antonio came from the kitchen, moved to the table, and whisked bread crumbs away with a cloth napkin, humming offbeat, "Celeste Aida." He bent his head low between Laura and Isaac and whispered that long ago he had played the cello, but because he was merely proficient he performed as a solitary, although this activity had brought him great happiness. Antonio's eyes were sad, but he was radiant with the power of his longing. The man of the bohemian couple at the adjacent table put the dark sunglasses back on his nose. He waved to get Antonio's attention. The white-haired pig-tailed woman sat, her great egg-like face naked of her sunglasses, she stared at Laura Providencia and blew rings of cigar smoke. Antonio said softly, "Farewell," and scurried to the table of the bohemian couple.

Laura thought of the kitchen in that first apartment on Broome Street. On the wall above the Formica table the hour and minute paws of the Felix the Cat clock pointed to the time;

Felix the Cat rolled his great eyes every hour at weeping Jesus on the opposite wall pointing to his heart in flame. Laura's mother and aunt had found work at the blouse factory, which was within walking distance to the apartment on Broome Street. It was in the kitchen that her mother emphasized Laura's special responsibility for her brother and sister. Her mother told Laura that because of her difficult birth, which had capsized and weakened her womb, she was only capable of bearing three children, a paltry size for a family, and so the safety of Angel and Rosita fell justifiably on Laura. Then as now Laura hadn't felt anything mean in her mother's communication. She was aware that for her mother all facts are the expression of destiny, and so there wasn't any reason Mami couldn't say anything.

Antonio returned to Isaac and Laura's table and whispered, "When you go, please, please do not leave the gratuity." Again he said, "Farewell," and marched off toward the swinging doors of the kitchen. Each time he went from the table he said, "Farewell," and each time he returned he greeted them as though he had just returned from a long and perilous journey. With great ceremony Antonio placed a carafe of wine on the table, which he said was a gift. "Wonderful to see you," he said, "Marvelous, hello, hello." Breathless and at home, Antonio rested, his arms propping him up on the back of Isaac's chair, his large arthritic fists grasped the finial spires of the chair, and he allowed himself ease.

Laura looked at the two rapt faces, the old man's face above the young man's face. Antonio had started to say several times that this month was the anniversary of his wife's passing, and he resented embarking on the adventure of old age without his Emilia. Laura patted Antonio's hand. He backed away from the table and went into the kitchen.

Laura was touched by Isaac's confession. She suffered a sense of déjà vu so powerful that she could no longer bear the dining room and Antonio returning again and again, coming through the swinging doors of the kitchen with a tray of red apples and bel paese cheese, which she knew he would recommend ardently, and Isaac gaping at her for eons with the face of an idiot savant. The moment would not pass. She noted that Isaac, like her brother Angel, had reached his eighteenth year a virgin. She guessed that she was supposed to understand something from this. Sitting there in the warm restaurant with the snow falling beyond the window, Laura wanted to get up and run out the door, away.

The wind rattled and hummed in the window. A couple, the man eating in his shirt sleeves and wearing a porkpie hat, and the woman ensconced in a mink coat, who had been sitting near the window, were moved to an alcove of golden stucco walls. The door to the street opened slowly, the force pushing at the door cracking the thin seam of ice that ran along the lintel, squealing from the wooden frame around the door. Isaac thought he could hear the bricks of the building grinding like teeth. The door pushed open a little further. An arctic breeze whined along the floor. The whole structure of the old tenement moaned, and the door flew open, revealing a funnel of night blasted to smithereens, the swirling bits the color of pewter, the brief glimpse of a building across the way swayed and was lost in a great roiling of silver. The wind and the calligraphic snow sketched in the doorway two huddled priests, their shoulders bent to the door in comic and blasphemous obeisance to the storm. They had opened the door a crack and that collaboration had been enough. A cloud of snow the size of a Volkswagen hurtled into the permanent pre-dawn light and dissolved in the warm air of the restaurant, as substantial in its several seconds of life as something Isaac would have sworn he had seen a moment ago. Laura Providencia caught the moisture of a flake on her tongue. Antonio closed his eyes and stepped between Laura and the wind. He called over his shoulder to the young apprentice waiter on the other side of the room to close the door. The waiter ran to his duty. The two glacial priests staggered through the open door to the center of the dining room. The wind had taken their hats. Vapor rose from the top of their heads, their frosted black suits crackled, the wreaths of ice around their pants cuffs chimed and dribbled puddles at their feet. Crouched and moving with the dignity of melting glaciers, the priests turned back to the hole of seething white-night from which they had appeared, and battled to close the door on it. The young apprentice waiter put his shoulder to the door, and the husky patron wearing the porkpie hat ran to join them; the men bunched up against the door, fought the heavy wind, whose full-throated cry was cut off before it reached its apogee, as the apprentice waiter turned the large old-fashioned key shaped like an exclamation point in the lock.

The closed door truncated the wind's scream. Antonio had closed his eyes, and Isaac had torn to bits a heel of bread as Laura Providencia's tongue flicked out to catch the mite of snow that dissolved in the air. It was in the last seconds of the wind's howling that Isaac began to live his life perpetually in an air of expectation, a feeling remotely like optimism, but hunkered down deeper in a more recalcitrant and dopey unreason. He knew he would disclose everything to Laura Providencia and still be laboring to a beginning. The bohemian couple and the woman in the mink coat applauded the men at the door. The woman of the bohemian couple clapped the loudest; from her lopsided grin, with her teeth clamped tight around the stub of her cigar, she puffed a string of ragged little clouds. Isaac startled, glimpsed a solitary drinker at the far end of the bar who sat with his back to the door. The man seemed at once to have appeared out of nowhere and have been sitting there forever, nursing one inexhaustible drink that was actually an endless series of drinks, replenished by the efficient specter of the young waiter who appeared at the penultimate moment of the nearly empty glass, topped the drink, and disappeared. Isaac noted this as another symptom of the miraculous.

The feeling of déjà vu, which Laura Providencia remembered Professor Sloan describing as "eternal recurrence," had reduced time to something like seasickness, and passed as Laura considered that her only option was courage; the incipient nausea subsided, she convalesced in the immeasurable moment. She no longer felt the need to remind Isaac that he talked like a book, even if her sympathetic listening made her a collaborator.

Antonio was extolling the virtues of bel paese cheese, he said that a taste for this cheese was not plebeian. He held out to Laura a red apple that he had buffed on his sleeve. "Yes," Laura Providencia said, "yes," and took a bite of the apple.

Antonio cleared the dishes, and with a hand that looked to Laura like the calcified root of a dead tree, brushed apple cores and bread crumbs into the apron tied to his waist. He bent over and held the edge of the apron out and away from the small swell of his gut, folding the apron into a hammock as though he were a midwife swaddling newborn life, and rushed into the kitchen.

He returned and said, "Hello, Hello! Wonderful to see you!" and swirled the fresh white tablecloth above their heads, flapped the tablecloth into a canopy, lanced the canopy with his arm, and laid the cloth out on the table. He turned his back and was busy at a little serving-table. He turned again and poured the espresso into small cups, set out a bottle of after-dinner liqueur, and two tiny bell-shaped glasses. He opened the bottle and passed the cork under Isaac and Laura's noses. Laura said, "Ah, anise." Antonio whispered, "Signorina, it is a more sublime relative of the same, may I?" poured the liqueur into the exquisite little glass, and trembling, lifted it to Laura's lips. Isaac reached out and held the old man steady as he swayed on his feet. "Yes," Laura said, "oh yes, delicious." Antonio wiped his eyes and glanced over his shoulder at the middle-aged bohemian couple seated at the next table. Under a cloud of cigar smoke they arranged heaps of cherrystone clamshells into patterns on the table and sipped wine. They bent over their work in progress in an attitude of meditation, during which they might overhear the world and be entertained.

Antonio continued to whisper, his voice perfectly pitched and clear. He composed his face so that those sitting close-by might assume that he was holding forth on the glory of wine and cheese. "Signor Isaac, if you will forgive my presumption," he whispered, "You must not be bitter. That you encountered the thing of inestimable glory in the house of ill repute and retreated is only a boy learning." Isaac almost blurted that he hadn't retreated, but held himself still and quiet. Antonio paused before Isaac's silence like a drink being offered, nodded assent, sighed, and said softly, "Escusi, there is a Sicilian adage, 'The world is made primarily of whores and spectators,' but the danger Signor Isaac is bitterness and hating the world, which creates the desire for vengeance, and the desire for vengeance can make life grotesque. When my wife Emelia died I hated God's world, I have not finished with hating it, and hating myself for hating it. A year before she was ill, when there was no sign of illness at all, our apartment, where we had lived for thirty years, was broken into by thieves."

The young apprentice waiter called Antonio. Antonio continued to speak, pretending he hadn't heard his colleague call him. "Of course it was the pride of the important criminals in our community that such things did not happen, but this age of drugs has made its own anarchy, and now all order collapses. However, I thanked all the saints for the safety of my wife. Emelia was out shopping when the thieves came. I was away working. At that time I was still blessed with work I loved; I was, despite the betrayal of my hands, a piano tuner."

The young apprentice waiter called Antonio again, his voice rising a little. Isaac saw the waiter clearly for the first time as the young man stood in the reflected lights of the bar. He was so defiantly ugly he was handsome. He wore his acne-scarred skin and bent nose as adornments. The ugly-handsome waiter had topped the solitary drinker's drink and stepped discreetly out of the aura of the lone drinker's space. The drunkard, speaking in a moderate tone of voice to no one present, said, "The good news is, nobody lives forever." The young waiter called Antonio again without raising his voice, but broke Antonio's name into three sharp syllables. "An-to-nio!" Antonio turned his head for a moment in the direction of his severed name. The young waiter gestured toward the two priests who hadn't yet been served, and had insisted on sitting under the large snow-glazed window, which the wind rattled, playing high-pitched grace notes from the glass.

The young priest had the pink, dazed face of a cherub, and appeared blissful, grateful for the adventure of the storm. The older, bald priest was bearing up under the many inconveniences of life. Antonio turned his head and acknowledged the young waiter, and displayed his arthritic hands to Isaac and Laura with the same swift discretion that he would slip the folded check next to the wine bottle. They saw the hands and the hands were gone, tucked under the apron tied around Antonio's waist. "Please," he said, "please do not go, wait," and he shuffled off.

"We should," Laura said to Isaac, "think about leaving." "Do you want to call home?" Isaac said, reaching into his pocket for change and nodding toward the phone booth near the kitchen's swinging doors. "Your family may be worried." Laura sat and thought, as though Isaac's suggestion were terribly complex; for the moment she couldn't telephone, didn't want to hear her mother's voice. She sat there. After a half a minute Isaac said, "Antonio's offering a story." Laura said, "Later, I'll call later." She smiled and said, "I guess we're obligated, we accepted his gift of wine." Isaac nodded, swallowed a sip of the wine, accepting culpability for the obligation of hearing Antonio's story, and whatever else the night would bring with a degree of comfort that was entirely new to him; moreover he knew, just knew, that he and Laura Providencia shared an affinity, a kindness of listening that was simply necessary if they were to avoid creating some brute karma to breathe ill will on all the rest of their days. She smiled and said, "Water, water everywhere and not a drop to drink." He said, "I don't know if the wedding guest will ever get to the wedding," and remembered that during the fall semester, when Laura had been in his literature class and throughout all the lectures on the *Ancient Mariner*, he hadn't mustered the courage to speak to her.

Antonio delivered two orders of chicken cacciatore to the priests seated next to the window. The priests turned from the spectacle of the window, and each gave a passionate and illicit glance at the chicken cacciatore. Antonio stood by, wearing his waiter's face, rhapsodizing, for all one could tell, some detail of gourmandize. The older priest dismissed him, waving his hand in a reflexive fragment of a genuflection.

Slowly Antonio backed away from the table of the priest's, turned, and shuffled into his pilgrimage back to Laura and Isaac's table. He tucked one misshapen hand under his apron and with the other clamped the top of the back of Isaac's chair; covertly and ever so slowly, he lowered and rested his backside on the edge of the small serving-table that was nearly the height of the table where Isaac and Laura sat, taking the weight off his legs. Antonio sitting, appeared to be standing, his face the anonymous and immobile mask of servitude, his lips which barely moved, whispered clearly: "Listen, the thieves stole our silverware, a clock my wife brought with her from Italy, and my cello. They made a great destruction of our kitchen for reasons I still do not understand. The loss of the cello was a special grief for me. For years I played this instrument as though I were nurturing a secret vice. My love of music is great, my knowledge considerable, and my ability as a musician as modest as my need to play is overwhelming. The loss of my beloved cello was a foretaste of the loss of Emelia. Emelia said that if we observed the necessary economies the cello might be replaced in seven, perhaps nine months. The thought of taking up with a new instrument was unthinkable. My old cello had accommodated itself to what time had done to my hands and seemed not to be offended by the music we made. My wife worried because I could not overcome my grief. Emelia was a woman of great resources and profound sweetness. She had lived through the loss of our one child, our son who died in infancy, and she survived the knowledge that she would not be able to have any other children, and of course she had known hunger and want in Sicily. When Emelia recounted her childhood it was never with bitterness, which astonished me always. My wife's fantastic dignity would have frightened people if it were not for her cheerfulness, which was surely her way of reassuring the world. She lived as though the pain of her life were a privilege, and the universe seemingly well-made and haphazard only in the matter of justice, provided the opportunity for faith. When I could not overcome my sadness at the loss of the cello, Emelia said my inability to gain a victory over my grief might bring down greater misfortune. After four months had passed and I had not played any music, my sadness became bitter and Emelia warned that my bitterness would bring a calamity on us. Three months after the thieves had stolen the clock, the silverware, and the cello, they returned. Emelia and I were in the laundromat. Before the theft she had been saving for a washing machine, which was a dream of great luxury for her.

"On the morning of the day the thieves returned, I awoke from a dream in which I was on my knees at the center of a great stony plain. I had my right hand thrust in a hole in the earth preventing a fire from escaping that would destroy the world. Emelia awoke and said that the fingers of her right hand burned and her knees ached. She had dreamt that she was lost in a forest, and although she could see through the trees to a plain where she knew I was in distress, she could not find her way out of the forest. She then reached under the mattress and showed me the sock with her savings, and said that in four months there would be sufficient money to buy a new cello. Amazing Emelia, if you gave her a dime she would save a quarter."

"An-to-nio," the syllables of his name tripped through the air, soft, distinct, and mocking. Another waiter, who had come from the dining room in the rear of the restaurant, waved a shovel in the air. The stout waiter waving the shovel looked like a barrel on stilts. The ugly-handsome waiter stood next to him at the door. The woman bundled in mink, so that only the crayon orange of the top of her hair showed, and her husband in the pearl gray porkpie hat and camelhair coat stood waiting, ready to leave. Antonio looked up, "They live just around the corner. Please excuse," he said, "I'm needed." Antonio's face went from the blank mask telling a story surreptitiously to a demonstration of Antonio's face in the story, yearning; and as he padded by the solitary drinker, still as an effigy under the fresco of smoking Vesuvius, Antonio's face was again a mask of willing service.

The two waiters positioned themselves at the door and pulled it open, slowly. The stout waiter went out with his shovel. The street Isaac glimpsed through the haze of blowing snow was a congealed ocean of white. Isaac and Laura waited for Antonio to return and tell the rest of his story. They looked at each other and laughed. The couple at the door startled one another with laughter neither recognized, and plunged into what had been the street.

The two waiters pressed their backs to the door. The waiter who looked like a barrel on stilts waved the shovel in the air, shouted, and laughed with a child's voice of near hysteria, "The whole block is buried." The priests were far gone in chicken cacciatore. The bohemian couple continued the arrangement of artful patterns of cherrystone clamshells, sipped wine, and with an air of neutrality waited to overhear again what would be told at the next table.

Antonio returned, stood smiling wistfully, and pulled a wine glass from beneath his apron. Isaac filled all their glasses. They toasted, touching glasses, saying nothing. Antonio repositioned his backside on the little serving-table behind him, so that he appeared to be standing, although he was sitting.

"You say," said Isaac, "that the thieves returned." Antonio did not answer; he looked with a persistent downward gaze at Laura. "Emelia," she said, "saved almost enough to replace the cello?" "Yes," said Antonio. "On the Sunday of the thieves' return, a little before noon, we had coffee and went to the laundromat. When we returned to the apartment I pulled the wire shopping cart with our clean, dry clothes and bedding into the kitchen. The kitchen was exactly how we had left it, orderly and silent; nevertheless, Emelia sensed a presence. She walked directly from the kitchen, through the living room, and flung open our bedroom door. Why the thieves had overlooked the bedroom the first time I do not know. The sock of money under the mattress was gone, of course, but more serious, the chest under our bed which held my piano repair and tuning tools had been emptied. Now I was to be deprived of the means of work I loved. Emelia acknowledged the catastrophe immediately, suggesting that we appeal to relatives for a loan, so that the tools could be replaced and I might continue to work. I could not bear the thought of going to anyone in our family for help. It seems that all during the years that I cultivated what music I was capable of, many opportunities to earn a comfortable living had passed without my notice. I knew that my family and relatives held me in a certain contempt. My younger brother, uncles, and nephew, referred to me as the poet; in the lexicon of our family the term reflects pity for one who is lame or a born fool. Emelia and I are also the childless couple. Moreover, there is a belief — here primarily I speak of my wife's side of the family — that I have somehow fraudulently used Emelia's life and wasted her beauty. You see it was impossible. I could not go to anyone in the family for help and I begged Emelia not to do so.

"When Monday morning came and I could not go to work or bring myself to telephone Mrs. Luftberg, a piano teacher living in Brooklyn and a very old client, Emelia refused to make the call for me. I could not bear to think about any of it. Emelia attempted to reason with me, suggesting various courses of action, all of which required my asking for help from relatives or petitioning Don Alfredo, the preeminent criminal of our community, himself a thief, and a third or fourth cousin to my wife. It was Monday morning. People were going to work. I went into the bathroom, locked myself in, and went to sleep. Before I fell asleep Emelia reminded me, on the other side of the bathroom door, that she would not telephone Mrs. Luftberg for me, that this was my responsibility. At that moment, God forgive me, I conceived a great bitterness for my wife. I remembered that through all the years of our marriage, no matter how loving Emilia had been, she could not bear to be embraced at the moment when she departed into sleep. Then she moved from me, did not want to be touched; sleep was for her a solitary and fugitive effort she could only embark on alone. But worse yet, I was abandoned by my wife's feet. My circulation is poor; very often, lying in bed at night my feet are cold. When I tried to warm my feet by placing them on Emelia's warm feet, she would move her feet away. She was adamant. I remember saying to her that the marriage vows included her feet, but she said no. This was a painful infidelity to me, and I was only able to make peace with these issues of our marriage by a willful and habitual forgetfulness. But now my cello was gone, and my piano tuning and repair instruments were gone, and every kind of bitterness returned to me. I remembered wrongs done to me as a child. Sitting on the commode, longing for sleep, my wife's reasonable voice on the other side of the bathroom door, I was haunted by another thought. It occurred to me that the arthritis in my hands had progressed to such an extent that perhaps the music I made was truly abominable, and only my wife's forbearance protected me from the fact, and too, the infirmity of my hands had made me slow and not greatly efficient in my work as a piano tuner. I wondered whether the charity of my old clients protected me from this knowledge. So it passed through my mind that the thieves who had come and taken my cello and piano tuning tools may have been an appropriate and critical expression of fate. I armed myself against this thought by thinking about the injustices done to me, and reflecting on the fact that the world is governed by thieves. Emelia's sweet, reasoning voice went on and on and I became as anonymous as her virtue. Sitting on the toilet, my head resting on the wall and drifting towards sleep, I realized that I had long ago reached the limits of my wife's love, the finite point of our marriage, which was also the innermost reaches of our intimacy, the point of sleep where Emelia could not bear to be touched. This was betrayal, although it is impossible to say by whom or what I was betrayed. I had married a beautiful and practical woman, and perhaps I was the one serious lapse in her sensible judgment. If anyone had harbored a dream of the infinite possibilities of love it must have been me, although I have no specific memory of this, but of course it was my heart that was broken, and there was a voice that spoke to me, just before I fell asleep on the toilet, reminding me of Emelia's innocence and my own, each of us carrying into marriage vast histories beyond our knowing that would inevitably set the limit of our capacity to love as indelibly as the size and weight of our skeletons, and the shape and life of things swimming in our blood.

"I awoke on the toilet seat enraged; in spite of my desire for sleep and oblivion, part of me believed that my wife should have been driven by an ambition of love as great or greater than my own. I could not forgive the denial of her feet. And in the world I was denied the one kind of work I loved, the only work I had ever truly been good at. The messengers of all this had been thieves, in the world governed by thieves."

Years later, Laura and Isaac would argue about what had happened next, and many years later they disputed the incidents in the argument about the argument, Laura Providencia declaring her innocence; she swore that the scalding water she had poured on Isaac's lap had been an accident, "The handle on the teakettle was loose." Isaac didn't remember that the teakettle had been defective, but the memory of his lap on fire was as vivid as the braid of scar that snaked from his lower right thigh to his knee like an aerial map of the Pyrenees, over which, during distracted moments, his fingertips would play, feeling through the cloth of his trousers the corrugated flesh. Isaac maintained that in the first argument, early in their marriage, he had only been stating the sequence of events in the restaurant and he was puzzled, not so much by Laura's disputing his memory, as her vehemence and then her rage.

He'd simply said that once more Antonio was summoned from their table. The old don had emerged from the door in the façade of the latticed fence of grapes and vines at the rear of the restaurant. The old man was surrounded by the maître d', the handsome young bartender, the barrel-chested waiter who had shoveled a path in front of the restaurant's door, and two sharply dressed soldierly young men. The maître d' clutched the umbrella, which he would open over the venerable head the instant the old man set foot out of doors. Antonio ran to help the old man put on his topcoat. The old man, dressed in the impeccable somberness of a banker, wore eyeglasses so thick that his eyes looked like large wet mollusks shorn from their shells, breathing moisture on the eyeglass lenses. The old man with the blind sea-creature eyes had clinging to his arm a young woman who bore a remarkable resemblance to the recently deceased Marilyn Monroe. Marilyn, who the old man addressed as "Cookie," excused herself and strode to the ladies' room adjacent to the bar. As she walked past the bar and approached Laura and Isaac's table, an overpowering aroma of tropical perfume preceded her; the closer she got the older she became, the cosmetic mask of her face an astonishing artistic accomplishment. The sweet and humid jungle reek of her perfume capturing its own brief and complete season as she approached, and a half-minute after she had past, the bohemian couple and Isaac and Laura sniffed and gasped. The older priest remained sunk in the mist of chicken cacciatore, the younger priest sneezed, sniffed the wave of candied air, and turned away from the scent as though it were an impertinent question. The solitary drunk at the bar began to choke and writhe, emerging into the world teary-eyed, the first thing he saw was Marilyn-Cookie's spectacular anatomy striding past him, and looking beyond that Laura Providencia's face. Marilyn-Cookie disappeared behind the tufted, red leatherette door of the ladies' room. The drunk at the bar stared at Laura, and then swore on "the eyes of his children" that this would be the last drinking night of his life. Laura turned her face away from the drunk's declaration. The bohemian couple began a commentary on what they said Laura

Providencia had inspired.

Laura didn't dispute that the drunk had declared that he would never drink again, but she insisted that he hadn't been looking at her when he made his oath, and she denied hearing any commentary by the bohemian couple on the subject of what she might have inspired. Isaac said that the man of the bohemian couple had raised his glass of wine in tribute to Laura Providencia and made some witticism about the wine turning into blood. Laura said that she had no such recollection. Isaac insisted, recalling it all again, describing the passing of the artfully wrought recreation of Marilyn Monroe, made for viewing at a distance, reeking the closer she got, the evidence of her aging, petrified beneath her strenuous art, glimpsed just before Marilyn-Cookie disappeared behind the red door of the ladies' room, the drunk gagging on the sweet stench of paradise, and emerging out of the alcoholic's dark tabula-rasa stupor to find a world — the world, the manufactured miracle of Marilyn, gorgeous, all that art could do, and then he saw Laura Providencia's face and made his oath because maybe booze wasn't necessary after all. In that first argument early in the marriage, about what had transpired at the restaurant, Isaac sensed Laura's resentment at being taken by his description of the disputed events, but he could not stop himself from continuing with his narrative. He noted that the barrel-chested waiter, whose name was Carmine, had been sent like the raven Noah had dispatched before he tried the dove, to test the tempest and report to the important man on the extent of the deluge.

Isaac couldn't resist his exegesis, and a decade would have to pass before the perception that Laura was at the point of screaming before she scorched his lap registered in his mind. "Remember," he had said, just before she set his lap on fire, "there were these biblical and religious references, the bohemian guy making his wisecrack about the wine and the blood of Christ, and my remark about Carmine being sent sailing like Noah's raven into the deluged world. And you coughed then, took a sip of wine and, and…" And she burnt him, and he howled and rolled on the kitchen floor.

Still he maintained years later, in the peaceful interstices of their marriage, that what she had told him first had been the provocation, and provided the confidence that night in the restaurant that allowed him to tell her how, when he was twelve, he wanted God to talk to him.

He was twelve and preparing for his bar mitzvah, he had started to explain in response to what she would maintain she had not told him. Laura, Isaac said, again and again, took a sip of wine, made a sour face, coughed and laughed; the laughter sounded to Isaac like a desperate improvisation, the breath of it keening. For the first time she told something that just fell out, as if the telling of it would stave something off, and when saying it didn't help, she wanted to bury it all in silence. Isaac didn't remember her exact words, but after she cleared her throat, her voice still rasping and strange, she told of the communion ritual in which she gagged on the wafer, the flesh of the Lord.

Finally, years later, when memory had begun to require an effort, and because he was still interested in the argument, and her, she acknowledged that she had undoubtedly told him, but she still insisted and would insist always that she had not told him then, that night, their first time out together; but yes, it was true she said, she had vomited up the Host, the priest jumped out of the way, and her mother had looked both mortified and vindicated, as if she had known all along that this daughter was foreordained for sin, for which God's forgiveness might have been invented.

In the restaurant, as Laura struggled to finesse the word "sin," and long before she ever denied that this had happened, Isaac was overwhelmed by her revelation. He felt in that moment that he was not merely delivering the all and everything of his life as another item of courtship. His voice recapitulated his adolescence, wavering, riding up to a cracked soprano and dropping to a droning baritone again; he had to rescue every word from being the last by telling it all in a hurry, and he was daunted because what had happened had of course taken longer than it would take to tell, which fact suggested that no matter how hard he tried, what he was about to tell was a kind of a lie. His swift and fleeting horror at the thought was as good as a red brick smash to the head and partial coma; and in the sweet bye and bye of the next infinitesimal moment, he was encouraged by the sense that he didn't have to understand what it all meant, what Laura Providencia had related had the quality of a melody he had always been trying to remember, and would continue trying to recall for the rest of his life, a song that resembled something crucial in his life.

He was happy, smiling, and didn't know why he felt like weeping. Isaac took a sip of wine, glanced at the restaurant's door, where the tumult of preparations for the important old man's departure was taking place, and he told Laura about the rabbi who had prepared him for bar mitzvah.

Rabbi Schlomo was a refugee, said Isaac, from the furthermost reaches of the Ukraine, someone left over from the nineteenth century whose ardent longing for home was the shtetl of the eighteenth century, where like his forebears, during the Babylonian captivity, he could dream of the lost conjugation of an Aramaic verb that would make "love" a moral imperative.

Isaac's father had found the rabbi wandering about the cemetery in New Jersey. It was just after the high Holy Days and his father had gone to visit the grave of his mother to say the necessary prayers. Rabbi Schlomo, like many of his colleagues, wandered about the cemetery in the hope of earning a few pennies helping American Jews recite the prayers in the holy language they didn't know. Isaac's father reported that Rabbi Schlomo, unlike his colleagues, seemed incapable of bargaining for a better price for his services, and he wandered about the cemetery as though he'd forgotten why he had come there.

Like the other drifting specters in their long, dark gabardine frock coats, Rabbi Schlomo also carried an umbrella, but his umbrella was all bent spokes with a few ragged strips of banners flapping in the wind, the beams of light shining through the skeletal umbrella, a radiant cage the rabbi carried above his head, shining all around him, and on the earth of New Jersey, America.

Isaac's father decided that Rabbi Schlomo was in need of charity and hired him to prepare Isaac for bar mitzvah. Isaac remembered the rabbi as a frail man with robust, wiry white hair growing from everywhere but the top of his shiny head, and an infinite number of soft words nestling in his beard. The rabbi taught him the Aleph Beth, and to show that he was not entirely out of sympathy with the modern scientific world, Rabbi Schlomo often used the word planet, breaking the word into two separate and heavy syllables, more like two distinct words. Rabbi Schlomo frequently invoked, and referred to the "Plann" — "Nett." Forever after whenever Isaac heard the word "planet," in any context, he heard "Plann" — "Nett" and an unaccountable laughter took him and squeezed drops of lemon-tasting water out of his eyes.

As Isaac told it to Laura in The Vesuvius Ristorante, he laughed and tasted his lemon-flavored tears, and had the odd sense that he was drinking a glass of tea rather than the Chianti he actually was drinking.

Isaac explained how Rabbi Schlomo had taught him several of Yahweh's sanctified aliases, and how the rabbi's whispered words insinuated certain stories from the Old Testament; the rabbi's tender words rooting the tales so deep in him that they grew into inexplicable deeds.

As Isaac recalled Rabbi Schlomo telling it, the boy Abraham of Genesis concluded that the idols his father made and sold, and to which men prayed, could not be gods. The artifacts were not deities but things of commerce, things. Abraham smashed them and told his father that the idols had destroyed themselves, committed suicide. Isaac couldn't remember whether Abraham's father had beaten him for being a smart-ass.

And so Abraham prayed to the sun and to the moon, a month to each, and neither the sun nor the moon spoke to him. At last God spoke to Abraham.

Isaac did the same. According to the Old Testament account Abraham learned that neither the sun nor the moon were God. Nevertheless, as a kind of protocol, a cautionary devotion to the same labor, Isaac prayed to the sun and then the moon. He stood at his bedroom window, looking out past the fire escapes and rooftops, the sunlight and moonlight forcing his eyes shut; at his back, past his bedroom door, from the living-room wall, he could feel Franklin and Eleanor Roosevelt looking on whimsically from their ornate frames. As Isaac told Laura about it, he remembered a sense of blasphemous self-striving, which he could only begin to name now, with her, but he had been without choice, he said, open to whatever all-making power was out there. God didn't speak to him, Isaac said, except perhaps in his most frightening dreams, the little of which he could remember for a short while upon waking was always beyond his understanding. He was afraid and his fear didn't feel like the requisite piety declaimed from the pages of the Old Testament. Still he remonstrated at the sky above the rooftops, as if his earnestness entitled him to something, he wanted God to talk to him, and telling Laura, confessing really, he was nearly as embarrassed as when he admitted he was a virgin.

The maître d' uttered the old don's name with an unctuous tremor that carried to the older priest's ear. The priest raised his head out of a stupor of bliss, above the plates of chicken, pasta, and olive pits, and dutifully recognizing the responsibility of one potentate to another, reflexively genuflected in the direction of the old don, the expert impersonality of the gesture a form of grace. The old don's face lit up, his sea-creature eyes ballooning behind the thick lenses, joyous as one granted an irrevocable and sweet longevity; and as if to confirm the old man's premonition, Marilyn-Cookie returned, walking toward him, splendid, perfect, and beautiful in the shimmying fathoms of his begoggled eyes. Antonio helped the old man put on his topcoat. As the handsome young bartender placed the homburg hat on the old don's head, Antonio helped Marilyn-Cookie get into her sable coat. The maître d', the two soldierly young men, the barrel-chested waiter, and the handsome bartender made a barrier with their bodies around the old man and his lady to protect them from the wind. The barrel-chested waiter pulled open the door and a chill splashed the knees of the patrons in the restaurant; the door opened on what looked like billowing lava. The entourage squeezed through the door, and once outside popped open a canopy of umbrellas over the precious ones at their center. Antonio pulled the door shut from the inside of the restaurant and Carmine pressed his stout body against the door from the outside.

Slowly Antonio made his way back to Laura and Isaac's table. He stopped and checked with his colleague, the ugly-handsome waiter with the pitted face and regal bearing, posted at the table of the two priests. The waiter, with a look of mild disdain, reassured Antonio that nothing was required of him in that quarter, and placed a bottle of cognac within reach of the solitary drunk, who was silently celebrating the imminent and unspeakable life of sobriety to come. Antonio continued, the gradations of his progress perceptible only after he reached each of his destinations. He made his way along the length of the bar, under glowing Vesuvius and into the kitchen, a bottle of wine the color of stone tucked under his arm, and emerged to deliver to the bohemian couple an incandescent, smoking red lobster that looked like it was about to come back to life, and the wine contained in the bottle that looked like stone. Laura held a handkerchief to her mouth. She noted the invisible speed of Antonio's slow movement. Hurriedly Isaac told Laura that he was still, from time to time, subject to fits of makeshift prayer. Laura squeezed Isaac's hand. Her palm was moist. For a moment she had looked disoriented, as someone who had suddenly awakened on a subway train at the wrong stop. In the next instant Antonio was there, lowering his backside on to the edge of the serving-table, taking the weight off his legs.

Laura and Isaac found themselves laughing uncontrollably, as if Antonio's arrival were a reprieve from an imponderable future about to commence any instant, and for which they could never be ready. Laura struggled to compose herself and asked, "Antonio tell us, please, so Emelia..." and she laughed.

Isaac wiped his eyes and smiled encouragingly at Antonio. Antonio clasped his hands in an attitude of prayer, sliced the air with his steepled fingertips, and swore he wouldn't detain them, although what was left to tell wouldn't take much time, but of course if they chose to go, he understood; and then Antonio was apologizing, speaking to Laura in Italian. Laura answered in Italian, her inflection reassuring, she threw scraps of translation at Isaac as she mollified Antonio. No, she insisted, she hadn't thought of Antonio's tale as a form of incontinence, and she and Isaac really did want to listen. Antonio allowed himself almost a direct gaze into Laura Providencia's eyes, and shivered. "My wife Emelia also could only tell the truth, even when she was lying." "So?" said Isaac, the word coming out of him in a sudden and surprising anger, the rhetorical "so?" a little boy's challenge, embarrassed both men. "Yes, of course," said Antonio, looking down at the floor where he found the remaining words of his story, "So, somehow over the next two months Emelia managed the household expenses. I didn't bring a penny into the house. I lived in a stupefied resentment which was my sleep, and a waking rage which drove me to an endless wandering of the city streets. Often I talked to myself; strangers replied to statements I did not remember making. Once a very pretty woman wearing a coat with a fur collar stood before me, the two of us were in front of a window of an exclusive jewelry store. The woman was crying. I realized that I had been cursing her with the foulest language I knew. When I reached into my coat pocket to offer her my handkerchief, she ran off. It was during this time that I must have conceived my plan for revenge. I have some recollection of my reasoning, which became clearer to me when the police questioned me; although I did not confess to the police what I had confided to the supermarket manager, whom I had mistaken for a man of philosophic disposition.

"The manager materialized just past a pyramid of oranges, in an aisle of shelves devoted to candy. There was something resembling music in the air. A young mother pushing a shopping cart loaded with groceries and her little daughter seated on top of the mound of groceries blocked my path. I was caught with a salami in my coat pocket, a can of anchovies under my belt buckle, and a bottle of olive oil in the inside pocket of my jacket. The manager of the supermarket told his assistant not to handle me roughly, and sent one of the young men off to get the police. The manager's name was Rodolfo Termini; he introduced himself to me and asked me into his office. He was a man of approximately my age, perhaps a little younger, but not young. Once in his office he offered me a chair and I was encouraged by his courtesy and kindly manner. I ventured to speak to him as a countryman in the dialect of our region and he responded in kind. In speaking to Mr. Termini I was not merely trying to justify myself but attempting to understand what I had done. Certainly I was embarrassed — oh no, yes, shamed is the truth. I explained how the need for vengeance had insidiously possessed my spirit, how in a world ruled by thieves of one kind or another, one's recourse is only to become a thief. However, I did not tell him of the theft of my cello and piano tuning instruments; this seemed some shameful impairment I could not admit. I did say that in breaking the law, in more or less openly being a thief, I had not corrupted the law and the possibilities of civility at its source, so that theft could still be seen as an infraction; I could not really be a significant criminal. The manager seemed sympathetic. He gave me a cup of coffee and offered a cigarette. But when the police arrived, there were four of them, which I judged to be a great and superfluous number, Mr. Termini flew into a rage.

"He ranted in English. He glanced at me with disgust, as though looking directly at me would make him ill. He said that for more than a year the supermarket had suffered a plague of thefts amounting to a loss of thousands of dollars, and always the thieves stole Genoa salamis, anchovies, olive oil, sometimes Spanish olives, coffee, and frozen veal cutlets. I offered that in my home the meat prepared for meals was fresh, purchased from Gandoli's, and that this was my maiden voyage as a thief. The manager orated at the top of his lungs, his eyes full of tears, his voice trembled. He brandished a ledger book showing how the losses due to theft were undermining his business. He said that he had listened to me bragging before the police had arrived and that I was perverse, clever, and undoubtedly the leader of a band of thieves. I had, Mr. Termini said, disgraced the Italian-American community, and I should be deported. I could see that the police, up to that moment, were doing their duty with professional indifference: one was writing in a pad, another stood just outside the office's glass door questioning the young mother whose daughter was still sitting on top of the mound of groceries in the shopping cart, and two stood flanking both sides of the chair I sat in; but when Mr. Termini had said that I had bragged of my exploits, the police began to undertake their tasks with greater vigor. One stood me up and put handcuffs on me, another seated me again with a little shove, and they spoke in consoling tones to Mr. Termini. I assured the police that I had never meant to cast aspersions on their profession.

"When I went before the judge there were questions concerning my citizenship. I came to this country when I was eight years old, and various official papers that I should have had in my possession had long ago been lost by me or my parents. I had no visible means of employment, and although the judge was not persuaded that I was the leader of a band of criminals, he did believe that I was a habitual petty thief — a shoplifter. Finally, some consideration was given to my age. I was convicted, given a suspended sentence, and put on parole. The conditions of my parole required that I be employed and live under the supervision of a family member. My relatives, through the intercession of my wife, provided the employment and supervision; I am subject to the authority of my nephew the bartender, the proprietor of this establishment.

"The legal proceedings concerning my crime, and the quest through various federal bureaucracies to validate my citizenship, lasted for almost two years. Emelia was stoic throughout. My despair became silence, which I relished. I answered when spoken to, or when madness selected my voice. The family used me as the principal example of folly to their children. I could not find within me a benevolent feeling for myself. Beginning my work here in the restaurant I did attempt to turn menial tasks into something artful, but my hands were like two separate old animals, each accommodating suffering in its own way. I broke many dishes. I had been here almost a year and was still on parole before I was finally proficient in my work. True, I was beginning to find pleasure again in listening to music, despite the fact that I could not make any, when one morning Emelia did not return to me after sleep. From all appearances it seemed that I had not exhausted Emelia's cheerfulness, but the family accused me of exhausting her heart."

Laura avoided Antonio's gaze. The bohemian couple at the next table applauded when he finished his story. Antonio glanced at them, surprised that his whispering had carried that far. The couple stared at Laura. They applauded as if she had been the source of all they had heard. Antonio stared at Laura, waiting for her to transform what he had told by some small gesture.

"Antonio," she said in Italian, "the weather — and my mother is waiting." In the silence of the next ten seconds, the portent of what Laura couldn't offer welled into an emptiness. Isaac gulped the last of the wine and stood up. He felt dizzy and bent into a crouch. His head cleared. Red-faced, he imitated Groucho Marx, flicked invisible ashes from an invisible cigar, and said, "Hello, I must be going." Laura said, "Are you all right Isaac?" and to Antonio, "Please." Antonio said, "Si, Si," pulled a pad from his back pocket, a stub of pencil from behind his ear, and added up the check. He folded the check and placed it next to the empty wine bottle.

Laura stood up to go. Antonio embraced Isaac. Isaac breathed deeply, smelled the pomade in Antonio's hair, returned the embrace perfunctorily, and saw over Antonio's shoulder the solitary drunk, more or less on his feet. Isaac had the distinct and disturbing sense that somehow his Groucho Marx imitation had set the drunk in motion, the karmic threads spawned from his Groucho imitation pulling the drunk from his stool. The drunk, in his business suit, staggered and thrashed towards them; dollar bills and coins fell from his hands and pockets; slowly, he stumbled forward, blinking his eyes, trying to see through the liquefied something that contained him, his vision found and fixed on Laura Providencia, and he gurgled something urgent. The ugly-handsome waiter saw it all from his post; he raised his eyebrows, and stepped off smartly from the priest's table, and blocked the path of the drunk. The drunk reeled back and stopped. Isaac held Laura's chair as she stood up. The waiter with the cratered face and the nose like a bent soupspoon made his large body a barrier, behind which the drunk swayed and blew kisses. Isaac helped Laura Providencia into her coat. The ugly-handsome waiter had handed the coat to Isaac ceremoniously, the garment draped over his outstretched arm. Isaac held Laura's coat as she slipped her arms into the sleeves, and he breathed in the scent from the back of her neck. He went far away for a while. When he came back he was still holding the coat, Laura was buttoning the buttons, and Isaac noted the audacious posture of the ugly-handsome waiter; the man's stance seemed to Isaac to demonstrate some principle of nakedness that was the obverse of the emperor's new clothes. The waiter had invented his handsomeness by the daring assertion of his scarred and battered face; and he gestured, his large hand palm up, indicating the path he made possible for the young woman who could not enter a room without it becoming an event. Antonio, standing in the shadow of his large colleague, turned his head to Laura, closed his eyes, and moaned, "Madonna." The man of the bohemian couple said, "Aztec princess"; the woman of the bohemian couple said, "the Madonna of the Long Neck." Antonio, no longer in control of the modulation of his voice, or his hands which fell from beneath his apron like dead birds, said, "Please signorina forgive the imposition, it is only that seeing you I remembered that for the first six years of my marriage each of my days were as splendid as any of the first six God invented."

With her coat on, Laura embraced Antonio so swiftly and briefly it seemed that a shadow had passed over his body. She made her way to the door. Isaac glanced at the young priest. He looked up from his chicken cacciatore and saw Laura; stunned, the young priest appeared suddenly lost in a heretical dream. The old priest ate blindly, and wiped his mouth with his knuckles. Antonio stood with his arms outstretched, trying to hold the shadow that had embraced him. The large ugly-handsome waiter rushed for the door. The bohemian woman pointed at Laura with a lobster claw, and said, "Not Gauguin, think if El Greco had painted the Tahitians." "Oh yes," said her companion, "oh yes!" Isaac walked behind Laura and wanted desperately to do something useful or heroic. On the wall above the table of the bohemian couple, in the mirror framed by naked cupids blowing trumpets, Isaac saw himself plodding in the wake of embattled majesty.

THE LONG WAY HOME

Six steps beyond the door and out from under the canopy of the Vesuvius Ristorante, the street disappeared. They were knee-deep in a drift of snow. A doubt made him smile; perhaps the delirium that followed looking into Laura Providencia's face was not the prelude to self-knowledge. She said, "You're half-drunk," and laughed.

Parked cars were enormous, glacial, half-buried eggs. The wind whistled, exploding great white plumes from the tops of the eggs, and the lamppost's lights went out. The windows in stores and buildings lining the street went dark. They turned and could no longer make out the Vesuvius. Laura said, "A power failure." Isaac sneezed. Laura shook her head, her long black hair jeweled with hail ticked as it swung about her shoulders. Still they inhabited a prescience; she knew what he thought and couldn't bring herself to disbelieve it entirely. His desire had provoked the sky into the deluge of white, this pause and quiet. They looked up through the densities of the ice-speckled night at the tenements which had become moon grottoes. Bone-white fire escapes floated in the air, pouring Niagras of glistening snow. They trudged through the drifts; sinking, climbing, ocean weight tugged at their legs. The street became a ravine. They climbed up and down. They walked in the narrow center. The white dunes that flanked them were worked and shaped by the wind to various heights and spires. Above the glazed white wall a street sign impacted with snow and impossible to read and a floating fire escape flashed, a window loomed, spotted with the beam of a flashlight, all quenched as the wind blew a gust of dark. The wind, which they could see from moment to moment in its effects, didn't feel especially cold. They thrust their hands into it like children in a surf.

They walked. The wet sky had fallen and disappeared; looking up there was only the infinite and shimmering constellations of snow drifting down, palpable and immediate. It wet their eyes; they breathed it in. They moved forward in the pelting mist in the direction of what they remembered to be Washington Square. What they could see wasn't anything they remembered. The sound of their shoes crunching snow startled them. Their voices rose, taken by the wind, and became other voices. Isaac, open-mouthed, tasted the flurry of wet on his wine-coated tongue. He said, "What?" Laura repeated, "My little sister walks in her sleep." He retrieved the sense of what she had said from beneath the sound of his shoes, squeaking over the snow, but he heard what Laura had said in the past tense, and was curious about how Laura's sister had been cured of sleep walking. And it wasn't important. Time had crawled through one of the blind tenement windows. Isaac knew they were beginning at the end, walking around in their afterlife. He held her hand in his coat pocket, and remembered feeling fearful about something long ago. He pawed the ground with his foot. She rolled her eyes. He stared. Her face was God's money.

The path widened; the dunes leveled out. In the distance they could see an icy pond surrounded by snow-heaped park benches, and a rising mist that looked like the shadow of Stonehenge; suspended beneath the enormous smoky lintel, a great eye cast a beam of light. Across the circle of light, the stick figure of a man, arms outstretched, sailed. A dog barked. Isaac felt his numb feet kicking through the snow. The man who had crossed the circle of light, still in the distance, came closer. Isaac said, "Look!" Laura said, "What?" Isaac said, "Please, look, look." It was necessary that Laura see what he was seeing or the moment would cease to exist. "Your glasses. Laura, put on your glasses." "Izzy, they're for reading." She laughed. He squinted and pointed, "Over there, see over there?" The bulky figure was carrying a shopping bag; the coat bulged in the vicinity of the hips. The dog of Isaac's dreams bounced in and out of sight behind the man's legs. The man came closer and diminished in size, as though Isaac were peering through the distancing end of the toy telescope his father had once bought him. He guessed that the diminution of his vision was the consequence of Laura's inability, or perhaps, her refusal to see, and for one astounded moment he was relieved that there was something about Laura that didn't entrance him. Laura said, "I hear a dog barking, I can hear that." Isaac looked again, and the man and the dog were gone. They could hear the dog's paws ticking over the ice,

and followed the receding sound until it disappeared at the edge
of the large frozen wading pool, surrounded by the snow-heaped
park benches. Laura sneezed. "Izzy," she said, "My feet are cold
and wet" — not merely to repudiate the claims of magic, as he
knew, but to interrupt living the story he was making, and the
possibility that she might turn into what he imagined her to be;
and she said, "Please, my feet are cold and wet."

Isaac scooped a seat out of the snow-covered park bench,
and swiftly sculpted and packed two massive armrests and gestured for Laura to be seated. Laura sat down. Isaac kneeled, removed Laura's stockings and low-heeled shoes. He rubbed her
feet, blew on her toes, and wrapped her brown bare feet in his
coat. Laura pointed and explained how the wind had shaped
the color and heat mist rising from the ground; the great bulk-
ing shadow that appeared to be smoking Stonehenge was the
arch of Washington Square, the great eye of light, a stalled bus
with one headlight out, just under and a little beyond the arch
on Fifth Avenue. "There, over there, beyond the embankment
of snow." Isaac, on his knees, turned his head and looked. He
listened. He marveled at her voice. It was crisp, empathetic, and
didactic; the pronunciation and chiming timbre something that
might have been created in the most devout chamber of an
anglophile's heart.

For a moment he remembered Speech 101, and heard his
voice, tinny and grating, coming from Professor Dearborne's
lips, the eloquence he had aspired to clogged his heart. Again he
heard the substance of his thought reduced to absurdity by the
mere sound of his voice, the ugliness of it; the voice made the
aspirations of his mind and heart ridiculous to his own ears. All
he had tried to say sounded like a conceit his spirit could neither earn nor had the right to desire. He shook his head, refus-

ing defeat, and he rubbed and blew Laura's feet warm, his lips brushing the arch of her foot. He put her stockings back on. With his pen and the hard cardboard cover of the little note-book he carried in his pocket, he scraped the snow from the soles of her shoes. Then he scraped the snow from the bottom of his shoes. Gently he slipped her feet back into her shoes. Laura stood up. He took her hand. They assumed the posture of ice skaters about to perform great balletic feats and slid across the frozen wading pool.

Holding hands, tugging and supporting one another, they climbed up the icy embankment into Fifth Avenue. A grand apartment house that must have had an auxiliary electrical sys-tem of its own cast a dazzling light on the avenue. They trudged to the center of the street and circled two abandoned cars that blocked the possibility of the bus' turning left, to go east on Eighth Street. Beyond the intersection, about a half a block, di-rectly in front of the bus the wind had built a frozen surf, its peaks three feet high.

The front door of the bus was open. Isaac and Laura stepped up and entered. Inside the bus was dimly lit and damp. A wet breeze blew down the length of the vehicle. All the side win-dows were covered with snow. The door toward the rear of the bus was closed, its glass windows beaded with ice. The light in the bus was gray. Where the driver sat, on the window in front of him, the windshield wipers swept back and forth, streaking two molten half-moons of the red and yellow of a stained glass window bled of its details.

The driver wore a peaked cap and was bundled into a sweater and an unbuttoned plaid mackinaw; his wire ear muffs were askew, his pink ears shining in nests of white hair. He turned toward Isaac and Laura with difficulty, puffed and swaddled as a child dressed by his mother for inclement weather. On the ring finger of the hand that held a portable radio to the side of his head, he wore a thick gold wedding band. The boyish face was not young. The driver labored to free himself from rapture. He smiled and babbled statistics. Laura asked if it was possible for him to back the bus up and drive in reverse, since there was no way to go forward to the subway stop at 23rd Street, and she asked, did he know by any chance, if the trains were running. The static from the little portable radio the driver held to his temple enveloped a voice passionately narrating a sports event, swooning statistics. The radio voice speaking through far away dismembered thunder affirmed something that brought a look of bliss to the driver's face, a message from heaven. As in prayer the driver answered the radio voice, reciting names, dates, and numbers. At some imperceptible instant the driver was no longer speaking to the radio voice, but to Laura, offering her his real- ization of a greater harmony. Isaac saw it happening and pre- tended not to notice, aware as he was now, that such events were invasions of Laura's soul, events she would have to fend off or domesticate to her own purposes; and he didn't want to be in- cluded in her collective experience of the male species. He was sure he was different, although it occurred to him that his will- ingness to die for her wouldn't necessarily set him apart from many of the others. Still Isaac was shocked when the driver ac- tually turned the radio off even though the game was far from over. Obedient, puzzled, the sports enthusiast touched himself under his sweater, fingering the place where Adam had felt an ache at the loss of that rib, and Isaac, with his wine-inflamed intuition figured that the driver thought too that maybe Laura Providencia was one of God's better ideas. The driver put the portable radio on the floor under his seat. He didn't look at

Isaac, who just happened to be there, only Laura was implicated in his epiphany. He handed Isaac a spatula-shaped tool for scraping ice. "I'm Sammy," he said in a surprised voice, introducing himself to his name, and rested for a half-minute. Then he remembered, "this window," he said, rapping the window to his left with his knuckles, "got to be scraped, and the back one from the outside." Isaac said, "Sure, of course." Laura said, "Thank you. Thank you so much." Sammy placed his hands on the steering wheel. "Oh yeah," he said, "you wanted to know about the subway. Some lines are running, the Lexington Avenue, I think, but the bridges are out and the Lex don't go no further than Third Avenue in the Bronx, cause the El is out too — the radio's been reporting."

Sammy the driver sat in the cloistered gloom with his hands on the wheel. He looked straight ahead, except for occasional glances at Laura, and recited the routes by which she might get home. Laura encouraged him to speak, she asked questions. Isaac climbed out of the bus with the plastic scraper in his hand.

Standing on an empty garbage pail he had hauled from the side of a building and turned upside down, Isaac scraped away at the rear window of the bus. His fingers tingled, his hands burned with the cold. He crossed his arms over his chest and tucked his hands in his armpits. It took a moment before he realized that he'd scraped the window clean; the window had the sheen of isinglass. Isaac couldn't see through to the inside, but he thought that was perhaps a peculiarity of the light, it was possible that the driver would be able to see through from the inside. Isaac climbed down, slid the trashcan over the sidewalk back to the building. He walked around the bus to the window on the driver's side. He grabbed hold of the stem of the side rear view mirror, lifted his leg, placed his foot on top of the front tire, and hoisted himself up. Perched there he dug at the thick beaded ice that covered the window. He jabbed and poked, the chips of ice flew in his face. The breath from his mouth and nostrils obscured the shadow forming in the ice. Isaac jammed the scraper into his coat pocket. He maneuvered his hand into his pant's pocket, the tips of his fingers searching, touching a coin he thought was the item he searched for. Finally he found it. With his house key he carved the oval shadow emerging from the ice. He blew his smoking breath at what he seemed to be sculpting. He blew on his fingers. He chipped, shaved, and carved the gleaming concavity; and there through the fog of his breath was Laura Providencia's face, feathered around in starbursts of frost. From the inside, through the porthole-sized circle of the frosted window, Isaac's face diamond blue, grinning, appeared to Laura. They heard one another's laughter; a sound a ventriloquist might have placed in a box. Sammy's pudgy hand appeared in front of Laura's face, knocked on the window, pointed; Isaac would have to scrape more ice.

Sammy's shadow moved in the frosted windows, wherever he wanted Isaac to scrape he rapped with his knuckles.

Inside the bus Isaac and Laura sat directly behind Sammy. Laura rubbed Isaac's hands, blew on his fingers. Sammy managed to back up the bus far enough into a side street to turn and drive forward in the direction of what would have been oncoming traffic. At least that's what Sammy said he was doing. Laura and Isaac watched Sammy's back, his hands turning the steering wheel. Beyond the tunnel of light made by the bus' one operating headlight, and the sweeping arcs of the windshield wipers smearing the driver's front window with two half-moons of pulsing yellow, Laura and Isaac couldn't see very much.

Looking out of the side window they glimpsed a lunar night,

the infinity of white spots floating in space. The floor of the bus rumbled. They couldn't see movement, but felt the vehicle ride a swell, as though they were in a ship. Isaac rested his head on Laura's shoulder. She held his hands in her lap. Sammy called over his shoulder, announcing various landmarks on the avenue, his voice a cheery exhortation to look and see. Isaac lifted his head from Laura's shoulder. Rocking in their seats Laura and Isaac peered through the large porthole shape Isaac had etched in the icy window. For all they could see passing they might have been floating in a diorama; beyond the glass, the fixed, white-pocked void. Isaac laughed and said, "Yeah, sure." He thought maybe Sammy, traveling the avenue for an eternity, possessed a night vision as acute as Braille, and he could read the city through some sense he didn't have to know or acknowledge. Perhaps the driver was reciting what he knew of the avenue by rote, reassuring them — Sammy a Coney Island maestro operating a great toy vehicle, shuddering on its axis, going nowhere, the illusion of travel enhanced by Sammy's enthusiastic calling of placenames and the deception of lights. Laura put a finger to her lips. They would honor Sammy's effort. Isaac said, "Why not?" They clapped hands.

The bus made a great hissing sound. The shivering of the vehicle stopped. Isaac whispered, "No kidding?" Sammy called, "Fifth Avenue and Eighteenth Street, Barnes & Nobles Bookstore."

Isaac struggled with his desire to kiss Laura. Sammy cranked open the side window, thrust his head out and yelled. He conducted a complicated negotiation with someone Laura and Isaac could neither see nor hear. They could hear Sammy. He hollered, "You too cheap to give me a minute? Alright already. Please, please, Wally, don't use that kind of language, I'm carrying my

mother's picture in my wallet, and I got a lady on board." Sammy
pulled his head back into the bus. Slowly he rose from his seat.
"Youse," he shouted at Isaac and Laura, without turning, "wait
here please." He adjusted his peaked cap and earmuffs so that
his ears were covered, and pulled at the mackinaw, tight under
his arms; he gave up trying to button it, and struggling inside
the bulk of his own flesh, waddled out of the bus. Isaac's nerve
failed him. Laura kissed him.

Isaac drifted up from the taste of Laura's mouth. She was
tugging at his arm. Sammy stood there in the aisle, holding the
shovel, "This is the deal," he said, and laid the shovel across Isaac's
knees. "Larkin, Wally that is, is willin' to drive youse as far as
Yankee Stadium, if he can get there. It still leaves you maybe a
mile or two from where you wanna be. Larkin says he won't go
into the South Bronx in any kind of weather. It's twenty bucks,
not on the meter. But anyways, first you gotta help shovel him
out. He slid into a drift. He's buried, and for now he ain't going
nowheres." Sammy studied the puddle at his feet. "Listen,
Larkin's a little weird, he got a mean mouth, but if he says he'll
drive you, he'll drive you — just don't listen, don't pay no attention. It's important not to pay him attention. Me, I gotta try to
get the bus back to the garage. It's time, power's been restored
in lots of places, lights going on, and some subway lines is running." Sammy stepped back in the aisle, his head inclining towards his chest. Laura and Isaac squeezed out of the seat, Isaac
with the shovel on his shoulder. At the open door at the front of
the bus, Sammy spoke to Laura's feet. "The cab's motor is running okay, you'll be warm in there, the heater is working … I
asked … and you could sit inside while they dig out." Laura
said, "Thank you," and offered her hand. Sammy hesitated, and
barely touching the tips of Laura's fingers, shook her hand. Isaac

said, "Thank you," and improvised a salute with the shovel.

They stepped down, out of the bus. A pool of light fell from the bus's opened door at their backs. Wet pelted their faces. They heard the door swoosh closed behind them. They squinted to see, and waited for their vision to adjust. They took three tentative steps forward.

The cab was sunk in a drift up to its fenders, its shining headlights partially buried, revealed their feet, their legs, and illuminated the white street as the footlights of an ancient theatre would gleam from the floorboards of a stage. The light that bounced up from the street and reflected from several piles of snow, the bookstore window, and two half-buried cars was isolating and selective; through the falling snow what little they could see of the city was in shadow. Laura and Isaac made their way toward the cab. The vehicle was stuck not more than twenty yards adjacent to the bus, off to the side of the bus' dead headlight.

The hack driver, Wally Larkin, stepped out from behind the rear of his cab. He swung a shovel, tossing snow in the air, thrust the shovel into a mound of slush, and leaned his elbow on the handle. Cradling his head in the palm of his gloved hand, he stood, legs crossed, his weight focused on the ball of his booted foot. He looked like he was wearing a birthday cake on his head, the scalloped rim of the cake crumbling, sifting in front of his face and around his face, a scarf which he wore like a kerchief, knotted under his chin. Laura and Isaac approached. The cabbie reached for the top of his head and the cake exploded into powder as he raised a pearl gray fedora toward the sky, and gestured with it in the direction of the great beyond. "What about this shit?" He leaned forward, aiming his face at Isaac. "Well, what about this shit?" Isaac shrugged, opened the

door on the driver's side that had been shoveled clear, and mo-
tioned for Laura to step inside. Heat wafted out of the open cab
door. Laura paused, smiled, and said, "It's good of you to help."
The cabbie glanced at her and frowned. Laura was one more
great natural calamity, like the stuff falling out of the sky. The
cabbie bent his head into the cab and nodded toward the dashboard, "Uh," he said, "Listen to the radio." Isaac and Larkin stood
facing one another. The cabbie wore a World War II leather
bomber jacket. He raised his fedora, which was turning into a
cake again, and shook off the snow. His eyes seemed gleeful.
Isaac studied him. The look on the cabbie's face was mirthful
and knowing.

"Sammy explain to you the deal? I take you to Yankee Stadium, if I can make it. I ain't going into the jungle, even if it's
snowing there, understood?" Isaac nodded. The cabbie shouted,
"What?" Isaac nodded again. "The shovel Sammy lent you is
mine." Isaac said, "Sure, of course." "Sammy heard you talking
in the bus, he told me your name is Isaac. Lissen Isaac, you gonna
have to work," Larkin said, "And what are you laughin' Isaac?"
Isaac asked, "Am I laughing?" and thought perhaps he looked
like he was laughing. Laura had kissed him and he couldn't
imagine what was on his face. In the throes of his joy there was
a tremor. He needed silence, a prayer untainted by any conceit
of language. He began to shovel slowly, deliberately, picking up
his pace. He caught sight of the bus moving in the falling snow,
in curling sheets of mist, like an ocean liner, except that the
tires made crunching noises, and this incongruity Isaac could
attribute to the disorder of his senses as his new life was being
born. And who knew what it would be? Sammy didn't call out a
last farewell. Isaac concurred with the bus driver's discretion.
He remembered Sammy's instructions, not to listen to Larkin,

and the advice felt like a talisman, the key to getting Laura back home. Facing Isaac, over the snow-capped roof of the cab, in the white-flecked air of the near distance, he thought he saw three robed figures bent over illuminated texts. As he shoveled, rocking as though he were at the Wailing Wall of Jerusalem, he wanted to see what he was seeing more clearly, but he couldn't stop shoveling. He shoveled furiously, digging deeper into his prayer, heard music, and realized that the music was coming from the radio inside the cab.

Isaac heard a flurry of garbled voices, "Wheat is up, cotton higher," an inane jingle, and then when Laura found the FM station, a Bach cantata, no less; and it came to him as he went on digging, digging, without even bothering to look, that the spectacle of the miraculous wouldn't impinge on his prayer; the three figures at study over the illuminated texts were mannequins in graduation caps and gowns in the window of the Barnes and Noble Bookstore.

The Bach cantata became an indecipherable hum. Isaac could feel the sweat running down his back and considered that he didn't know what his prayer was, except that he didn't want it to be a petition; he only wanted to say "Yes" as quietly as possible. In the moment he knew he wanted the prayer to be this, he knew he wanted, and he wasn't praying anymore. He shoveled snow.

He paused with his shovel in the air and saw that Laura had rolled the cab window shut. She said something and turned away. She turned her face to him again. He thought she said, "I'm okay." He mouthed, "How do you do." She looked puzzled. She'd been crying. It occurred to Isaac that beneath the radiance of her beauty he didn't know who she was. She waved at him in the window. He pointed, indicating that he was moving over to

the next fender steeped in snow. But he moved slowly, willing
his body on, nearly caught again in the act of staring at her
until he lapsed into a forgetfulness that would conjure its own
mental life, and he would wake for the thousandth time that
minute to find himself where?

Larkin was muttering. He couldn't contain himself another
minute. Isaac almost answered and peered around the side of
the cab to the right rear bumper. The cabbie's shovel was stuck
vertically in the snow. Larkin grasped the shaft in one hand
and orated into the handle. The shovel was a microphone. He
shrugged his shoulders, cleared his throat, and testified; his head
tilted heavenward. His tone suggested that if he were saying
anything provocative, it was merely the truth, which was an
accident that had happened to him. He was innocent. He chuck-
led. The joke was not lost on him. He hoped God had a sense of
humor too. "Lissen, I had no choice, I was sent to the university
of life, and this kid from Catatonia University comes stumbling
from nowheres to help me outta the storm. An Isaac he is, which
his father is probably the president of a bank."

Isaac told himself not to listen, as Orpheus had told himself not to look back. The cabbie's eyes shone like two freshly
minted nickels. Larkin yanked off his hat and crumpled it to
his heart, a gesture of abandonment and sincerity at the utter
hilarity of the ineffable, which he hoped the ineffable appreciated. With the scarf wrapped like a kerchief around his head,
and his wrinkled face clenched against the weather, Larkin
looked to Isaac like an illustration out of Mother Goose, the
little old lady who lived in a shoe. The little old lady croaked,
"They own Seagram's, and they own Canada." Isaac heard the
wind, and something unaccountable, unseen trees groaning, a
promise of the future, and the wind like sea water splashing his

face. He found himself thinking of Eskimos and whales, and the Eskimo belief that the whale offered itself for the nurture of the Eskimo people. He thought how some indigenous people kept the wolf as a totem to represent cunning, a lion to represent courage. So his people, city dwellers, had an affinity with the natural world after all, they too were creatures who had a metaphorical function, were an aid to moral imagination. Isaac, upright on his hindquarters, holding his shovel like a baseball bat, smiled. Larkin was holding forth on the second deadly sin. "Tell me," the cabbie said to whomever might care to answer, "tell me what the hell don't they own?" And the light flashed behind Isaac, above him, exploded in all the windows of the avenue. Larkin illuminated, would not be taken in, and outdone by the lights; he shrugged his shoulders and raised his voice, "This Isaac here, he's probably studying at Catatonia University how the Jews can give the niggers the atomic bomb so the niggers can take over the world." Isaac reached out, wanting the dark back, flailing after the lost silence. He heard the knock against the glass. He turned. Laura knocked on the cab window, and struggled with the handle to roll down the window. Isaac wanted to say, "wait, please wait," but couldn't speak. Larkin's eyes followed Isaac's eyes. The cabbie laughed, "I don't know what I'm gonna say 'til I say it, see it's just the truth that comes out." Larkin lowered his voice, "You think I never been in love?" Larkin stepped closer to Isaac, he seemed about to put his hand on Isaac's shoulder. "My old lady," he whispered, "when she was young, she had a mink-lined cunt, and for that I been carrying her around on my back my whole natural life — some deal!" Isaac took one step back. He heard the cab door open on the other side, facing the curb and bookstore window with the mannequins in their medieval garb, bent over the shining tomes.

Larkin glanced in the direction of the cab, and then looked up to all the windows lighting up the city, he raised his voice to address one and all, "You can get your ass off the table Mabel, the two dollars is for the beer."

Isaac didn't know he was going to swing until he felt the pull of his body, the balls of his feet pivoting, his upper body turning, the joy of it, Isaac the two-sewer home run hitter going for the roof, the sky over the roof. The flat of the board metal spade caught Larkin flush in the face.

The body lay still. "Is he dead?" Laura asked. She stood stiffly beside Isaac. "I don't know." "Check." Isaac looked. The body appeared not to be breathing. The face looked like squashed fruit. The wind had taken Larkin's hat; his head was still wrapped in the scarf kerchief, and his arms were outstretched in the snow, as if he had fallen in a swoon. Laura began to rant softly in Spanish. Isaac looked around. The voice sounded like an old woman's. Isaac was able to translate, "My cross," and "crazy." She glared at him and turned her face quickly away, "Well, is he dead?" she demanded; and as Isaac marveled at the old woman's voice becoming the young woman's foreign voice and the long hissing sibilant "s" in "Iss he dead?" Laura crouched down and felt the pulse in the cabbie's neck. "Alife," she said, and then, "Alive, turn him over quick." Isaac bent down, rolled Larkin over, and lifted him from the waist. The cabbie coughed, drooled blood and bits of teeth. He didn't come to. "Put him in the back seat," she said, "we're not far from St. Vincent's." Isaac stood there, his arms around Larkin's waist, the cabbie's body draped over his arms, hanging head down, threads of blood swaying from the smashed mouth. "The back seat, Isaac, put him in the back seat of the cab! We'll take him to St. Vincent's hospital. What's the matter?" "I can't drive," he said. "You don't know how to drive?" Isaac nodded yes. Laura said something in Spanish he didn't understand. "I," she said, "have had driving lessons, two anyway, I'll drive." She looked very unhappy. Isaac thought that it was quite possible to live a whole life in New York City and never need to know how to drive. This was not unusual, and he wondered who gave Laura the driving lessons. "Isaac, put him in the back seat."

She helped him, lifted and held the cabbie's feet as Isaac loaded Larkin into the back seat. She told Isaac to undo the knotted kerchief under the cabbie's chin, to help him to breathe easier. Isaac leaned into the cab, struggled with the knot, smelled what he thought was the cabbie's bloody, rancid, boozy breath, and remembered that he hadn't seen Larkin drinking. Perhaps he was smelling his own wine-soaked breath. He sweated, he struggled. The knot might have been made of wood. Laura looked over Isaac's shoulder. "Okay," she said, "Never mind, I'll do it." He watched as her fingers began to loosen the knot. She paused, handed him the car keys, "Collect the shovels," she said, "put them in the trunk."

He did as he was told. He put the shovels in the trunk, slammed it shut. He walked around the cab, got in, and sat down in the front passenger seat and waited.

Laura went around the driver's side and got behind the wheel. She looked like she might cry. It took her a minute to collect herself. Isaac sat there, waiting, not believing, and ready to accept that he could be found wanting for not knowing how to drive. "You," she said, not looking at him, "you didn't do it for me. Not because of me. I know crazy. You want to prove you can live the things you want to write in your stories. You're making up your life, that's why you hit him. Not for me! I never asked you to commit crimes for me"; and she turned to him and said more things in Spanish, balled up her fists and looked like she would punch him, or cry, if he contradicted her. She waited. Isaac said, "Okay." "Okay, okay what?" she shouted in his face. "Okay, okay." he said, and thought there was truth in what she said, but there were other things true in what had just happened. But he knew better than to argue. If he quibbled he'd lose her.

Isaac looked out of the cab's front window at the winter. Laura turned on the ignition and the headlights. The snow-spotted trunks of light traversed the street, illuminating a clothing store window festooned with Christmas green. In the middle of the white thoroughfare there were tracks the bus had left. Buildings, windows, lit up again, the remembered world, apparently inhabited. Isaac couldn't see any footprints in the snow-covered sidewalks.

Laura jerked the clutch back and forth. The gears screeched. The wheels spun, waves of slush geysered up in the air. Isaac smelled smoke. His head snapped back and they were off skidding down the avenue, the ride as good as anything in Coney Island. She screamed all the way in a kind of delight, if he could believe her face. She was driving, no matter what, she was behind the wheel and then he was screaming too. They sideswiped a parked truck and hit something head on, inanimate, a box; it flew over the roof of the car, and stuff, potatoes, he thought, maybe apples, rained down, drummed on the windshield. The thumping spilled clusters of webbing across the window. Beads of light flashed in the circular fretwork chasing the dark. Globules of light fluxed in the shattered mosaic of the windshield, and an unseen power grabbed and yanked him about. His ass half-out of the seat, his torso was bent over Laura's head. She was hunched over the steering wheel, driving. He strained against lurching, stretched out his arms, and braced himself against the passenger window and the roof. He heard Larkin roll off the back seat. He wondered if he was supposed to beg her to stop, if she would only stop or slow down if he begged. He closed his eyes. He thought, she is fleeing away into her own life. He felt the pain in his back radiate out several inches beneath his neck, and the index finger of his left hand oddly dead and tingling, as if the finger had taken a shot of Novocain.

The car slid into a slow half-spin. Isaac flopped back into the seat and bounced. The engine shrieked, stank of burning, and they stopped. He peeked through one squinting eye. The car was at a horizontal angle, blocking the snow-filled narrow street.

"You can open your eyes now," she said. Her hand was shaking as she pointed to the entrance of St. Vincent's Hospital. "Are you okay?" he asked. She said, "por que no, muchacho?" Behind them they heard gurgling and cooing. Larkin rose slowly from the floor. Isaac could feel his heart beating. The cabbie held the scarf to his face as a Muslim woman might hold a veil. Only one eye was visible. In the dim light of the cab's interior Larkin's eye appeared dove-brown, an eye that might have lived in the face of one who had resided since the invention of time in paradise. Laura put the car keys in Larkin's hand. She pointed to the hospital's entrance. From beneath the veil came a cooing sound. Larkin batted the one visible eye. He moved, slumberous and obedient. He stumbled out of the cab and shuffled toward the hospital entrance.

On the sidewalk Isaac assayed the damage to the car. The front fender on the driver's side was bent, the grill dented, the windshield intricately cracked and rippled, and a deep, wide gouge ran the length of the car's side. Above, way above, the night sky was tranquil, clear and full of stars. The blizzard was earthbound, roof high, blowing through the tunnels of streets, between buildings, the wind gathering the snow from roofs, fire escapes and gutters, and scattering it in the air.

Laura called to Larkin who paused at the hospital door. "In there, go ahead, yes that's it, through the door." He turned. The scarf fell from his face. One eye was completely closed, a purple mound, the mouth carnage. The cabbie turned and went through the door. Laura turned to Isaac. "Let's go, hurry. We're not far from Sheridan Square." She offered her hand. He took it.

Isaac, wild with gratitude, held Laura's hand and attempted to trot, to keep up with Laura, but the pain in his back slowed him to a hurried walk; the tingling dead feeling had spread to three fingers of his left hand, the index finger, and the next two. He touched his cheek with the fingertips; the fingertips felt nothing. "Are you alright?" he asked. "Alright? Of course, let's get out of here." Isaac, with his good live right hand, felt her shoulder, her arm, "nothing hurt?" "Yes," she said, "yes, I told you, I'm fine." As hurried as she sounded, her eyes took him in slowly, concerned, "and you?" "Okay, sure, fine," he said, bathing himself in her solicitous look.

Going down the steps of the Sheridan Square subway station, they heard the train roaring in and Laura let go of Isaac's hand and ran ahead, down the steps, as Isaac continued slowly, his back aching.

Laura held the train door from closing. At the rear of a small crowd Isaac ambled in, behind a middle-aged, huge, smiling black woman, who announced to the others getting on the train that she was going to appeal to the Pope, her uncle, for help, because Clint Eastwood's former wife was jealous of her, and blamed her for the breakup of their marriage. "The crazy white bitch is fixin' to kill me." Next to Isaac a young Hispanic man carried a large carton on his shoulder. The young man was sweating. The black woman turned to the young man with the carton on his shoulder, "Youngblood honey, now don't sprain your milk, you got pleasure waitin' on you at home." Someone said, "Amen!" It sounded to Isaac as if the black woman's statement had been made out of a great disinterested love, a gift of her madness perhaps. Isaac looked into her face. She looked back and smiled. Isaac noticed that people were looking at one another openly, pleased and curious. He'd never seen anything like it in this city. He looked to Laura for confirmation. She seemed to be seeing what he was seeing. They sat holding hands. The graffiti was still there covering the walls of the train, and the filth, and smells. Isaac remembered that they had been together since early afternoon, a day of eons. The train pulled out of the station.

The passengers were wet, chastened, thawing out; and the atmosphere on the train was festive. The machine of the city had been stopped, Isaac thought, a blizzard, all lines down. For a while there was no way home in the dark, with all the signs buried, routine, even destiny interrupted, a reprieve from all our inventions. People on the train were talking to one another, laughing. A young man with a shaven head, wearing a drenched, white, woolen robe, cymbals on his fingers, made his way down the aisle of the train. His legs were spread wide, like a sailor negotiating a pitching deck. Water dripped from the hem of his robe. He smiled, reached into a cloth bag hanging from his shoulder, and distributed handfuls of raisins and nuts to the passengers. One old man said, "Pistachios I like, not this kind." An old woman sitting nearby reached into her purse, and said, "I can offer you an orange if you like." "An orange is good," the

old man said. Isaac whispered to Laura, "Everybody looks goofy."
Laura and Isaac looked at one another and laughed. She asked
the Hispanic man sitting across from them what was in the carton near his feet. The man smiled and shrugged. He looked
embarrassed and puzzled. He opened the carton, peeked inside, and withdrew a narrow silver-colored tube. He shrugged
again, placed the tube on the floor, and held it gently in place
with his foot. He reached into the trembling carton set on the
train floor and withdrew a wheel with gleaming spokes.
"Cecilia," he said, si, si, Cecilia, a baby carriage." He reached
inside his jacket, took out a screwdriver, and got on his knees;
swaying in the moving train, he attempted to screw the wheel
to the silver tube axle. Laura suggested to him, in Spanish, that
this was not a very good idea. The project could wait until he
reached home. The man appeared grateful for the advice. He
sat down, holding the silver axle and wheel in his lap.

Laura rested her head on Isaac's shoulder and closed her
eyes. Isaac let himself drift towards sleep.

They awoke in the dark, their bodies lurching sideways, the
booming roar of the train filling the dark. Exquisite pain traveled Isaac's spine and the lights came on as the train pulled into
96th Street. Many passengers had gotten off the train. The man
with the unassembled baby carriage, the robed novitiate who
had distributed raisins and nuts, and the stout black lady who
was going to speak to her uncle, the Pope, were gone.

A prince of the streets entered the train. Tall, his powerful
body moving in the creaking black leather coat, the fur collar
pulled up, framing his handsome head, he wore one ruby earring, a plum-colored ascot, velvet trousers, and a burnished gold
homburg hat. Next to the majestic African, an exhausted looking Chinese man carrying a newspaper entered the train. The

prince, regal and enormous, sat opposite Laura and Isaac. He crossed his legs and held a *Time* magazine by his large manicured fingertips. As he turned his head, studiously attending to the page, Isaac and Laura saw his other ear, and the trickle of blood from inside the ear wetting the edge of the fur collar. The prince willed composure, his implacable and ferociously blank face suggested to Isaac that the man believed he would perish from acknowledging his wound. Isaac thought of Larkin and the injury he did the cabbie. The thought came and went. Laura sneezed, her eyes were tearing and she was choking, laughing. Laura laughed, doubled over. Isaac said, "What is it?" and glanced from her to the huge prince who appeared chagrined. Isaac watched the prince rise haughtily from the seat, and find himself again at the pinnacle of some dream of who he ought to be. He glanced dismissively at Laura and Isaac and strode with a gliding motion to the door that would lead to the next subway car. "This country," Laura gasped, "I can't help," wiped her eyes, and harvested breath from the laughter shaking her body. She shouted above the screaming train. Isaac tilted his ear to her mouth, catching each word bludgeoned by the train's howling. "America, when I first came here, how strange, big buildings, such machines, like living things. It wasn't him," she yelled, waving her hand toward the train car door the black prince had gone through. "I wasn't thinking about him. My aunt, her, Titi, I was thinking of. She is like, well, another mother to me. And she is a healer, she knows many things. As a youngster I accepted her authority on many subjects. When I was sick and had a fever, she would make one of her teas and change the weather in my body. When we came to America and I saw those young Jewish boys with those long, how do you call, kosher curls at the sides of their heads and those long black coats, I thought my brother would have to wear those curls and that attire in school. And my aunt explained, no that is only for Jewish boys; these children, my aunt said, are dressed for penance to atone for the many sins of their forbears, and they have their own schools. I was relieved when it turned out to be true that my brother didn't have to wear the penitential uniform. See, I accepted almost everything Aunt Titi said about America. In my class at school there was a Chinese brother and sister and I couldn't pronounce their names. When they spoke to each other their language sounded even stranger than everything else I heard and couldn't understand. On the day I asked my aunt about the Chinese children we were walking in the street. A piece of dirt, a cinder, something blew into my eye. It hurt terribly. I couldn't see. Immediately I felt Titi's hands on my face pulling my head down, and her tongue darted out and washed my eye, and whatever it was that attacked my eye was gone, and the hurt was gone, and my eyes felt wet and new. Then my aunt Titi said, "Well, do you know how the Chinese name their children?" I shook my head no. My aunt said, "Well, they go to the cupboard and take out an armful of pots and pans, then they toss the pots and pans across the room. When the pots and pans crash on the floor, bing, bang, bong or ding, bang, ding, that is how they name their children, by the sound the crashing pots and pans make hitting the floor. I didn't," Laura Providencia yelled, "believe that."

The train came into the Third Avenue station and stopped, the roaring noise diminished to a throbbing rumble, and Laura was still shouting, "but anyway, I think everybody in America should name their children that way." People turned and stared. She was still laughing, tears squeezed from her eyes. It sounded to Isaac as if she were in pain. He felt alarmed, self-centered he knew, but the despair he heard at the heart of Laura's story named him as part of some general condition. He was desperate. He would do something extravagant, heroic, carry her on his back through the snow, singing all the way. He wished he could, like the biblical Joseph (who had prophesied fat years and lean years, outwitted famine, resisted the Pharaoh's wife's advances), be an infallible reader of dreams, interpreting for Laura her dreams and memories; and he would never have to falsify fate since he was ready to throw his life into the balance to make sure things came out right. Maybe before the night was out, on the way home, they would be attacked by muggers. He would defend her, fight and die, but no, he wanted to fight and live. The pain in his back said something else, disabled that dream. Perhaps he would only jeopardize her and so he should dream something else.

The train didn't move. The doors were open, the wind blowing through the car was brutal. The public address system squawked. Finally Isaac and Laura and the other passengers figured out what was happening by the fragmented sounds of words, the length of time the train sat in the station, the doors open and the wind blowing through the car; and at last the conductor stuck his face in and barked, "Everybody out, this is it, last stop, out." The train was above ground, on the El, blocked by snow. They could go no further.

Laura and Isaac and the dozen or so passengers climbed down the steps to the white-heaped streets.

Within a minute everyone had disappeared in ones and twos, moving off in different directions. Laura and Isaac looked at the fading evidence of footprints. It wasn't snowing, but the wind rose the dust of snow up from the hilly street in spumes. Laura and Isaac peered through the rippling snow, high as a wheat field, white, shimmying. The apartment houses above the waving sheaves of snow dust, glazed monoliths, a replica of the South Bronx Laura remembered, a colony on the moon, yellow windows promising human presence, the frozen drop of moon, a reflection of the ghostly planet she and Isaac wandered.

"That way," Laura said, pointing toward nothing Isaac could see. "We're twenty, maybe thirty blocks from my house, I think." The snow underfoot crackled like crushed glass. They hunched their shoulders and lunged forward, marching against the wind. Isaac's pants ballooned as the wind reached under him; he had the sensation of sustaining effort, treading water and inching forward. Laura pulled her hands into the sleeves of her coat, tucked her head into her shoulders, and pushed on ahead of him. She called back over her shoulder, "Come, come." Isaac struggled forward, remembering WW II newsreels of Russia, soldiers, refugees staggering across an endless winter desolation, their feet and heads bundles of rags. In the blue black sky far above the swirling snow, Isaac saw the rags grown huge in the form of clouds still traveling west, driven by the wind. He marched, thought of *Dr. Zhivago*, and the Jack London story, "To Build A Fire"; and when he could no longer see Laura, called out, yelled, ran in circles. He cursed himself for diverting himself with such thoughts. He promised to respect the given world forever, to be attentive, and he screamed, "Laura!" He went backwards and forwards in the snow. He wondered if he had been too hasty to vow, to make a deal that said forever, as now he would have to march and search forever before seeing her again, and how could he outlast forever. He'd made a mistake, and after all, the bit of diversion he'd occupied himself with, trudging onward, was not evil in itself. "Laura!" he called, "Laura!" and heard his name come whistling back to him, mockingly, as a reprimand for his egotism he was sure, and his toes were singing with the cold. "Pendejo, loco, ven aca Isaac." He followed the sound all the way to the door, into the hallway of the tenement where she waited, warming up.

Five or six times they stopped this way. In hallways of buildings they rested and warmed themselves before going on. They compared blue fingers and red faces. They stamped their feet.

The topmost stories of the public housing project reached into the lucid night. The door to the lobby, with its broken lock and the doorknob missing was propped open with a wooden milk box. Laura and Isaac stumbled out of the wind and snow.

The four walls and ceiling of the elevator were covered by graffiti. Laura pressed the button for the 12th floor. The box they stood in jumped. Laura and Isaac staggered and regained their footing. The machine groaned and swooped up. Isaac and Laura held on to one another. The encompassing hieroglyphics of numbers, names, cartoon renderings of animals, humans, parts of animal and human bodies blotted out by ballooned letters, shuddered; the whole shotgunned alphabet exploding, layered, image over image, over every square inch of the walls, the closed elevator doors and ceiling, thick with the markings of scores of scribes trying to speak at once. Isaac closed his eyes. The elevator smelled of piss. He heard his teeth chattering, and once more had the feeling that he knew all along he would get here; this too was something remembered, his former lapse of memory, or faith, a reflex of struggle in the physical world.

A bell chimed above them as they came through the door. Isaac smelled the pine-scented disinfectant that had pervaded his childhood. They stood in the overheated vestibule, under a ceiling light fixture made of three electric candles, giving off three drops of orange light. Beneath the purgative odor of the pine disinfectant Isaac caught the scent of melting wax.

Laura's mother's progress down the narrow corridor was quick and stately. Her large round face, Isaac thought, like a great finely cracked brown boulder, repose holding the design of old trauma, the face of a shell-shocked Buddha, seeing the world clearly enough out of a meditative sleep. Laura recited, in Spanish, what Isaac assumed was a repetition of the explanation of their long night together. In the morning Laura would explain to Isaac that she had not told her mother that they were on a date, a notion her mother could not understand or honor. What she had told her mother was that she had been at an end of semester celebration at City College, attended by many students, and when she learned that the snow that had begun to fall during early mid-day had become a blizzard, and stopped the New York City transit system, Isaac volunteered to see that she got home safely. The blizzard lent credence to Laura's story.

Señora Milagros thanked Isaac for seeing Laura home safely, three times, twice in Spanish and once, the last time, in English. She said, "Thank you." He said, "My pleasure." Beyond the throes of her first gratitude Señora Milagros sniffed his breath and turned her nose away. Laura said, "Pardon me Isaac, I'll be right back." She walked down the long vestibule, disappearing around a curve into the dark. Laura's mother excused herself and followed Laura. Isaac stood there dripping; it was wonderful to be warm again. He heard the toilet flush and more discussion, hushed, in Spanish. He pressed the three fingers of his left hand into the palm of his right. The three fingers tingled. He pushed the fingers of his left hand harder into the palm of his right hand. Pain, sharp then dull, pulsed at different points in his spine, and he played each swell of pain in the keyboard palm of his hand, speculating on the injury to his back.

Smiling, Isaac wiped the tears he had brought to his eyes. The little woman appeared out of the blur of water and darkness, taller than a dwarf. She padded down the dim vestibule into the faint orange light. Her quilted robe, with the sash pulled tight around her approximate middle, squeezed the bundle of lady into two prominent spheres; the two feet in carpet slippers protruded from the bottom sphere, clapping softly along the floor. Her head was thrust forward, turtle-like. Above the gray head and face, wrinkled and colored like a walnut, was another head on a long stem of neck, pretty, sleeping. The half-opened eyes of the sleepwalking girl reflected nothing in this world. The young, sleeping face bobbing above the venerable, squinting face it would someday become, Isaac thought, noting a family resemblance. The old woman and the pretty adolescent girl, barefoot and in a bathrobe, shuffled around the curving wall of the vestibule. As they approached the orange light from the overhead fixture, Isaac saw that the sleeping girl was clinging with both hands to the long, thick, gray braid hanging down the old woman's back. The sleeping girl made a long drawn-out sound, the kind of murmur one might make sipping a delicious broth.

The old woman whispered in Spanish. When it became apparent that Isaac didn't understand her, she patted his arm encouragingly and began a pantomime with her hands. Her hands flew, stitching the air. She looked into Isaac's face expectantly. The pretty adolescent girl's head rested on the old woman's shoulder, a spit bubble blooming in the corner of her mouth. The girl clung, anchored to the braid, snoring. The little bubble in the corner of the girl's mouth burst, and drool ran down the old woman's shoulder. She ignored this, gesticulating, trying to endow Isaac with speech, her hands inventing a language in the air; if only Isaac made a sufficient effort his eyes could be ears.

A bright light went on down at the far right end of the vestibule. Laura and her mother stepped into the light. They walked toward Isaac, the old woman, and the sleeping girl. Laura's mother's arms were loaded with bedding.

The old woman spoke to Laura, urgently. Laura answered and sighed, each phrase weighted with enduring and courtesy. Laura's mother said something, she seemed to disagree with both the old woman and Laura. The hushed argument went on. The sleeping adolescent girl's head rested on the old woman's shoulder, the girl snored, her eyelids fluttered. Isaac stood there in his soaked shoes. "Please excuse me," Laura said, her voice rising above a whisper, "Isaac, we didn't intend to be rude. May I introduce my aunt, Titi, you've met my mother, Lucia, and my sister Rosita. She sleepwalks sometimes, I think I told you." Isaac said, "How do you do." Laura's aunt nodded. "My aunt is insisting, although I have tried to explain that she is exaggerating the significance of the late hour, she still insists that you be informed of certain things." Laura's mother said something. Titi answered. Laura enjoined the argument, which sounded civil and imperative.

Finally Señora Milagros, her arms loaded with bedding, signaled with her head that they follow her into the living room. Isaac was not sure this included him. Laura followed her mother, Titi followed after Laura, Rosita shuffled in tandem, clinging to the long braid. Isaac stood in the vestibule, damp and warm, listening to the conference that continued in the living room.

"Isaac," Laura called, "please come, come."

The living room was dim and glowing, and reminded Isaac of the marine room in the Museum of Natural History. Radiant shadows of aquamarine drifted along the walls and flowed over the ceiling, like the tide of an ocean's surface seen from the bottom of a sunlit sea. The cluster of penny-sized flames of the votive candles, surrounding the milk white statuette of the Virgin Mary on a table, fluttered in the calm depth of a rosy corner.

Laura's head was bowed. Titi stood facing Laura, Rosita stood directly behind Titi, her head resting on Titi's shoulder, Rosita snored and clutched Titi's long silver braid. Titi grasped the sides of Laura's face, as though she were testing the ripeness of a melon, and sniffed Laura's scalp. She lifted Laura's face and examined the whites of her eyes. She patted Laura's face as a potter might shape a rare vessel. The tranquil smile on Laura's face buckled Isaac's knees. Señora Milagros opened and prepared the bed that extended out of the convertible couch. Laura's drowsing voice said, "Isaac, you'll find it a comfortable bed." Señora Milagros patted the freshly made bedclothes. Isaac said thank you and sat down on the bed. He looked to Señora Milagros to be certain that he understood her wishes. She nodded approval. Titi completed her examination of Laura's eyes and scalp, and reached up to her shoulder to caress Rosita's sleeping head. Laura, no longer being handled, spoke, her voice ascending to wakefulness, recovering the conviction of one who can believe that the world she sees is not just a reflection of what resides behind her eyes. Isaac thanked Señora Milagros, Titi, and Laura for their hospitality. He said, "Gracias." Laura dropped her voice to a mock baritone and said, "De nada, mi casa es su casa," Titi said something. Señora Milagros answered. Laura smiled at her aunt and mother, and said to Isaac, "My mother and aunt exaggerate the ambition of your affection." A fever flushed the inside of his head, and his ears rang. His face went dumb and eloquent in search of language he didn't find. Aunt Titi, Señora Milagros, and Laura saw the declaration he hadn't spoken. "Alright then," Laura said, as though she were bored. "I'll tell you what my aunt insists you know; my mother never taught me to sew." Isaac said, "Sew?" and followed the bubbling shadow of a current of water on the wall, above the large, fluorescently lit tank of tropical fish, an undulating tide washing over the velvet tapestry of the face of the recently assassinated president. The eyes of John Fitzgerald Kennedy under the glimmer of water, nubbly as deep sea vegetation. Aunt Titi began to stitch the air again with her hand and shake her head, vigorously, no. Isaac, trying to be agreeable, nodded in affirmation, agreeing to her "no" shaking his head "yes." The shadow of water falling from the ceiling across his lap, the reflection of fish swam over his thighs. "You see," Laura said, "Neither my aunt nor my mother would teach me to sew, so I wouldn't wind up working in a factory; although they have both expressed concern about the ways a college education might lead a young woman astray." Isaac continued to nod his head "yes" and "yes," and he saw on the wall above the sofa bed, a flock of tin doves pointed at the wall clock replica of the sun, each extending spoke of sunlight ending in a flowered candelabra. On the wall above the sun clock, all the way to the rim of ceiling, casting its tropical shadow of emerald water and fish, another velvet tapestry, "The Last Supper." All the apostles, under the shadow of water, the apostles, talking, agitated, whispering. Isaac wondered, doesn't the rabbi see, but Jesus, at the center in perfect repose, stared ahead, indifferent to the rampant Eden before them.

Señora Milagros said something emphatic to her sister, who nodded in agreement. Laura Providencia said, without much conviction, "No, I will not translate that," and, "por favor, Alright, Okay, yes. Isaac, although my mother believes my aunt is granting you too much importance, my mother wishes me to repeat what she claims, it is probably unnecessary for you to know; well, um, no one has ever been allowed to touch my face; that is discipline me. No one, not the man who says he is my father, no uncle, no relative has ever struck me. If anyone hit me, his hands would die, and he would die; and my mother and aunt would devote a lifetime of prayer to insure that such a malefactor's tenancy in hell would be eternal. My mother thinks it is only fair that you know this."

Isaac heard himself make a sound, the noise of an evolving language, part of what he'd wanted to say, as best as he could tell, was, I'm not that kind of folk hero. The squawking coming from his mouth was sincere. Aunt Titi and Señora Milagros looked satisfied. Isaac recalled a recent past when he'd worried that he might be a brilliant talker; at the head of the table in a bar near City College, the other students sat listening to him talk about a book they were all reading. They listened, willing to buy him beer all night, so long as he kept on talking, and he had become anxious that his capacity for talk would undermine a more scrupulous use of language in which he might find the truths necessary to write stories. Now he struggled against the aphasia his heart decreed. He coughed, cleared his throat, and groaned. Titi tilted slightly toward Laura and took one last premonitory sniff at Laura's head.

Señora Milagros, Titi, with sleeping Rosita in tow, turned and left the room. Laura lingered for a moment. "You may," she said, "use the bathroom if you wish, wash, bathe; you'll find some dry trousers, socks and a shirt you can wear to bed. Angel's things." Isaac nodded, squawked affirmation. "They are," Laura said, lowering her voice "satisfied that 'el damage' hasn't occurred." Isaac made another noise in the inchoate language, the inflection sounded like an inquiry. "My aunt and mother," Laura whispered, "are persuaded I'm virgo intacta — Titi's science is imprecise. Anyway, I told her you slipped on the ice and hurt your back and hand. She says you've pinched a nerve. She is preparing a special tea to help you sleep, and a poultice to make your back better. Trust this. Go, go ahead, use the bathroom."

Isaac walked slowly down the vestibule to the bathroom. He found that he could believe that he would resume speech again when he no longer struggled to will it, and whatever the new language brewing in him, it too would come to fruition in its own good time. Isaac moved slowly in the nearly dark vestibule toward the bright light at the far end, where the bathroom was located. The silhouettes of potted plants and ferns and narrow tubs of flowers bracketed to the wall were vivid in the dark. He wondered what kind of plants could flourish in the gloom. Maybe all the vegetation in the vestibule, unlike all the stuff growing in the living room, was plastic. This plant life gave off no scent, although the air was pervaded by the odor of the pine-scented disinfectant that his mother also favored. He glimpsed foliage on the wall, and protruding out of the leaves, Christ's bleeding feet. At once he saw his mother's tortured feet, and remembered their insistent and pitiful speaking, and he hoped the new language gestating in him would subsume the sad tales of his mother's feet. As he came closer to the brightly lit bathroom and its partially opened door, he saw a small end table, where a stalking black panther with a cactus growing out of its back was poised before a bowl of wax pineapples and bananas; and towering up from the table's shining surface, behind and above the bowl of opalescent bananas and pineapples, a pair of white plaster of Paris hands clasped in prayer, rising above the bowl of fruit and the black glass panther, frozen in a stalking posture, and humped with a living cactus, growing thick and prickly as an obscene finger pointing up. And there on the wall was the luminous framed picture of a woman saint, offering her eyes on a plate to heaven.

Whatever it was that Laura Providencia said next, calling from behind him in the dim vestibule, perhaps saying something about the location of the soap and towels, and then, just after, or later, something more; the content of that moment would be taken by the innocent skepticism and longing in Laura's voice, telling Isaac that the saint offering her eyes on a plate to God was Saint Lucia, her patron saint; and not because, she, Laura had chosen, but this was the patron saint given to her, as her mother had been given Our Lady of Perpetual Succor. Laura's voice conveying this, whenever it actually happened, would not be a point of contention. It was only that her voice saying this, carrying backward or forward, in what, Isaac, for want of a better word, would have to call time, so that he heard, stepping into the startling whiteness of the immaculate bathroom, and viewing the same white and pink swans on the shower curtain his mother had chosen for his parent's bathroom in Brooklyn, Isaac heard what Laura hadn't yet uttered. But he was too busy anyway, coming into, if not possession of her childhood, an odd temporal proximity putting him there in her past as well as her future, and he cared about and would honor all of it, the bric-a-brac of her longing for faith, and her astonished skepticism, which was her faith; and he would use these items of memory to identify himself, when in the next century she awoke from a nightmare, screaming, and demanded to know who the old Jewish man lying in bed next to her was.

Isaac had showered. He sat on the edge of the bed that extended out of the convertible couch. His feet were warm in

Angel's socks. He sat and swayed, his torso wrapped tight as a mummy in the safety-pinned, large white bath towels holding the hot mustard plaster in place on his back. Angel's cotton trousers fit him perfectly. The warm damp poultice of rags, leaves, and twigs crowning his head had the fragrance of eucalyptus. Pungent mist drifted up from the tussock of his head, and steam rose from his back. He sipped the warm greenish tea; it had the consistency of cod-liver oil, a smoky mentholated scent, and tasted like the Coney Island Atlantic laced with brandy. And it was good. Beads of sweat dripped from the tip of his nose, and balm on his temples. Woozy, he looked out of his half-opened eyes. Laura and her mother stood over him, smiling, studying his face. Titi asked him to stick out his tongue. He opened his mouth and stuck his tongue out. Titi bent forward, as Rosita, upright and holding on to the tip of Titi's silver braid, which was bowed in the middle like a skipping rope — Rosita pendulating to and fro, stirring her sleep deeper. Titi bent forward and brought her eye closer to his tongue. "Duerme," said Titi, although it was not clear whether her statement was a diagnosis, or prescription, or both, treating fire with fire, returning cause and effect to an original oneness. Titi spoke, her nose almost touching his tongue, she appeared to scold the organ of speech hanging on his chin. "Duermase!" she commanded. His eyes closed, his tongue curled into his mouth, and he drifted down into the pile of pillows.

Isaac, buoyant, full, awoke dreaming. He made his way down the dark vestibule toward the light seeping under the bathroom door. Titi stood guard in front of the door, her arms crossed over her breasts. Rosita stood draped over Titi's back, still clinging to the braid, her head on Titi's shoulder, snoring. Isaac understood. Laura had had to get up and pee too; and when she had stirred in the bed and sat up, Titi's anchoring arm slipped from Laura's waist and Titi awoke. Rosita, clinging to Titi's braid, spooned as tight as a shadow against Titi's back on the furthest end of the bed, rose too. Titi and Rosita followed Laura to the bathroom, where Titi stood sentinel, awaiting Isaac's arrival. He said, "I only came to pee." Titi smiled.

Morning and he awakes like Rip Van Winkle and finds the world vaguely familiar, imaginable. He, the husband, looks at his wife. He desires her, still. He remembers when she was beautiful. His wife knows his thoughts, nods in the direction of the mirror on the wall behind them, laughs, and says, "We were beautiful long enough." He glances over his shoulder at the mirror. He sees; they are growing wider and shorter, bell-shaped. The mirrors in the house have turned into the trick mirrors at carnivals, where they see themselves transfigured into funny fluid shapes. He considers the way the earth's gravity is tugging and molding them into queer shapes, perhaps in preparation for the next mortal form they will inhabit, the whole morphic burlesque, he thinks, a rehearsal for eternity. Nevertheless he wants her. But he has to pee. That happens almost always now. For the moment he finds it interesting. He wanted her when she was beautiful, and he wants her now that he has encountered something he will provisionally call character, and it has it's own prurient interest, for which he is grateful. Is this, he wonders, that inevitability some people call becoming a dirty old man. He is surprised. But his most immediate need is to urinate, and it occurs to him that he really doesn't know how they became truly married.

Almost awake and desiring the second cup of coffee he is

no longer allowed to have, he recognizes his wife as the white-haired woman he'd seen holding hands with the white-haired man reflected in the hardware store window, pixilated as adolescents, and he and the woman in the kitchen are that cute old couple.

Now she is placing before him, on the breakfast table, a bowl of oatmeal. He doesn't like oatmeal, but he is supposed to eat it because it is good for him. She reminds him of what the doctor said, the connection between high cholesterol and prostate disorder. He would prefer a doughnut. The doctor described the prostate as doughnut-shaped, and Isaac's doughnut, the doctor said, was very enlarged and acutely inflamed, which accounted for the frequent urination, the chronic feeling of fullness in the bladder, the lower back pain, and the blood in his urine. The various tests indicated the necessity of a biopsy. Among the options, should surgery prove necessary, the doctor said, was penile prosthesis, life could go on.

Isaac sits rigid in the chair gripping fistfuls of his trousers, bunched up at the knees; he stares down into his lap and thinks that the organ that has been a reliable and indispensable instrument of love is also the thing he pisses through. This fact is no longer funny, God and or nature, whatever the all-fashioning power, comedian or frugal engineer, now the functions are confused, and he can't laugh. Not this morning. He doesn't want to eat his porridge. His wife sprinkles a handful of raisins into the bowl and stirs the muck around with a soupspoon. She smiles at him encouragingly. Eunuched by time Isaac listens as his wife of forty years declares cheerfully that she'd be quite content if he learned how to tickle and suck artfully. Isaac knows that Laura is trying to make him feel better. She tends to take an upbeat, practical view of the difficulties life presents. He remembers; her capacity for happiness is what has moved him again and again, this woman, his wife so very different from the woman who was his mother. Isaac recalls his mother trying to give what she could give, impart her gift, "Isaac darling, don't forget, life is shit." And even then, in a long ago, so long ago when he was a boy ... or was this something returned to him during his troubled sleep, or the longing that passes for sleep, a piece of the pieces of narrative clamoring in a tantalizing anarchy that makes night exhausting, and Laura asks, "Are you awake?" A good question Isaac thinks but does not answer. "Did you sleep well?" she asks, relenting, pouring him a second cup of coffee against the doctor's orders, for which Isaac is very grateful. He sips the coffee and reviews his nights. Often the excruciating dark finally leaves him near morning in oblivion, where he sleeps like the dead. Then dawn is deliverance, a delirium he is addicted to. Moments of glorious morning so brief he can't be sure whether he's remembering it or wishing it, but he feels for an instant a kind of happiness that is quite new, a happiness in which he is able to believe in acceptance, and senses an immensity not inimical to his human delight; but each dream of morning gives way to afternoon that yields evening and inevitable night, and he must be very quiet to elude being mugged by dread. It gets dark earlier and earlier. The preponderance of his mornings, in the moment when the conceit of the never ending present insinuates the world, are mostly disorienting, then like old Rip Van Winkle he finds the world strange, something vaguely recollected. Still, he is sure that even as a boy he understood that his mother wanted to give him the gift of her understanding, the gift given as a scream, nevertheless coherent, or perhaps he had become a boy adept at reading screams. She wanted him to know life was a swindle, something that used her for its own purposes without regard for her specific humanity. She would be unstinting in her effort to wise him up, protect her son, marinating his heart as she did herring with bitter condiments, leaving him forever susceptible to Laura Providencia's smile.

Isaac looks out of the kitchen window. Across the road, in the gleaming white meadow that is part of the Bothfeld farm, a red cardinal is perched on a glazed tree limb. The strange winter weather, balmy, then wet and white and cold again, has turned the trees into crystal. Out past the glazed tree and the cardinal, a dollop of flame shimmying in the austere branches, an ocean of snow heaves mists, brilliantly particled sheets of white flying in the sky, flapping like wings the chestnut mare has discarded, the horse stands in the cushions of white, steaming.

The wind hurls sleet against the window. Howling envelops the house. The roads are closed.

His pillow is a bog. He tosses off the quilt. That the deep night fantods stalk him almost two decades after he's given up drink strikes him as vengeful. Now in the night he reminds himself that his memory of the day may be faulty. Laura is in bed next to him, her leg touching his, her skin still feels like a girl's, although the buffo snoring that is a new feature of her ripe middle age has the sound of an oboe not yet invented, one with comic possibilities, a music made in collaboration with a great silence. Earlier, just before going to bed, he'd put a record on the stereo. The melody beat through his blood but the name of the tune absconded. He panicked. Couldn't name the tune. He thought, yes, I'm in the early stages of the disease. Mother had it, Uncle Yussie died of it too. I'm genetically predisposed. Could I write faster? Complete the stories I must write before memory dies, and before the aging generations out there, those quaint atavisms who still read, die away. Then he remembered and was saved — "Limehouse Blues" played by the sublime Django Reinhardt. He'd clutched the record album to his chest as though it had runic properties and hummed softly, "Limehouse Blues."

In a stupor that is neither sleeping nor waking, he refuses to consult the clock, but because he has been to the bathroom to piss three, or has it been four times, he guesses that it is somewhere between three and four in the morning. The pianissimo of Laura's snoring swells the breathing nest of quilts.

The bedroom emerges out of the murky light. He tries to remember the day of the week. If it is Thursday he will have to go directly to the library, as he is the faculty chairperson of the Library Committee. He should get out of bed. The committee meets at ten.

He sits and struggles to fight off dozing. He nods. Laura's toes caress the vertebra at the base of his spine. He sits at the edge of the bed with a slipper in his hand. The massage feels good. The light in the window bears a resemblance to morning. Laura advises that he go to the bathroom. Isaac rouses himself. Laura's foot helps launch him into motion.

Meditating over the toilet bowl, Isaac waits for his faulty plumbing to do its work. He can feel the heat rising around his ankles from the forced hot-air vent in the floor. The bathroom window is a flood carrying away the morning. He hears the tiny splash in the bowl and feels the drip-drop of relief, but not the emptiness he yearns for. Through and between the rivulets streaming down the window, he can see the bare winter architecture of the apple tree in his backyard, the glazed cross hatching of branches forming bowls within bowls in the greater dormant circumference of outreaching limbs, dripping. He thinks of where he is and the conventions for saying it. My house. My backyard. My apple tree. Astounded by the transmigration of his spirit, he is more certain than ever that he is not in a subway train hurtling underground through the stone bowels of the city dreaming of an apple tree: and the incredible story his mother-in-law told in a recent telephone call from Puerto Rico — can he ever live long enough to tell it with the seeming ease and power she told it, undaunted by the truth and its implications. She told it and laughed. Her daughter told it to Isaac and laughed, and Isaac, standing over the toilet bowl, hears the several splashes he makes and wishes with all his heart for the longevity that may allow him to tell the story with sufficient skill. Meanwhile, his wife's voice calling from the bedroom is not strident but louder, a more imperative beckoning. Isaac thinks, now when they take their clothes off they are no longer nude but naked. And they are embarrassed when they look at one another. He thinks as he makes his way back to the bedroom, that what he hears in her voice is not so much desire but the idea that she should be desired, and an old anger at an old hurt hones some ancient aspect of his will, but finally in the bed, bending to her mocha-colored knees that are still pretty, he remembers also that latent in the idea is the real something beyond anybody's idea. She, his great friend. The inside of her silken thighs press his cheeks. His nose burrows in the wiry tuft. In this dark, his tongue busy, he tells himself, think of Beethoven deaf, Homer blind. He hears his wife moan. Her hand reaches down to pat his back, as if she were burping a baby, preparing him for the greater dark.